Saga of Dead Men Walking

Insanity's Respite

Book I of the Auramancer's Exorcism

Joshua E. B. Smith

DEDICATION

"One book," I said to myself.

"One book," I said to others.

"Just one. One book to bridge Akaran's journey from Toniki to the hundreds of pages I wrote a decade ago that I got stumped on and stalled out that has been an emotional albatross around my neck."

"One more book, and I'll be ready to face that challenge. One book, and Akaran will be in the middle of the Golden Shores of Sycio with the Heavens at his back and the Abyss yawning at his feet. One book, and Draedach will rise."

"One book," I said, "and I can put my mind to ease. I can write the story I wanted to write when the idea to write a short story called Snowflakes in Summer popped in my head and demanded attention first in 2016."

Over, and over again, I said, just one book.

Welcome to Insanity's Respite, Book 1 of the Auramancer's Exorcism.

I'm working on part two, Insanity's Rapture,
and part three, Insanity's Reckoning,
as fast as I can.

Because it was just supposed to be *one* blessed book...

OH HEY!

Make sure you sign up for the email newsletter! Get free things, news on upcoming releases, and more!

http://www.sagadmw.com/email.html

CONTENTS

ACKNOWLEDGMENTS

Between the time that I released Favorite Things and the moment that I am sitting here at my desk writing this acknowledgment (the 27th of February, 2020, for the record), I've had so many incredible adventures and had so many outstanding people enter my life in one way or another.

The number of people that deserve a shout out are legion. I am not gonna lie. It's nuts. Between my beta readers, my ARC readers, my friends in the industry, my fellow authors, to the random Facebook groups that offer suggestions for authors and marketing plans to my mom and my amazing girlfriend (who puts up with WAYYYYY more crap than she deserves)...

...I don't think I can list all of you. I want to, but I can't.

That said, I can say this:
Thank you to Danielle V. who won a contest to get to name one of the taverns in Basion City, the "Sow's Teat." That was a fun little thing to do.

There's one more special shout-out I have to do.

At several conventions and events in 2019, I donated a portion of my book sales (online and in-person) to a couple of different charity groups in my home state of West Virginia for LGBTQ+ rights and local food pantries.

For everyone that either:
Bought a book
Bought a trinket
Made a direct donation
Allowed me to put up special signage
Helped share the word

...thank you for helping me make a difference, no matter how bit or small.

For those of you that make supporting others your life's work,
you are true heroes, and you have my utter respect and adoration.

Thank you.

~Josh

Joshua E. B. Smith

The Battles of Coldstone's Summit did not come without cost.
It was supposed to have been a simple haunting, a simple test.
What it became was a bloody battlefield rife with corpses;
the majority of which were still walking, albeit not breathing.

Akaran had been sent there to prove his mettle,
to show he could wear the mantle of an exorcist of the Order of Love,
simply to prove that he had learned his lessons and was ready to serve.

He proved that he knew how to bring the Will of the Goddess.
He proved that he knew how to survive.
He proved that he knew how to fight.
He proved that he knew how to banish the damned.
He proved he would do anything and all things,
sadly, without regard for the costs of his actions.

That disregard came at a price.

An act of contrition was imposed on him for his acts of disrespect to the Mount.
We had no idea what the true nature of it was,
only that it brought him suffering, and cruelly left him bereft of magic.

To heal his body and recover his magic, I sent him to Medias Manor.
A haven. A place of recovery and peace. A sanctuary.

Basion City had nothing of note for interest by any outside party.
No grand military plots were hatched there. No truly excessive industry.
No grand structures for the Queen. No risk of invasion.
The 'safest place in the Kingdom,'
minus one little storeroom owned by the Order of Love.

It was an inland haven, a day's ride away from the closest military outpost.
A simple city, yet one full of thousands of souls,
all of whom that wanted to live in peace.

I sent him there knowing there was no chance that he would
be embroiled in bloodshed, violence, suffering, or pain.

I should have known better.

~Sir Steelhom
Office of Oversight, New Civa

1

PROLOGUE
Wundis, the 2nd of Greenbirth, 513 QR

Rain pounded against the window as two women curled up across from each other on a pillow-covered bench near each other. It was late, and the only light to be had came from a flickering fireplace in the corner. "It's cold out," the youngest of the two lamented, "and the wind it... it's blowing my hair everywhere. Making it... making it hard to see."

"But you aren't using your eyes, are you?" the other woman asked as she sipped tea from an old ceramic mug. The light from the fire made her gray eyes glimmer silver.

The younger woman shook her head, her white hair hanging limply down on her cotton robe. "No... yes, but no. What I see? What I hear and see aren't -"

"Tell me what you *can* see."

She took a nervous breath and tried to calm her shaking hands. She couldn't bring herself to look up at her friend, and no matter how hard she tried, she couldn't stop her fingers from twitching. "I... see a man. We're outside."

"Outside where?"

"The... it has a picture, a... a pig? It... engorged teats? It's... disgusting."

Her confidant made a show of slowly setting her mug down before picking up a feathered quill and a piece of parchment before make note of the design. "You've never mentioned that before in our sessions. Is it new?"

"Yes. We... we haven't been there before."

"What else do you see?"

"Him," she replied, "and a man below us. His aura. Loud but refined. The... the ether around him? It's... orderly. Arranged. It's vibrating. Ready. Looking for more. But it's not swirling. It's not... not chaotic. He... has to be a Gran. Has to be. Too refined."

The other woman made a note of that, too. "A Granalchi? What does he look like? Can you tell?"

She squeezed her eyes shut tight and focused on the thought. "It's so high up here," she complained. "I can't... I can barely tell. He's... a brown cloak. I can... sometimes see his reflection. He... he has a white mustache."

"Okay, that's good. What more do you see? Do you hear anything?"

The wind is blowing her hair. There's more rain coming. Their prey feels it, too. She can feel his heartbeat pounding through the ether. He's rushing, and they follow him for a few short blocks until another man appears. He's wearing a round, flat-billed hat that's hiding his face from overhead. "That one. That one," she repeated, "dangerous. Aura is death. Not... not from here. He is... other."

Her metaphysician leaned in closer to listen to her whispers. "Do you know his name? Can you hear *him*?"

"Just... he wants in the vault. The... Miral. Miral's vault. He wants in there. He thinks that... thinks that the brown cloaked. He... can get him in there. The man in the hat wants in there."

"What about the Granalchi?"

"He... he doesn't. Wants the other man to leave him alone. He's... agitated. The aura around... the one in the hat. It's the opposite of his. Chaotic. Maddening. I can't stand... please, let me stop..."

The healer gently cupped the younger woman's shaking hands with one of hers. "No. You have to. You came to my room tonight. You know something is wrong. We've discussed this, Bistra. The way to wellness is through confronting the things that you can see."

Her patient looked up at her, her amber eyes brimming with tears. After a little sniffle, she bent her head back down and tried to focus again. "The bad man leaves. He was wrong. Not what we wanted."

"We?"

"The... the shadow. The one with me."

She made a little soft 'ah' sound in response.

Following him again. It's getting windier. His cloak billows about, and when it blows open, a bag falls out of it. He bends down to pick it up, and catches a glimpse of them in a puddle. His silver eyes flicker with light. The shadow realizes that it's been seen. It tenses up. They lunge through the air as he starts to turn. There's a scream. "That's... that's where it ended," she panted, swallowing air.

"Your dream ended?"

"Not a dream!" she shouted, eyes huge with tears streaming down her cheeks. "Oliana... I, I mean... Lady Oliana, it's not a dream. And... not. Not. Not ended. *He* ended. Started ending."

"I've told you before, child, you may call me Livstra. Hardly anyone calls me by my surname," the other woman said with a smile.

3

A closed fist whips out and cuffs the man across the back of his skull. There's a scuffle, cursing. Rough hands slam his face into a wall. He's stunned, he's disoriented. He starts to utter an invocation. His hands move like lightning in the air. Then the shadow grabs them. Fingers snap like twigs. We shove him again. Send his head against a post. He's unconscious now. We're dragging him.

"Bistra, it's a dream..."

She was too lost in it to hear her voice, and her eyes grew cloudy as she saw the scene play out again in her head. *We stop dragging him. He's against the wall. Rain is falling now. Can't wait. Can't watch but can't wait. Know it's coming. It always does. Like this or not. It happens. Sound. Little whimpers. A groan.*

Clattering.

That sound. Know that sound. A short scream and a clatter. Little pebbles hitting the cobblestones. A glimpse of one of the stones, shiny and ivory, fresh from his mouth. Clattering on the stones.

"It's a dream. Focus on my voice, Bistra, it's a dream."

Another sound. Things dropping into puddles. Wet sounds. Wet things. Terrible sounds. Stomach is twisting hearing them. Body is screaming. His. Mine. Ours. Can feel it. Can hear it the noise in the ether is so loud. There's... a blob. A mass with bits of things attached to it. She looks down at it.

The eye in the gutter looks back up at her, and she screams.

When she came to, she realized that Livstra had her head in her hands. The healer's eyes are shut, and she's repeating the same words again and again as a faint pink hue radiated from between her palms. "*Ashadi fa Solina, ashadi; ashadi Solina, ashadi,*" she repeated. "Peace, peace from Solinal. Listen to the Peacebringer. Let Him help. It's a *dream*, we've been down this road before. It's a dream."

The spell made the broken woman sag down into a relaxed heap as the invocation took hold and snuffed her panicked hallucination. "Not dream," she sniffled. "It's him. The shadow. It follows. Follows free. Fangs. Fangs are here."

"*No,*" Livstra stressed. "There are no fangs here. This place is safe. You know that. That's why you're here. It *has* to be a dream because those things don't happen here."

"Can't be. Can't be dream," she insisted.

"Why do you think that, hm? You know you don't leave the Manor at night. You almost never leave your room at all. Your window was open and some rain got in. That's why you're cold and wet; we'll move your bed tomorrow. No more nightmares after that."

Bistra sniffled again and shook her head slowly. "I'm wet because I was... I was... here, maybe now you'll believe me," she replied as she reached under her robe and pulled out a copper medallion.

It had been banged up, dented, and streaked with dried blood.

4

All of the color in Livstra's face drained away as her eyes went wide in shock and disbelief. "Where did you find that? How did you *get* it?! That belongs to Adept Odern! He's from the... the Granalchi Annex..."

"Shadows," she whimpered. "The *shadow*. The *fangs*. *He* gave it to me. Said... it was a gift."

On the other side of town, a few blocks away from the *Sow's Teat*, passersby found a body nailed to a wall of a local tannery. There were screams of horror and shouts for help. Guards rushed down rainy, cobblestone streets. One of them slipped in something squishy and immediately fell into the bloody mud. On a nearby building that overlooked most of the city, an old sign creaked in the wind.

"*Welcome to Basion City,*" it read.

If the corpse could've laughed at the irony, it would've.

"*The safest place in the Kingdom.*"

I. THE SAFEST PLACE
Londis, the 3rd of Greenbirth, 513 QR

"First time to Basion City, exorcist?"

"First time," Akaran answered, looking up from the back of the creaky wooden cart he'd been stuck in the last four hours. "Don't know that much about it, honestly."

Truth be told, there wasn't much to see approaching it either. Basion City – the oft said 'Safest Place in the Kingdom' – sat in a crater in the back end of Yittl Canyon, and was a bit of a slog to reach. The mouth of the canyon was a bit less than a day's travel by foot from a port at the edge of the Alenic Ocean. From what his escort had said, there was only one feasible way into Basion from the ocean once you arrived at Port Cableture, and that was to trudge north through the length of the canyon and try not to get stuck in the muddy deposits left behind by the Orshia-Avagerona River that coursed right down its throat.

Of course, even with only one primary way *in*, the safest city still needed a wall. And what would the point of a wall be if it didn't extend over the top of the canyon? It'd do the guards no good if someone decided to scale the cliffs and then just hop in over the edge (or get to the edge of the basin from the other direction and do the same).

At least, for right now, that was the only excuse he could think of to justify the massive stone edifice looming before them. It wasn't like it could've just been built to stroke the ego of the city planner, of course. The fact that you had to travel through one giant choke-point to even *make* it to the city or that the only way *into* the canyon was through a naval base that the entirety of the 2nd Naval Fleet called home?

Well, that alone should've done away with the need for a wall around the entrance. Yet, there was one. A very large one that towered over their heads as some grand symbol of the Crown's Might.

Or at least, the Crown's Wallet.

So, surely, there couldn't possibly be any other entrances into the city.

When he voiced as much, his escort referenced the book he *should* have been reading on the weeks-long trip here. Specialist-Major Badin looked back over his shoulder at him and rolled his eyes. "Weren't you supposed to read that travel guide that Evalia handed off to you?"

Handed was an interesting term for it. Toniki felt like it had been years ago, though really? It had just been a month. After escorting him off of the mountains and down back to Gonta, the Commander of the 13th had some choice phrases and suggestions while the so-called doctors in the equally so-called City of Mud worked to patch him up.

Not the least of which was to shove a letter in his face before saying, "I swear upon the Lady of Destruction and Reformation, if you *don't* study this I am going to have you jailed for idiocy ill-befitting an Agent of the Crown."

"I skimmed it."

"You know if she finds out..."

The priest sighed and pulled himself up on the cart with one hand as he looked towards the imposing gateway ahead. "...then I know you're the one that told her and I'll hit you in the face with my cane."

"Gotta be able to catch me first," the battlemage laughed back. He flashed his friend a smile through a face full of graying stubble. "How's your knee feeling?"

Akaran ran his left hand down over his leg and cursed. "Like I'm never going to walk again."

"It can't be that bad? They cut you open how many times?" he asked as he wiped a few errant raindrops off of his cheek.

Behind him, the exorcist clutched at his thigh with a grimace and a shudder at the thought. "Twice. Without magic to numb me, too."

"Still don't get it," Badin replied after thinking about it for a few minutes. "You took a hit from that monster in the tower, and suddenly you can't use magic anymore? And magic doesn't work on you?"

As he gave his leg another squeeze, the exorcist shook his head. "It's a lot more complicated than that. Can we not talk about it? I'm going to have to explain this when we get to wherever it is they told you to take me."

"Fair enough. Gotta admit after that mess? I think I picked a shoddy time to give up drinking."

"You gave up drinking because that old bat Hirshma told you your stomach was gonna end up permanently hanging outside your mouth if you kept it up."

Badin just laughed. "Gonna miss you, you know that, right? Soon as I get you delivered, it's back to the mountains. Gonna try to stick around for a few days first, see if I can't get a rest before trekking back."

"Yeah, because it was such a hard trip for you."

"We've been traveling for three weeks. Two of which was on a boat. I don't like traveling by boat," he whined.

"I don't like traveling tied to a cot," Akaran grumbled back. The cart crested a small hill and the glory that was Basion City's stone wall was spread open to them – and for a moment, the exorcist let himself enjoy the sight.

The mage quit laughing and sighed in vague frustration. "Okay, so someone's gonna give you the grand tour later, I don't doubt – so let me hit you with the highlights."

"The buildings look like the ones on the grounds of the Queen's Capitol."

"Should," the battlemage retorted. "Some of the Second Queen's architects worked on it. Or so I heard."

Akaran glanced at him out of the corner of his eye. "You hear a lot about building construction?"

"I'm a drunk. I hear a lot about a lot of things."

"Fair enough."

They pulled up to a slow halt in front of the semi-imposing barbican as a pair of chainmail-covered guards flagged them down. "You two. Didn't know there were any transports scheduled up from Cableture."

Badin pulled a writ of passage from the inside of his coat and passed it over. "We're technically not from Cableture."

The soldier looked at the wax seal and arched an eyebrow. "This says you're from there."

"Well, yes," he quickly corrected. "But we're not *from* Cableture. Just had to pass through it to get here."

"So then answer the question," came the quick and gruff snap back.

Akaran cleared his throat and pulled a silver coin out from his coat and held it in front of the guardsman so he could see it. "Medical transport. Order of Love."

"Oo-lo. You the medic?"

"The transport."

With a grunt, the guard opened the seal and scanned over the letter as a misty drizzle started from the miserably cloudy skies overhead. "Manor or Repository?"

"What repository?" the exorcist asked.

"The Oo-lo one. Are you going to it or the Manor?"

Badin shrugged at him. "He goes wherever he chooses. That signet says as much. Trust me, spend some time with the man. You'll figure out how that works in a hurry."

Akaran tilted his head slightly and looked his friend in the eyes. "Thank you...?"

"...and I go where I choose," the mage added.

The guard looked over at his partner, who wasn't doing anything other than holding the city wall up with his shoulder. With a roll of his eyes, he shot them both down. "Not today. Nobody gets past the gate without bein' 'honest an' forthright' about their business in the city. Orders from up high."

"What? It's *Basion City*," the battlemage stressed with a whine, "the quote unquote 'safest place in the Kingdom.' What's got the Overseer pissed off?"

"Orders didn't come from the Overseer. He's out-ranked."

"By *who?*"

"Paverilak Tyreening," he answered with a shrug as he handed the writ back.

Akaran finally cut through it with a wave of his hand as he shifted around in the cart to stare the guard square in the eye with enough intensity that it made the underpaid footman flinch back. "I don't live here. I don't know local politics. I don't know what's going on. I am tired, I am in pain, and I am hungry. I am an exorcist with the Order of Love, *he* is a Specialist-Major with the 13th, and we have papers. Are you going to let us in or not?"

The guard sighed and shifted uncomfortably in his boots. "Look, sirs. Are you two going to the Manor or other? I gotta make a note of everyone that comes through the gate on my shift, or the Captain will have me feeding Paverilak's pigs. I *don't* want to get on the bad side of the Captain and I *don't* want to get stuck tending after the Betrothed's livestock."

Before Akaran could offer suggestions on other things he could do to the livestock, the battlemage interjected a question. "That Paverilak fellow is the regional...?"

"Yeap. Maiden Esterveen's Betrothed. He's in the city for the damn wedding celebrations starting next month, curse every single cock-suckin' royal that's come to town. Makin' absolutely all our lives a livin' pisser," he groused as he gestured back behind him into the city proper. "So, please. The Manor or the Repository? You're Oo-lo. Whatever you do once you're in the walls is your own business, I just gotta fiskin' know *where* and *how long* you're staying."

The travelers looked at each other for a long moment before finally giving him an answer. "Medias Manor. I'm being sent to the Manor. I don't know for how long."

"I'm just here long enough to get a drink," Badin added.

Flummoxed, Akaran turned back to him. "You just told me you were going to quit drinking."

"But there's a wedding. Have to drink for weddings."

"He just said it's next month!"

The guard spit something decidedly green and foul on the ground and corrected the priest before he could continue. "Said the *celebrations* start in a month. Weddin' ain't for at least three."

Smiling, the battlemage patted his friend on his shoulder. "I can stick around. I didn't promise Evalia I'd get my ass back anytime quick."

"You forgot that I've met the woman," Akaran protested. "She will have your ass *hauled* back if you don't."

Finally at his limit with the two of them, the guard straightened up and put his hand on his sword. The move immediately made Akaran reach for his until his escort squeezed his arm as tight as he could. "Dammit, how long are you two chucklefisks staying?"

"He's staying until they fix him," Badin answered, "I'm staying until I have to go back. Kinda upset the Commander and she said to keep this boy company until I was satisfied he was taken care of."

"Fine," he growled. "Undetermined, and one week. You stay any longer than that, it ain't my fault. An' since you decided to be so damn roundabout, you can tell me where exactly you came from, an' if you say Cableture, you can go back to it."

Akaran dropped his face into his hands and winced as he felt a familiar pull in his injured arm. "Goddess what did I..." he started before he composed himself. "I got hurt in a frozen little pisspot of a town called Toniki, in Weschali Province. From there, they sent me down to Gonta; same province. Gonta couldn't help, so after they stitched my knee and arm back together, they sent me here. Came by boat to Cableture and from Cableture I got stuck here with *you*. Now you are going to let my tired ass inside or so help me, I will use what rank I have left to make sure that you don't *feed* the damn pigs, you're *fed* to the damn pigs."

"Well you don't have to be so nasty about it, do you? That's all I bloody needed to know."

"ME nasty? I will show you what nasty is the second I -"

Badin coughed loudly and interrupted the priest before he could finish the thought. "*Thank you*, guardsman. We'll be on our way."

"No you won't," the soldier quickly interjected. "He's Oo-lo? Needs to check in first."

"I just did?" Akaran asked with a frown.

"You just got through the gate," he corrected with a sniffle. "Standing orders from one of the Maidens. You gotta register at the waystation if you aren't going to the Repo first thing. That's the rule."

The battlemage raised his hand and spoke up. "Excuse me, did you say *Maidens*? As in, more than one?" When the guard nodded, he adjusted the dangling pewter sun hanging off of his neck and looked back to Akaran. "Who did you piss off to get stuck in a city with a plurality of *Maidens*?"

All the exorcist could do was wordlessly shrug and sputter out a, "Damned if I know?" before turning back to the guard. "What waystation?"

"I dunno. Some Oo-lo thing. Not far from here. Go two blocks. Take a right. Can't miss it. Go there first," and added, "and no you *don't* have a choice," when Akaran started to protest the order.

Badin had the cart moving before the exorcist could utter a retort. After they passed under the portcullis and were well-past the gatehouse, Akaran made a rude gesture at the guardsman's back. "Soon as I can walk again..."

Now that they were *inside* the city, he was sad to say that the architectural theme matched the dull-gray and depressingly imposing wall outside. Or at least, the *construction* did. Every building within eyeshot had been built out of the same utilitarian stonework and perfectly matching drab masonry work. The only thing that made the buildings look less like a pinnacle of army planning and fashion were the occasional second and or third-story walkways that connected some of the structures to each other.

That started to change about two blocks in, albeit briefly. While Badin looked around and commented on the surprising military presence out and out, all Akaran did was just sit and try to figure out why in the world there would be two Provincial Maidens in one city. As it turned out, there weren't. Not exactly, at least.

The waystation was a little more formal than it had sounded at the gate, though not by much. It was an otherwise nondescript building that looked as drab as the others they'd seen so far. That was except for the copper bust on a dirty marble pedestal just outside the front door, and the sign etched into the stone above it. "*Eldot... ta iah...*," the battlemage tried to read before giving up and looking back at his companion.

Akaran looked up from the back of the cart and frowned. "*Eldot ta iah hass ma hassers*," he recited. "'Love for Those Whom Harm Harmers.' This is the place, alright."

Badin pulled open his cloak and very carefully set a gloved hand on a straight steel knife at his belt. Despite his rank in the army, he hadn't bothered to wear his uniform – so instead of traveling in a chain tunic and the rest befitting his station, all he wore was a thick wool tunic and a brown leather vest. If it wasn't for the sun-shaped sigil dangling from his neck (or the red wool cloak over his shoulders), you'd be forgiven for not realizing he was army. "You... you're in the Order of *Love*, right?"

"I am, why?"

"That doesn't sound loving."

The younger man shrugged under the bewildered gaze from the grizzled veteran. "Do you enjoy killing people?"

He blinked his slightly-jaundiced eyes in surprise. "No, of course not. We do what we do when we must."

"Same," Akaran groused as he started to pull himself out of the cart before giving up halfway through the effort, "but nobody is gonna assume that an army barracks is full of daisies and apples, are they? They're going to see swords and maces and shit in the cabinets?"

"Probably, yes, but -"

"My job is to punch things that need punched and I do it because the Goddess tells me to. Or She tells people who turn around and tell me to in Her stead. Or She tells people that tell their people to tell me to go hit something," he added as he pointed up at the sign. "I promise, you walk in there, you will be greeted with honor and respect and if you need help, they'll give it because if you follow Her, you are tasked to love all and defend those that seek aid."

Badin rubbed at his coal-black stubble and narrowed his eyes slightly. "I'm sensing a 'but' in there."

"But don't look in the cabinets," Akaran warned, "because they'll have worse things in there than swords."

The battlemage started to reply when an oddly creepy person in a pale white cotton robe stuck their head out of the door. "The drawers are what I must warn you away from; the cabinets mostly have mildewing vestments," the caretaker suggested with a voice that was so universally bland that it was impossible to tell if it was a man or woman, or even how old they were. "Though neither are filled with things to be discussed on the street." With the heavy hood obscuring their face, neither priest or mage could see the face it belonged to, so wisely, they decided to be as respectful as possible.

Just in case.

"Apologies...?" the priest replied, leaving the question open to fish for a name.

"Templar," they answered – and didn't offer anything else to go with the title. "Exorcist? Why have you not yet showed the respect due to the Lady?" they asked with an accusatory gesture towards the bust by the doorway.

"With respect, Templar, it's not because I don't want to," he admitted in reply. "I'm hurt."

"We all hurt, child. That is no excuse for showing dishonor."

Badin cleared his throat and interjected himself before things could turn for what felt like a quick way to worse. "Templar, a moment."

"Yes?"

"He really is hurt. His knee's just about been destroyed, and magic ain't helping him. We just arrived and we're on the way to the Manor, where he was told to find help."

The figure shifted around in their robes and peered into the cart from the doorway. "Ah. And I suppose the fools at the gate instructed you here...?"

"Yeap," Akaran grunted.

"Ah," the templar sighed again before vanishing back into the station without a word. The priest and Badin exchanged bewildered looks and shrugs as they wordlessly tried to make sense of anything that had just happened. A few moments later, and the caretaker stepped back outside with a quill and a piece of parchment.

"There's no slight to the Lady intended, Templar, I promise, I simply -"

"You are an exorcist with wounds that cannot be healed. The Goddess does not judge the broken for things that they cannot do within reason, and as such, nor shall I. But I do need to register your arrival for Order records, of course."

That request turned into a quick back-and-forth from both the exorcist and the battlemage. Most of it was the same information they'd offered at the gate, but a few more questions were asked that Badin had never heard before. "Five-one-one, six-three-nine," was the answer to a question the templar asked about 'numbers' and, "Upper left arm, scalp, rear neck," for a question about where his 'words are written.'

Seemingly satisfied, the caretaker stuffed the scroll back into their white cloak and started to address Akaran like Badin wasn't even there. "The Order welcomes you to Basion, Brother Priest, but I have to warn, this is not an ideal time for a new arrival – although at the same time, it is most fortuitous. I have a small job for you."

"Respectfully, Caretaker...?"

"I am a Templar, child. Speak accordingly."

Badin cringed for him at the tone in their voice.

"Templar, respectfully, I'm not up for any tasks..."

"You will be for this one. A further explanation will be offered when it isn't pissing the rain, but please, in short: while you stay at the manor, please be mindful of the other guests. It would be nice to have a resident of that place be able to tell us how our fellows are healing."

Akaran wrinkled his nose and wiped some of the rain off of his face. "You're not getting reports now?"

"We are," the templar clarified, "though they come from staff. Well-meaning staff, of course, but staff the same. Voices in other levels often provide a broader picture."

"Oh look. You're getting your knee fixed *and* turning into a spy," Badin dryly interrupted.

"Love is Love, wherever She goes," the caretaker chided, "though Love does not always see clearly."

The youngest of the three flinched and stopped himself from covering up his eyepatch with his left hand. "Of course. I'll do as asked. Who do I report to?"

"In all likelihood, Maiden-Templar Prostil," the templar replied.

"Prostil?" Badin interrupted, "I thought that Maiden Esterveen was the Provincial...?"

The templar turned their head and even without being able to see their face, you could *feel* the disdain they had to even have to *look* at the other man. "Maiden Sanlian Esterveen *is* the Provincial Maiden of Kettering Province, yes."

"But you just said her name was Prostil...?" the mage asked, slightly bewildered.

"Maiden-Templar Catherine Prostil, yes. She oversees the Repository of

Miral, in the eastern corner of the city. It is an outpost for the Order. You'll have to head there once you are ambulatory."

Akaran sat there and slowly mulled the information over in his head. "So there are two Maidens in the city right now. Who has rank?"

"One *Provincial* Maiden," their host clarified. "Sanlian's Betrothed, Paverilak Tyreening, is currently in the city acting in her stead – though Sanlian herself is not. The only responsibility that Prostil has is with the Repository and claims no Betrothed of her own. You should have no reason to be bothered *or* to bother any of Sanlian's interests. Do not concern yourself with reporting to her staff."

"Just Prostil's?" he asked.

The templar nodded firmly. "Just Prostil's."

The priest was quick to agree to that with a short, sharp nod. "Spy on the manor, avoid the Provincial's interests. I can do that."

"The suggestion that we want you to spy is untrue. Simply expect to be asked about how you feel that the staff is treating the other residents when you eventually arrive at the Repository," the templar retorted indignantly. "Or, that is to say, if he is capable enough. Mage? Are his wounds worse than a broken leg and the breath of an addict?"

"An addict?!" Akaran protested. "Excuse me but -"

The person in white hushed him with a wave of their hand. "I smell the cocasa on your breath from the doorway. For the odor to be that pungent you must have ingested a sizable amount. Thus, you are addicted, or you are foolish, or you are both. It is to treat pain, I presume – but that is neither here nor there. Battlemage? Is he capable of interaction or has his mind been assaulted?"

He looked at the exorcist and sized the boy up slowly, and let the question hang in the air for several long moments until Akaran growled out, just under his breath, "Badin..."

"Yeah, he's fine. Cranky, but fine."

"Well, we are the Order of Love," their inquisitor replied, "not the Order of Sunshine and Happiness." After saying that, Akaran was handed the scroll and quill. A few moments and a poor signature later, and the Order representative sent them on their way.

"That... that was strange," the battlemage muttered after they were safely out of earshot.

"Would expect that if we were closer to the border," Akaran mused, "not this far towards the Kingdom center."

"Guess we arrived at an ideal time," Badin replied as they worked their way through the streets. It only took them another block before the tone of their surroundings changed measurably. Gone were the drab, militaristic buildings. Gone were the ramparts and loopholes decorating the sides of random shops

14

and stores. Instead, the houses and shops were much friendlier and even painted in soft colors here and there (although not uniformly, and most of the places that were, weren't done well).

"What do you mean?"

"Get a chance to rub noses with royalty from all over the province, apparently," he answered. "Can't imagine what a big deal it must be if the Provincial is sending down her right-hand man to handle it."

"Do not know, do not care," the exorcist retorted as he stared at the multitude of banners draped from doorways and walkways and archways. It wasn't just that – people scurried back and forth, shouting instructions at each other to hang bows and wreaths and trim bushes and trees and arrange flowers down the main street from the gate. "Maidens defend their Provinces with the full backing of the army. Their Betrotheds handle governorship and local laws. We give them a wide berth, they give us one. Only gets to be a headache when the Maiden in question is in the Order itself."

"Like that Prostil woman he mentioned?"

Akaran nodded and watched a happy couple singing and dancing through the drizzling mist falling on everything. "Just like. Sure, we take orders from them, just like anyone else, but our permissions in the Kingdom let us work outside of their influence. Mostly."

The buildings may have been dull, but the trimmings were garish to the point of over-compensation. "Some free advice?" Badin offered.

"What?"

"When Maidens start moving their Consorts around, keep your eyes open. If it ain't for money, it's for blood."

"I don't have any money. And I've only got one eye."

"But you've still got blood. For now."

Akaran ignored *that* particular comment and the thoughts spreading from it. "They said this mess is for a wedding?"

"Which *guarantees* it's money *and* blood."

The exorcist couldn't dispute that by any stretch, so he just stayed silent for a few minutes as the cart rattled along the cobblestone streets. "So what's so damn magical about this city? The safest one in the Kingdom? Bit of an egotistical title for a town in a pit."

Badin chewed on his lip and waved at a gaggle of children that stopped to beg for coins as they passed by. "I can't say that I know all that much, to be frank. Read the regional guide when you get some free time. 'Till then: Basion is so named because way back when at the dawn of time or some shit, one of the Gods got all pissy and put a holier-than-thou fist into the ground. Punched a crater and a half in the dirt."

"Which one?"

"Which what?"

"Which God got pissy and decked the countryside?"

He shrugged and turned down a side street without slowing down. Every bump he hit made the priest grit his teeth and clench at his leg. "Oh, who knows. You're the priest."

Akaran's reply wasn't worth repeating.

"Anyway: some other idiots not as long ago decided that it'd be a good place to build a village. Whole place is surrounded by a cliff with only a couple of easy openings into the basin. Saved on building walls, I guess."

"Except for that giant wall."

Badin shrugged at him. "I did say the Second Queen had her architects involved."

"So there are some other ways in and we took the one that made us get covered in mud. We couldn't have gone through one of those?"

The battlemage shook his head. "No, and if you quit grousing, I'll get to the why."

"Fair enough. But... wait. How do they keep it from flooding? Big pit in the middle of the ground? Feels like it should be a lake more than a bustling center of commerce."

He didn't see Badin's smile. "Finally, a good question. The Orshia-Avagerona River winds down into this province from somewhere up in Lowmarsh, and spits down over the northern lip of the basin. It circles around the edges of the walls on both sides and drains out along the south-eastern quarter. There's a bridge ahead; once we're over it, we're over the river and into the city proper. Right now we're just passing through the barracks and around some of the local merc postings."

"Oh. That explains the fortress feeling."

"Now for the bad news," he cautioned.

His shoulders tensed up so hard it made the ache in his arm absolutely throb. "There's bad news?"

"You won't be staying in Basion City," he clarified.

"Then what am I doing here?"

Badin pointed up in the sky and off somewhere past the throng of buildings ahead. "Well, my orders were to get you up to Medias Manor. *That* delightful little place is all the way on the other side of Basion and then up the wall on the western side."

There was a very long pause from the exorcist before he spoke up again. "If we don't *have* to go through the city, why, again, did you make us go through all that mud and now through a town I'm not even staying in...?"

"Because I'm hungry. And I don't feel like hacking my way through the trees. Didn't you notice the woods around us?"

"I'm in a cart. All I notice is the shit back here that I'm trying to keep from bouncing out whenever you hit a bump."

His friend didn't even try to hold back a chuckle. "Alright, listen. It ain't just the basin that keeps the city safe. The Fel'achir Forest stretches from about a week's ride east all the way through this entire province and halfway into Mulvette."

"I suppose now is when I tell you I'm garbage with directions, right?"

"Aren't you supposed to be a traveling priest?"

Akaran flung up his left arm with an exasperated shout. "I travel with a map!"

"Then I suggest you read one," the battlemage scolded. "It's in the guide-planner. That thing you're supposed to have read by now."

There was another grumbled bout of profanity from the back of the cart that Badin didn't give much effort to making sense of. An elderly woman passing by, however, slammed her hands over her ears and hobbled away from them as fast as she could. "And when I'm done doing *that*, then I'll read the damn thing," he continued to grouse.

"*At any rate*," Badin continued, "while the Fel'achir is thicker in some places than others, along the edges of Basion, it's damn-near impenetrable. So, going *through* the city is easier than going *around* the city."

"So what you're ultimately telling me is that you're dropping me off in some fisking medic's hut that sits on the edge of a basin surrounded by trees that are so thick that you can't climb through them?"

"More or less."

After another long pause, Akaran spoke up with a bit less bravado in his voice. "I really am being punished, aren't I?"

Badin turned his head to look at the somber, sad stare in the exorcist's eye. "That I don't know."

"Well, wonderful," he sighed. A few moments later, he shifted around until he could face the front and see where they were headed. "So, any idea what the Repository is that guard was going on about?"

His friend thought about it for a minute and gave an answer that almost satisfied his curiosity. "Not much of a clue. I know that your Order has a fortress here of some kind. Been here as long as I can remember. Don't know anything about it, really. He seemed to think you would."

"My Order owns a lot of things. Just because I don't know what it is doesn't mean anything."

"Well. Surely someone will tell you."

"Speaking of telling you," Akaran said as he changed the topic, "you know she really will have your ass if you don't get back to Toniki."

"Who, Evalia?"

"That's the her I was thinking."

"No, she won't," he replied with a half-sigh. "I guess I didn't tell you, did I? We had a bit of a... falling out."

The priest passed forward a flask of something that wasn't entirely water from the inside of his cloak. "I had heard. When you, her, and Mariah went after the fracture at Usaic's cabin?"

"Yeah. Things didn't go well."

"Want to talk about it?"

Badin took a swig of the not-water and blanched at the taste of... stale awfulness. "Not... really. The long and short of it is that I'm on leave from the 13th as long as I want. Gonna make sure you're safe here and then I'm gonna find somewhere else to head to. Maybe Mulvette for a while, if I can find an open posting." He swallowed hard and looked down at his bottle. "Belianberries? These spoil a week after harvesting..."

He took the flask back and nailed a swig of it himself before putting it away. "You're the fan of fermentation. How'd you manage to get the time off?"

"You mean aside from the two of us nearly killing each other when that... when the mana started to seep through and...?" he asked in return, letting it trail off.

Akaran nodded knowingly. "You got exposed to something you shouldn't have been exposed to. I can relate."

"Yeah. Yeah, bet you can. So I didn't tell you, I guess?"

"Tell me what?"

The cart rolled to a halt at a busy intersection while a squad of soldiers marched by, the red and orange Dawnfire flag on full display as the misty drizzle made their chainmail clink sharply with every heavy stomp down the wet street. "After you did the deed in Toniki and got kicked to Gonta, Maiden Piata and her consort rolled in. Took over operations."

"That was fairly expected, wasn't it?"

"But not welcome."

"Considering her title, I'm not surprised."

Badin grunted in half-amusement/half-misery. "Once the Madwoman got a handle for what was going on – Gods above, I am so glad I wasn't in charge of that mess – she reassigned the 13th. Sent half of us back to Gonta, the other half marching off towards Anthor's Pass."

"She did what? Evalia isn't in Toniki anymore?"

He shook his head. "No, she is. Promoted. Working with the Maiden directly now, until she has her kid. After, maybe, too. Rest of us that survived that nightmare were given the choice of remaining, taking a year personal leave with half-pay, or permanent reassignment."

"And I'm gonna guess that after you and Evalia..."

"I love the 13th. I have a lot of friends there. Lost a few to that damned thing you killed off. Don't want to leave them. Just don't..."

"I get it," he answered with a sound that was almost like a sigh, but more of a quiet sob for a single tear.

Badin stopped the cart suddenly (much to the chagrin of the people around them) and turned to look the exorcist head-on. "How do you do it?"

"Do what?"

"Deal with... it. I saw inside that portal. That... what'd you call it? A breach? I saw..."

"Things you shouldn't've?" he asked knowingly.

His escort nodded and wiped some rain off of his face. "I mean, I get it. I throw lightning bolts at people, for the sake of all fisk. I know it comes from somewhere, not just inside my drunk ass, not just from the air around us. I know there's places but..."

"But there's knowing, and then there's *knowing*."

"That's it. How... how do you deal? All I know is that I picked the wrong time to quit drinking." He pointed at the flask still in Akaran's hand. "*That* doesn't count."

The exorcist just looked down at his leg and couldn't meet Badin's gaze. "I don't know."

"How do you not know?" he questioned as someone shouted slurs and assorted other colorful words at him for blocking the street with the cart.

"I can't sleep at night. I hear that wraith in my ears half the time. I'm the wrong guy to ask because I'm *not* dealing. All I want to do is hop out of this wagon and go beat someone up that deserves it and all I *can* do is sit here and chew on cocasa and pray that I can get past this."

That wasn't good enough for the battlemage — not that he could blame him. "How about the things before Toniki? I know you're new to the job but you stopped other things, right? Surely you had training against liv... well, can't call them living, I suppose."

"Well... yeah."

"Then how do you manage it? *Knowing* what's there?"

He took a deep breath and looked up at the miserable sky. "All I can say, I guess, is that I know *it's* there, the Abyss knows *I'm* here. I know that when I kill them they go someplace bad and that I know, at least, that a good place exists and if I don't fisk up that I might get to go when I get dead."

The mage blanched like he'd just been hit with a dead fish across the face. "So you cope by knowing there's a place that *might* let you in if you keep them happy? That doesn't give a lot for the rest of us to work on."

"Who said anything about that helping me through it? It's a big *might*. I don't understand it, don't really know how it works, and I sure as piss don't know what the Goddess has in mind for me. I just know that She wanted me to stand in front of that shit and punch it in the face. So I go punch shit and hope that it helps."

"Coping by stabbing things, huh?"

"Until I get told to quit. Then I'll do something else."

Badin's eyes started to twinkle just a little, with a slight bit of hope in his voice. "Drink?"

"No," he half-lied, "though it's not like I don't make enough bad decisions sober for it to count against me."

The soldier just snorted and went back to navigating them through the streets. "Fair enough. Well, if that's how you deal, maybe I'll look into that. I can't say I *like* knowing what's out there."

"Nobody does," he honestly answered. "You either face it or you run from it."

Badin didn't say anything for another five minutes at least. "Suppose so. Can't really ignore it."

"No. Really can't. Not once you *know*. Having belief is one thing, but *knowing* is..."

Silence reigned between them for a little longer as the military-styled structures gave way to more pleasant buildings with fewer hard edges and more windows. "I think I understand you a bit better now. So, either way. I'll be staying here in Basion for a while. Grew up near here. Father would drag me down here on occasion. No, doesn't mean I know anything about that Repository," he quickly added, "because... well, let's just say that dad? He didn't exactly look at you people in a friendly light. And honestly? I got a feeling that until you feel up to punching things again, you might need a friend."

More windows, more smiling faces, and more gaudy trim. Somewhere in this city, a horticulturalist was making a killing – he just knew it. "Thank you, Badin. I mean that."

"Don't doubt that at all. In the meantime – find a taberna for some food?"

"Yeah. Food. Thank you, my friend. I mean that. Both parts."

Badin finally joined the ranks of the smiling as he waved someone down to ask for directions to the closest tavern or bakery that wouldn't kill them both. "After what you did in Toniki? Playing bodyguard is the least I can do."

Yeah. After what I did in Toniki, he sighed to himself before he tried to keep smiling as they went deeper into the city.

II. MANOR-ISMS
The Late-Afternoon of Londis, the 3rd of Greenbirth, 513 QR

After they ate, the rest of the trip through Basion went by in a crawl. Or at least, the trip through the city proper. Badin hadn't been kidding – Medias Manor was on the far north-western side of the crater-turned-city, and it felt like it took forever to get there. And it was actually *on* the side of the city, beyond the cliff wall and on a hill that overlooked the urban center.

Getting there...

That was harder than it had sounded. Sure, if he could have walked on his own power, it might not have been so bad. Puzzling their way through the city streets took a few hours on its own. The trip took them through at least four distinctly different districts before the exhausted pair reached the western wall.

Which itself posed a different (albeit obvious) problem.

It was the first thing that Akaran had seen since arriving that didn't look like it was trying to be imposing. In fact, the internal wall was as beautiful as it was brilliant and answered a major question he had since he had first heard about the nature of the region: how do you feed a city without sprawling room to farm?

You farm *up*.

As best as he could tell, the northern wall of the city had been converted to one gigantic stair-stepped garden that spanned more than two-thirds of the rear face of the cliff. The upper edge was framed by another stone wall and wooden ramparts to his total lack of surprise. However, while providing a way to feed the masses, the problem the two of them faced was as obvious as the nature of the farms: they were stair-stepped. The locals called it both the Wall of Gardens and the Northern Stairwall, depending on who you talked to (and why).

Akaran and stairs were not two things that had been mixing well as of late.

Finding an alternative path that the two of them could manage to take in a cart served to be even harder than finding their way through the city even with Badin's experiences growing up in the area. He defended himself by saying that he had grown up in East Giffil, some district that was on the other side of the city. The exorcist didn't believe it and his companion didn't try to justify it further.

Once they found a path that the cart could ascend, it was as well-trodden and heavily packed as you could imagine. That slowed things down further and managed to wear out not only the two humans, but even Akaran's horse. By the time they reached the top, Nayli was expressing her namesake *repeatedly* and *loudly*.

It was an opinion that he couldn't argue with.

Nor was it the only complaint that they could hear.

From a distance, the first thought that Akaran had when he saw the manor was that it was some kind of low-budget castle. Up close, he regretted the 'low-budget' part. The manor stood three full stories tall with five jutting half-towers with gabled roofs and dormered windows complete with thick frosted glass and a balcony that stretched around the entire upper level.

It was beautiful in a decidedly imposing and somehow depressing way. The second and third stories were more wooden planks than they were stonework, while the bottom level had been built on heavy bricks that were the same color as the dreary clouds overhead. What was markedly *less* dreary were the four marble statues out in the yard, and the two busts by the main entryway.

Isamiael, Solinal, Niasmis, and Pristi, he mused as he looked at them from left to right. *Goddess of Medicine, God of Peace, Goddess of Love, and Goddess of Purity. At least they're giving attention to a good mix of the Pantheon. Wonder who the two heads by the door are.*

The glory of the manor was almost taken away by the heated argument between a middle-aged woman in a burgundy dress and a much taller (and in much better shape) man from the local garrison. Judging by his red cloak and the pair of short spikes down the mid-line of his bronze helmet, he was a Lieutenant-Commander, which likely pegged him as the head of the local garrison. "Any idea on who those two are?"

Badin shook his head as they approached the wrought-iron fence around the Manor grounds. "No idea. Looks like he's from the 4th, and they manage the security detail for the province."

"You have any friends with them?"

"Just a couple. He's not one of them though."

They stopped talking once they caught sight of the two travelers parked at the gate, although the woman gave the lieutenant-commander a hateful look and spat one last barb at him. "When you find out who, you *will* tell me. I will make sure there is assistance rendered in the meantime."

He flicked some dirt off of his shoulder as he stared her in her eyes. "I will do as the Queen's Law demands. Nothing more, nothing less."

"See to it that you do," she growled as she brushed past him and composed herself as she walked up to the gate. "You two. Bringing supplies or requesting assistance?" she called out with a deep, almost baritone voice.

Akaran dug into his cloak and pulled out one of three different letters granting him passage and permissions for his trip before handing it off to her. "Akaran DeHawk, Order of Love. Exorcist. Requesting medical assistance and admission."

"What about you?" the guardsman interrupted, pointing at his friend. "You're not one of mine and I didn't authorize any transfers."

The battlemage looked at the priest out of the corner of his eyes and silently mouthed a, "This is going well," before digging out a letter of his own. "Specialist-Major Badin, on leave from the 13th. Providing escort for this priest."

His superior officer scanned through the letter before he puffed out his chainmail-covered chest (painted red, like everyone else in the army) and crossing his arms. "I prefer to have warning when soldiers are being transferred under my command."

"With all due respect sir, I'm not being transferred to anyone's command, as it states in that Grant of Leave. I'm just carrying out my last orders prior to my break."

"If you're in my city, then you're under my command," the lieutenant snapped back. "I expect you'll be demanding use of my barracks?"

Before the battlemage could answer, Akaran quickly lifted his hand. "No, Commander. He's being extended an invitation to find lodging with the Order of Love for the next month. A gesture of thanks."

Badin turned slightly and tilted his head just a little. "You can do that?"

"Do you want to bed under his roof or one of ours?" he replied under his breath and out of the corner of his mouth.

He cleared his throat and pointed his thumb in Akaran's direction. "What he said. Lodging with the Order until further notice."

After a long drawn out stare, the garrison commander flashed them another look dripping with irritation out of his pale brown eyes and huffed in annoyance. "Just don't cause any trouble. I don't need some *hedgewizard* on *vacation* besmirching the reputation of *my* garrison while we prepare for the wedding. Or so help me, you *will* be shoved under my command and I *will* find ways to put whatever talents you *think* you have to work," he snarled just before he stomped over to a tan-haired horse that looked just as happy to be there as everyone else.

Nobody said anything until after he was well out of earshot. "Well isn't he just a bag of roses and fairy farts," Badin finally said to break the uncomfortable silence.

"You will have to excuse the Lieutenant-Commander," the woman in red replied. "Henderschott has had a bit of an issue land on his plate this morning. A headache he feels obligated to share with everyone that crosses his path today."

"I got chewed out by the gate guard when I got here. What's going on?" Akaran asked.

"It's of no matter. You must be Akaran. Welcome to Medias Manor – we've been waiting for you. I didn't expect you for another couple of days; forgive me for not having someone meet you at the gates."

"Thank you...? I wasn't expecting anyone. In fact, I honestly..." he let it trail off as he gestured at the manor "I... I don't know anything about *any* of this."

She gave him a matronly smile. "Of course you don't. What were you told about us?"

"Just that this was a hospital. That you might be able to help me."

"We are a hospital," she said before adding, "of sorts, that is. Of course, is anything really just one thing? Aren't all things a mix of what makes them?"

Akaran looked at Badin with a nervous little frown hovering across his eyebrows. When the battlemage just shook his head and tried to scoot back a little in his seat, he replied with a quiet and nervous, "No?"

She tucked his letter into the rope sash at her waist and matched his frown with one of her own. "Is that so? Are you just one thing? Are you just an exorcist? Or are you a soldier? Are you a priest? Are you a loyal agent of the Crown? One title begets another."

He shifted back and forth in his seat. "At the moment... not really much of anything."

The woman sighed and rolled her eyes. "Oh, wonderful. Someone that takes pity on themselves. You'll find that attitude doesn't get you too far here."

"It's not an attitude, it's a fact."

"Bones heal, child," she scolded. The warmth in her voice had faded to nothing and was quickly being replaced with irritated scorn.

He shook his head and pointed his finger at his head. "It's more than just bones."

"We can heal that too," she quickly retorted. "Have faith. Peace will be with you soon enough."

Akaran shifted around again and scooted himself to the back edge of the cart. "You say that like I should expect hope. Forgive me for being less than optimistic."

"We don't deal in hope here, child. We deal in healing," she said as she circled the cart until she was facing him head-on.

He wiped dirt and rain off of his face and glowered up at the sky. "With all due respect...?"

"Lady Oliana," she answered. "Or as most of the residents call me, Livstra."

24

"Then with all due respect, Livstra, can we deal inside?"

She followed his gaze to the heavier clouds looming overhead and nodded. "Yes, suppose we must. But first, a thing. The letter we received said that you were currently somehow unaffected by magic?"

"Can't use it. Can't cast it. Can't feel it."

She rolled her sleeves up past her elbow as she looked him up and down. "Doubtlessly a diagnosis placed on you by someone that doesn't know what they're doing," she scoffed before she placed her hand on his knee. "*Naffin, naffin, Almed Isamiael; vetchins takint uldas beneal,*" she chanted. As she did, a pale gold light pulsed out of her eyes and from the palm of her hand.

When absolutely nothing happened more than a blank look growing on Akaran's face, Badin cleared his throat. "You may wanna give it another go. First try with him doesn't always go over well."

She didn't deign to give a response to that, and instead just cleared her throat and tried again. "Ah... ahem. *Naffin, naffin, Almed Isamiael; vetchins takint uldas beneal.*"

All it did was get his curiosity riled up. "I recognize some of those words..."

"Well, yes. They are *purgalaito*. Any priest should recognize the tongue of the Gods," she groused as she looked back and forth from her hand to his tightly-wrapped and bloodied bandages.

He couldn't help but roll his eye. "Talk in *lythrivol*. I'd understand you."

Without looking up at him, she started to undo the wrapping. "Oh, yes. I forgot. Exorcists of *Love*. Your Goddess lets you speak plainly to Her and makes you learn the language of the damned instead."

"It works."

"Apparently not well," she retorted.

"So... what did you...?"

She looked up at him with a mixture of confusion and disgust on her face. "*Please, please, Goddess Isamiael; bones mend bodies heal.* I felt a spark but... you extinguished it like water poured on flame. It felt almost... intentional? And yet I don't think by you?"

"Sounds right," Badin quipped.

The exorcist, on the other hand, couldn't manage to get up the energy for sarcasm or the desire to be shocked. Instead, all he did was just sag down and slump against the side of the cart. "Can you help or not? I can't... I can't stand my leg. Please. Either help patch it up or... or..."

She looked at the ugly gash in the side of his knee and bundled it back up before he could. "Oh there will be no *or*, child. Though am I to assume you've done something worth being ostracized by the God of Medicine?"

Akaran looked over at Badin and held a lingering gaze at him before turning back to her. With a little shrug, he answered as truthfully as he could: "I pulled a demon into Tundrala and left him there."

Livstra stood there in stony silence for several very long moments without so much as even blinking. "You... oh, lovely. You take pity upon yourself and are an embellisher of tales."

"Not embellishing," he argued. "I pissed off the *episturine.*"

"Mortal men have never *seen* an *episturine*, child," she responded with a wave of her hand. "You are no different."

The battlemage lowered his head into his hands and sighed. "Well this is off to a great start."

As she tugged the bandage back on tight, she continued on. "You can explain yourself in full to the lady of the manor then. I promise you though: she's less tolerant of spun tales than I. One supposes you will have to learn the hard way."

He grimaced and uttered a bit of profanity under his breath. "Great. The hard way."

Frowning, the older woman gestured at a man dressed in garrison attire who had just stepped outside. "No doubt the cocasa is affecting your judgment. I can smell it on your breath."

"It's not that bad, really. You get used to it," he protested.

The glare she gave him could have cut a ship in half. "Oh, I know how easily people 'get used to it.' You aren't the first to find it special; you won't be the last."

"Could you be less ominous?"

You couldn't say the look on her face was a *smile* as much as it was an unspoken *condemnation*. "Simply foreshadowing your fate, if you don't mind yourself. The Maiden will not tolerate abuse of it any longer than you must take it. *Do not* doubt me."

He raised his hands in surrender. "Lady, I just want the pain to stop. Please? Please help me with the pain?"

That succeeded in getting her to sigh in agreement. "Yes, we will. You. Officer...?" she asked as she pointed at guardsman trying very hard to be unnoticed in the doorway.

"Sargent-at-Arms Telpid, ma'am," the guard answered after giving Badin a short salute. "Ronald Telpid. I've been stationed here for four months," he said as mopey voice hung in the air. "I've said hello to you every morning since -"

"Yes well. My apologies," she interrupted with a dismissive wave of her hand. "Sargent Telpid. Would you please help me get him to his new room?"

"Be happy to, ma'am," he sighed with a roll of his eyes.

A roll that, for some reason, Akaran completely agreed with.

Almost two hours later, Badin had gone about his merry way to find the berth the exorcist had promised (or so he said; Akaran figured that he was out looking for a tavern no matter *what* he claimed) and the priest had been introduced to his new room. It was small, simple, but comfortable enough. There was a small fireplace in the corner (which he was told that not every room had), a single sconce on the wall near the bed, a dresser, and a basic chamberpot safely squirreled away in the corner.

It could've been worse, all told. The bed wasn't even that stiff. Still, there was barely enough room for his crutches and the oblong trunk that had followed him from Toniki. *Hopefully*, he mused, *I won't be here long enough to care.* The only seating available was either the bed or a *very* odd chair that someone had put wooden wheels on.

It was like a cart, only for one person, and no room to carry anything in it. He had never, ever seen anything like it before and Telpid had shrugged it off as some kind of 'wheelchair,' and said it was, "A new thing one of the healers had come up with after seeing some noble prat get pushed around the city in a carriage."

He figured it was just a matter of time before the royalty decided to claim it for their (and only their) use. In the meantime, it made getting around a bit easier... though the thought of having to face stairs in it made him cringe.

After the sargent-at-arms had taken him to his room and helped him get set up, he was jostled awake from a half-doze by a knock at his door. Before he could answer, a pale and almost waifishly thin young woman (even younger than he was) with loose brown hair slipped into his room. "Ah, Sir DeHawk? So very sorry to bother you, but Lady Medias is ready to see you now."

"If she's ready I guess I'm ready. Who are you?"

She smiled and bowed her head respectfully. "My name is Raechil. I'm one of Lady Medias's handmaids; I'm here to assist in some of the more rudimentary tasks, and you may call on me for as long as you're enjoying a stay here at the Manor."

He looked out the slightly-frosted window in his room at an otherwise bland landscape outside slumped his shoulders. "I... I don't know what there is to enjoy about being here. The little I've seen looks..."

Quickly (and disturbingly quietly) she slipped through his room and pushed his wheelchair out into the hallway before he could protest. "It can be a little off-putting to new arrivals, I will agree. I do have to apologize for that. While the Manor has had open doors for twenty-two years now, it was first built in the 456th Year of Queen's Rule. It first served as a boarding house for the Hunter's Guild, and later, the Grand Army."

"Impressive history," he mused quietly.

"There are places with far greater pasts to be admired. The truth is that this is simply a safe haven in an even safer place in the world, and that's what matters. Even if it is, sometimes, a little intimidating."

Akaran tried to crane his head back and look at her. "Intimidating? I wasn't...?"

She quickly stopped the chair and placed a hand on his shoulder. "Oh, I meant no disrespect. This place is a haven for the mind, and most maladies of the psyche have a basis in fear. Intimidation is a base building block of things that strike a chord in a dark way."

"Maladies of the psyche? A haven for the mind? You make it sound like this place is an..."

"...an asylum for those that need it," she finished for him. "Please, do not take it with disrespect. The work that people like you have been tasked with claims a price from even the strongest of the willful. Give it time, and Lady Medias will have you fit to return to the field in due haste – or provide you comfort for as long as it otherwise takes for you to adapt to a new calling."

A deep sense of dread fell on his shoulders as he sagged down into his seat. "Steelhom, I swear... listen, Lady Rae -"

"I am no Lady. Raechil is fine, I promise," she corrected.

"Raechil, sorry. Listen. I haven't lost my mind. My leg is what's broken, not my head or... whatever else you think might be wrong."

She started pushing him through the wide hallway and past a series of rooms on his right. "If it was only a matter of bones, you would not be here. There is no shame in it, no reason to play it down. We have numerous souls here that have been exposed to too much for too long. We do not judge them and we will not judge you."

"Sounds like you already did," he grumpily retorted.

"Paranoia, I see," she accused as she made a soft 'clicking' sound with her tongue. "You do realize that such a feeling is a common enough dalliance of an unhealthy mind. Have no fear. We will overcome it with you."

Akaran put his good foot down and stopped her from getting him to the end of the hall as he fidgeted around to look at her. "Lady, I don't have fear. But you are giving me a headache."

The page just shook her head and nudged the chair until he lifted his foot back up. "Another sign. Nor am I a Lady; as I said, I am one of her handmaids. Paranoia and confusion both. You may be more challenging than you first appear."

"Aren't you a little too young of a healer to make that distinction?"

"Aren't you a little too young of a priest to be in this shape?"

He started to retort a nasty comment back before he shut his mouth and gave up arguing with her. "So. It's an asylum. Tell me about it."

Raechil ignored his lack of a 'please' and started to recite the history as quickly as she could. "There's quite a lot to tell. As I said, it was built in the mid 450's but eventually abandoned. It was consigned to Lady Medias in 491 after being given the land by the Sisters of Love themselves. While not every healer or resident is a follower of the Mother, the Manor is dedicated to Her."

"The Sisters got involved? That's... huh. They normally don't get involved with things like land ownership."

"Yes," she agreed, "it comes as a shock to many. It's no secret that the Manor exists, but there's little point in telling Her soldiers that there's a place for their minds when they inevitably crack. We have found that the knowledge of such a place only causes more stress as they think upon what may happen to them and where they may end up at the end of their duties."

Cannot fisking imagine why you'd think that, he groused inwardly as they passed by a corner office with some tacky painting of flowers by its door. "So this whole place is to help treat people like me?"

"Absolutely," she quickly replied. "It was during the Third Imperium War that Lady Medias realized the need for specialized assistance for people like you. You, and others who have been paid in horrific memories and broken souls as your wages in the war against the dark."

He cocked his head and thought about it for a minute before piping back up with another question. "I was always told that we would be treated at the Grand Temple if something had gone that wrong...?"

She smiled and wheeled him down the main hallway and past the main foyer. "Some are, of course. Some afflictions are more spiritual than physical; it would be safe to assume that if you were corrupted by the taint of the Abyss or were battling corruption of your aura that you would be confined to Temple grounds until your soul was cleansed."

"Huh," he grunted. "Then I wonder why Steelhom sent me here instead of the Temple..."

Raechil shrugged and took a look at the bandages wrapped around his arm and leg. "From the look of you, I don't know if you could have made the trip. My understanding was that you traveled from Gonta, yes?"

"Toniki. Near Gonta."

"It is another eight or nine weeks to travel from here to the capital by horseback for the able-bodied. Nearly a month by boat." She paused and frowned as she realized what he had just said. "You weren't exposed to the madness of the Abyss in a way that would have...?"

"Not directly. Mostly just the River Solindal," he slightly lied. "And Tundrala. Some exposure to magic from Frosel, but I kept that to a minimum. Not enough to cause lasting harm, I don't think," he added a bit too-nonchalantly, "though there was a minor possession." *On second thought,* he sighed, *that sounds worse when you say it out loud...*

She stood still and chewed on her lip before shaking her head and sighing at him. "The upper and lower elemental planes of ice? The River of All-Souls? Possession? I see. Delusions, too. How wonderful."

He glowered into his hands and hung his head. "You know, if I wanted abuse, I'd go back to Toniki."

"Seems you have been abused enough as it is," she replied before taking a deep breath to resume her story. "The Manor has twenty-two beds for the weary to rest their heads. At current, there are fourteen residents."

"That's not too bad, I guess..." he mused under his breath.

"Five of them were exorcists," Raechil added with a grave tremble to her voice that made him cringe. "The other nine are a mix of priests from the Orders of Light, a be-maddened Adept from the local Granalchi Annex, and a pair of mundane nobles that came face-to-face with an agent of immortality."

He blinked and tried to crane around to look at her again. "An agent of immortality?

Her nod was so slight it was barely noticeable. "You know as well as I that assorted creatures that poke their way past the veil can be overwhelming to minds that are incapable of comprehending them. In their case, I believe that it was a *cirtage* that assaulted a funeral service."

Akaran's brow furrowed and he quickly shook his head no. "They don't do that. They're soul-eaters. They live past the Veil. They don't cross over. I don't think they even *can* cross over."

"You would need to ask the Auramancer Exorcist," she replied with a sad twinge the name. "She brought them here not long before succumbing to a breakdown herself."

"Not to sound like I'm repeating myself, but who's that?"

His guide smiled just out of his line of sight as she parked him by a large double door at the far east end of the south hall. "Bistra Enil. She's lived here for... hm. Three years now. In her past life, she was well-renown in the western provinces; a truly capable soldier of your Goddess. Truly a pity what happened."

"Bistra Enil," he repeated slowly. "Think I vaguely heard her name while I was training."

"I would not be at all surprised. I wish I could say more about her but I must respect some measure of her privacy. However, I can tell you that the circumstances around her arrival were more grim than not: she encountered Circle cultists."

The name sent a chill down his spine and he felt his stomach start to roil. "Fisking bastards. Just got done dealing with one of their messes."

"Really? I thought you were forced to face off against some wizard?"

"The wizard made the mess. The Circle made it bigger."

"Ah," she said with a nod. "Well. I can't say anything more about it. She slid progressively down into a state of unwellness before she finally consented to treatment. I..."

"You...?"

With a deep sigh of resignation that belied her age, she finished the thought before knocking on the door beside them. "I wish I could say she was one of our successes. It only appears that she's grown worse since her stay – and I've only been lucky enough to call the Manor home for almost as long as she has."

"Oh. That's... too bad."

She quickly forced a new smile onto her face and straightened up as she opened the door and started to push him through it. "But! That is neither here nor there, and now we are here. Lady Ridora Medias, as you requested: this is exorcist Akaran DeHawk, your newest patient."

Ridora stood up from her huge elm desk and quickly sized up the exorcist while he did the same. The differences between them were striking: he was barely a third her age, and she had a lifetime full of wrinkles that he probably wouldn't live long enough to earn.

Her silver-streaked auburn hair was tied back in a regal bun and streaked with gray. His blonde hair hadn't been touched with sheers for weeks, nor had his face met a razor in even longer – resulting in a mane that would have done a troll proud. She had a pair of pale blue eyes peering out over sunken cheekbones while his blue-gray eye was so bloodshot and red around the edges that you could barely tell. The patch over his right eye had a simple gold swirl embroidered into the brown leather, though it was drooping like it didn't fit quite right.

In other words, it was the difference between someone that had either never seen perdition (or had escaped it unscathed) while the other probably wouldn't survive his next encounter with it. "Ah, wonderful," she replied with a warm chime to her voice. "Welcome. I've heard a lot about you."

He took a deep breath and tried not to be intimidated by how purely *regal* her room looked. "Can't really say the same, but thank you."

Lady Ridora smiled and straightened out the velvet royal-blue dress she was wearing. "You have many questions, I'm sure. Has Raechil been helpful so far?"

"Yes m'am. She's been a font of knowledge," he replied as he looked over his shoulder in her general direction with a very slight smile.

That warmed Ridora up slightly, and she bowed her head towards the young page. "Wonderful. Well then, as she said, my name is Ridora Medias. This is my home, and for now, yours."

Akaran took a nervous and rough breath before expelling it in a half-sigh. "Please don't take this the wrong way but I hope I'm just passing through."

She gave him a knowing nod as she walked around from behind her desk. "Of course. Only a handful of us truly *wish* to stay. And of those that do, they are ones that find staying to be how they best can provide help to others. You never know; the Manor may be your calling."

"It's not," he quickly responded before she could go on. "I already know. No offense intended."

Her smile didn't falter even for a second. "None taken, of course. Not everyone is well-suited to being a velvet glove, as it is."

"Right," he slowly replied as he caught the reference. *Wouldn't have pegged her for one of the Goddess' flock. Maybe this won't be so bad.*

The Lady picked up a letter off of the clutter on her desk and scanned over it. "So then. Akaran DeHawk, exorcist. Born...?"

He braced himself for the questions he *knew* were coming after he answered. "I think around 493. That's what they guessed."

Lady Medias gave him a puzzled frown. "Guessed? You don't know?"

Nodding in response, he clarified as best as he could. "The Temple adopted me when I was about nine. I don't... I don't remember what happened. Or where. Or anything before. They found me, took me in." He shrugged and shifted slightly in the chair, moving his leg a little to the side. "Woke up one day with my head bandaged up and a Sister taking care of me at the Grand Temple."

She continued to study his face before speaking up again. "That is utterly fascinating. I wonder if we can't help you recover some of that. They should have sent you to me ages ago."

"I'm sure they have their reasons," he returned with a tense shrug. "They told me not to worry. So I don't worry."

"Even still. I would have loved to have helped. Of course, you're only around two years older than the manor itself but still, you could have come here anytime," she mused. "*Intriguing.* I do wonder if they're keeping anyone else in the same circumstances."

He tried not to snort. "That's a word for it, I guess."

"So you don't remember...?"

"Anything," he reiterated. "The temple is my home. Goddess is my life. Without Her, I'd probably be dead somewhere. Whatever happened before then doesn't matter. Just serving Her in the now."

She looked down at the letter again and resumed reading while talking to him. "I see. Devout even against your past; impressive. So then. Adopted by the Temple when you were ten, and graduated..." she paused and looked up from it, an entirely new and different frown on her face, "...all of four months ago?"

"Yes m'am."

"What made you decide to serve as an exorcist?"

It wasn't the question he expected, but he went along with it. "I didn't. She did."

"How so? All of the ones I have ever met have always said that they had to truly search their hearts and souls to decide to put their lives on the line."

He continued to fidget, this time plucking at the edges of his coat until she glared him into motionlessness. "When I was twelve, they tested me for magical aptitude. I couldn't heal most wounds, couldn't do much for divination or anything that'd make me interesting to the Granalchi. Didn't pass through any of the six schools."

Ridora's frown somehow deepened and made her eyebrow start to twitch.

"But an exorcist? If you failed to pass through the six...?"

"I wandered into a lesson hosted by an Arch-Templar on demonology," he explained, "and they had a *corpusal* wandering around that they were using as an example. I didn't mean to but... I made it... well. Go away."

She pursed her lips and looked down her regal nose at him. "Go away? You chased it off? I imagine that was quite difficult, if it was properly behind suppression wards."

"Blew it up," he clarified. "They figured it'd be safer for everyone involved if I got training after I got done scrubbing down the walls."

Her criticism died in her throat as developed a mental picture of how that might've looked. "I... see. Well, a calling is a calling. Now from what I have so far, next you graduated from the Temple, were sent to go deal with your first exorcism, and... and you immediately ended up here. Is that correct?"

"It is."

"Maybe it wasn't your calling after all."

Akaran dropped his head as her words cut deeper than Gonta's surgeons. "Maybe it wasn't. Won't really know until you take a look at me."

"That part will happen momentarily, I do promise. I want to know more about what happened before I make any additional judgments."

He didn't say it, but he surely thought it: *Additional. Lovely.*

If she noticed how hard he was trying to hold his tongue, she didn't say anything. "Allow me to explain the rules of the Manor before we delve into the reasons for your stay."

"I'll do my best to honor them."

"Good. Breakfast will be delivered to your room no later than an hour after the first rooster's cry; dinner served at six marks after the noon sun. You may stop by the pantry at any time for fruits or cereals. There is no alcohol of any kind permitted on premises, and if you ever come onto Manor grounds while inebriated, you will spend the night with the pigs."

That might have been the only thing that could've hurt worse than her callous remark about his career. "None... at all?"

"None," she repeated. "Our guests have troubles enough without adding to their muddled minds. Is that going to be an issue?"

Yes? "No, Lady. I'll abide." *Except when I can get away with it.*

"Good," she replied sternly – and then added, "I do mean it. *Don't* imbibe. It is not worth the results. By the same token, there are to be no herbs or other concoctions that affect the mind or the personality. As needed, we will provide medication to treat what ailments the land can treat, but use of others will have you evicted – no exceptions."

He squeezed at the pouch of cocasa hidden inside his jacket in alarm. "Okay, just so you know -"

"- you were given cocasa to treat your pain and you brought it with you," the Lady interrupted. "Yes, I know. Raechil will take it from your possession after this meeting and it will be dispensed to you as you need it. I've already spoken to Livstra about your case; however, you'll need to explain a great deal more."

"I have to... Yes m'am. I'll abide."

"I am happy to hear that. We do offer prayer services and worship to Niasmis, Isamiael, and Solinal. There is a Shrine of Light in Basion that offers services to the other members of the Pantheon, if you feel that you owe any of them an apology or conversation to help balance your soul."

That third name brought a cringe that you could've seen on the other side of the city, if you'd been looking. "Solinal... Lady, I hate to say this, but I do not think that Solinal is overly pleased with me."

"Oh? And why would the God of Peace have an issue with you?"

"I spent a month drinking from His river."

From behind them, Raechil cleared her throat and interrupted them for the first time since wheeling him in. "Ah, yes. I should warn you, m'ladly: Akaran here believes that he has been drinking from the River Solindal." She dropped her voice down into a conspiratorial whisper that was as insulting as she intended. "I fear that we will spend some time treating his delusions."

"It's not a delusion –" he spat at her before Ridora cut him off.

"Not to say that *I* don't believe you, but if that is what *you* believe, I can see why you may think that He is not on your side." She waited until he calmed himself down and then went on. "*However*, that aside, the services for the Gods that watch over us are offered thrice a week. You will be strongly – *strongly* – encouraged to bow your head to at least one of Them twice a week."

The idea that he wouldn't was almost as rude as Raechil's insistence that he had lost his mind. "I offer my heart to the Lady every day. I don't imagine I could have survived what I did without Her at my side."

She finally let herself smile at him again after hearing that. "Good. Still, you are to be at the services as long as you are able to leave your room and are have reasonable stability. Speaking of leaving: once can move under your own power, you will be encouraged to find tasks either on the Manor grounds or to provide aid to the downtrodden in the city. No good can come from a man that stays confined to his room when he is capable of providing works."

"Not being able to provide works is why I'm here, m'am. There's nothing I *can* do."

"For now," she stressed. "There are a few other rules to follow but they are minor and I'll allow Raechil to explain them later. I *will* say that the privacy of our residents is paramount. Do not enter anyone's room without their permission for any reason, and there are several people here that are incapable of granting it."

He nodded and squeezed his pouch of cocasa through his coat again. "I promise not to compromise someone's privacy."

"Good. You are not confined to your room but while you are on the grounds you are limited to travel to my office, the atrium, the kitchen, the study, and the commons. The other areas of the Manor are off-limits unless you are being escorted by one of my caregivers. Do you understand?"

"Yes m'am. Are there many other areas?"

"It's of no business either way for now. If you haven't been told you can go someplace, presume that you cannot. There is a room for surgeries and other parts for personal care when and however it may be needed."

Akaran nodded again and started to quietly wish that they could get this over with already "That's fair. Not like I can walk much."

She flipped the letter over and read a few more lines on it before giving him a steely look down into his eye. "About that. I have not yet received the full report on why you were sent into my care, so I am going to need you to explain what happened."

He looked up at Raechil and then shook his head no. "I can't."

That must have caught her off guard, because her mouth worked for a heartbeat before any sound came out of it. "I can't help you if you can't be honest about the maladies that have befallen you."

"I can't because the exorcism that landed me here has been placed under Seal of Order. I am not able to divulge everything I experienced in full to anyone except those serving as Paladin-Commanders and higher," he clarified before looking back up at Raechil again. "In part, I can. Just not the full story. I don't think your page holds that rank...?"

"Under seal? By whom?"

"Paladin-Commander Steelhom, m'am," he answered as he pulled another letter out from his coat and passed it over to the Lady, "and with not-so-tactic request by the Priestess of Stara from Gonta to rarely speak about the matter in general, as well."

She held onto the letter and checked the seal – twice – before cracking it open. "On your first exorcism? What exactly did you do?"

"Steelhom explained it in full in the letter, m'am. He's the one that sent me here."

"Interesting," she mused as she began to read the first part of it. "Well then, as Lady of the manor, I can assure you that anything said to any of my staff is to be considered held in the strictest of confidence."

Akaran wrestled with that for a minute before giving way to another uncomfortable refusal. "Sorry m'am. Not to argue you, but I'm *part* of that order, and I have to be careful with what I say and how. If your page will leave the room, I can explain."

"Paranoia too, I see," Raechil sighed.

Ridora waved her away with a quick flick of her hand. "Now now, be kind.

He isn't wrong — if he's part of the seal, then he does have to be careful about what he speaks. Condemning the damned and state secrets oft go hand-in-hand." Her voice drew to a slow stop as a little bit of color drained from her ruby cheekbones as she scanned the note. "Is... is this true?"

"Which part?"

She cleared her throat, walked over to a bookcase, and pulled a dusty tome off of a shelf without looking away from the parchment. "Rae, step outside, please."

"Lady? Are you sure that's wise?"

"Quite," Ridora snapped. "Leave us, now."

Chastised, the young woman mumbled an apology and slipped out of the room. "So... which part?" he repeated.

She let all pretense of experience and understanding drop from the tone of her voice. "It isn't uncommon for this manor to receive souls that have suffered at the hands of the Abyss, or whom have been corrupted by magical influences. But you traveled...?"

"It's not recommended."

The lady set the letter down and folded her hands over themselves as she sat back down. "Explain, please. I'd like to hear your own words about how you came here. What caused your injury and what has interfered with your ability to use magic?"

He sighed and looked down at his knee. "It should've been a simple exorcism. That's what they told me that it was going to be. A simple haunting."

"Two words that aren't always easy to combine."

"No," he agreed. "The truncated version? I was assaulted both by an *abogin* and an *arin-goliath* by the name of Daringol. The *abogin* — Makolichi — shattered my knee in our final encounter. Did this number on my arm, too," he added, pointing at the bandages around his left bicep. "The *arin-goliath* attempted to infest me several times, and I managed to be host to a singular *arin* for a few days without realizing it."

"Both a revenant *and* a nesting wraith? *And* a documented possession?"

"*Corpusals,* too," he added, "along with a pair of *giata.*"

There wasn't any hiding her shock. "That is NOT a simple exorcism!"

"That's what I thought, too."

"How did you not realize you were a host to it?! It seems that as an exorcist that would be a thing you'd be intimately familiar with the signs..."

Akaran raised a hand and sighed in tired frustration. "In my defense, it jumped into me while I was being swallowed by the *goliath*. I had other issues to contend with and it wasn't one I had previously encountered, so I didn't notice it right off."

She had to pause and drum her fingers on her hand for a moment to take that one in. "That is a defense. I am unsure if it is reasonable."

36

"I was also exposed, repeatedly, to waters from the River Solindal."

She shook her head and glanced back down at Steelhom's letter. "That is something I am having trouble believing. Solindal is past the Veil. It does not travel into this world."

He coughed and shrugged slightly. "Does when there's an asshole who decided to crack open breaches into the Sands, Frosel, and Tundrala and leave them open."

"I was hoping that part of the letter was an exaggeration," she sighed. "So you touched the river, you say? Did anyone else see you do it?"

Another shrug. "They watched me drink it, too."

"You... what?"

"Never again will I drink a water so pure," he lamented.

Her jaw worked silently again before she found the right words to say. "Never again *should* you. If you aren't leading me down the garden path with this story as it is..."

"I... yes, m'am. In my defense, I recognize that it was a bad idea. It was necessary though, in each circumstance."

"Why, exactly, was it necessary?"

"Because I needed to heal fast and hit harder," he returned with a slightly apologetic bow of his head. "One of the first things I tangled with up in Toniki were a pair of Abyssian hounds. Between those two and the *abogin*, I'm pretty sure I got killed. Mostly dead, at least. I only managed to recover because Eos'eno took me into Tundrala with her and then she and an alchemist and Steelhom all tried to patch me up after."

"They claim you died?"

He gave her reluctance a bit of leeway. "Yeap."

She lifted a finger and pointed it at him with a matching lift of her eyebrow. "The fact that you're still here makes me doubt that."

"I had help from very grumpy healers," he clarified, adding, "and I didn't lose my connection with magic until the very end of the incident." Then, sheepishly, "I also drank a lot..."

She brought her hands to her face and breathed deeply into them, "From Solindal, I presume?"

"And the local inn."

She didn't find that half as amusing as he had hoped she would. "I... see. So then, Eos'eno? Who is that – and how did she have the power to travel into Tundrala?"

"She's elemental-kin," he explained, "a wisp, of sorts. Her story is a bit more messed up than that, but... she could teleport, and her method involved passing through Tundrala."

Ridora let out a breath she didn't realize she'd been holding. "Oh? 'Messed up,' you so casually claim. I expect it's more worse than that, if it holds true to the rest of the story so far." When he shrugged at her, she shook her head and continued to egg him on. "So you... only went *through* Tundrala. Not...?"

He didn't hide the slightly bemused smirk at her discomfort. "No. She dropped me off in there twice. It was not fun. It wasn't... right." He took a deep breath and closed his eye tightly before continuing by saying, "Imagine looking at a snowy mountain. It's beautiful. Tall. Miles wide. Wider and bigger than anything you've ever seen. Stunning and *perfect*."

The lady cracked a smile. "You know, when I was a little girl -"

Without missing a beat, he interrupted her and went on as the joy in his face crumbled into something not quite as delighted. "Then imagine that mountain sprouting legs and walking away while snowdrifts open impossibly wide eyes made of immaculate crystal and fly over you while a blizzard chases it and they both laugh at each other." As her smile drooped again, he shuddered at the memory. "You know, at least with the Abyss you know where you stand... I don't... I don't want to go back there..."

"I think I have heard enough delusions to know when I am hearing one."

"It gets worse," Akaran quickly warned, "that's just what *I* dealt with."

"I am having a hard time seeing how this fantastic tale of yours could possibly get *worse*, young man," she retorted. "Even with the seal on this letter, I am having a very hard time believing any of it."

"I have to be honest, I don't blame you. But it happened. There's witnesses. Some magical, some mundane. Random villagers to members of the Queen's Army. Commander Evalia Wodoria from the 13th, for one, and Specialist-Major Badin, another. He accompanied me to town. You can bring him in for questioning for some of it, but he's *also* under seal. In fact, everybody involved is."

She listened to that then looked back down at the letter as she drummed her fingers on her desk. "I may just do that. I am, of course, taking this seriously – this letter *is* signed off by and bears the seal of a Paladin-Commander of our Order. Yet 'taking seriously' and 'taking easily' are not one and the same."

The young priest nervously ran his hand up through his hair as he continued to try to convince her of the truth. "It's hard for me to argue that, m'am. The more I talk about it the less it feels like it's something that could've, or even should've, happened the way it did."

"Yet it did," she said with a dry tone.

"Yet it did," Akaran sighed right back at her, "and I am paying for it."

She nodded and took a long drink out of a horned flagon on her desk and sat there thinking quietly to herself. Finally, she summoned enough patience to get to the next part of his story. "About that. How is it you lost your ability to use magic?"

"I mentioned that Makolichi was an *abogin*, right? You're aware of them?"

"Not intimately. Revenants, yes?"

"That's them. *Abogin* is the *lythrivol* name for the bas... monsters."

Ridora drummed her fingers on the desk and wracked her brain for a moment. "Let me see if I remember correct. They are... hmm. Their essences tend to be bound to physical objects. Unless the object is destroyed, they continue to come back after you exile them? It makes returning them to their divinely-ordained resting place difficult?"

"Also them," he confirmed. "Makolichi had *two* that I was aware of, which isn't natural, and *still* came back after both of them were destroyed. I didn't have much hope that he didn't have a third hidden somewhere. I really hope he isn't – hiding somewhere, I mean – but I have my doubts."

"I can see how that would be a problem, even for an exorcist. What does that have to do with your inability to call upon the holy words or even magic of other natures?"

Akaran reached down and gingerly placed his hand on the side of his leg. "After he broke my knee... it was a rash decision. I didn't have a choice. I still don't think I did. I don't think any of us would be alive if I hadn't..."

Her eyes narrowed at his trepidation and she studied his face intently. "Hadn't what, exactly?"

This was the part that had been the hardest to admit to everyone so far. His mentor had nearly knocked his head off of his shoulders, Hirshma had howled with laughter, Commander Evalia had to scrape her jaw off the floor, and Deboria? The High Priestess of Stara?

He *firmly* intended to request that the Temple add 'Never piss off a psychic' to the Exorcist's Field Guide. "I had Eos'eno grab him, and me, and told her to take us back home. Her home. Tundrala."

She just sat there.

Then she blinked a few times as she leaned back into her chair. "You took an abyssian... into the Upper Plane of Ice?"

"...Yeah." *Here it comes*, he groaned to himself.

Unfortunately, her voice didn't stay neutral for long. "You... allowed... a demon... to bypass Pristi's Gate and... into the realms of the Pantheon?"

"...Yeah..."

"And you still live?" she breathed out incredulously.

Meekly, he looked up at her and gave the tinniest of smiles before he replied meekly with, "...not well?"

The Lady just kept staring at him with her hands wringing nervously on the desk. "There are those of us, *simple* mortals, who I imagine would want to see you dead for doing that. I can *only* imagine how angry the creatures of the Mount are if what you say is true."

"The Order of Frost isn't happy with me," he confirmed.

"There are a *lot* of people that would like to see you die for that if they knew," she stressed. "The Order of Frost would be one group, I am sure, but...

do Pristi's followers know?"

Akaran coughed into his coat and shrugged. "I don't like to talk to them anyway."

Her shoulders tensed up as she struggled to get a grip on his story. *Any* grip. "This... this report? It isn't something you are simply making up, is it? Your injuries are severe, this letter seems sincere – as do you – but please, tell me...?"

All he could do was shake his head no. "One of Istalla's guardians, an *episturine*, took care of Makol... no. No, that's not right. They let him *go* and tortured *me*. Left me like *this*. Said my punishment was to lose magic. So it did. It cut me off from magic and I can't feel I can't do nobody can do anything and they... *it*... let him *go*."

"I doubt that he was allowed to roam free," she argued, even as her mind whirled.

"Oh, I heard the episturine clearly. *'Your taste of purity, as part of what it is you have earned.'* A taste of purity."

It was her turn to sigh aloud and she shook her head right back at him. "Only a *part* of what he earned, I am sure. If he was as vile as a beast as you suggest, then I assume that his ledger had many things in it to show what he was owed."

"I don't know. I'll never know," he spat. "They surely punished me for it though."

"How, exactly? What do you remember?"

Akaran took a deep breath and tried to calm his suddenly-shaking hands. "I... I remember crystal knives. They cut me, but... it didn't... I didn't bleed. Started at the back of my head, went along my jaw. Hirshma – the alchemist – had to hold a mirror up for me to see that I hadn't gotten sliced open after I got kicked back to our reality."

"Interesting. Then what happened?"

He looked down at his leg and traced over the edge of the bandages with his fingertips. "Then it forced every drop of Solindal out of me and stripped me of magic. It... without magic... I felt everything. It..."

"You had been using magic to dull pain, hadn't you," she stated with a faint knowing smile.

"Yeah."

"And you haven't been able to stand being without, have you?"

He didn't move but for squeezing at his leg again. "No. No I can't stand it. If it wasn't for the cocasa, I wouldn't be able to even have this talk right now."

Ridora clicked her tongue inside her mouth semi-silently and looked him up and down. "You're doing a remarkable job for seeming to be clear-headed if you're on as much of it as you suggest."

"Pain is a focus," he grumbled before resuming his story. "They patched me up with what they could. Hirsh... she did a lot. Some fisking asshole at the garrison in Gonta cut on my leg, said it was the best I was going to get."

She flicked a finger up and pointed it in his general direction. "Language, Akaran. We do not tolerate profanity on these grounds."

"Great," he grumbled – this time forgetting to direct it inward.

"What was that, exorcist?"

He quickly cleared his throat and went back to fidgeting in his chair. "I mean, I'm sorry."

"Much better," she said with a snippy tone to her voice. "I am to assume that after Gonta, they decided to send you here?"

"No, m'am. Steelhom wanted me to come here himself even before that. He spoke highly of you."

Her eyebrows lifted quizzically. "Interesting. I don't think I've ever met him."

"I wasn't under the impression that you had," he replied. "I believe you treated some people he knew during the 3rd."

Ridora nodded and then shrugged it off. "Imperium War? That is a possibility. Ugly spot of work that was. Be happy you missed it."

"Got a feeling there's more ugly on the horizon, m'am."

Her face offered faint smile that appeared and disappeared as quickly as it arrived. "There always is. You are intriguing, no doubt. I do have one more question about this order: what parts of it are under seal? I assume there's things you can talk about...?"

Akaran thought for a moment and quickly ran through everything that he'd been told prior to leaving Toniki. "I can talk about the *arin*, the *abogin*, the *giata*, the *corpusals*, though I'm not allowed to talk about Tundrala other than to say it exists."

"That's a fairly wide window," she replied.

"Well," he started to explain, "the existence of rifts is known. We couldn't keep that hidden even if we wanted. We do, but that's blown. I am not, under any circumstances, allowed to talk about *how* the rifts were opened. I'm not to talk about what I saw in the Veil or what glimpses I had of... the other place. Either place."

She pursed her lips. "Not giving people instructions on how to breach the planes is reasonable, I agree. I don't think it will pose a problem with your recovery, given that *you* didn't open any of those gateways." Ridora paused for a moment and started to ask, "You didn't, did -" before he interrupted her.

"No, I didn't."

"I couldn't be so sure."

The priest cleared his throat. "I'm to keep talk of the coldstone to an absolute minimum. In fact, I'd be happy if you never asked me about it again."

"As critical as that relic is to your condition, I cannot promise that you'll be so lucky to avoid it. Why are your superiors so firm on that?"

"Because of those flame-worshiping assholes up north. If the Civans realize rocks that can mitigate the very thing the Divine Matron of their Empire is known for, they'll move the Mount itself to topple us while we screw around with it trying to make it work. It'll be the 4th Imperium War," he gravely replied before he looked her dead in the eyes. "*If* we're lucky."

Ridora narrowed her eyes and then looked down at the letter like she was searching for something in it before speaking up again. "You certainly managed to play a dangerous game, didn't you?" Before he had a chance to reply, she went on. "Any other limitations I should be concerned with?"

"The exact nature of the haunting," Akaran added. "The public at large doesn't need to know that a demonic cloud of black ice tried to spread down the eastern seaboard after hiding in plain sight for almost half a decade."

"This letter says that it attacked Gonta. That fact and this order don't seem to line up."

He shrugged. "A demon attacked the city and there were spirits with it. It got hunted and stopped and the populace assured that it was some rogue wizard who did it and died painfully. That's all people needed to know. Anyone that thinks that they know more will get *spoken to* by the Order and their attempts to glean more than what we're telling them will get stonewalled. The Kingdom doesn't need to know that everybody's safety was in as much danger it really was."

She sat there and studied his face carefully for a long minute. "Does your side of the Order do that often? Engage in half-truths and cover-ups to hide things from the rest of us?"

"Depends," he answered, "on how much you actually know about what we do."

"I know a great deal," she slowly replied with a sudden lack of confidence. "I have taken care of many an exorcist since I founded this sanctuary for the be-maddened.

"Then you know. Or at least, you know that we do things that don't always end well." He gave her the faintest of unpleasant smiles. "Makes you wonder about how many things do."

For the first time since he had been wheeled in, the lady suddenly looked completely unnerved and he could tell that she wasn't used to having someone speak frankly to her – and that she didn't like it. "Well. Then. That's a discussion for another time. You mentioned that you weren't permitted to talk about the things in the world between and the worlds after...?"

"As little as I can get away with," he replied slowly.

"Those things may be important to your care. You can trust myself and any of the healers in this manor to keep your secrets."

He sighed and looked over his shoulder to make sure the door was still shut. "M'am, again with no offense, I don't know them. I don't know you. Steelhom said you had permissions equivalent to Maidenhood, and that's about the only reason I've said this much. I'm just hoping that nobody can hear through that door, if you want the truth of it."

"I assure you, the doors here are very solid."

He gave a deep sigh in relief. "That's everything then."

Ridora gave him a warm smile that he doubted she actually felt. "I'll keep your restrictions in the forefront of my mind. What do you know about the Manor?"

"Not much, just that you treat people that need treating."

"Yes, that's... a fairly succinct way to put it. Some of the people we give aid to are people that have seen things from the other side, and maybe have seen *into* the other side," she explained. "Not all of them are as able to keep their tongues with themselves as you are, seals be concerned or not. Everyone in this manor has heard one secret or another, one time or another. All of my people know well to keep their mouths shut – and as such, a few things uttered at one time or another is not unexpected."

Finally getting some news he could relate to, he sagged his shoulders in relief. "Thank you. I... in all honesty, I don't want to talk about it anymore than I have to. I still..."

"You still...?" she prodded.

"I still see it in my dreams. Daringol. I see it swallowing me and trying to crawl inside me. At... at night? I swear, I still feel it trying to squirm around. It's not. It's gone and I *know* it's gone."

She made a soft little 'ah' sound, as if she had finally figured him out. "You would not be the first, young priest. Those that come here have seen far too much far too often. We do have people here that will be able to help you through that. It may not be easy at all times, but they will help you through it. We even have a phrase to describe what you're experiencing."

"So you can make it stop?" he asked, a twinge of hope in his voice.

"We can show you how to stop it, yes," she replied with a tender smile.

Akaran closed his eye and dropped his head. "Thank you."

"I must say, it is hard for me to believe all of this, even if it is signed off on by a man of Steelhom's reputation."

"I kinda figured," he returned. "Like the others said, you're used to people dealing with paranoia and delusions and other insanity, right?"

Ridora nodded her head at him and folded the letter up before setting it aside. Yes, I am afraid so. We expect those that come here to embellish their tales a little bit, even if they come under their own power."

He grit his teeth and squared himself up before continuing. "Then this is the other reason I'm under the seal."

"There's more? I thought you said that was everything...?"

"There's this," he said as he flipped his eyepatch up and pulled a small blue rock out from the lining. "Eos'eno wanted me to keep it. Said I'd need it." He stopped for a second before handing setting it on the desk. "She said a lot of things, none of which made me comfortable, if you really want to know the truth."

Her eyes went as wide as they possibly could as she straightened up and stared down at the rock, then back at him. "You have it?"

"Part of it," he clarified, "just a shard. The rest of it is safe with Steelhom and Maiden Piata. I assume, anyway. They didn't say and I don't want to know."

Ridora stared down at the pale-blue stone and looked at it incredulously. It was hard to imagine that such a simple rock was the end result of dozens of deaths, a plague of walking dead, and demons the likes of which hadn't been seen in the Kingdom for decades getting loose from the Abyss. But it was. This one small shard itself had power that nobody had managed to completely decipher – fitting, given that it wasn't just *infused* with otherworldly energies, it was *part* of another world. It came, quite literally, from the Upper Elemental Plane of Ice, and broke all of the Laws of Normality simply by *existing*.

"You were *allowed* to you keep it? Given all of your other issues? Does anyone else know you have it?"

Akaran nudged it closer to her with the end of his finger. "As best as anyone could tell, the shard isn't causing me any grief, and when an emissary of the Goddess of Ice tells you to keep a freezing pebble and gives you an appropriate title, you keep it."

"A title, hm? What did she call you?"

"Guardian of Winters," he replied with a vague cringe. "I've been called worse, but…"

The lady reached for the stone and jerked her hand back before she could touch it. A cold aura stabbed out of the relic and poked at her fingertips, almost as if it was lashing out at her intentionally. "But it is a bit lofty, isn't it?"

"Pretentious as all," he grumbled.

"Does it do anything?"

Akaran shrugged again. "I haven't let anyone touch it. Your guess is as good as mine."

"May I?" she asked as she bent down to peer at it closer, risking a second attempt to examine it.

"I… I'd rather you not," he answered, "but if you're going to help me get back to normal… be my guest."

Cautiously, she picked it up between her fingers and started to study it. It wasn't much bigger than the last bone of her thumb, and after the initial chill, it felt… calming. "Interesting… let me…"

He realized her intent before he could stop her and his attempt to grab her hand didn't make it in time. "No! I wouldn't! The full stone -!"

44

Just as a warm white glow pulsed in the palm of her hand, a sudden sharp aqua one lit up the room and a sudden chill enveloped them both. The spark of frozen energy disappointed almost as quickly as it appeared, but it left her staring at it with her eyes wide and mouth agape. "*Goodness!* That's a *shard* of the full stone?!"

"Just a shard," he replied as he reached out for it.

She hesitated instead of handing it back right away. "I am not at all sure that it is safe for you to have that in your possession. Nor do I think it is a good idea for you to have it *here*. Or around people. Anywhere," she added a little breathlessly.

He reached for it a second time and shook his head. "Respectfully, m'am? It doesn't leave me. If I can't keep it, I can't stay."

"That's an odd demand for a man in your position," she countered.

"M'am, in all honesty? This thing was created from blending magic from three different extra-planar realms, the woman that gave it to me said it was built by the express instruction of the Goddess of Ice Herself, *and* she listed off a prophecy to me where that thing holds some significance. If it goes, I go."

"There may be a time when it comes to that," she cautioned. "Are you prepared to defend your right to carry it in the face of losing treatment for your condition?"

There was absolutely nothing jovial in his reply to her and not even a hint of sarcasm when he answered. "I feel like I'm going to die either way."

Taken aback by his cold honesty, she let the stone fall back into his hand. "Not if I have any say in the matter, I promise."

"I appreciate that," he said as he slipped it back into its pouch.

"As much as I *loathe* the idea, there are two people in this city that will be able to help you with that stone more than what I can. One of them is a Maiden in her own right and the other you will have to decide if you feel safe speaking to or not on your own."

Akaran took an almost nervous breath. "Who are they?"

"All things in time," she replied. "Now, I will be digging deeper into your story – that I can promise. In the meantime, it would be best to send you to your new quarters and let you get a feel for the grounds while I consider what exactly to do about you."

"I'd like it if you helped me walk without crutches. Sleep would be nice, too."

She nodded with an understanding smile. "In due course. Before we operate on your knee, I'd like to know what and how we need to address your immunity to magic."

"More surgery?" he groaned.

"Oh, please. You cannot deign to tell me you felt that the hackjob they did in Gonta would be enough? In the meantime, I suppose we will have to see about the weed you're holding."

He clenched at his coat before he realized what he was doing. "You're not a fan of it, are you?"

"No," she tersely replied. "However, your knee? Until it is repaired, there is little sense in forcing you to be rid of what eases your pain. It will, itself, deaden your ability to use magic – to an extent. I hate to admit it but it is something we are forced to administer to some of the patients that come through these halls if they are unable to control their own skills with the ether."

Looking down at the bulge in his coat, he picked his words carefully. "So... I need it, but it's ruining me."

"I do not expect that it is helping you, no. It will be tolerated, for now, but the longer you consume, the worse it will feel when you are purged."

He nodded, then looking up at her with a pleading look, he took one more try at avoiding the inevitable. "I had really hoped there wouldn't be any more cutting. Or purging," he added.

"You had best to give that up," Ridora cautioned. "Our resident surgeon claims to have more knives than the army owns; soon, many of them will be pointed at you."

Resigned to his fate, Akaran dropped his head and sighed. "Better than teeth."

Unfortunately, those would be an eventual concern, too.

III. MERCHANT OF SECRETS & THE BLADEBANE
Wundis, the 4ᵗʰ of Greenbirth, 513 QR

Basion City has many faults. In the rainy season, the Orshia Overflow tends to flood heavily and displace families throughout the Lower Naradol, Piapat, and Akkador districts. Overpopulation is another; for a place christened the safest city in the realm, it tends to attract those that are unable to protect themselves. In the winter, the stairs and pathways leading from the bottom of the basin up to the lip of the city become so slick that they are almost impassable. (Salt merchants and enterprising blacksmiths, however, adore it.)

However, for all of its faults, having too few taverns, inns, corner food stalls, tabernas, and other open-air bakeries was not one of them. The *Cherished Atonement* on the border between the Upper Naradol and West Giffil districts was one of the ones that catered to a specific audience of priests and pages – along with other well-wishers and well-doers in the city.

The walls were decorated with sculptures and paintings declaring the glory of the Gods and the joys of creations. Every hour, you could hear the head cook say a prayer of thanks off to Goddesses of Health and Nature. Sometimes you could hear his wife utter one to the God of Gluttony, too (but never around Pantheon faithful).

It was the last place a not-so-pious hypocrite like the high priest of Stilamatheric of Basion – Altund Obermesc – belonged, and one of the absolute last places that Lady Anais wanted to be. Stuck with his slovenly self and morbidly-obese company for hopefully the last time, she wrapped her pale pink lips around a pewter tankard and took a very long drink that was more water than wine. It wasn't enough to make up for having to endure his presence, sadly.

But it would do.

"And you're sure?" he quietly grunted with a gravely voice.

Anais rolled her muddy-gray eyes and took another drink on the barely-wine. "Yes, Oldstone. If you hand this coin off to the customs officers, you'll be able to get your shipment of *golluthum* without paying a tithe to Merchant-Master Hannock."

"Who exactly gave you this authority?"

You can read, can't you, you pebble-minded oaf? she muttered to herself, before replying with, "As you can see, that coin was issued by Merchant-Master Eran. You know as well as I do that the two have a working *arrangement* with each other."

He poured over the coin, and Anais thought she saw little multicolored glimmers flash in his eyes as he stared at it. "Looks real enough."

"I assure you, Oldstone, it is no fake. I wouldn't risk our newfound relationship on trying to do something underhanded."

"Of course you would," he grunted, "you've earned a reputation for getting what you want from people. Nobody that professes that they're an *information broker* can ever be trusted. As if that's even a real thing."

She kept a forced smile on her lips as she reached over and placed a single finger on the coin. At the table behind her, a man in brown leather with his back towards them very deliberately reached for the hilt of a knife at his side. "Again, Oldstone, and with all respect intended: my name and reputation have been carefully crafted over the years. When you make a deal with me, it is within my interest to ensure that you get exactly what's wanted."

The old man scoffed and set the coin down on the rough wooden table. "*Carefully crafted*, you say. As are most well-made fakes."

"If you don't think that what I offer is true, you are welcome to leave the offer on the table, of course," she said with only a hint of bile seeping into her words, "but then we would both walk away unsatisfied. What good would that do us?"

"It isn't the offer I doubt," Altund replied. "Just the merchant... *and* her bodyguard," he said with a nod towards the man behind her.

"A lady can't be too careful," she said, still smiling (although less and less friendly by the moment).

He chortled again and pulled out a carefully-folded letter from inside his muddy cloak. "I assume you can read?"

Anais felt her eye twitch and took a drink from the not-quite-wine instead of rising to the bait. "I shall assume that's the report I requested?"

His fat fingers started to open it up, tearing the edges of the parchment in the process before she covered it with her hands and deftly slid it out of his grip. "The only person I've ever heard of that'd even care about how deep that awful pit goes."

"Well. A blight like that thing *can't* be good for the Unders. I'm so glad that you feel the same way about it as I." Her eyes twinkled as she peered down at it. "Such awful things that get buried. They can cause all kinds of disruption to the natural order."

"That so-called *temple* absolutely reeks. It's an offense to the Stonehewn that the Oo-lo dared to put their magic so deep into the world... and that's to say nothing of the unstable toxic... *whatever* it is that they have in there."

"The *whatever* is the source of my concern. There are a lot of people that would love to know how much danger those heretics have placed the city in."

That same glimpse of color flickered around his face as he peered at her. "And what they would love to know, you would love to know."

She quickly tucked the paper into the bodice of her faded-pink gown and smiled. "That is the name of the game, isn't it?"

"Whatever you're thinking, I wouldn't."

"Oh, and why is that?"

He stared her in the eyes with such intensity that it made her flinch. "They've no business putting their garbage in the realm of the Grand Mason, but they did. And they're guarding it. All of it."

"All of it?" she asked with a slight tilt of her head. "You make it sound like they have more than a few things gathered there."

He let a faint little smile flicker. "I'm sure you already know."

"Maybe I do. Maybe I don't."

Altund leaned back in his chair and smirked at her. "It'll cost you, either way."

The lady matched him smirk for smirk. "I see you learn quickly, Oldstone. Yes, I would, actually. There is something else I'd like, too."

"Oh?" he boomed, almost loud enough for the rest of the tavern to hear. "What could a lady like you want from an old man like me?"

Half the eyes in the room turned to her, though if it bothered her in the least, she didn't show it. "There are times in the life of a traveler like myself that finding a warm place to stay is harder than not, but there's no shortage of caves as one travels. I would love to know that if I hopped in one that I would have the blessing of the Stonehewn to protect me."

The old priest sat there and continued to give her a smirk that showed off his disgusting yellow teeth. "It's a *blessing* you want, is it?" he said with a leer. "I'm a bit too old to be handing those out, but maybe I can find one of my younger assistants to come around..."

Her body shivered with revulsion before she could recompose herself. "There is no call for such crassness, Oldstone. I am a businesswoman, nothing more, nothing less. Many of my travels have me going through the Equalin Mountains. I was always raised to respect and seek the protection of those that bless the paths I travel."

"It's an old business. All of it."

Anais flinched back away from him. "*All* I am looking for right now is a blessing I can travel with. An amulet, a bangle – something that I can safely carry."

Delighting in knocking her off-balance, Altund scooted forward and leered at her. "It'll cost you. Maybe more than you're willing to pay, since you want it so badly."

"Cost me, yes, but not what *I'm* willing to pay. I'm sure you know that

Bendolynn Gavasti recently died, yes?"

Pursing his lips, he thought about it for a minute. "Don't know him."

She straightened up a little and folded her fingers into a steeple on the table. "He owns – owned – a small quarry located behind the Orshia Overflow. Master Hannock has placed a lien on his estate and has refused to allow his heirs to take possession of it."

"And?"

"And," she said with a smirk that belittled his, "I know that he dug several tunnels that went far deeper into the dirt than most people think. It would be a *wonderful* location for the Unders to take over and dedicate to the Grand Mason Himself. You could have room for three, even four times the number of devotees to call it home than what you have space for now."

"If Hannock owns it I'm sure his masters in the BeaST have claimed it already. What's your point, woman?"

Anais turned her head and let a few locks of her ruddy-brown hair trail down the front of her dress. "The point is that a lien is just a piece of paper and paper can be burned. If the right deal could be presented off to the good Overseer, then I imagine that I could get your name inked onto it instead."

The disgusting old pig of a man sat there in confused silence for a minute before slowly speaking up. "That's a big offer for a piece of jewelry."

"The jewelry is one thing. For a deal like that, you'll be giving up a few baubles more. A girl has to eat, you know," she replied with a warm smile. "There's no way I can do this without a finder's fee."

"Business is business," the priest reluctantly agreed.

"That it is."

"If you travel so much why don't you already have a blessing?"

She gestured over her shoulder without even looking at the muscle behind her. "I had one. My bodyguard was carrying it."

The priest smirked and sneered at him. "And he lost it? Surprised you're keeping him."

"I didn't," she replied coolly. "That's why this one is so on-edge."

The *thunk* of her escort's tankard hitting the table made the Oldstone jump slightly. Question answered, he sucked on the air and finally nodded his head. "How much?"

"Five *evanes*," she replied, "and the amulet. I imagine that a future favor would also be appropriate."

"Five evanes?! You're asking five thousand crowns?!"

Her bodyguard didn't pretend to hide his laugh at the priest's outburst. "Five is fair for a quarry that's still producing; let alone one that's not just producing, but one that will give you plenty of room to expand the influence of your God, too."

Altund shook his head. "Even if it was birthing a mountain of gems, I'd still need someone to extract it."

She just smiled. "As if a geomancer such as yourself would *need* people to extract from the land when you are more than capable of waving your hand and conjuring it forth. If the BeaST were to allow Hannock to sell it on the open market, do you really think it'd go less than eight?"

"You say that as if there's anyone in this city that could afford it."

"Who's to say it would be bought by someone in this city? I know you have a desire to keep the interests of Basion located *in* the basin. There's little doubt that there would be many others that would just delight in gaining access to it."

"Three," he countered.

"Four and a half, the blessing, and a four-percent payout over the next year of production."

His flabby jaw dropped open. "That could end up being more than five!"

Anais shrugged. "But it would not be required to be paid upfront."

"I will do four," he agreed with a snarl.

"Four and the other terms?"

She could hear his rotting teeth grinding together as he brooded over her offer. "No. Just four."

"Three and three quarters, with two-percent and a favor owed in the future," she countered, "and this is the lowest offer I make. The blessing is *not* that important to me to pass my hand at this much coin. I could always trade this offer with the Lovers; see if they are more willing to tell me what I want to know. If that blight on the land needs room to expand, maybe they could stick it in Gavasti's quarry."

He ignored the idle threat and waved her off. "But asking *them* without the question being turned back to you is a bit harder, isn't it? That's why you're coming to me and not going to them directly. They won't tell you what you need to know, and you don't dare approach them."

The lady pursed her lips and tried to read his face. "I sense you know more about what they do and what I seek than you've been letting on, Oldstone."

"The Stonehewn feels what is in the ground and what things should stay buried in it," he said as he peered at her closely and the smile he gave her was neither friendly nor did it imply anything holy. "Your apparent interest in pissing off the followers of the Harlot is the *only* reason I haven't called attention to that yet."

"It is true, I do have an interest in what they've put in the Repository."

"You are well aware of what I meant. They've buried many things. Some that were buried before."

"And if you knew what I searched for," she slowly replied, "I would offer a great deal more. Yet you already know that – so I know that you *don't*, do you?"

He ground his teeth like a petulant child and slumped into his chair. "You'll find that the Repository is more of a grave than a vault if you push against the door. I wish to be one with the mountains, yes. *Not* one with that blighted pit."

Her smile never faltered. "Then we have an agreement. As a gesture of good faith, I would ask for that amulet sooner than later."

Allund's laugh grated on her ears. "I give nothing for free. You deliver the contract, I deliver the payment. Nothing stopping you from taking it and leaving, is there? As you said – you're a traveler."

"But a woman of honor."

"No woman has honor," he spat, "not when she wants something from you."

For what felt like the tenth time since he sat down, she rolled her clay-gray eyes at him. "I *assure* you, Oldstone, I am a woman of honor. Besides," she added, "what good would it be for me to accept a holy item and then turn on the person that blessed it? The Divine have never shied away from turning a favor to a curse when and if it suits Them."

"Think you know a lot about the Gods, do you?"

"Well," she slowly retorted, "I am a merchant of secrets. Who has more secrets than the Gods?"

"People that try to hide from them."

Her laugh was nowhere near as grating as his, and lasted longer. "Fair enough. Do we have an accord?"

The priest gave her a short nod and raised his tankard up. "Consider it done. I'll find something suitable and send it to you."

"I assume that means you already know where I'm staying?"

"And who with," Altund replied. "People don't think to realize how much knowledge the ground holds."

"Something I won't soon forget," she mused. "Then the deal has been done. You have no idea how much of a reassurance it will be to have His blessing once again. As I said, my travels often take me towards the Midlands and -"

He stood up and dropped the mug on the table. "I don't care, woman. But I'll tell you now – if you *don't* get the contract? You'll find out how deep the pits of this world go."

"I am a woman of my word, Oldstone. I promise."

"Believe it when I see it," he grunted before he morbidly sulked off, with the coin she had given him rolling between his pudgy fingers.

"If I *ever* have to deal with that foul-smelling pile of lard again, it will be far too soon," she seethed once he was out of earshot.

It's often said you shouldn't judge a book by its cover – but in this case, you'd be right to judge her bodyguard before you got close enough to examine the pages. "He did not seem the most forthcoming," the short and stocky man grumbled in a raspy voice.

Anais rolled her muddy-gray eyes and took another drink on the barely-wine. "Forthcoming? To hear him speak of it he had the secrets to the kingdom."

"Did you get anything of value?"

"Yes, thankfully. The Repository goes much deeper than expected; and unfortunately, even sewer access is guarded. The rest we need from him will come our way in the future."

"So little, and yet you still rewarded him."

She raised her eyebrow up in her wrinkled brow. "You feel that it was too much? It was a necessity, I am afraid."

"Doesn't matter how deep it goes if we can't get into it."

"While true, the protection he offers will at least let us get a closer look. That alone is worth the favors I'll have to exchange."

He sat there, utterly unimpressed by the pointless explanation. "And you can replace those favors easily enough, can you?"

"People will pay for many things," she returned as she mulled over the ways she could take advantage of it, "including the Bearer's Guild, who will be most unhappy that Altund has been using his influence to avoid paying dues on the ore they so painstakingly transported across the province. No matter the what or the why, someone will pay for what we know now."

"Doesn't sound like much. You could get more and faster. Use wine. Use whores."

"Wine and whores leave trails," she answered with irritation inching into her voice. "Donta, we've been searching for the Urn for years. I refuse to pass up any opportunity to find any nugget of information, no matter how unlikely the thread may be to the payoff we seek. Yes, it may be a small and subtle approach but it is a means to an end for our larger goal."

He stared at her, unblinking, before finally giving up and sitting back on his stool. "Wine and whores. Still faster."

"And how well has that worked for you so far, hm? Have you been able to corrupt a scribe yet with promises of willing women, or a guard with booze enough to cough up the names of everyone on the watch? Or get *any* kind of confirmation about *anything* or *anyone* that calls the Repository home?"

"I watch. You bribe. I gave you the names I've found."

"You did. And every single one of them is either uncomfortably pristine, touched by the Gods, or too restricted to know anything about what we're after."

"Did my part. Waiting on yours."

With a huff, Anais pointed her finger at him. "Then until what you've accomplished thus far actually gets us closer, I will not have my judgment questioned. I will, however, question some of yours. Have you heard or seen anything worth noting the last few days? Anyone new enter the city?"

He let her tone pass without challenge. "Wedding guests. Clan of bankers. An envoy from Karastag's Thunder. A *shiverdine*."

She pursed her lips and pondered the arrivals. "Karastag, hm? I wonder if they remember us. We might be able to use them to get access to the Guild. And a shiverdine? How repulsive. What is a slaver from Sycio doing this far into the Queen's territory?"

"Flesh is trade, trade is flesh," he replied with a shrug.

"Disgusting. Simply disgusting," she spat with revulsion. "Any new arrivals from the Orders of Light, by chance?"

He nodded and took her tankard from her. "Oo-lo."

Anais tensed up and leaned forward. "You should've lead with that, my dear."

"No," he grunted. "Nobody useful. New arrival for the Manor. Some fool. Broken leg. Exorcist."

"A limp doesn't get you sent to the Manor," she contested.

Donta shrugged it off and refused to give her sudden interest any real merit. "Manor guests don't get you to the vault."

"Depends on how shattered the mind is that's attached to the leg."

"They don't attach that way."

She pointed her finger at him again. "They are closer than how a shiverdine can ever hope to be towards the Repository, at the least. Do you know where he came from?"

He took a swig of her drink before answering and gave her a condescending glare. "Gonta."

Anais narrowed her eyes even deeper. "Gonta? We were just there a trio of months ago. What could've possibly happened in that sad little claybog that would have condemned another exorcist to suffer under Medias's misguided attempts to lead a healthy life?"

"The Circle was there," he pointedly reminded her.

Almost insulted that he thought she would've forgotten, she gave him a stoic glare. "I hadn't forgotten about him. Pegilo, wasn't it? I made sure that the Civans knew about him before we left. Should have been a quick disposal."

"Maybe they didn't kill him. Maybe they used him."

"I sincerely doubt that such a putrid piece of wrinkles and bile could have done anything to a trained exorcist to warrant a stay here. If our benefactor hadn't instructed us to expose them whenever we found them, I'd have left the odoriferous wretch alone."

Continuing to be utterly nonplussed by her tone, concern, or general presence, he barely answered her. "Doesn't matter," he grunted.

Resisting the urge to strangle him, Anais struggled to keep her voice quiet. "If an Oo-lo arrives injured from a place where the Circle was working, it's hard to imagine the two situations aren't somehow related. This bears a short investigation."

"You credit them too much. They just preach."

"*Don't* underestimate them, Donta," she warned. "If they were truly worthy of our scorn, we would be done by now. I will keep my ears open for whatever cause could be responsible for his arrival; you do the same. In the meantime, find out where the Karastags are staying and whoever holds the highest rank in their motley mercenary crew."

With a sigh, he set the empty cup down and he lowered his head. "Yes, mistress. You're tense. Why?"

"I had word from *him*," she replied, drawing out the word for several extra syllables. "He grows *impatient*."

That was the first thing she said that elicited any kind of emotional response from him worth noting. He clenched his jaw and looked her in the eyes before responding carefully. "He always is."

"Yes, it does seem to be so."

"We've only had a month."

"A month here, a year there. He knew how difficult the job was before he hired us."

Donta snorted and crossed his arms. "Hired?"

Anais looked askance at the other patrons in the tavern and kept her voice low. "It is a word for it."

"Not the right one."

She ignored that and looked up towards the sky. "I fear I may be running late now, blasted be all. I am due to meet with some minor functionary from the Blackstone Trading Company... Gistan? I believe? Just another BeaST, but the more of their members we can put in our purse the better. As it is, the Granalchi have started making some odd purchases throughout the province for some new research project, and I'd like to know more about it."

He twitched and followed her gaze. "Be wary around them. Do you need me...?"

"No, and the no is because I *am* wary. It's why I seek the counsel of the BeaST, instead of the council of the wizards themselves... for now, at least. It may be nothing, or it may be something. Find out what you can of this new arrival to the Manor, and then resume your task with the Repository. If the Urn truly is in Basion, then it will be there."

"As you will it," he grumbled.

"Yes, as I will it," Anais half-sighed. "Oh, and Donta? Before I forget -"

"You don't forget." he interrupted.

"So glad you realize that," she snidely replied. "I did need to tell you: I received word from our good Ettaquis."

Her bodyguard-come-assistant blinked and tilted his head to the side in confusion. "Only word? He's late."

"Yes, he is," she agreed, "though he has a reasonable excuse. Apparently the ship I had booked his passage on never arrived at its port of call, and he had some difficulty finding one that was coming back this direction."

"Ships sink," he grunted. "Better before than after. After would... be worse."

Anais pursed her pale lips and nodded. "Said that way, I will remember to do better to keep my patience with him in check. Warships don't oft do so in peacetime."

"It's Dawnfire. Even peacetime isn't."

She couldn't hide her smirk at the rare arrival of his sense of humor. "All the best for us, that."

Donta shrugged. "How did a lowborn like him get on warship?"

"He's not that lowborn, and he didn't get on it – which is part of the problem, though I think we can *both* consider ourselves grateful he wasn't."

He sat very still and she could almost see the pulse start to beat in the side of his neck. "The package wasn't -."

"No. No, he still has it."

He visibly relaxed and let out a deep breath. "Thanks be to the after for that."

"Yes, many thanks," she quickly agreed with a half-hearted gesture towards the various Pantheon-inspired artwork in the tavern. "I made the arrangements for him; it felt safer to have him under guard on his trip than trust him to make his own plans. I hired a ship for him out of Gonta before we left. The... *Q. R. W. Hullbreaker*? I believe it was."

Donta grunted his disgust. "Dawnfire sailors. The biggest failures in the Kingdom. Worse than the army. Not surprised."

She replied with a very un-ladylike chortle. "It's worse for them than you realize; my understanding was that it was carrying *sylverine* destined to the Chief Metallurgist... I paid quite well to make sure they had room for him after they finished their delivery at the capital. If you want to speak of a waste, consider the gold that they just cost us."

"Could be worth it," he grunted. "Maybe knowledge to be had from their corpses."

"It sank, Donta. It didn't beach itself and break apart."

"Bodies float."

Anais didn't quite dignify that with much more than a silent snort of derision. "Well. If you happen to find one, I'm sure we can find out something. I would not get your hopes up. That said – Ettaquis and Moira will be here within the next two weeks."

He looked up at her and his eyes slowly changed from navy blue to a stormy gray. "Then we'll know."

"Then we'll know."

Basion City.

The safest place in the kingdom.

Sent spiraling in the air from the mage at the end of the street, a glowing manabomb detonated on the side of a building over the head of a cloaked warrior in steel chainmail and studded leather. Bits of sharp brick and glowing embers caromed off of his shoulders as the huntsman wrapped his hands in pulsating shadows before he sent them through the air after his assailant. The shadows snaked through the assembled crowd expertly, only to vanish in a pale fog before they could even come close to their target.

The combatants paced back and forth on the street, barely able to move to the sides without running into people. Flanking was all but impossible (though they were trying). It didn't look like a fair fight; the battle was stacked three-against-one. That as fine as far as the mercenaries were concerned – the Hunter's Guild never cared about fighting *fair*, they just cared about fighting and getting *paid*.

Their target, on the other hand, wasn't about to be dissuaded by such trivial concerns as *being outnumbered* or debasing himself by fighting with a *sword*. He was barely concerned about *fighting*, and had no qualms about dabbling into showmanship as much as he did about embarrassing his opponents in front of the assembled onlookers. Of course, that kind of behavior was expected from a man from the Granalchi Academy. Mages, as the old saying goes, are a general's best friend.

And their worst enemy.

Smug from effortlessly handling the deflection, the garishly-garbed Granalchi flung his hands up and conjured a thick wall of rocks and mud in front of him to block an angry blow from a second hunter approaching him from the side. One of his swords bounced harmlessly off of a chunk of stone, while the other ended up so mired in thick mud that he nearly broke his wrist jerking it free. With a growl of frustration, he abandoned his smaller blades and unsheathed a bulky, two-handed broadsword from his waist and used it to hack through the floating obstruction.

The Adept tucked his hands into his tan and gold robe and let raw willpower alone dictate the effects of his next spell as he laughed at his opponents. While people watched and cheered, he began to levitate and let an arc of thin, yellow electricity leap from the air in front of his chest and knock the sword out of the melee-minded mercenary's hands.

A third hunter wasn't having anything to do with his tricks. He barely managed to move his head before the knives she threw did more than just slice through the end of his beard. While he was able to dodge that, he didn't have as much luck avoiding the concussive burst of sound and light from her fingertips that left stars in his eyes.

She charged across the street and sprinted for him as he held his hands up over his eyes – and realized that she missed another one of his cocky little tricks. Her fist went right for his face and connected flat on his jaw...

...or it would have, if there was a jaw for her to connect with. Her hand and arm went through his face and out the other side without meeting any kind of resistance. The crows-feet along his navy blue eyes crinkled as the projection shook with laughter before it vanished into thin air.

While the huntswoman recovered her footing, the mage stepped out of the crowd behind the sword-swinging mercenary who was trying to get free of the mud wall that was covering his feet and boxing him in. A hand on the back of his neck and a whispered invocation later, and the mage's melee-minded assailant passed out in a heap on the ground. "One down," the Adept boasted to the adulating crowd, "which one will be next?!"

His boasting gave the other mage time to fling a fresh bolt of magic at the adept. The shadowcaster had the bolt cloaked in twisting shadows that licked at the heads of the cheering onlookers as it arced past them. While the smoky tendrils from the tail end of the bomb wilted a few loose strands of hair, that was all the destruction he managed to accomplish. The Granalchi held his hand out and caught the bomb in the palm of his hand before he squeezed his fist closed and snuffed it out.

The hunter wouldn't be so lucky. Before his spell was completely crushed, the mage jerked his other hand up and willed a chunk of mud from his earlier spell to launch straight up and punch the mercenary hard under his chin. The impact popped him up to his toes... and knocked him out cold.

It cost him though.

A shower of electrified sparks erupted all around his head, startling him and forcing him to cover his eyes again. This time, the huntress managed to get up close and personal and had her dagger almost to his throat before he could do anything to stop her. This time, instead of dirt or fire, it was nothing but water – and it welled up from the ground in such a torrent that it knocked her feet out from under her.

He caught her when she fell face-first into his shoulder. She got out a muffled, "You frustrating bastard," before he twisted her head up with his left hand and kissed her firmly on her lips. Before the huntress could protest the assault, he kicked her feet out from under her and let her land unceremoniously in the mud.

"That would be three!" he crowed to the crowd as they erupted with shouts of delight and clapping hands, "and *that* is why they call me the Bladebane!"

The huntswoman looked up at him and pushed strands of wet golden hair out of her eyes. "That's why I call you an utter asshole."

"You do that out of love."

"I do that because you always make a grab at me," she grumbled.

He grinned down at her and helped her up. "Yes, but can you blame me? I mean, look at you. Even covered in mud you are... exquisite."

"Yes," she huffed, "yes, I can. You're gonna pay for this mess, too."

The Adept smirked at her and then gestured wildly to the crowd. "So then! These are three of the best Huntsmen that the Southern Guild has to offer. What you *don't* know is that any of these three could kill half the men in my employ with ease, but? An Adept, a true Adept? One that from a mere Affinitist to an Arch-Adept and beyond? One that bears our titles with the power that they have rightfully earned through studies and willpower? We have magic unknown and unseen! The Academy only takes the best, the strongest of minds, those keenest of wit, those -"

She calmly grabbed him by his hair and wrenched his head back before she placed the edge of her knife at the beating jugular on the side of his neck, saying, "- those who can still be taken when they drop their guard. Mages may be hard to kill, but it is not impossible. *Is it,* my love?"

Her 'love' coughed and very carefully slipped himself out of her grasp. "Ah.... no. Death does come for us all."

"And the Guild *is* death," she went on to tell the onlookers. "The Academy may seek those with the patience for scrolls and books and musty tomes. The Guild?" she asked before giving a short nod to someone standing on the side of the street, "The Guild seeks those whom have earned contracts on their heads – and those with the means to fill them." She punctuated the declaration with a flick of her knife towards the crowd, and the blade went spinning into the thigh of a seemingly-random passerby.

As if on cue, someone lunged out of the crowd and grabbed her victim from behind before he could do much more than grab his leg and howl. A few feet away, the shadowcasting hunter had managed to get back to his knees. A grumbled invocation escaped his lips and he used his magic to bind the bleeding spectator's hands together with thick black shadows.

The spectator-turned-mark tried to fight his way out of the spell and the hands on his shoulders. Nothing did any good, and while he fought, the crowd melted away around him. "WHAT ARE YOU DOING YOU STUPID BITCH?!"

"That's simple," she replied with a happy yet cold smile and a happy tilt to her voice. "I said it once already: the Guild seeks those whom have earned contracts on their heads. Mikan Shelboat, you're being detained by authority of a Writ ordered under the hand of Dawnfire's 10th Garrison."

His mouth opened wider than the wound in his leg as he voiced his protests. "I didn't -"

"- run fast enough," she countered. "B'tril. Cassanol. Muffle him, please."

The first mercenary nodded and pushed his cloak off of his head enough to reveal his dusky brown skin and bald, rune-covered head. "Yes, Huntsmatron," he answered with a raspy voice. "Your will be done."

The so-called Bladebane kept rubbing his throat over the red mark that the feisty huntress had left behind. "Oh, and tell Henderschott I said hello when you see him, please?"

"A delivery and a greeting," B'tril answered with a half-smile. "I would never deny the wife of our Huntsmatron."

"Husband, you mean."

The hunter cast his pale-pink eyes at the Bladebane and smirked. "I said it as I said."

Before her husband could give an undignified response to the insult – and as the crowd dejectedly began to move on – the woman quickly spoke up to interrupt them. "Oh, and if that fisker gives you grief, cut his balls off. He won't need them where he's headed."

"WHAT?" Mikan managed to shout out before a spell from the shadowcaster wrapped a black fog around his lips and throat.

The unlikely pair watched him kick and fight all the way down the street as three mercenaries carried him off. With the show over, the crowd dispersed back to their day-to-day lives. When they were finally gone, the Bladebane turned to his beautiful, albeit filthy, wife of eight years and wrapped his hands over hers. "My love? I need to ask a favor, now that this is done."

"After you drenched me in mud?" she challenged indignantly. "Unless it involves you scrubbing my back tonight, I'd chose your *favors* carefully."

"Sadly, no."

She arched her eyebrows at him and gave him a look that could've stopped an army in its tracks. "No?"

"I mean, yes, I will," he hastily added, "but that's not what I need to bother you with. I actually saw Henderschott this morning. That's what I need to talk to you about, the prospects of what a bath could do for us aside."

Her eyebrows lifted halfway to the top of her head. "Oh? Then it must be important if you're passing up on a chance to go home right now and -"

"One of my students was found dead this morning."

The flirtatious look on her face crumbled in an instant. "Oh. Oh, Tel, I'm sorry. Were you close?"

"No, not very. I'm more surprised than heartbroken."

"Spell went bad?" she asked.

He shook his head and squeezed her hand worryingly. "Could not be so lucky. He was murdered."

The huntress let go of him and tensed up before she realized she was even doing it. "Murdered...? One of yours?"

"Shocking, I know," he lamented. "Defensive arts are one of the first things trained these days. Imagine my surprise when it was Instructor Odern, at that"

Dismay turned to intrigue as she struggled to remember the name. "You've mentioned him before. Isn't he the, oh, what is it...?"

"Instructor-Adept of Defensive Magics of the Basion Annex?" he finished for her. "Yes. His entire job is to teach the students how to defend themselves against those will ill-intent."

She quickly wrapped her arms around him and gave him a tight hug in support. "What happened? Mugging? Jilted lover?"

The Bladebane cleared his throat and grimaced. "Hung by his feet in an alley, heart stuffed in his mouth, upper body flayed clean. Needless to say, we are feeling upset in our hallowed halls."

"Gods," she breathed into his chest. "Why didn't you tell me earlier? Mikan could have waited."

Her husband kissed the top of her head and leaned into the hug. "After the way that prick earned his writ? Hardly. No. Now I need to petition the Guild for one of my own. Not as the man who took your hand in matrimony, I'm afraid."

"And not as the mother of your daughter."

"Correct. This, I am afraid, must be official."

She sighed and stepped back from him – and any trace of compassion in her eyes suddenly turned into something that was cold, hard, and almost violently unpleasant. "Then, Headmaster Adept Telburn Gorosoch, as Huntsmatron of Basion City and Interim Guild Executioner of Kettering Province, your petition is accepted for negotiation. Name the writ."

Telburn's gaze nearly matched hers. "Huntsmatron Elsith, the Granalchi Academy requests a Writ of Investigation and Naming into the death of Adept-Instructor Odern Merrington. We also request that the writ contains a provision to allow for modification into a Writ of Execution, pending permission of

Maiden-Templar Catherine Prostil, or her Betrothed, or another duly recognized individual capable of and charged with serving as the legal authority of this city and province whom holds such power under the Crown."

"Given the nature of the murder in question, the Guild will consider this a high-value and priority writ," Elsith returned matter-of-factually. "The negotiated cost will also reflect the potential danger to any contractor that accepts the hunt."

"We are aware," he acknowledged as he continued on, "and as such, the academy is prepared to offer seven hundred and fifty gold crowns for the writ."

Elsith shook her head no. "Eight-twenty-five," she countered. "We also request access to the Basion Annex Rune Vault for no less than three Runes of Alloyance."

"Seven-seventy-five and one."

"Seven-fifty and three, or a full *diandra*."

The Adept had to fight to keep his composure steady and his voice down. "A full diandra? A thousand crowns? You are aware that I could request a Collector for less from the Offices of the Dean?"

"Yes, but a Collector will likely review your teaching methods."

He winced and lowered his head in defeat. "Fair point. I need justice, not an audit. Seven-fifty, two runes. Writ of Investigation, a Writ of Naming and an Execution provision attached to both."

The Huntsmatron didn't miss a beat. "Headmaster Adept, the Guild accepts your terms." And just as suddenly, she dropped back into a warm and loving smile with a gleam in her eyes. "Now let's go find the sonofabitch."

Gorosoch chuckled and reached for her for another hug. "I do love the way you think. Want to stop and get Valina a bowl of sweet pudding on the way home tonight?"

"She eats too much of that as it is," she protested, "you spoil her."

"My dear," he chided, "there is *no* such thing as *'too much'* pudding."

IV. CAUSE AND EFFECT
Londis, the 5th of Greenbirth, 513 QR

In the east wing of the ground floor of the Manor, Akaran was having to answer questions that he *truly* didn't want to. "Tell me about it," she insisted.

"Do I have to?"

In his defense, nobody would. "If you want peace, you have to confront your demons," Livstra countered with a slight wag of her finger.

He shifted in his wheelchair and wished – for the umpteenth time – that she would open the curtains on her window. "Confronting my demons is how I got here. Well. Somebody's demon."

"That is the nature of your job," she argued. "You survived through it, so you must have done something right."

"There's a *lot* of debate on that," he grumbled.

Ridora's Lady-in-Waiting styled herself as something of a psyanist, he had found out, having studied at the Granalchi Academy. She had turned her talents for empathic observation and aura manipulation into treating the chronically maddened instead of... doing whatever those wizards would do for gold instead. A noble profession, but there was only one thing worse than a mind-mage that Akaran could think of that he wouldn't want to be sitting aside from. "As I have heard. So tell me about it. The dreams. How much do you remember?"

"Enough," he sighed with an uncontrollable spasm shooting down his leg.

She stood from her chair and began to wiggle her cotton-gloved fingers in the air around his head with little flicks and twists. Something in the air started to shift, though the moment he felt it, it suddenly shut off just as quickly. Liv frowned and tried a few more times before resuming her irritating line of questions. "Do they feel real? Or is it more of a fog, a snippet...?"

Akaran closed his eye and slowly shook his head. "It is real." Even awake, it was real. All he had to do was close his eye and give a halfhearted effort to focus on the memory. They'd been growing progressively worse since the fight, but they always started out the same. "It doesn't *feel*. It *is*."

She nodded slowly. "Then is it truly a dream, or a memory?"

"Both?"

"The mind works in many odd ways. You would not be the first to think it be both."

It's dark all around him. There's enough light that he can see that he's standing on a perfectly-white sand dune. It's shifting, rolling back and forth. As his eye focuses he realizes it's already swallowed his feet and is halfway up his shins. There's a fog there, a growing pool of shadows billowing up from the grains around him. Little green lights start to flicker in it as it begins to ascend his body as he began to sink into the ground.

He squeezed his eye shut even harder. "It didn't happen. But it's real."

"Is it the same dream?"

"No. Different. But it starts the same way almost every night," he said as he let it boil to the surface. "I wake up, only I can't move. I'm paralyzed. I can move my head a little back and forth. That's it. And I'm not where I was."

"You are someplace other than Toniki?"

He shook his head. "Yes, but... no. I mean, whenever I go to sleep. I'm there, but I'm not. It's like the room has moved. Or I've moved. Or the bed has. It's like while I'm asleep someone moves the walls slightly and tilts the bed and opens the door and shines a torch through it. Or I'll see just... nothingness where a wall had been joined to another wall. It's like... the world has *broken* and I see that it's *broken* and I can't move because I'm stuck because it's *broken*."

Ridora's chief therapist made a note in her journal as he talked. "What you describe is not uncommon. We speak of it as the *paralidrieam*; a torment of the mind. It could be a sign that you've been cursed by Nia'valth. Did you happen to encounter any of Her followers?"

"Nia... no. I mean it's possible, but no, I don't think so...?"

"Well, it's worth testing you for. There are many causes of nightmares; allowing oneself to land on the bad side of the Dreamer is one of them."

"It's not a dream. I swear it's real."

Livstra never let her eyes waver from his. "If it never happened, then it isn't real."

"Lots of things can happen to a soul that don't happen in the flesh," he countered. "Doesn't make them any less real."

"Yes, but those things have a cause. If you had an influence acting upon you, the wards at the gate would not have let you in." She hesitated for a moment and carefully added, "At least, not comfortably, by any stretch."

He glanced at her and failed to hide a self-loathing smirk. "So I assume that since my skin didn't turn black and char that I passed the test?"

"Yes."

"Were you going to warn me about it?"

"No."

"That's not a recurring theme or anything at this point," he grumbled.

She answered with a little laugh that came with a look in her eyes that was anything but humored. "Continue with the dream. There's little time today."

The world around him melted away. It did it every time. The bed he was on would just disintegrate into nothingness, leaving him standing on the mound of sand. It was like that in every direction – sand, as far as the eye could see. Eternal sand, under a cloudless, bright blue sky.

No matter what he tried, the sand wouldn't let him go. No matter how he struggled, it kept on him. The fog started to rise and it slowly swallowed his legs to his knees. That's when he felt them in the fog – shapes. Hands. Faint touches on his naked skin from things that felt rubbery in parts and crisp in others.

The more he struggled, the faster the fog covered him. The more he tried to kick, the faint touches turned to rough tugs. When the fog reached his hips, it developed features. The rolling mass of blackness turned into a face. The flickering lights in it turned into coldly lit eyes.

The fog smiled. He screamed and shouted at it. When it swallowed his hips, he started to punch at it. Bits of fog flickered away each strike, until the mouth clamped down and caught his fist. Hands in the fog grabbed him and started to methodically break his fingers. He screamed each time, and couldn't stop screaming. His toes bent backward and shattered. His knees twisted inward and followed suit.

As it swallowed his chest, he felt the first wound that Makolichi had inflicted burst open front to back and the fog welled up through him. He felt the blood pour out of the wound but the shapes in the cloud swallowed every last bit of it. The entity continued to swell as he heard other screams joining his. Some he recognized, some he didn't, and then he heard Mariah-Anne scream his name in a sharp screech that -

"Ah, there he is," a young woman's voice interrupted. A moment later, and the voice had a body to go with it – Raechil, and she looked exceedingly flustered. "I've been looking all over for him. Finally. You'd not think that a cripple would be hard to find."

"That's almost uncalled for," he muttered as he worked himself out of his reverie.

Livstra closed her journal and sighed. "We were just getting somewhere, too. What is it you need, Rae?"

"Your patient, Lady. It's time for him to meet Keto."

Akaran watched her shudder hard and look down at her paperwork as she quickly found a way to busy herself with anything *but* him. "Well. Then. Let me... let me not be the one to keep you from that."

"Keto? Who's Keto?"

Raechil wrapped her hands around the handles on his chair and started to pull him away. "It will likely be a few days before he can have another session with you."

"Oh, child. There is no wondering of that."

He put his good foot down to try to slow her incessant tugging as he asked the question a second time. "Who's Keto? Why will it be a few days...?"

The faint, pitying smile from Lady Oliana was the only answer he got.

While putting up with a psyanist may have been the second-to-last-thing he wanted to deal with today, there was absolutely no doubt that the wrinkled forty-something (maybe fifty) man with a white mustache sitting next to him was the last. "I suppose you're going to tell me that the men who worked on you called themselves physicians?"

At least he was easy to get along with.

"Some priest at the Temple. Didn't get his name," Akaran replied to the surgeon.

"Presumably because he was too busy butchering your leg and lying about his qualifications," he grumped as he twisted the offending limb back and forth to take a closer look at the poorly-healing incision. "Tell me, did he attempt to anesthetize you for the procedure, or did he chase after you with a skillet until he hit you in the head enough times to leave you loopy?"

The offended limb made sure that he knew *how* offended it was every time Keto twisted it around. "It wasn't much of a chase," he answered back through clenched teeth and the hint of a tear coming out of his good eye.

"No, I don't imagine that it was."

He let that slide (hard as it was). "Can you fix it?"

The codger looked up at him and blew a loose hair away from his upper lip. "Fix it? I'm insulted."

"Can you fix it while being insulted?"

He snorted and straightened Akaran's leg back out until the exorcist unleashed a pained cry. "I can do a better job than *this*. Tell me, what do you know about the human body – joints and bones?"

"Hit them with hammers they break and cut them with swords and they fall off," he managed to gasp.

Keto sighed and rubbed his eyes. "Oh blessed be. I thought you were a priest."

"Exorcist," Akaran countered.

"A violent priest."

There was a brief moment of silence while he thought the description over. "That's not inaccurate."

None of the poking and prodding would have been as bad if it wasn't for how the surgeon had decorated his room. There were bleached bones in glass cases. Jars of unidentifiable bits sat on dusty shelves. There was a flowerpot on the floor filled with plants that he was *sure* wasn't safe for human consumption (or even animal, after giving it a closer look).

If he didn't know better, Keto would've been a prime target for a Temple Inquiry. Even knowing better, it was hard not to voice that request. *I wonder if the local Stara priestess knows that he's keeping bones here. They frown on that.*

While he'd been lucky enough to enjoy Livstra's office on the ground level – and his own room was on the first floor too – getting down to the basement and the surgeon's lair (office) had taken more effort than it was worth. The lair (office) was a small room barely big enough for the two of them as it was, and the added... stuff... made it claustrophobic. "What did you say did this again? Some kind of... what was it?"

Wouldn't kill the man to put up a tapestry, something with color in it, would it? "An ice demon. I hurt it a few times. It hurt back."

The old veteran of a medic didn't even pretend to look surprised. "I'd say so. Alright then boy, your kneecap is fractured. I can feel tendons that have rolled up the inside of your leg which means they've been severed from the bone. Part of your upper leg seems to have been shattered at the joint, and I can feel bone shards in the bone below it. Do you understand any of that?"

His face paled as old memories from the Temple popped up in his mind. *'Where and How Bits Are Connected'* was a non-optional course in the Temple. Anyone picking up a sword got a lesson on the basics of anatomy – both human and non. The reason was because many Abyssian monsters tend to share traits (or even bodies) with living beings on the mortal plane, so knowing what fastens to what was supposed to help you know where to stab.

It wasn't his favorite class then, and being able to draw on it didn't make him feel any additional fondness now.. "Goddess... I... that explains why it hurts."

"Hurts?" the quote-unquote surgeon replied with a raised eyebrow. "Quite frankly I'm surprised you're still conscious. There *are* spells that are used to combat this kind of injury, you know. You are a strange man to have an aversion to magic, as a magic-flinging priest."

"They won't let me use them."

"Who?"

"The things that took away my magic," Akaran obliquely clarified.

Keto studied his face for a moment before he shrugged his shoulders and moved a few steps away to wash his hands in a simple basin against the wall. "Ah, yes, the other thing. I want you to understand that I serve Isamiael. He has blessed me with the ability to enhance natural healing and to ease the pain of those in suffering. Yet for some reason, I can't even channel a hint of ether into you. Would that be related...?"

"I got punished for abusing wild magic," his patient replied as he desperately tried to find a way to make himself feel comfortable on the surgeon's cot.

"Punished? What possible human has the ability to...?"

"Wasn't human."

The surgeon stood perplexed until he finally shrugged his shoulders and went back to scrubbing his hands. "Well, I shall assume your stoicism on the subject means that it's far out of my pay-grade, so I will let others with more experience deal with *that* part of your treatments. I can fix you. You will not like me fixing you, but I will fix you. What are they giving you for pain, if magic cannot do the task?"

Somehow, he didn't even trust Keto with the water and he tried to scoot further up the bed. "It was belistand and Iarochi in Toniki, then they started giving me cocasa-root in Gonta."

That got his attention, and for none of the right reasons. "Cocasa? In what dosage?"

Akaran pulled a package out of the quaint wool robe they had issued him with his room. "As much as I need to sleep."

"Please tell me that someone told you the dangers of abusing that."

"Not really," he said as he slid it back away, "just that it's a little addictive. Dangers?"

"Yes, *dangers*," Keto said with an exasperated sigh. "That root is a horrid substance. You're playing recklessly."

The priest sank slightly against the cot and looked slightly guilty for reasons he couldn't explain. "What did I do now?"

"You began taking one of the most addictive drugs in the kingdom," the doctor said as he pointed at him. "It's prohibited outside the manor and the lesser clinics in Basion. Not that it stops anyone, but it is prohibited."

"I mean I've heard of it before but -"

Keto raised his hand and interrupted him. "Have you been feeling depressed?"

"Uh... yes?"

"Tired?"

"Very."

The doctor leaned in close enough that Akaran could almost smell a hint of rum on his breath. *So much for that rule about drinking on the premises*, he grumbled inwardly. It was almost like he was *trying* to get Akaran not to trust him. "Short-tempered?"

"Getting there," he grumbled.

"Shakes? Nightmares? Paranoia? Restlessness; memory issues?"

The holy warrior rolled his eye up to the ceiling and tried to stop the babbling inanity pouring out of Keto's mouth. "About half of those. Can I point out that my leg is shattered? It hurts like fire. All of those seem reasonable if it makes it hurt *less*."

The surgeon just sighed at Akaran and crossed his arms. "Thus the problem with cocasa addicts. You take it for valid reasons, but when those reasons end... pay attention. I want you to listen close to me."

"I've been listening. So far all I've gotten out of this is that I'm screwed."

"That you are," he agreed. "After I fix the mess the fisking guttersucks in Gonta left behind, you're going to hurt worse. You're going to have to take more of the root unless you can regain your pathway to the ether or whatever it is that's wrong with you. I can't say it any other way; what I must do will *not* be pleasant."

That much blunt honesty was as refreshing as it was distressing. Thankfully – or so he thought at first – someone new to the exorcist decided to interrupt. "Ahem, Keto. You know the rules on language in the manor."

"In this case, I am not using enough of it," he said without even facing the young woman that had appeared at the entrance to his lair (office).

Akaran ignored her too (although that was difficult for reasons best described as 'blonde,' 'thin,' and 'almost-sheer white cotton tunic'). Instead... "Will I be able to fight again?"

The surgeon sized his leg up one more time and then looked over the rest of him for good measure. "Walk, yes. Fight, I don't know. That is up to you to decide. I can't do much for your recovery, just the fix."

"Then I'll deal with it," he promised.

Keto gave a nod of his head and poked his patient's chest where the bag of cocasa was tucked away. "That's the best answer I suppose you could give me. *Now,* keep in mind, if you start taking more of the root, you *will* become addicted."

"I think I -" he started to interrupt, but he failed utterly.

"No. I don't care *how* strong-willed you are, you *will* become an addict. Watch for the signs. When your leg turns into a tolerable throb, please, for the love of Isamiael, stop taking it."

"You're being pretty adamant about it," Akaran whined. "It's just a weed. What's the worst it can do?"

"I've seen the damage it can do," he said as he sat down on a nearby stool. "There's an epidemic in the areas immediately outside the city. Dozens of smaller villages. It's been making inroads for months. It's gotten bad in Lower Naradol. *Please* be careful with it. I implore you."

As the intruder in the doorway impatiently tapped her foot, the priest finally gave a slow nod of his head. "As best as I can. I promise."

"Good. You seem like a nice boy, maybe a bit dense, and I feel bad for what's gonna happen to you."

"Not as bad as I feel."

"Not as bad as you're *gonna* feel," Keto promised.

He blanched and tried to curl up in a little ball to little effect. "When do we start? I think I want this over with."

Their uninvited guest cleared her throat. "Not for a bit yet, I'm afraid."

Akaran finally took the time to size her up past the first impression. She was shorter than him, smaller than him, slightly older than him, and a lot prettier than he ever would be. The only blemish he could see was a trail of poxmarks that started on the side of her neck that trailed down her shoulder and to places unknown under her dress. "Ah, Seline. I don't believe I said it yet: it is an unexpected pleasure to see you this morning."

She smiled sweetly at Keto and stepped into the claustrophobic room. "Unexpected pleasures are the best kind. Are you done with our broken little soldier?"

And just as quickly as he had been enamored with her looks, he lost his taste for her attitude. "Broken little... wait just a minute, would you? I don't need -"

"You are a soldier of the Goddess and you're currently broken," she pointed out. "As you can't straighten up, you appear little. I stand by my statement."

"I'm as done with him as I can be until I can start cutting the boy open. I really should do it right away. Are you sure you need him?"

"A brief wait, please?" she asked with a smile. "He's been requested by Lady Medias. She has several people she'd like him to meet before the operation tomorrow."

"Oh? Who's the lucky...?"

"Lolron and Risson."

Keto cringed and made a quick sign of warding. "Together? At the same time?"

"Together, and at the same time."

"Ick." He let the statement hang there while Akaran swore he felt a noose tighten on his neck. "Hah. Well, boy, have a good time."

He looked back and forth between the two of them. "Who are they and what does she want?"

Seline handed him a crutch and the surgeon helped him stand up. "She's called in for assistance to help your magical deficiencies."

"Deficiencies," he grumbled, "isn't that a quaint word."

"You don't know her like I do," she said with a faint little chuckle. "You should hear her other quaint words."

"She's right, you should," Keto added, "and if you stay here long enough you will."

Akaran sighed and caved to their insistent offers to help him stand up. "Fair enough. Thank you, Keto. I'm not looking forward to it, but I appreciate everything you're going to do."

The surgeon stopped and leaned back slightly, blinking in surprise. "Huh. Now that's something I don't hear often. You're... welcome, I suppose."

"Not used to your victims thanking you in advance?" Seline chimed in.

"Please don't use the word 'victim,'" he quietly pleaded, "he's going to operate on me, not..."

"...not flay you to the bone, core you from the inside out, and stitch parts of your body you've never seen before to each other as you as you lay on a cot screaming in agony while large men hold you down so you don't mess up my knives?" Keto finished for him.

The priest blanched and felt the color drain out of his face. "Yeah. That."

Seline gave him a reassuring pat on his shoulder once he steadied himself on his cane. "Cheer up, exorcist. We will find a way to restore your touch to magic and you won't have to worry about barbaric methods to regain control of your leg."

"It's only barbaric because of the screaming," Keto argued.

"I don't think that's helping, my friend."

"The blonde girl is right," Akaran agreed.

She smiled and walked him out to his wheelchair waiting in the hallway. "See you soon Keto!"

Akaran very distinctively heard him mutter, "Don't need to rush it," as she wheeled him away.

Before he had a chance to chew on that thought, Seline offered her own. "It's good to finally meet you. A full and detailed report from your superiors at Toniki finally made its way into the Repository and I had a chance to read a good bit of it."

"The what?"

"Oh you don't...?" she asked before kicking herself internally. "No, why would you? Record-keeping is not an advertised hallmark of the Oo-lo."

He craned his head around to glare at her. "No need to be insulting."

"No, no insult in the least," she quickly answered with that same irritatingly chipper smile. "Those that train as Her warriors have far more important things to do than to worry about musty old books and smudged papers."

For some reason, that didn't sound like much of an improvement. "Well, I mean, we study them and learn from them..."

Almost ignoring the comment, she started to explain. "The Repository of Miral is named after Miral, one of Niasmis's Three."

"The Guardian of Love," he added.

"Yes. And as such, the Repository stores everything. Whenever an exorcist, or paladin, or templar, or any of us, really, records an 'encounter'? It goes to the Grand Temple for review, and then after, a copy is sent to storage. Leaving the knowledge in two places keeps the risk of losing it all to a minimum."

All of this was news to him and he was having a hard time not showing it. "So... every encounter?"

"Yes. If a report is filed, it ends up there."

The hallway went by in a blur as they talked. "I didn't realize that we had a place for that outside of the capital."

"Most don't," she said, "and I've never seen anything past the foyer, myself. Much as I would love to."

"How come?"

She coughed lightly as they went past a staircase that went deeper underground. "There's been a measure of dispute between Lady Ridora and Maiden-Templar Prostil. They do not get along so well."

He frowned and nervously fidgeted in his chair. "How 'not along' do they get?"

"Lady Ridora has banned all those that work here from visiting there unless it's a matter of importance," she said. "No such restriction is on those that are simply staying here – though that's largely because we have very few patients who are capable of leaving the grounds on their own."

The idea of an archive full of anything and everything that the Order had been up to recently was strangely not unappealing. "Might be worth seeing at some point," he mused.

"Depending on the length of your stay, it may be for more than 'just seeing,' if she deems you fit," Seline cautioned. "Lady Ridora hates to have a mind go to waste. It has one of the largest libraries in the province."

Akaran bit back a bit of derision. "Because if there's one thing I enjoy doing, it's sitting down trying to read some chicken-scratch inked down by someone too out of shape to work in a real profession."

She must have picked up on the lack of enthusiasm behind his boisterous claim. "You never know. Your injury could lead you to carrying a quill the rest of your life, instead."

"Please don't threaten me."

The aid flicked her hair back over her shoulder and otherwise ignored him. "Of course, none of this is important right now," she said as the hallway gave way to a long ramp headed up. "What *is* important is that after a review, Ridora and some of the other healers and I have an idea how to treat you, if it pans out."

Somehow he felt that the offered glimmer of hope was less substantial than she was trying to lead him to believe: not the least of which was because he had no idea who she was. "So you're a medic...?"

She paused as she pushed him forward. "Oh? I didn't say, did I? I am sorry. My name is Seline Valdin. I am one of Ridora's healers. We'll be spending a lot of time together in the future. But first... have you seen the atrium?"

Akaran shook his head as they reached the top of the ramp and went through a small doorway. "The atrium...?"

The moment that he saw it, he realized that he was going to be spending a *lot* of time here. The garden was smack dab in the middle of the manor, with three of the wings serving to wall it off from the outside world. The north wing, on the other hand, closed it off halfway with a large bronze gate serving to provide a way into the exterior grounds.

Part of what made it impressive was the way that the second and third levels of the manor overlooked it. He quickly realized that the atrium was sunk at least half a story lower than the ground floor – and primarily illuminated from the sun through a set of wooden support beams overhead. Suddenly, the entire building looked so much more imposing than he had given it any credit for since he arrived.

He could see iron lamps along the dark-gray brick walls and from the acrid smell of it, someone had filled them with pine oil. It didn't quite mix well with the unseasonable petrichor from yesterday's rain, but that was easy enough to forgive. It did, however, delightfully mix with the smell of the daises, roses, belian-berries, honeyblades, and assorted flowering trees that filled the garden from top to bottom.

In the middle of all of it – and surrounded by a shallow moat that lazily sluiced towards a grated drain near where Akaran sat in his chair – three statues stood honoring a trio of Gods. With a cloak of bronze, a body of silver, eyes of amber and hunched over a living oak staff, the Goddess of Health and the Matron of the Order of the Hand stood tall on a sandstone pedestal to the left.

Across from Isamiael, and bearing a cloak of poppies, Solinal stood tall. The God of Peace had a clay jug in His hands that poured a steady stream of water into the moat below. The terracotta statue had been decorated with streaks of silver through His beard and across the scaled tunic that His robe didn't quite cover.

In the middle was the one statue he hadn't expected to see at all. Niasmis stood tall, carved out of marble and inset with golden eyes. Unlike the other two, nothing grew on Her, but a soft white light emanated from the base of Her feet. While the others bore cloaks or robes, She stood there in nothing but Her glorious stone skin with a sword in one outstretched hand and a glowing gold torch in the other.

In front of the three statutes – and looking fairly impatient – were two men that flanked Lady Ridora and she was the only one that was smiling. When they realized he had finally deigned to arrive in the garden, it was the one to her left that spoke up first. "Ah, is this the one?"

She nodded at the slightly pudgy man beside her. It wasn't hard to tell who he represented – the Signostica of Stara dangling from his neck gave him away as a Lower Adjunct from the Order of Light. "This is the one."

The *ladjunct* peered at him and started to look him over from head to toe as Seline wheeled him closer (and Akaran did the same in turn). He was an older man – not *old* old, but easily twice as old than the exorcist (and then some). "He doesn't look too damaged. Nothing that we haven't seen before."

That encouraged the other person in attendance to give a nod and a snide look. "I agree. A broken leg isn't an abnormality. His aura seems quiet enough." There wasn't a damn thing priestly about that one – in fact, the gray tunic he wore was ratty enough around the edges that you might mistake him as a pauper. Although if the cocky attitude didn't give it away, the copper coin hanging from his neck surely did.

Granalchi, Akaran groaned to himself, and then he groaned even harder when he looked closer at the symbol. There were six circles etched into the coin, and on the outermost, a trio of stones: white agate, hematite, and a green-and-gray ore of some kind. *An ulta-keneticist*, he recognized. *Great. Just great. I know those stones say what he's good at, I think, but damned if I know what they stand for.*

"That would be the problem, I am afraid. His aura is **too** quiet," Ridora chimed in.

"All I know is that I can't use magic and magic doesn't have a lot of an effect on me anymore," he blurted out – both to clarify the situation and because he felt much too much like a *thing* they were preparing to dissect.

"Both a resistance and a retardation? Intriguing," the Granalchi mused.

He felt the hair on his neck start to stand up as he straightened himself in his chair. "You didn't just call me -"

"*Intriguing* is what I just called you," the Adept clarified, "nothing more, nothing less. How did you lose your connection to the ether, again?"

That was a little bit more than he felt comfortable answering right away, and his pleading look towards Lady Medias didn't go unnoticed. "M'am, who are these...?"

"Ah, yes," she replied with an absentminded flip of her hand. "Sir DeHawk, this is Lower Adjunct Risson from the Ellachurstine Shrine of Stara."

Risson stepped forward and placed his hand on top of the exorcist's. "It is a pleasure. I heard that you had opportunity to work with Deboria Ult from Gonta?"

A faint smile danced across his face for a heartbeat. "I did, Ladjunct. A bit maddening, but she was of massive assistance in the fight in Toniki."

"Maddening? Then yes, you do know her," he replied with a chuckle. "Her habit for rooting out truth is a bit aggravating, I must agree. That aside, she is a truly lovely woman. Anyone that she finds worth her time is assuredly worth mine. When you're eventually able to make it out on your own, please feel free to visit – we are located on the eastern side of the basin, in the Chiadon district."

It wasn't typical for the *Oos* to offer a place for one of the Lovers, and the offer made Akaran blink in surprise. "You honor me, Ladjunct."

"The honor wears off in time," the waif-thin old man beside them muttered.

"And this charming fellow -" Ridora started to say, before he cut her off.

"I am capable of providing my own introductions, Lady. My name is Adept Lolron Essinge."

She cleared her throat gave the exorcist a pleading look and a whisper of, "*Show patience with him*," before continuing with a more proper introduction. "Lolron is a ulta-keneticist from the Academy Annex in West Giffil."

"Not familiar with that town."

Lolron rolled his mossy-green eyes. "It isn't a town; it's a district. I wouldn't bother remembering it – fairly obvious there'll be no reason for you to ever visit."

"Manners, Adept," Ridora chided.

He gave her an askance look that would've made a lesser person cringe. "I am not being paid well enough to be considerate to every broken toy that you hoard in your house, Lady," he quipped before he turned back to Akaran. "I'll assume you don't know what it is a man like myself is capable of doing."

"Getting an idea," he grumbled.

Seline choked back a laugh that was unconvincingly masked by a cough as the mage's eyes narrowed. "Say again?"

He cleared his throat and politely attempted to clarify himself. "I mean – yes, I do. It means you are a specialist in healing, divine influences on ether, demonology, and sometimes even a bit of necromancy."

Lolron perked up just a little and lifted an eyebrow in semi-surprise. "Well then, he knows a few things. Healing and an understanding of the practical applications and study of the end results of divine influences. Theology of such things is pointless to debate when you can actively experiment on what happens when They get involved."

"Risson and Lolron are here to help determine the exact root cause of your curse so that we may do our best to relieve it," Ridora explained with the faintest of annoyed sighs giving away a hint of the headache that the two of them had caused so far.

"Yes," Risson added, "the Lady already explained to us that you somehow were able to cross into the next realm? How exactly were you able to do so and how long were you able to stay?"

Before Akaran could reply, the Adept waved his hand at the Ladjunct. "Oh, ignore those questions. It's long been established that men are able to project their auras from this world and into the next with the right spells and training," he interrupted as he crossed his arms and stared at the exorcist so intently it could've burned a hole in his shirt. "Where did you learn to project your astral form to other planes? Is this a new training regimen being established by the Order of Love? That will go a long way to understanding how you were unpleasantly disabled."

He gave a pleading look back towards the lady of the manor. She nodded her head before he could ask – but he did anyway. Just to be sure. "M'lady I...?"

"By my authorization, you may. They've agreed to go under seal as well – though please omit details on *how* certain things came to pass. That you *did* was enough, the *how* is less important."

Lolron bristled at the mere mention of it. "An unnecessary requirement. There's nothing you can say about projection that needs to be kept under lock and key."

"Wouldn't count on it," he muttered, "since it wasn't projection."

The incredulity in the mage's voice was so thick Seline wondered why they couldn't see it dripping onto the ground. "Come again? You expect us to believe that you crossed over in the flesh?"

Akaran calmly pulled up his left sleeve and showed off the badly-healing gash that went through his bicep. "Earned this and the leg while I was there."

Risson frowned and drummed his wrinkled fingers absentmindedly on his hip. "Well, there are some cases where it's established that men have managed to cross into the Sands before. I suppose this shouldn't be considered too much of a stretch."

"Skipped the Sands. I landed in Tundrala." Both the mage and the priest opened their mouths to argue, but he kept going before they could get a word in edgewise. "Before you ask, no, I wasn't welcome, no, I didn't do it of my own accord, no, it wasn't a fun experience, no, I don't know how to do it again on my own, and yes, I'm aware that this is an offense to theology and an even bigger offense to Pristi, considering what I did when I was there."

There was a moment when Lolron started to ask another question and it was Seline that interrupted for a change. "And, *no*, he may not give details on how it was *possible*. In short, someone very smart did something *very* stupid. Then he," she continued as she pointed at the exorcist, "found ways to make it worse before it got better."

Ridora cleared her throat as her guests stared at Akaran in equal parts disbelief and wonder. "His claim seems outlandish at the least, and I will admit that I shared the same reaction you're both experiencing. However, his claims have been signed off on by a Paladin-Commander and undersigned by the Priestess of Stara you think so kindly of, Risson."

"Forgive me for not having the same faith in either as you two must," Lolron replied with a half-sneer.

She was apparently waiting for that. "The situation he was involved in is currently being probed by an Understudy of the Arcane. I believe he is from the First... what is it you name them? The First Orbit?"

The Adept didn't say anything at first and just stood there working his jaw and biting on his upper lip as he considered what she said. "Well. The *Understudy* of the First Orbit isn't much too special, *although* I suppose that lends some credence to the claims. Though I must say: I am very interested in the *how*. In details as specific as you are allowed, of course."

Medias nodded back at her patient as he sat there trying very hard not to tell Lolron where to shove his disbelief and in what direction to turn it first. "You may tell them."

"I really don't think that I should," he pleaded.

"You run the risk of being bereft of magic should you not," Seline cautioned him from behind.

Caving, he took a deep breath and explained things as much as he could. "I was being assisted by a wisp. We were fighting an *arin-goliath* and an *abogin*. We were both injured and she opened a portal to Tundrala. The inhabitants didn't like us dropping a demon there and liked it less that all of us were bleeding everywhere."

"More unbelievable by the moment," the Adept protested.

Risson was quick to agree, although without the bile. "It does strain credulity. Are you certain that Priestess Ult signed off on this?"

"With her own seal accompanying his arrival," Ridora replied with a half-smile. "I have made arrangements for it to be sent to your office."

The ladjunct pursed his lips and looked the exorcist over again. "Well enough for me, though I am not at all surprised that denizens of the upper realms took a dim view of something abyssian thrown into their doorstop. I cannot even begin to imagine the stance that Pristi Herself has taken in regards to this. If it is, indeed, a truth."

"Do I understand that it was an episturine that did this, you claim?" Lolron interrupted.

Akaran tilted his head and started to reply with an, "I didn't -"

"I did," the Lady clarified.

"Oh," he said as he sighed in defeat. "Yes, Adept. That was the creature that wasn't happy about what we did."

"Did it give any indication that it planned on letting you regain your strength?"

"No."

It was Lolron's turn to purse his lips. "So as far as the inhabitants of the next world are concerned, you could be stripped of power for the rest of your, and I can only assume, likely miserable and possibly short life."

Ridora cleared her throat again and turned slightly to him. "Lolron. Your tone leaves a great deal to be considered."

"Only attempting to inquire as to if he knows if this is a disability designed to fade over time or one that has a more permanent durability."

Akaran hung his head and squeezed the side of his chair in a mix of irritation and disgust. "The ice-bitch that did this to me wasn't exactly eager to make me feel better. Although Eos'eno implied that I'd regain it. She said she 'knew things' that the 'ice' had shown her. She didn't say when or how."

"Oh, how irritating."

Risson glanced at the Adept. "Irritating?"

"Prophecies," he explained, "and divination are two of the most *annoying* issues that the modern Granalchi deals with. It circumvents half of our understanding of the real world and eliminates certain concepts of what it means to be human that don't sit well with my peers. Using magic to sort through the threads of time. The very art itself is so poorly understood that many of us wonder if the very act of doing so doesn't rob one of conscious will. As an ulta, I feel as if I have the right to say that, before you protest."

The ladjunct protested anyway. "Every Order in Kora has their own set of prophecies and predictions."

"Yes," Lolron replied, "thank you for clarifying my point." Then, to Akaran, he let his voice take on even more scorn. "So you traveled to a place no human has any capability to withstand, dallied about in it, offended the entities that call it home, and were stripped of the ether as a result – only to be loosely *suggested* that you will somehow gain it back at some point in your life with limited understanding of how?"

He dropped his head and sighed out a tired, "Yes."

"Prophecies," the mage grumbled back at Risson.

"I'll grant, they are not a perfect thing," the priest reluctantly admitted.

"Shall you go first or I?"

Risson brushed his hands down his white robe and straightened it up as he walked over to the injured priest and set himself to work. "It's said that the episiturine are spiritual creatures, guardians of sorts to the Queen of Ice. If he did in fact delve into the upper planes, then this may be a punishment of the soul more than a punishment of the ether."

He couldn't help but bristle slightly at the implied accusation. "Not *if* I did. I *did."*

"As you say," the priest murmured as he placed his hand on Akaran's chest and began to pray. *"Naffin, naffin, Almed Isamiael, rodel Imin rodel lumin eldein Lethandra's goshiat!"*

After evoking the spell, a warm light erupted along Risson's arms and rolled over – but didn't touch – Akaran. It probed the air around him, brightly shining over some parts and going dim around others. The light around his leg and arm pulsed a dull gray and the light around his face turned brighter than anywhere else. Still, no matter how hard he could *feel* the light struggle to touch his skin directly, it didn't. After a few moments of trying, it quickly flared and faded away into nothing.

The ladjunct frowned ever so slightly. "Well, there's nothing dark about you, but for those injuries. Quite odd tho; wounds don't typically give off an ill-aura. You must truly be in pain."

It may have been the dumbest thing anyone had said today. "Yesss," Akaran said, drawing the word out as he glared up at his supposedly-elder like he'd grown a second head.

"Well let us see what we can do about that," he said as he took the challenge. *"Almed Isamiael, Almed Isamiael, rodel solin rodel lumin rodel nia rodel kayba'a proppa!*

Another light flared up and washed over the exorcist with pale silver streamers that rolled off of Risson's fingertips. Seline smiled and sighed in blissful relief as part of the aura unintentionally washed over her skin and banished every ache and pain she had. Akaran, on the other hand, just sat there, staring up at the ladjunct with a look like he had just sneezed on his tunic.

Every time one of the streamers tried to touch his skin, they just bounced off. After a few moments of abject failure, Risson's confidence melted away into a stupefied look on his face. "Uh..."

Silence reigned before the exorcist spoke up again. "Was that supposed to do something...?"

"That... no, that's not right," Risson mumbled. "May I touch your leg, brother priest?"

"Be my guest," he offered. Off to the side, Lolron watched intently and made small gestures in the air with his finger.

The priest placed his hands above and below Akaran's knee and gripped just tight enough to make the poor boy wince and try to pull away. As he did, he repeated the prayer twice – first in purgalaito and then in Queen's Common. *"Almed Isamiael, Almed Isamiael, rodel solin rodel lumin rodel nia rodel kayba'a proppa!* Goddess Isamiael, Goddess Isamiael, bring peace bring light bring love bring pain's anathema!"

Akaran tensed up as he felt the pressure of the spell wrap itself around his leg. Everyone in the room watched as the streamers tried to wrap themselves around his knee and almost violently lashed at the air as they tried to find something in his aura to latch on to. After a minute's worth of effort, he begged him to give up through clenched teeth. "Brother... please, stop I -"

Risson didn't have to be asked twice. He let go as a sheen of sweat began to drip off of his face. "In all of my years of study, and in all of my years able to hear, never have I heard of a man that was able to *reject* a call of *peace*. Never have I heard of a man that wished to!"

"I didn't do it on purpose!" he protested.

"My boy, there was a *pushback* against me with that spell," he scolded. "Why were you trying to resist it?"

"I didn't," he growled through his gritted teeth. "I felt pressure. Felt like you were trying to crush me." He took a deep breath that was so ragged it was almost painful. "Like you were trying to crush it all over again."

"That was not a spell I can invoke, nor one I would know how to."

"*Phekenit*," Lolron interjected, "*Ghosner's Invocations of Physical Adjustments of Mal- and Other-Intent*, page one-six-three."

"Pardon?"

"*Phekenit*," he repeated. "a spell used by elementalists and mattanics. It's quite simple, really. You can find it in Ghosner's. We have a copy at the Annex."

Akaran took another breath and tried to force himself to relax. "That stopped him from healing me?"

The adept blinked and shook his head. "Oh, no. What stopped him was something else altogether. 'Phekenit' is a spell that causes compression around the object of the caster's will," he said with a vaguely vile smile over towards Risson. "Now you know the invocation to use when you wish to channel that desire. Of course, you have to have an aptitude for it by way of either telekinesis or some form of elemental magic – but I am sure that someone that wields light such as you can will have no problem with it if you sit down and practice for a few months."

Risson's glare outclassed anything that the exorcist had managed to pull off to this point. "The lesson, Adept, is appreciated – although the timing could be better."

"Always a delight to have my talents be useful," he said as he stared at the exorcist as Ridora started to warn him back some. "You will not, however, find any luck in using spells of that nature on him."

"I don't know what happened. Any of it," Akaran sighed. "Just that it hurt."

"That you don't know what happened I find less likely to believe, but I will humor you." He glanced back and forth between the two priests. "May I have a turn, Lower Adjunct? I don't think that the result of using another call from one of your vaunted Gods is going to do more than make the boy wince."

The ladjunct stepped back and gave a slightly mocking bow to the Adept. "Be my guest, if he's up for it."

Akaran grimaced and offered himself up without much hesitation. "Just do it, please. The moment I can channel Her will again, the faster I can heal this on my own."

"Her will does not work that way, Akaran," Medias corrected him with an irritated twinge to her voice. "I have studied the workings of Niasmis for longer than you've drawn breath; while She can and does heal, I do know all too well that those of your rank are only able to tend to minor wounds at best."

"It worked in Toniki."

She didn't rise to the bait. "And what worked in Toniki is why you are here. Adept, you have an idea...?"

"A few," Lolron replied as he started to dig into an old worn pouch tied to his tattered belt. After a moment of rooting around, he pulled out four different gems – two a pale pink quartz, and two that were some kind of clear crystals. He placed one each of the pink stones in each of Akaran's hands, and then made him spread his arms out away from his sides. While they watched, he placed one behind his chair and shooed Seline away.

She backed off quickly and managed to ask "Is this really safe?" before he put the stone down.

He never bothered to give her an answer. After he placed the final rock in Akaran's lap, he took several steps back and smiled contentedly. "Let's ignore any such constructs as the perceptions of dark and light, shall we? Far more interested in what is between."

The exorcist bristled again and glared up at the Adept. "Listen mage, just because you don't believe in them -"

"Oh, no," Lolron said with a dismissive wave of his hand. "I believe in them. I have seen hints of the things that lurk in the shadows, and the things that look through the light. I simply think that both sides think far too much of themselves – and that people like you only give them reason to."

He almost rose to the bait, but the Lady quashed it before it could begin. "An intriguing stance from a mage. Considering all the ways you manipulate the ether, I would think you would have a greater respect for the places that oversee it."

"No more than necessary, I assure you," he quipped. "Now, exorcist?" he said with a smile that wasn't at all warm nor loving.

Akaran blanched and suddenly wondered what exactly these rocks were supposed to do. "I've seen that look in someone's eyes before. I didn't like what happened."

"If this works, you won't," he said with a smug smile. He took a few more steps back and cracked his fingers before uttering a command at the world itself in a language that nobody recognized. "*Pitida, adi, miyok – DEVIST!*"

The exorcist would've jumped out of his chair if he could've. As it was, he nearly flung the stones out of his hands at the sight of the twisting mass of churning black lightning that started to swirl in the air behind the Adept. "IS THAT A MANABOMB?!"

"No," Lolron answered, before shouting, "*TSIVED!*" at the top of his lungs. He clapped his hands together and the charged ball of mana shot forward. Akaran unleashed a curse that should've caused an instant condemnation from the aura of all three of the statues in the atrium just before the bolt split into two an inch away from the crystal in his lap.

The split-spells hovered over his thighs and spun around like flies trapped in a tornado before they bounded into the crystals in his hands. The twin impacts sent the pink stones flying before the bolts slammed into the stone behind him at the same time. More curses rushed from Akaran's lips as he fought every ounce of his being to hold still and not roll away.

Bits of burnt grass rained down on the exorcist as he sat there shaking and cursing as Lolron examined his handiwork. "It was a shadowbomb, actually. Not potent if it impacts on the flesh, but does wonders on a man's aura." An errant burnt leaf landed on Akaran's nose, causing him to add a brief emphasis of, "*As potent, I should say.*"

When he finally stopped swearing, the exorcist threw a chunk of topsoil off of his lap at the adept. "*YOU FLUNG A BOMB AT ME!*"

"A small one," he admitted as he effortlessly waved the projectile away with a flick of his fingers.

Ridora, to her credit, almost threw something at him too. Seline stepped between them while Risson prayed (loudly) for Akaran's soul. "Blessed Pantheon, he is young and scared and in pain, and knows not what he says in his distress..."

"YES I DO!" he shouted at the ladjunct. "And YOU! You could've killed me!"

Lolron lifted his finger and waved it at the priest. "At worst, it would have provided a moderate amount of discomfort. It did exactly what I thought it would, however."

"You're not going to get my magic back by scaring it into me!" he half-growled/half-shouted back. "I'm pretty fisking certain none of this works that way!"

"That would make it much the simpler, wouldn't it? Were that the case I'm sure we'd all just send you to the Cult of Hovoth and see what comes of it. No. Given the opportunity, the spell avoided you and channeled itself into a different path that offered lowered resistance."

"What exactly is *that* supposed to mean?" he growled as he gingerly picked up the clear crystal in his lap and handed it to Seline (who didn't really want to take it, but Ridora quietly insisted from the other side of the garden). "Lowered resistance?"

Lolron took the stone from her and glanced at it before stuffing it back in the pouch at his waist. "Yes. The shadowbomb should have gone from me to that crystal in your lap. Instead, it was ripped in half and followed the ether to the two channeling stones you were holding before reuniting at the one behind you."

"Adept," Ridora interrupted, "I realize that it may come as a mild shock to you, but I do prefer that our treatments do not involve potentially murdering a patient." She glanced over the exorcist's shoulder and her frown deepened. "Or damaging the yard."

"Oh, he would have been just fine," he murmured back dismissively. "I don't think that would happen unless I attempted to use a spell that... let me see..."

Akaran shifted in the chair and gave him a wary look. "See what!?"

The mage extended his hand and willed a small flame to life on his palm. "Your hand, please."

"No."

"It's important, I'm afraid."

"You want to burn me."

The mage nodded in agreement, then clarified ever-so-slightly. "Only briefly. I need to check my assumption."

Lady Ridora tapped her slipper-covered foot on the mossy grass impatiently, even as she sounded concerned for his safety. "Go ahead, Akaran. I have *full faith* in the Adept not to harm you irrevocably."

He didn't stop glaring at his waif-thin tormentor as he did as instructed and let the mage bring the flame closer. It wasn't all that surprising that exposing naked skin to a burning fire ended up painful. "Ow, Lolron ow that -"

Before he could continue his protests, Lolron extinguished the flame and nodded sharply at the red mark forming on the exorcist's palm. "As I thought."

"That fire is hot?" Akaran unhappily grumbled.

"That magic based in manipulation of the physical world still has an effect, but magic based in the etheric doesn't. I have one more test... please hold still."

His hands clenched up as he fought the desire to pick up his cane and beat the Adept half to death with it, but he eventually forced himself to hold still. Once he settled, Lolron etched a glowing, semi-circular rune into the air that evaporated into nothingness after brief moment. "You're of the opinion that divine and demonic won't work on the boy?" Ridora asked.

"Yes and no?" the Adept replied as he started to explain his idea. "I would presume someone that was strong enough would be able to make an effort to do so could. And anything physical, of course – he seems to be prone enough to knives; I assume claws would fall under the same frame-set, were I to conjure some and fling them at him. I strongly suspect they would hurt."

"Reassuring," Akaran muttered, and it was just loud enough that he made damn sure that everyone realized he didn't care if they heard him or not.

"I would not classify it as a blanket immunity, either. Allow me to demonstrate," the mage warned as he stepped in again and placed his hands on either side of Akaran's head without touching him. The exorcist had a moment to tense up and start to sputter out a demand to know what he was thinking about doing before Lolron quickly shouted a spell at him. "*Donola... donola... donola-CHA!*"

A briefly visible spark of lightning popped out of the fingertips on Lolron's left hand and bounced across his patient's scalp and face before it landed with a nasty sizzle and a handful of tiny embers in his other palm. Akaran reeled backwards and slapped at his face, cursing as he batted at little red welts on his skin. "WHAT THE PITS!? OW FISK OW!" An errant ember started to make his ponytail smolder while the Adept quickly backed away.

"Your language!" Ridora scolded while Seline moved in to make sure his hair was completely extinguished.

"That fisking hurt!" he shouted back. "What in the thundering goatpiss did you do that for?!"

She huffed loudly enough for the room to hear as she crossed her arms. "LANGUAGE! Pain is no excuse for a lack of manners!"

Silent for the first time in an age, the mage listened to their bickering as he studied his palm. Then, face ashen, he cradled it and called out for the other priest. "Risson...? A moment of your time, please?"

"Cursing from a priest and manners from the adept, how odd," the ladjunct mused.

"Please, Risson," Lolron implored as he lifted up the bloody, blistered mess that the inside of his hand had been reduced to. "I think... my assumption of.... his metaphysical injury is correct."

Akaran went pale at the sight of the damage and quieted his own complaints. "Oh... oh shit. Adept, I didn't do that did...?"

He shook his head and played down the discomfort as Risson went to work on his palm. "No, not... not directly. It will be easier to show than to tell." He closed his eyes and then began to draw a circle in the air with his left hand, a streamer of orange light following his every gesture. He painted a circle first, then added three triangles with one point each intersecting the center.

The magical geometry hung there for a few moments as it emitted a cool orange glow in every direction. He waved his hand a second time and the runes floated over Akaran and settled down around the top of his head. As they all watched, it stretched out in every direction until the exorcist was surrounded by a cone of light and vibrating streamers.

Then, as the runes settled in place, he whispered another spell even as his hand shook and sweat started to bead upon his forehead. "*Isava, annoia, castata.*" Inside the cone, a wall of interlocking lines appeared just over top of his skin. They crackled and twisted but every time they touched Akaran's body, they changed from orange to blue and recoiled away. "I think you can see the problem," he whispered through slightly-gritted teeth.

Akaran sat perfectly still with his eye wide as he tried to make sense of whatever madness the mage had pulled out of his ratty robe this time. "What in Her name is this? What did you cast on me?"

"I didn't cast a spell on you. That, while not impossible, will be exceedingly difficult," Lolron answered as the ladjunct started to whisper a spell of his own that encouraged little tendrils of silvery light to wrap around his ravaged palm. "I cast a spell at the ether around you. Your issue, little exorcist, is not that you are somehow immune to magic."

"Then what is it?"

He waved at the energy field as it started to fade from few and shrugged his shoulders. "Your issue is that your energy is no longer in-tune with this world."

Risson tilted his head to the side and bit his lower lip while Lady Medias stopped her incessant tapping and raised a finger in the air before letting whatever thought she was about to express die on her lips. Seline made a soft 'huh' noise, but Akaran... he just looked at the mage like he was debating shoving him off a cliff. "Please. Just tell me what that means."

"Hmm. How to say this," the Adept started before going silent for far, far too many heartbeats before answering the question with another question. "You are aware that when you mix oil with water, that the two will eventually settle as separate compounds, yes?"

His curiosity-turned-patient-turned student sat there bewildered. "I... yes?"

"And as matter of course, you are aware that some substances are able to absorb water, or absorb oil. Soaked in water, a rag can clean mud from your face. Soaked in oil, a rag won't clean, but it will burn."

"Every child knows that..."

Lolron nodded and then looked at his mostly-repaired hand and quietly thanked the other priest. "With humans, magic works in much the same way. Magic, ether, floats all about us. We can't always see it, but it is there. While a rag can soak up water or oil or tar or blood or sap – humans that have the natural attunement to the ether can absorb the energy around them and channel it based upon how their natural essences interact with this world and the next."

"Ah, yes. This is the basis for all of the Granalchi's schools of study, isn't it?" Risson curiously interjected.

"By and large, yes it is," the Adept replied with another very brief nod of approval, "to the extent that if you are born with the aptitude to absorb magic and express it in one way – you are able to engage the raw elements of the world. In another, you're able to craft illusions. You absorb ether, or a type of it, and are able to channel it outwards, much as a wet rag is a medium for water to clean."

Akaran couldn't quite keep the frustrated growl out of his voice when he spoke back up. "I *know* this. I *can* use magic. Please get to the point!"

"You use a *type* of magic," Lolron scolded. "Were you not enshackled to the Gods, the Granalchi would likely consider you an ambianist or an ulta-keneticist like myself."

"I'm not enshackled to anyone but this damn chair," he grumbled.

The mage let it slide as he placed his hands behind his back and rambled on. "With this knowledge: consider that you yourself are the rag. Magic, as an abstract, is what you absorb. People without an aptitude are unable to siphon and condense and make use of the ether around all of us."

"Adept, please," Akaran sighed, "the longer you take to get to the point the more I'm starting to get scared."

"The place you went. If it was actually Tundrala, or a manifestation of the plane on a different level, or simply if it was from where you were soaking yourself in the waters of the etheric river – that place has so soaked into your body that you are no longer able to attune yourself to the magic of *this* realm. You are still very much a rag, but you are a rag that is so drenched that you cannot absorb more."

"You're saying that it's not that I can't use magic, it's that I'm so full of it that I can't do anything with it?"

He nodded slowly and tried to demonstrate what he meant in a different way. "In a sense. Back to the analogy of oil and water? I believe that you have been so soaked in the water of the next world that you are simply unable to burn the oil of this."

"If that's the case, what of the episturine?" Ridora asked.

"I didn't see one – did you, Lady?" he quipped. "Are you sure that we know it exists and it wasn't simply a misinterpretation of a manifestation of magic that human minds aren't designed to comprehend?"

"It was there, I saw it, it *did this to me*," Akaran seethed.

Lolron shrugged it off as if he didn't care. "If it was and it did, my *assumption*, and I have no way to prove it either way, is that spiked your aura so that you're unable to discharge the magic you absorbed. Ridora claimed that it cut you somehow, yes?"

He shuddered at the memory. A series of crystal daggers had erupted from nowhere and dug into his neck and the back of his head. "Yeah. Didn't leave a mark. But it cut me. Felt every single blade digging into me."

"Then I think that – again, if your story is true – that it must have drained you of the ether you were full of. That would explain parts of your tale. However, nature abhors a void; this is a truth that is regardless of what realm you exist in. In the process, your body may have instantly absorbed the magic of the next." He paused and tilted his head slightly. "Again, this presumes that what you say is truthful and accurate, and not some kind of delusion or misinterpretation of the metaphysical."

The exorcist sat there silently as he tried to process all of it, leaving Ridora to speak up instead. "So then; our goal is not to mend an etheric anomaly as much as it is to cleanse his aura? Find a way to drain him of the magic that isn't capable of being bled off naturally?"

"Bled off is a phrase for it, yes," he reluctantly agreed. "I don't think that there is any way for us to safely siphon it off. At the moment... well. He is like an oily rag in a jar of saltwater that's been thrown into a freshwater lake. There's no place for the magic in him to go, because it doesn't naturally exist in this plane. *Forcing* it out may not ultimately be wise."

Akaran nervously took a deep breath and gave the mage another pleading look. "That sounds an *awful* lot like there's no cure."

"An argument could be made for finding a way to get you back into Tundrala – or whatever constructed plane that you were in – and discharging your essence there would work, but..."

Risson stopped him from going on with an upraised palm and a very firm cough. "I hate to place a refusal on a potential treatment, yet I have my doubts that returning him to a place where he was so cursed would be wise in the long run. The influences that have caused him so much grief may not approve."

"I think we can *all* agree that further exposure to them would not work in his favor," the Lady agreed. "By the same token, the parts of the report that weren't made available to the two of you fairly effectively rules out any hope of searching for aid within the Order of Frost. He is not, shall we say, currently held within high regard."

None of them said anything for a moment before Lolron started to look into his pouch before pausing and giving Ridora a quizzical look. "There is a way to test. It isn't a cheap way, so I will have to ask the Lady if she is willing to devote gold to it."

"If he is so 'soaked' as you put it, I would expect that there are dangers inherent that may have an effect on the other souls in this manor."

"I can't rule it out, no. I don't believe he is at risk of exploding or suddenly turning the manor into a glacier overlooking the basin, though Akaran, were I you, I'd be very careful about romping through first snow this year."

"Yes, you have my promise that the price will be paid, within reason."

"Reason is always negotiable," Lolron replied as he pulled out an oily black pearl. He set it on the ground and took several steps away before shouting *"Edsfion!"* at the top of his voice.

A trickle of pale blue light started to stream off of the top of Akaran's head and curled through the air towards the Adept. Both of them started to sweat as the mage's fingers danced in the air for almost a full minute before he jerked his hands down and willed the tendril towards the pearl. The gem began to absorb it — at first.

At second (and mere seconds later), it shattered.

Akaran hunched forward and coughed loudly, clutching at his throat with both hands as he groaned in pain. "Goddess... ow..."

"That's... unfortunate," the mage mused aloud while Ridora stormed over and stepped in front of him with a decidedly angry look in her eyes.

"I believe I mentioned that I would prefer it if you didn't destroy my home or ruin my patients."

"I would have preferred not to lose that rock," Lolron grumbled back as he carelessly walked past her to pick up the shards. "That was a Gem of Nullification. We use them time to time to soak up ambient energy or clean up broken... projects. I've never seen one shatter before. Whatever magic he imbued *did not* come from this world, *that* I can unequivocally state."

As he grumbled, Risson finally asked a question that she'd been holding in the back of her mind for the last few minutes. "If he's so steeped in it, shouldn't he be able to direct it out himself?"

"If I drain a pregnant cow's worth of milk into your mouth, would you be able to feed a calf through your own nipples?"

He shuddered as he answered him with a repulsed gagging noise. "Uh... I would presume not."

"I would *hope* not. Suppose we could always test it."

The ladjunct blanched and raised his hands in surrender. "No thank you, Adept."

Lolron smirked and answered with a flippant, "Pity," before turning serious again. "But, no. Simply because you are full of a substance, even magic, does not mean you are able to channel it outwards. You could violently expel the milk, of course, but it would not be pleasant nor helpful nor useful to the calf in question." At that, he looked the broken exorcist over and shrugged. "In his case? I expect it would have the same result as if he was full of tar and decided to expel it into a bonfire he was standing in."

Akaran sat there and stared at his hands for the longest time before speaking up again. "So... so there's nothing. Nothing I can do to...? No way to bleed this out? I'm willing to actually bleed."

"No," the Adept said, almost apologetically. "No, I don't believe so. There have been a few recorded cases of this in the Grand Library before – not many, and I am sad to say that I don't have much knowledge of them. But I think I like you, boy. If nothing else, a living example of this phenomenon would be advantageous to study."

For some reason, that idea made him bristle to no end. "I'm not some... experiment!"

"Life is an experiment," he admonished, "it is just that sometimes it works out better than expected and sometimes not..."

Risson answered him before Akaran could (and was happier about it). "That's a deeper philosophy than I expected from someone from the Academy."

"...but other times it serves as a warning to those that follow," he said as he ignored the interruption. "Though I am going to wager that he is more the latter than the former."

"That sounds more akin to you," the Order of Stara's priest quietly conceded.

Akaran sat there in silence as he started to feel more and more crestfallen. The world around him could've come to a fiery end right there and then and it wouldn't have unsettled him more than he already was – and in a way, it just had. "And... you're sure? I'm going to be without forever?"

"I would not automatically assume so. This analogy is not perfect, but it is the closest that I can express. I will take your case to the Archmage Adept and attempt to see if he has any other ideas on how to solve this issue. As it stands, however, I think that time may be the only true cure." Lolron sighed deeply and spread his hands wide. "For that, I am sorry."

"Why do I not believe you?"

"Truly, I honestly am," the Adept replied with another sigh. "The thought of never being able to weave the ether again? The very idea makes my skin crawl and my interest is primarily academic. To be so devoted to a Goddess above and beyond this world that you live to serve – and *then* have a base function of your life stripped away? I imagine that it would be maddening, to say the least."

"Maddening?" Akaran said before whispering it a second time to himself. "I think I'm in the right place for that."

It was Seline, of all people, that tried to offer comfort next. "A place that will take the best care of you as we can."

"My assistant is correct," Ridora added as she turned her attention on the two guests of the Manor. "Well then, gentlemen. A pleasure to have you both on hand, as always. If there's nothing more we can do for him with magic, there are other things that we have to see to for his sake."

"Such as?" the exorcist nervously piped up.

"A sincere apology that we will not be able to use magic to dull the pain of your surgeries."

Risson and Lolron both cringed as he uttered one last curse. "*Fisk*."

"Language!"

V. TOUR AND DUTY
Londis, the 26th of Greenbirth, 513 QR

The ice was so cold Akaran's naked feet stuck to it, but the biting wind? That was so much worse. There weren't clouds overhead as much as there were obscene and grotesque shapes moving through the sky above. Even though it was pitch black, it wasn't quite dark – light came from somewhere, just enough that he could see the jagged pieces of bloody gravel under him.

A cloud of embers blew past his face, little cinders burning against his skin. The place felt... wrong. Bad. Like it didn't belong, or that he didn't belong in it. A shouted, "Hello?" into the wind went unanswered while an imploring, "Where am I?" received an echo that bounced back and forth through the void.

He started to walk and tried to think. The last thing he remembered was being in bed in the Manor, and desperately trying to find some semblance of sleep. Several steps into his journey and his knee blossomed in fresh pain and for a moment, it felt like the cut on the side of it had split back open again. Only this time, it felt like something was being pulled out.

His scream went as unanswered as his questions.

At first.

A distinct crackling sound of ice crashing against the shore took his attention away from his leg while he struggled to stand up and find his footing again on the rough landscape. A dull green sheen moved through the rocks under his feet and illuminated his body, causing him to realize that wherever he was and however he got here, someone had stripped him down to his skin on the way.

More cursing, more stumbling. Against his best judgment, he walked towards the sound of the crashing waves. Another cloud of embers lashed against his back, burning so hot for a few short heartbeats that tears welled up in his eye. "Nightmare," he muttered, "has to be a nightmare."

"You'd be surprised at what things have to be," a woman's voice called out from the black din.

He straightened up and looked around, bringing his arms and hands up in front of his chest protectively. "Who's there? Out with you – now!" When that did no good, he tried shouting, "By Order of the Queen and the Goddess, I said out!"

That same voice just laughed. "*Which one?*"

"Of Dawnfire and of Love."

Her laughter grew louder and her voice sharper, shriller. "*Neither hold sway here, little lost boy. Sooner find mercy at an executioner's blade.*"

It almost sounded... familiar. Close, but not... "Where am I?"

"*Where you should be. Or where you shouldn't. Those that should often think they shouldn't. I don't. Not here. But here I am. Here you are. If I am here, of course you can be too. We each served our own. And rewarded how? With this. With misery.*"

Ahead, another crashing wave delivered a cacophony of shattering ice that buffeted against his ears. "I don't have time for riddles. I'm cold, I'm tired, and I'm in pain."

A shape moved off to his side just out of the corner of his eye, and was gone just as quickly before he could face it. "*Then this is the place for you. Bring your tired your ravaged your agonized, let them thrash upon these blackened shores. One of us once you're here. One of us before you arrive.*" A pause lingered in the air before she added, "*Be in no hurry to leave the rocks. The stones may bleed your feet, yet you will not be allowed to stay on dry land for long.*"

Turning around again, Akaran did his absolute best to find the source of the voice, but the harder he looked, the harder it was to see more than a few feet past his own face. With a mutter and a snarl, he crouched down long enough to pick up a loose chunk of rock and continued to head towards the water.

Every step on the rough stone was bitingly painful and finding purchase on the rocks felt like an impossible task. Something swooped past his head at one point with a drizzle of cold rain that fell behind it and over his shoulders. He started to see pale yellow sparks twirling in the air ahead, faint glowing shapes locked in rapid pirouettes before burning away to nothing.

The lights egged him on, and the further he walked, the louder the sound of cracking ice became. He wasn't sure when and where the slick gravel became submerged in freezing, brackish water, but he felt compelled to keep going no matter what. When the gravel gave way to wet ash, the darkness gave way to light, and everything gave way to horror.

"*Our shores beckon you; our waves demand you,*" he heard her call out.

Of that, there was no doubt. The lake looked like it might go on for eternity, with a shoreline that had no end in the darkness. There was a steady pulsing glow out of the water – the faintest of gray-green light to make sure that those cast adrift could see their fates.

Misery *always* loves company.

And to make sure that those who were waiting for their turn could see those that went before. Bodies thrashed in the awful water. Some were missing limbs, others missing skin. None of them were close enough to each other to do more than just watch as horror after horror fell upon their neighbors. Floating islands of sickly yellow ice prowled through the rough choppy waves, and those souls unlucky enough to be in their way were scooped up by hundreds of questing claws and stuffed into gnashing maws of rock and razor-thin shards of frozen oil and burning sulfur.

Crane-like monstrous birds swooped through the air and scooped up other souls. He watched them fly to the edge of his vision before they would rip the body into shreds before they cast them into the lake. Almost at the edge of the horizon, a mammoth shadow welled up as a miles-wide waterspout took form and sent monsters and men alike flying through the air.

"*Our shores beckon you; our waters welcome you,*" the voice repeated again. "*My home is your home,*" she went on, "*and once you are home, you never get to leave...*"

She was right, too. Despite how hard he tried to turn around, he couldn't. A thick oily lump spewed out of the back of his knee and splashed into the water over his feet. It anchored down into the gravel and wouldn't let him back up or get away. "This isn't my home. These aren't my shores," he protested willfully as the sludge forced him forward and drove him back into the water.

"*You are here. So it must be that it is.*"

He dug his toes into the sharp rocks and struggled against the muck. "I don't belong here."

"*That's not how it works. If you are here, then you should be. You've earned it if you have come here. As you cannot leave, it is now your home. Your home. My home. Our home.*"

A glistening piece of metal caught his eye and nothing tried to stop him from pulling it out of the lake. While it wasn't much of a weapon, a rusty sword was better than a craggy rock. "I know where I'm at," he snarled, "and I do *not* belong here. Set me free, or risk Her wrath."

The disembodied woman's voice laughed as a sheet of frozen bile peaked in the water to his side and shattered as it crashed along the ashen beach. "*This world is nothing but wrath; wrath risked, wrath delivered.*"

"Whatever it is you're suffering, it pales in comparison to Her rage. You know it does," he growled back. "Don't know how you got me here, but you'll have eternity to regret it." He waved the rusted sword in front of him to try to intimidate the speaker – not that it did any good at all.

"*My last mistake was trusting you,*" she crooned.

He stopped dead in his tracks and mouthed the words "Trusting *me*?" before he saw the body floating face down a few yards away. It bobbed ever-so-steadily closer and closer, and closer still as whatever was compelling him to wade into the lake forced him to step next to it.

The body was covered from head to toe in bloody burns and huge gashes that went down to the bone in some places. The wounds were festering and some of them had strange spines jutting through them like stitches sewn in by a demented physician. He saw a vaguely eel-like *thing* squirming under its chest that he couldn't quite make out in the cloudy water.

He didn't get time to see what it was before the body pushed itself to its knees and obscenely displayed the ruins of her flesh for him to see. She had horrific burns that trailed down in huge swaths that went from her forehead down past her thighs. Most of her face was gone, reduced to nothing but a few loose tendons and strips of skin left on her cheekbones. Her eyes and her temples had been left unmolested, though her lower lip had been reduced to melted fat.

"YOU!" she shouted, "*Trusting YOU! You offered me justice! YOU SENT ME HERE LIKE THIS!*"

She lunged at him, twisted and ruined arms attempting to wrap around him as skinned fingers dug into his shoulders. Akaran thrust his sword at her and watched horrified as the blade didn't do anything more than just core out another bloody gouge through her chest.

"*YOU! BELONG HERE! WITH ME!*" she screamed, and he finally realized who it was. And when he saw the tentacles erupting out of her chest, he understood that Daringol hadn't forgotten her either, even on the shores of the lower elemental plane of ice.

She'd been an ally in the first few days of the investigation in Toniki – except she wasn't, not really. She had been a spy, a murderess, a liar, and probably a thief. You couldn't call her a traitor to the Crown, as she had never pledged loyalty to it; but she was executed for it. Another near-victim of the wraith, the infection in her soul had lead to her untimely (and unexpected) capture after a daring (and bloody) escape from Toniki before her crimes could have been exposed. She had been arrested by the city guard in Gonta, imprisoned, and assaulted – the latter of which was *against* orders, and the man that had done it lost his head.

Akaran had seen to that.

Personally.

And soon after, she was burned alive by the Commander of the 13th for her crimes against the Kingdom. He'd seen it, he'd objected to it, and he had been powerless to stop it. She wasn't, apparently, understanding or forgiving. Given where she ended up? It was hard to blame her.

Not that it made the revelation of where he was – or who she was – any easier. "*FROSEL CLAIMED ME! FROSEL CLAIMS YOU!*" Rmaci screamed, bloody froth covering his face. He pushed back and fought to try to force her off of him, but no matter what he tried, he couldn't get her to let go. He freed an arm enough to take a backhanded swing but something else grabbed him and stopped him from connecting.

He panicked and struggled to try to free his arm as a different voice started to scream in his ear from just past his shoulder. He tried to kick and couldn't connect; he tried to push Rmaci's shade away and all it did was give her even more purchase to grab on. The screaming behind him got so loud that he couldn't even hear the crashing of the waves or the agonized screams coming from her torched throat.

The screaming got so loud that the world changed.

It kept going even as his room came into view, and as he saw Seline holding his left fist in a vise-like grip. "AKARAN! STOP – ENOUGH!"

"Get the *FISK* off of me you thundering cu -!" he screamed as he continued to thrash in the bed, just barely slowing down as his room came into focus.

"SAFE! Akaran! You're *safe!*" she shouted.

"I don't belong here I'm not going to... to..." he shouted as the last vestiges of the vision-like-dream faded away. "Sel... Seline?"

She let go of his hand and watched as he started to curl up on himself. "Safe, Akaran. You're safe. I promise. You're safe, here at the Manor."

He looked up at her with streams of tears and sweat pouring down his face.

He forced himself to take a series of deep breaths and made himself stare at the belt on her waist, just to have something to focus on. "No, I was, wasn't here, I was... Daringol and Rmaci and ice, *Goddess* so much ice and the smell, that awful smell... I was there I..."

"*Nightmare*, Akaran. It's a *nightmare*," she repeated. "It wasn't real. You didn't go anywhere."

"I went -"

She sighed and reached over with a wet cloth to wipe his forehead off. "To sleep. That's all you went, where you went. You haven't been anywhere since you went to bed last night. I promise."

He took another deep breath and swallowed hard. "I didn't?"

"You didn't."

"Oh," he half-whimpered as he tried to pull his leg tighter to his chest.

Seline looked down in his eye and smiles gingerly at him. "Who was Rmaci? A friend?"

As he wiped himself clean with her washcloth, he gave her a truncated version of who she'd been (and why she was there). "Civan spy. Executed for crimes against the Queen. Murder. Espionage, too." Akaran shuddered and then quietly added: "It wasn't a clean death."

From the look in his eye, she didn't feel the urge to press. "It was just a memory of her. Whatever you saw, it wasn't real."

"Exorcists get rid of echos and memories all the time," he pointed out, "and some of them would happily argue with you about what *is* and *isn't* real."

"As they aren't in this room with us right now, they are not," she chided, "and what was real were your screams."

He blanched and reached over to the small table next to his bed and started rooting through it. "I'm... I'm sorry. What are you doing here?" he asked while he pulled out a little pouch full of enough cocasa to tranquilize a horse.

Seline stepped back and pulled the curtains aside from the lone window in his room. "Interrupting your dreams and getting you out of the Manor."

Exhausted panic slid off of his face and turned into a cold wariness. "I'm fine here. I don't want to go anywhere else."

"No. You need to get up, get moving, go out and do things."

The sunlight made him wince and caused him to painfully try and roll to his side. "It's quiet here," he argued with just the faintest hint of a whine. "I like it when it's quiet and safe and comfortable."

She shook her head at him and carefully pulled some of his blankets away. "It's only quiet and safe when you're not screaming your head off, which is making things less comfortable for the rest of us."

"Not like I mean to. If you slept like this you'd scream too."

"Meaning is immaterial. You're starting to unsettle even the mad. Lady Ridora feels you have been cooped up for far too long since your surgery. It's been three weeks; and have you left the grounds even once since you arrived in Basion at all?"

He groaned in pain as he started to lightly flex his bad leg. "Haven't had a good reason to yet."

"Now you do."

Akaran narrowed his eye and glared at her. "No I don't."

"There *won't* be an argument about it," she warned as she laid out a long clean tunic and loose wrap for him. "Will you help me get you dressed or do I need to have the other caregivers come give me some help?"

Nothing he grumbled back was suitable to repeat.

Suffice it to say, it took more effort than anyone wanted to give to get him up and out of bed. Between her insistence that he wipe himself clean in a few strategic locations and his grousing about needing to wrap his legs up in something that resembled leggings, they nearly came to blows. When she came just short of demanding to be in the room while he used the chamberpot, the argument got so heated you could hear it halfway down the wing.

Eventually, *thankfully*, the two of them came to an agreement that saw him reasonably dressed and presentable enough to leave the manor. This came at a cost of leaving him unshaven, wearing a tunic that hadn't met a scrubbing bucket in a week, and allowed to carry his bag of cocasa with him. Though she gave in on that demand a little too easily for his taste...

The latter caused more problems than not. Much as he wouldn't have admitted it, he couldn't stop himself from chewing on the root even *before* the surgery. For the first week after, he had been taking twice as much as they had been comfortable with. For the week after that, he had continued. It took a borderline intervention to begin to get him to even start weening himself off of the drug – and a few of the healers wondered if it wasn't too late.

That was partly their own fault, he rationalized. If they had done due diligence, they'd have found the extra he had brought with him. They kept bringing him more, too, and sometimes more than he actually needed. Keeping some stored away was just an insurance policy of sorts.

At least, that's what he kept telling himself.

Nor did they know that he was keeping a small stash hidden near the chamberpot where nobody would look for it. *Just for when I can't sleep at all,* he had justified to himself. *Can't heal if I can't sleep.*

As it was, leaving his room took longer than actually getting him dressed. He painstakingly made sure everything he owned was where he had left it last. He was careful to ensure that the blinds were pulled shut so that nobody could see inside while he was gone. He hobbled back twice to make sure that the door was locked.

She even overheard him complain that the chambermaids that were responsible for keeping his room cleaned were going through his belongings. When she pointed out that their job was to do just that, he snapped back with, "But any clothes that *need* to be washed get tossed in the corner," and, "They've no right to look in my drawers!" It was all she could do to remind herself that he was probably just irritated from being stuck in his room all the time instead of out and about with the rest of the world.

A situation she had a long set of plans to implement to rectify that.

The first stop on his tour of Basion was only a few minutes away by horse-drawn cart. Seline quickly hopped out of the front and spun around, waving her arms happily. "I've lived in Basion my entire life, and in all honesty, there's nowhere as beautiful as the view from up here," she exclaimed. "The Orshia Falls! Right where the river meets the city."

He wasn't quite as impressed.

Sure, it was pretty enough, and he had to begrudgingly admit that the view from up here could probably be described as 'breathtaking,' if you had interest in such things. Though you could hardly say that this is where the Orshia-Avagerona River met the city so much as it was where the river poured into it. The surprising part of it was that the river was at least a quarter of a mile across (if not longer) and that there were two different bustling docks on either side. One of them was so close to the lip of the waterfall that a series of cranes had been installed leading all the way down into the city.

There was actually a moment where he considered how utterly brilliant it was. With the woods being so dense on either side, the locals were using the cranes as a quick and easy way to haul cargo in and out of the city and upriver to places north. That wasn't to say that there weren't a pair of roads leading up the wall on both sides of the falls – but they were steep, covered in stairs, and less-than-helpful to carts and carriages. "It's pretty, I guess."

Of course, while he studied the functionality of the bustling port, Seline was all too happy to continue to gush about the aesthetics. "You guess? Look out there! You can see the entirety of the city on a clear day," she exclaimed as she gestured out to the far southern side and towards the towering gates he could see in the distance. "Everything from the start of the Yittl Canyon to the Overflow. If you look down there," the ginger-blonde healer pointed down at the gatehouse at the southeast, "you can even see the Ellachurstine Chapel and the Order of Stara temple."

The Chapel definitely stuck out like a sore thumb. A massive, almost glowing, gaudy thumb – but still a sore thumb. For reasons he couldn't figure out, and from what he could make of it from such a distance, the building stood next to more than a dozen different marble columns all around it. Out in front (and presumably) on the ground, he could make out what looked like a pinkish clam-shell-shaped amphitheater no more than a block away.

"That's... odd. What is it?"

She immediately perked up and stood beside him. "Ah! It is the favored destination for all bewedded couples-to-be. A truly gorgeous building. The inside is covered in mirrors and flowers and silver. Walking into it is enough to take your breath away – it does mine every single time. Maiden-Templar Prostil shares oversight duties there with Lower Adjunct Risson. Lexcanna Jealions is the High Priestess of the Stara shrine right next to it."

He blinked and stared closer at it and realized that it didn't stand IN the columns, it stood ON them. "Are those... is it built on stilts?"

"Well... yes," she said after a moment, "but they're actually hand-carved marble pillars."

"So, stilts."

Seline sighed and hung her head for a moment. "Well... yes. That district is right against the Avagerona Shallows. Unlike the Overflow on the other side," she said as she pointed off towards the west, "the Shallows are... shallow. They tend to flood in the spring and midsummer."

He pursed his lips and gave her an utterly confused stare. "So they put a temple in the middle of a floodplain and then decided that stilts would be the way to go?"

"It's a very pretty view, and the Temple used to be curated by the Aquallans when it first opened," she protested. "It's currently being tended to by Solinal's priests."

"What happened to the Aquallans?"

She coughed and turned away from him. He *thought* he heard her say that they were ousted when people objected to putting a shrine somewhere that would need stilts, but then she said, "I wasn't planning on going there today, but as long as the weather holds out, we just might. Everyone that lives here in Basion ends up there at one point or another."

He smiled. It was faint, it was brief, but it was there. "That many happily married couples in the city, eh?"

"And multiples," the healer added. "You know the Queen; always encourages her subjects to find as much joy in this life as she can."

That got rid of the smile. "Always tries to have as many children populating the kingdom as she can get away with, you mean."

"Children are a joy," she said as she rooted around in one of the packs in the cart before triumphantly pulling out a patch and a letter.

"No."

"Of course they are."

"Absolutely no."

For a moment, she looked slightly crestfallen and let the faintest of frustrated sighs escape her lips. "Well. I suppose fatherhood isn't for every man. Oh, but I do promise you. The chapel is so well-loved that any chance anyone can get to go there? They go. Thus, everyone here gets there eventually. If nothing else, the Wedding of Dusk and Dawn will be there in another two and a half months or so."

"Is that what they're calling that big shindig that the servants were gushing on about?"

"The one and the same," she replied. "Malik Odinal from the Odinal Tribe in the Southern Midlands is being married off to Basion's own Baronessa – Hylene Tessamirch." After saying all that, she gestured at the docks closest to them. "Well, this isn't all about looking at the view today – though I'm going to add that you should come here at night and enjoy the ways the moons reflect off the Falls."

"We've got other tasks?"

"Just me," she clarified. "I need to arrange for a shipment. Fish is a bit pricier up here, but it saves from having to transport it up from Lower Naradol or Piapat, *and,* you don't get that strange taste to the ones that feed in the lower districts. All the tanneries and things, I'm sure."

His shoulders visibly relaxed and he leaned back against the cart in relief. "Oh thank the Goddess, so that means we don't have to go down into the city proper?"

Seline stopped and looked at him quizzically. "What would make you think that? Of course we do. This is just one stop. I have business today here and down in Piapat. Might have to go over to Akkador, too... don't think that I need to stop in East Akkador, though we do have business at the Repository, so we'll have to go through Chiadon or Giffil."

Just like the smile had vanished earlier, the knots in his neck came back just as quickly. "What in the name of the Pantheon do you need to do today?"

"The Manor may run itself but we don't have an infinite pool of supplies," she half-chided. "What we need has to come from somewhere, as all things."

"Yeah, I suppose," he grumbled, "but you want me around for all of it? I don't think I'm going to be of any help."

"You aren't confined to the Manor," the healer pointed out, "and in fact, of all of the residents, you are the only one that's able to be up and move around the town. Don't expect that Ridora won't put you to task – every able-bodied soul helps. She served in the army for three years, and then worked with the medical corps for another six. Her rule has always been that if you're able, you work."

He pointed down to his knee and frowned. "In case you haven't noticed, I'm not able."

"Only your body," she pointed out. "Your mind is otherwise just fine for the most part. I'll be back in a few."

Last I checked they're attached to each other, he gloomily whined to himself as he squeezed at his thigh and rolled his left shoulder in a painful circle, *and you'd fisking think that my arm'd feel better at this point. Been two bloody months since that bastard skewered it. If this shit doesn't stop throbbing soon, I'm going to end up killing someone.*

With nobody hearing – and nobody caring what he thought – the only real choice he had was to stand and grouse to himself or hobble around on his cane and grouse around people. Never one to let misery starve for company, the cane was in-hand moments later to aid his efforts to be the target of everyone's attention and or pity.

Sadly for him (and only him), the effort to find pity on the cobblestone path ended up being a futile endeavor. It did give him a chance to finally observe the non-convalescent and non-nursemaid citizens of Basion up close and impersonally. While the docks weren't an *ideal* place to study the locals, it was better than nothing.

It didn't take long to dispel that notion. 'Nothing' might have been more entertaining. Peasants wore peasant dresses and tunics. Workers labored in outfits that had more in common with sackcloth than anything else. Glove-less hands were either covered in callouses or wrapped in bandages. Glove-covered hands were torn and ratty. Most of them had roughly shorn hair and despite the fact that they worked *literally on the edge of the river* it didn't look like any of them had taken a voluntary bath in weeks.

In other words, there was absolutely nothing impressive about them.

Not that he was one to talk at the moment.

It wasn't until he overheard a conversation between a frumpy-looking middle-aged man and... and someone that made him grit his teeth for no apparent reason at all. "I'm telling you, I don't have it!" Frumpy exclaimed, just barely managing to avoid shouting.

Teeth-Grinder, on the other hand, didn't have to raise his voice to be heard. "Pay up. That was the deal." He was an ugly, waxy-skinned man with a wide-brimmed woven hat. Akaran had never seen him before but the priest had an utterly *intense* desire to bash the thug's face in with a rock. "You barter with her, you pay her."

Just some bitch's bully, he mumbled to himself, *so maybe I don't have to **kill** someone to feel better. Maybe a decent maiming.*

As priestly thoughts went, it wasn't a particularly noble one.

"I can't pay with what I don't have," Frumpy whined as he wrung his hands together and started to sweat exponentially more than was warranted for the heat. "Donta, I -"

The waxy-skinned thug stepped in closer and gripped the edge of the merchant's tunic tight in his left hand. "She expects payment."

"Then she can wait! I know that she knows that I lost money on that last shipment out of -"

Donta tugged at the fabric tight and yanked the merchant so close that they could've been kissing. It was all Akaran could do to hear him growl out, "I don't care. You know the terms of the deal. Honor it."

"I can't honor with what I don't have," he protested.

"Telpeth. I know you have a lot."

His eyes went wide and he unsuccessfully tried to pull himself away from the debt collector. "I have a stake in two fishing trawlers and that's it!"

The priest would've sworn he saw something move under the back of Donta's hat when he leaned in even closer to threaten the tradesman again. "You have an investment in the silver mine outside Tiaxadin. You have an investment in the claypit in Tvonn."

"Neither of those are here!"

"You have a tax... investment... with Petriv Chinndin."

Telpeth-the-Merchant went dead pale as the threat to name him Telpeth-the-Tax-Thief hit home. "Shut up! How do you know about that?!"

"Anais wants her payment," the other seethed. "From *you*. One way. Or another." The way he said her name – ending it with a *hiss* for an 'is' - made Akaran's skin absolutely crawl.

It had the same exact effect on the victim of the shakedown. "Keep your voice down! Let's make a new deal."

His accoster stepped back and grimly smiled at the frumpy grift-ee. "You didn't hold up your end of the last one."

"But I'm good for this one!" he protested a *lot* louder than he should've. "Look, let's go... elsewhere. Find an elsewhere. People are listening," he added, gesturing over at the impolitely-eavesdropping priest off to the side.

Donta looked at him for less time than it would've taken to swat a bloodbeak out of the sky – and with just as much interest before he turned his attention back to Telpeth. "It's not the cripple you should fear."

"Don't talk loud enough half the city can hear you then," Akaran piped up with a nod and a gesture with the tip of his cane.

"Mind your business, boy. Unless you want to lose your other leg," the frumpy merchant snarled.

In turn, the collector grabbed Telpeth by his shoulder and gave him a smile full of yellow teeth. "Be mindful of your own. They break so easily. Wouldn't you agree, *boy*?"

Before he could retort, Seline shouted out for him (much for the luck of everyone involved). "Akaran! Time to go!"

Invoking his name made Donta *immediately* turn his head to look at him again, and Anais's bodyguard rolled his name around his mouth slowly, almost like he was tasting it. "Akaran."

The priest twitched and felt a sudden, overwhelming urge to go over and shove his cane down the thug's throat and out a lower orifice. The feeling went away almost as soon as it came over him, and he turned around and hobbled over to her, calling out with a, "Right, coming," as he returned to the cart.

"What was that ruckus about?"

"Who knows," he answered as he shook his head. "Something about owed money and a tax arrangement."

"Wouldn't at all surprise me," she sighed as she steered their cart towards a waiting crane. "Taxes in the city have gone up to cover the cost of the wedding celebrations. Lots of people are trying to find ways out of it."

"Don't people always?"

"Yes, but more than usual. Half the city is excited for the wedding; the other half wants nothing to do with it. Neither are enjoying the new rules put down by Pav or the Overseer."

He grunted while giving an exceptionally nervous stare at the platform ahead. "Why does that not surprise me. Know anything about the man in the gray cloak?"

"Hm? Nothing, why?"

"A... feeling," he replied as he squeezed his cane again. "A bad one."

Seline handed a trio of coins to a worker manning the platform and he flagged down some of his companions. A few minutes later, and the cart was firmly fastened to the wooden lift. "Do we... do we have to go down like this?"

"It's that or walk," she cautioned. "Walking is better for the body."

"Not this one." Akaran lingered for a minute and looked back where he'd seen the argument. "I don't want to wait. That guy... I'm telling you. Something was wrong about him."

She made a 'tsk tsk' sound with her tongue and rolled her eyes. "With as much of that accursed weed you've been chewing on, quite surprised you don't have that feeling about everybody."

"Who says I don't?"

"Not a good way to validate your point, Sir Exorcist," she returned with a roll of her eyes as two burly men pulled a lever that was bigger than either of them. With that, the wood, chain, and rope elevator began its slow descent down the side of the Northern Stairwall.

Getting down the wall wasn't as simple as a slow drop. The slow part was accurate, but it wasn't only just one. Working down took three different stops and necessitated two different elevator changes as they plopped down into the city. Even though it took nearly an hour to go from the top of the wall to the bottom, not having to manually climb the twisting (and in some places painfully narrow and unpleasantly steep) was a lifesaver.

The journey gave him the opportunity to discover some interesting facts about life in Basion (starting with wanting to know why Badin hadn't taken him up the damn lift the first time). He had guessed that the city was sunk fairly low into the ground, but the average depth went down nearly two hundred feet, leaving even the tallest of the buildings to be dwarfed by the magnificence of the natural walls around it.

Most of the basin wasn't a straight drop from the lip. The Northern Stairwall was only passable as such because of a steep slope along parts of it. It was also, he discovered, where the vast majority of the food for the city came from. While Basion was supplied from the river overhead – and some from the fishing trolleys at Port Cableture from the far south – huge tracts of the Stairwall were considered part of the Wall of Gardens. Everything from fresh fruit to protesting mutton could be found growing (one way or another) all along the walls under the hands of Houses Eran, Essinge, and Hannock. The Blackstone Trading Company also owned some property there, as did some other unaffiliated growers.

When he saw a cluster of laborers that looked much worse for the life than others, she was happy to tell him that while the city had its poor, Merchant-Master Hannock had decreed that anyone working the wider steps the Wall for even two hours a day would be allowed a meal. For some, it was the only way that they could keep themselves fed. He claimed it kept crime down; the exorcist wondered if it just wasn't a way for the BeaST to save some coin.

As they reached the bottom, Seline was more than happy to point out a singular statue to Aqualla that sat in the middle of Avagerona's Rest; a simple thing of iron and steel with rusted blotches all over it. "Every year, they have to repair it. There's a Hall of Sea's Song on the coast a day or three from Cableture. It's at the um... oh. Village of Mardux? I think? The Aquallans make a short pilgrimage here to bless the waters and provide maintenance."

"For the sake of honoring Aqualla or other?"

"I never have figured that out. What I can tell you is that right after they erect a new one, the colonies of backclaw crab in Lower Naradol explode."

He suffered an involuntary cringe. "Violently or other?"

"Deliciously," she said with a smirk. "I mean they're not bad anyway – the leftovers from the wall feed the fish really well. It's one of the few things worth a rat down in that district."

He tried to study the statue as they worked their way along the outskirt of the Rest. Aqualla wasn't known for detail, and his craftsman captured that lack of distinctiveness with precision. He stood as tall as the average man, and he had scale-covered legs, shoulders, and what almost looked like a seashell girdle. There was a long, gold-tipped spear that held his attention until he remembered the one thing that always stood out on one of His edifices.

As they circled around the Rest, a secondary sculpture made to depict four squid-like tentacles that were wrapped around his upper shoulders and the back of his hips like folded wings. He couldn't look away fast enough before he saw *other* tentacles start to appear at the edge of his vision that seemed to sprout from everywhere in the air as they reached for the tendrils carved from pumice in the middle of the bay. Seline must've noticed his panic and she quickly grabbed his hand to shake him out of it.

"I saw it, Akaran. Just a statue. It's not what you think it is."

"You don't want to know what I thought it was."

She sighed and shook her head again. "The crab is about the only good thing that comes out of Naradol, sadly. The poor congregate there, unfortunately. Anyone with means stays away."

"Why?"

"The largest tannery in the province sits in the middle of it."

This time the flinch was accompanied by a gagging retch. "Oh, Goddess, no. I used to work with a blacksmith back at the Grand Temple, and he'd have me go back and forth to Annamelia's Leather and Weaving. The smell it... you never get it out of your hair. Can't imagine living next to it."

"Some people don't have to imagine," she pointed out. "Count your blessings, hurt as you are, that you aren't as ill-off as they. Still..."

"Still what?"

"Nothing in that district but whores and the illicit. If Lady Medias ever sees you there, you're out on your ass."

A bit later, and the errand-runners arrived at their next stop: the towering (as they always tended to be) spires of the Granalchi Academy Annex. There were few things about the wizards that could be considered hard and fast rules; after all, their entire reason-for-being was to study and experiment and challenge the Laws of Normality with magi-craft and 'scientific advancement,' whatever that meant. They were always adapting, always evolving, always doing something new (which in and of itself was a bit of a rule).

But what they weren't known for was experimental architecture.

If you saw a single spire somewhere, it could be anything from a grain silo to a watchtower from the local militia. If you saw two, there was probably a gate or a bridge attached somewhere. If you saw a minimum of three with one in the center, then at least two more at points that were doubled in distance from each other on a perpendicular angle from every other building and substructure within the always-circular wall that would be around it in a strange, non-overlapping orbit from the central tower?

Then you had either found a member of the Mason's Guild that needed to lay off the Ogrebund Ale he was obviously chugging, or you had found the Granalchi. It was a dead giveaway every single time. This Annex was no different – and while Annexes in smaller cities or the few that dotted the countryside might have at most three or four towers total, this one had seven, each decorated with copper-gilded archways for doors and not a single one of them was less than four stories each.

That was to say nothing of the smaller stone buildings scattered between the established circuits and 'orbits' that the towers represented. While he could make all of that out from outside the gate, the rainbow-robed guards wouldn't let both of them in at once. He assumed it was because the silks they were adorned with weren't breathing as much as they should be and the heat was addling their heads to make them less inclined to be helpful, but Seline corrected his misconception.

"You'll have to excuse them. There was an incident with one of their own recently. They've been dealing with heightened security for weeks now. If you're not known, you don't get in."

"What happened?"

"Nothing you need to worry about, but they'll only let one of us in at a time today." She pulled out a hefty purse laden with coins from her belt and dangled it for a quick inspection by the guards. "Lolron wasn't kidding about the cost."

Akaran whistled slowly as he saw one of them pull out a full evane from her bag. "Blessed be. I am sorry for that."

"Don't be. The Manor receives a stipend from the Crown for this very thing. We are quite popular with the resident Merchant-Master every time we receive a new guest for just this reason."

He weighed that on his tongue for a minute before finally begrudging her with a simple, "You're... welcome?"

"Much as I hate to say it, war is a profitable sport," she lamented. "That aside – even if it wasn't for the security, I wouldn't let you come inside with me. The Lady told me that you are in possession of an item that isn't to be cataloged by certain parties?"

"That nobody is to be told about at all," he groused, frowning at her.

Seline gave an exasperated sigh and ran a hand through her hair. "She assigned me to be your chaperone, exorcist. She had to tell me what exactly it was I was caring for. Your safety and mine."

"I... I guess."

"Do more than guess. You're a ward of the Kingdom right now. Let us do with you as best as we can. And that, for the meantime, is going to involve you going for a walk. In the other direction," she said as she nodded towards a gaggle of mages walking across one of the man bridges that connected the towers inside the Annex. They were paying just a little *too* much attention to him to make him feel *entirely* comfortable.

"Right..."

What that particular round of instructions failed to do was to give him any idea what to do to find a sense of comfort. Or peace. Or to fit in. Sure, there was a lot to be said for standing idly on a street-corner, but after the first person that went past tried to donate a handful of *keps* – not even a full crown's worth – he decided to go see what he could do that *wouldn't* leave him looking like your average bum.

That meant it was time to wander aimlessly. Which he hated. Aimless lazy loitering accomplishing absolutely nothing and being of no use whatsoever was driving him nuts. While not a poor idea given a beach and a bottle of something from the Grand Temple's vineyard, Basion was decidedly short on beachfronts and Ridora had so far been cruelly inclined to hide the wine.

Yet, somehow, he felt like everyone staring at him assumed he knew where it was being kept. Nobody was being overly mean, but either he was imagining it, or he was getting side-eye stares from everybody that went by. The truth was? He wasn't. The other truth? He didn't think he was imagining it. After a few minutes of feeling like that, he felt inclined to do the same in return.

At least it was something to do.

While Seline took her sweet time capering through the halls of the Annex, doubtlessly receiving multitudes of compliments on her hair and that pretty, plain peasant's dress (pretty plain, depending on your standards) and otherwise basked in the adoration of countless magic-oriented suitors within, he studied faces. He watched people shuffling through the crowded district streets carrying boxes of tools, bags of grain, and irritatingly noisy children doing nearly everything they could to get in the way of everybody else. It was such a stark contrast from Toniki and Gonta both that if he didn't know any better, he'd be hard-pressed to say that he was in the same Kingdom as the muddy bog and frozen armpit he'd spent so much time in recently.

That was the key to it. Sure, the style of clothes were the same – peasants were peasants, merchants were merchants, soldiers were soldiers – but it was how they carried themselves. Even the poorest and unwashed looked like they were happy. Or at least, not entirely miserable. The pallor of dread he'd gotten used to was gone; the looming specter of suicide en masse just waiting for the first person to jump; the gloom that had saturated the air in the east...?

It just wasn't here.

It was a breath of fresh air it was to be away from that toxic psychic mess of battered down souls and chronic hopelessness. Those things weren't there – after finally letting himself *see* the people, he could *feel* the people. But he was wrong about the happiness.

Sure, enough of them were smiling and prancing around as they went along their humdrum lives doing one thing or another, but there was another undercurrent. While a balding man with an amber robe haggled over the "Utterly outrageous – how can you charge this much?!" cost of a skein of silk, a boy maybe half of Akaran's age whispered to his friends that his father had told him to avoid any coins, "With a crow's feather on 'em, 'cause ain't nobody born low gonna have a use for silver cut high," whatever *that* was supposed to mean.

Another woman complained bitterly (and at length to anyone that would listen). Her three brothers had been evicted from their home in the East Akkador District to make room for, "Baggers an' lugs," who were trying to, "muscle in on the *honorable* men of swords of the Queen's Lands." It had nothing to do with failure to pay taxes to the Crown, of course, or any other reason that would involve even the barest hint of personal responsibility.

So while he was convinced that Seline was flirting her way mindlessly through middle-aged bookworms by the dozen (even though she had spent the last half-candle sitting in the lobby being thoroughly overlooked by *everyone* – including a bored and otherwise brazen bloodbeak), the exorcist realized that feelings of dread had no place in the city because it had been chased away by a surge of frustration, hate, and disgust. It was still a nice enough change (at least there wasn't the omnipresent sense of an impending apocalypse) even if it was unsettling to say the least.

It was what made one particular encounter stand out all the more.

When he finally gave up putting weight on his leg, he hobbled down the street until he saw a sign for a taberna that looked decently promising. 'Cromular's Keg' had a quaint ring to it, and the inside of the oblong structure fit the bill for just about any other taberna you'd see anywhere across Dawnfire. Nothing about it made it special – a handful of wooden benches around a circular counter, a pile of old casks along one wall, an oven. A sweat-soaked chef roasting a mottled assortment of probably-not-fresh vegetables inside it while a young woman lazily swatted flies away from a half-eaten loaf of bread on the counter.

What caught his eye – or rather his ear – was a gravely exchange between three people he'd never met before and didn't need to in order to recognize who they worked for. The three were quibbling around a table in the furthest reaches of the *Keg*, and an opportunity to listen to an argument between two of the most powerful guilds on the continent (and one of the most dangerous people in the province) was too good to pass up.

"Please tell me you've heard news," the first of them implored again. That one was a Granalchi – even though his back was turned and his sigil hidden, you didn't wear robes in those tacky rainbow colors without the ability to back up the affront to good taste.

The woman standing beside him, however, with the sleek, short, and tied back gold hair? The steel crest cut as a four-sided diamond on her cloak marked her as a Hunter, and the pair of embossed swords that were knocked on either side of a downward-facing bow either locked her in as the local Huntsmatron, or someone that was going to get killed for pretending to be one. "You know that if I had, the Headmaster-Adept would already know."

"Do I? The two of you have as many reasons to keep secrets from each other as you do truths," he charged in an angry hushed whisper. "Blood and knowledge go hand in hand but the pursuit for both at once are ill-mixed together."

"Much like your own secrets, Adept?"

"I don't know what you mean."

She shook her head ever-so-slightly. "Of course you don't. But I do. Which is why Gorosoch sent me to talk to you out here, instead of in there," she said as she flicked a finger in the rough direction of the Annex. "I don't know what you know, but I intend to find out."

The Adept stepped back with his hands raised slightly before the third member of their little dispute stepped in between them. His blackened-steel armor creaked so loudly when he moved that Akaran was pretty sure it was done intentionally. "She asked to meet us both in neutral ground, Adept. I doubt my presence here is muscle only; she's plenty of that of her own without bothering *me*," he grumbled before affixing a glare through a slatted helmet at the Huntswoman. "That *is* correct, isn't it, Elsith?"

And that is probably the most dangerous man on this side of the city wall, the exorcist mused to himself as he tried to figure out what was going on over a tankard of "It's ale," that the serving wench had handed him. It was a lie, but it would do. *If someone decided to summon the Provincial Maiden's Consort-Blade into this little pisspot of a drinking pit just to get him to play the heavy, then I am not going to have time to hop and hobble the fisk out of here before the whole damn building falls on my head.*

"I only asked you along because of Tyreeing's interests."

"What does Maiden Esterveen's Betrothed have to do with Odern's murder?" the Granalchi sputtered.

"Because in the course of the Guild's investigation, he was found to have outside contacts – past the typical for your lot – with suppliers and archanists in the Midlands. We are unable to rule out that his death was an assassination from someone from the Odinal delegation or one of their enemies."

"You're afraid that it would cause an *incident* should that be proven true," the Consort-Blade grumbled after a prolonged silence.

She nodded again and pulled out two different scrolls from her cloak. "Very. Could you imagine the chaos that would erupt if one of the most-respected wizards of the city was found dead at the hands of one of those barbaric northerners?"

"Utter bedlam," the mage whispered. "It would be akin to a declaration of war. The Academy would have to respond to that – a very minimum would be the denial of services to Clan Odinal and that would spread well past just *here* and would be imposed upon their entire tribe. The repercussions for them in the Midlands would be so significant that it would likely result in their collapse." The Adept paused for a moment and pursed his lips. "Which, may I add, would be a poor development for the Kingdom – I am quite sure that the last thing that the Queen needs is a bunch of angry and disenfranchised barbarians throwing fits on the northern border."

The big man beside them crunched the scroll in his fist before squirreling it away in a pouch at his hip. "Even the threat of that sanction would be enough to wreck the wedding."

"Which means it could be an enemy of Odinal's, as well. Now you see why you're both here – you, Ishtva," she said as she pointed at the Adept, "and you, Leadir, may be the only thing that can stop the city from descending into a riot. Ishtva, you even have an added bonus, given your secondary employment with the Order of Love."

Well, this sounds like all kinds of fun, he almost purred to himself as he took a drink of his now-seasoned not-ale. *Murder assassinates and intrigue? Safest place in the Kingdom my fuzzy white ballsa-* he thought to himself before being rudely interrupted with a blow from what he could only assume was a charred bundle of carrots across the back of his head.

"Get out of here, you! OUT, NOW!"

"Wait what? I haven't done anything!"

The barmaid smacked him again as the chef pointed a fat dirty finger at him and barked out the same command, adding, "Don't need any of that filthy weed in my bar, you disgusting coscer!"

Now all eyes actually *were* on him, including the trio he'd been struggling to hear. The trio said nothing, but Ishtva focused on his sigil with a frown, and Elsith studied his face for future reference. Vantage point completely ruined (and a fear that he'd be thrown in jail for good measure), he grumbled and left the taberna for better pastures.

Those pastures were otherwise known as 'a shady spot across the street.' That was where he was standing until Seline finally showed up another quarter-candlemark later. "You look grumpy. What's wrong?"

He gestured down at the mug that they didn't stop him from taking with him. "You could have told me that cocasa is *illegal*."

"I did, don't you rem..." she looked at him with her face turning aghast. "You didn't bring some with you, did you?"

Akaran looked at her like she'd just declared the sky was green and grass was blue. "Of course I did. Just stopped at that marketplace to drink something with it."

She sighed and ran a hand over her face before steering the two of them down the street as quick as she could. "Oh, you poor man. Public possession is strictly banned. The populace at large is forbidden to carry it with them, and it is only tolerated in public when in the hands of a licensed alchemist or physician. You'd best hope that the taberna doesn't call for the garrison."

"I didn't know," he sighed as he lowered his head, crestfallen. "I am sorry."

"You're not a well-traveled man, are you?"

He shook his head. "Six years at the Grand Temple, and we never traveled too far from it. Before being sent to Toniki, only other places of note I've been have been the Queen's Capitol and off to Panidillic."

"Panidillic... that's... capital of the Imaii Province, yes?"

"Yeah. For 'field training' with the Order."

"I don't dare ask what that is," Seline quietly said, before looking up at the sky. "Then no, you've not been far from home too often, have you?"

All he did was shrug. "Don't know how I got to the Grand Temple, so... I might've."

She couldn't quite hide the look of general irritation his response deserved. "Then no, you haven't. The city overseer has been taking a dim view of the root for a year now. The local garrison is tasked with, well... rooting... out the local dens, but no sooner than they close one, another opens."

He grimaced and squeezed the pouch through his shirt protectively. "Wonderful. I'll leave it back at the room then."

"That would be a decidedly wise idea," Seline replied as she patted him on his knee. "I've no desire to have to explain to the guards why I'm carting around a coscer any more than you wish to hand it over to them or pay the fine."

"A coscer, huh? That's a quaint name for it."

She ignored him and tried to explain the problem. "The weed's been growing in popularity for years now. It flows openly from the League to the southern sea and into the Ogibus Bay regions, with Dawnfire stuck in the middle."

He idly fingered at the pouch through his shirt. "If it's become such a problem, why hasn't the Queen been doing anything more about it? I can't imagine that she wouldn't direct the army to clamp down on it..."

"Because like all things that man wants that he should not have, the desire to partake in it overrides the sense of one's purse. With sacks heavy of coin, it's no surprise that enough gold slips loose to encourage the wheels of justice to roll elsewhere."

Akaran just grunted. "As pissed as the tabernesta was, should I assume that the wheels of justice don't always roll through here as often as they should?"

The healer made a little 'mmm-hmm' sound. "Just as cocasa flows out of the League, the head of the Orshia-Avagerona River itself is close to the Missian border. At least, for your sake, it means that you don't have to worry about your supply being interrupted."

"The Goddess smiles on me in ways I wouldn't expect."

She looked at him askance. "I'm not sure that's smiling. However! You're soon to be able to ask Her yourself."

The way she said it made his skin start to crawl. "Um... I will?"

"Oh, it's nothing bad," she unsuccessfully tried to reassure him. "*Look!* The Repository of Miral!"

There's a lot you could say about the Order of Love, but one thing was for damn sure: when they built a building, they *built* a building. Or in the case of the Repository, they apparently built a hill and then put building-like adornments all over it. The sheer effort that had gone into it was mind-boggling and borderline ridiculous.

To start with, the *how* they built it was just nuts. The maybe-a-temple? had been built onto a hillside (and presumably inside it) that was on the opposite side of the Avagerona. The grassy hill terminated about a third of the way up the northeastern cliff-face, and on top of it – and recessed deep into the dark brown stone – there were four archways that flanked a giant dome that jutted forward over several yard's worth of the hill's slope.

Nor was this a small hill, either. There were no less than two pairs of five flights of steps leading up to the top, arranged in some kind of figure-eight layout. They crisscrossed each other in the middle and the fifth flight lazily trailed to the top of the hill by itself. Four small gatehouses/entryways leading inside the hill were stationed at the top of the first and third flights (and on both sides) of the stairways. Each of them had golden gates protecting the doorways and whatever else hid beyond.

With all of that mess complicating the outside of the Repository, it was apparent that someone (or an army of someones) was in charge of the grounds proper. As they pulled up to the gold and copper gate that blocked the bridge leading over the river, it was hard not to pay attention to the countless orchids, bluebells, wild strawberry bushes, and miles worth of grapevines that were just starting to bloom. Not a single blade of grass looked like it was out of place, and not a single weed had taken hold in any crack on any step.

If they were taking that much care of the plantlife, it defied the imagination to wonder the kind of care they took on the rest of the outpost. *And why*, he mused. *Whomever built this had something in mind other than horticulture.* Then, out loud, he made a less-stunning observation. "They weren't kidding about Miral, were they?"

"Ah, so you noticed."

Akaran looked up at the giant statue midway up the hill and then looked back at her with his face as blank as a slate. "How could I not?"

"I'll confess. I never studied much about him."

"Miral?"

"Yes. I know he's one of the Archangels of Love but there wasn't a lot that I learned about him. All I really know is that he's called the Guardian, and he has a poor reputation."

He cringed a little and reluctantly nodded at her. The statue itself was three times the size of your average person and crafted out of solid marble. The full suit of armor it wore, however, was actual steel and over-sized leather straps – like the sculptor had wanted to be prepared for the eventuality of the stone coming to life and going to war. "Yes and no."

Seline looked puzzled and quizzically turned her head to the side. "How can an angel be disliked?"

"Well, he's liked because he's considered the Guardian of Love. The one tasked to personally defend the Goddess against all those that would wage war against Her." He pointed up at Miral's face and added, "It's also said that he was tasked to bed Mother Adrianne after she established the new Grand Temple in Dawnfire, after the fall of Agromah."

"An angel sent to bed a human?" she said with her eyes wider than he thought possible. "Why ever for?"

"Ask Brother Lanodry."

"Who's that?"

He couldn't quite hide the smirk on his face when he answered. "Twenty-five years after, he became the first Paladin-Commander of the Reformed Order."

Seline still looked lost and finally turned to face him. "Wouldn't that mean he was a nephilim?"

"Yes and no."

"You said that earlier."

"You aren't asking simple questions," the priest pointed out. "Adrianne never said either way if he personally visited her, or if he blessed her union with another man. She wasn't married at the time, so..."

Seline wrinkled her nose a little. "So it could be that the entire story was a lie she offered to protect her honor? It wouldn't be the first."

Akaran just shrugged at her. "It's a matter of contention. Lanodry and his heirs are some of the strongest fighters and the most potent of the healers we've ever produced. So sayeth the historical scrolls, at least."

"How does that make him untrustworthy?"

"It's not that he's actually *disliked* as it is. It's... well. He did it once, and he's a bit of an excuse now."

"An excuse...?"

Akaran shrugged. "The phrase 'Miral did it,' is not uncommon after a bad winter or around nine months after a sudden outbreak of peace."

She looked at him with her mouth agape. "I mean, I... I follow the Goddess of Love. I have respect for Her. I've never made it to the Grand Temple. I had heard a few stories but... that actually happens? I thought it was a myth...?"

"Nope, no myth. Of course, I've heard a few men use a similar excuse."

"How?"

He coughed into his hand and leaned in close to her. "Let's just say that the Goddess is of *Love* and *Love* tends to last longer than a few minutes in a barn somewhere."

Her face went beet red and she couldn't even stammer out a reply.

The exorcist sighed and looked up at the Repository. "That... all of that. That's incredible. I hope I can walk up those steps one day."

"Sooner than you'd think," she said, "and unfortunately, this is the end of the trip for us."

He let out a deep sigh of relief and squeezed at his leg. "Okay. In all honesty I'm tired and I'd love to go back to my room."

"You're not going back to your room."

Alarmed, he squeezed his leg a little harder as his eye went wide. "You just said -?"

"That it's the end of the trip for *us*," she clarified as she started to guide him out of the cart. "You need to report in, and you'll be spending the night."

"I will be? I didn't bring a change of clothes?"

"You will be," the healer repeated. "No need to worry about your clothes. Clean vestments will be provided, I'm sure."

"I don't have a choice?"

"You don't have a choice."

Akaran sighed again, a bit softer but not by much. "Dammit. What part of 'I hurt' did you miss?"

"None of it. You're going in on your own though."

"What? Why? What now?"

She cringed a little bit and came clean. "I wasn't completely truthful about why we went on this trip. Maiden Prostil requested you personally, and Medias agrees that until you can walk, you can study."

"So, this isn't a joke? I'm going in there?"

"You're going in there."

"But you're not coming," he pointed out.

"I'm not coming."

He ran his fingers through his hair and stared at her with his mouth slightly open and a frown giving him early wrinkles around his eyes. "Why not?"

"I'm forbidden," Seline replied with a little shrug of her own.

"Is it Order only?"

She shook her head and steadied him as they started to walk to the silvery gates of the Oo-lo outpost. "No, it's... well. I don't quite know how to phrase this in a way you will be receptive to."

"Truthfully would be nice. Bluntly optional."

"Fine," she sighed, then went on to explain what she could. "I think I mentioned earlier that Lady Ridora and Maiden Prostil can't stand each other. I don't know why but the last time they got close to each other it took three people to hold them back. Ridora has forbid anyone in her service from entering the Repository unless absolutely necessary."

"Oh. That's... strange. Any idea why?"

Seline shook her head and shrugged slightly "Us women are fickle creatures. We do not always make sense."

A brief look of mixed horror and relief flashed across his face. "So you're not allowed in but I am? Am I being kicked out?"

"No. You're a special case," she quickly elucidated. "You're... unwell... but you can still think. That means you are able to be out on your own from the house. You're not able to move as well as others, which means that if a use is going to be found for you, it's going to be with your mind," she said as she cast a long, sideways stare at him, "unless you think you'd be happier folding the cottons."

He tried to suppress a shudder and looked the gate over. "So... Ridora doesn't know what to do with me and this Maiden Prostil wants me?"

"Effectively. There are many worse places to work than at a library."

A brief flashback to his time in the academy and the last week of hearing the manor servants grouse about shit-covered blankets caused him to shudder hard. "I'm not going to argue that."

"Good. I'll be back tomorrow after the noon sun hits the sky."

"Alright, I guess."

She gave him a friendly squeeze on his shoulder. "Cheer up, Akaran. This is a shrine to the Goddess. Take the opportunity to relax in Her warmth."

He waited until she was back in the cart and out of earshot before he groused under his breath. "I haven't felt warm since I got to Toniki." And then, louder, "My name is Akaran DeHawk, Exorcist. I've been told to report to this temple," he called out, with the assumption that someone would be able to hear him.

A few minutes of relative silence went by as he leaned against his cane before a voice spoke up just out of sight. "Ah, there you are. The Maiden asked for you two days ago. We were beginning to wonder if you'd ever be permitted to come here."

The priest looked up to the top of the gatehouse and immediately bowed his head back down with a brief internal, *Oh, shit*. "Paladin-Commander. My apologies, sir."

"At ease, brother exorcist," the other man called down. "We're not frequently so formal here."

Akaran looked up at the presumably-forty-something paladin at the top of the gate and relaxed some. "Yessir. If I had known about the request, I'd have been here sooner."

"To be fair, boy, I just found out about it myself. The guards knew, but nobody bothered to tell *me*," he said with a grunt. The guard at the gate visibly tensed up and made sure that he was standing at *complete* attention.

It seemed prudent.

For Akaran though, the statement let him take a breath of relief. "Then it's a pleasure to meet you, Sir...?"

"Spidous Nel'don," the other man replied as he pulled off his helmet and showed off a head full of curly, medium-length black hair and a matching beard with streaks of gray in it.

"Paladin-Commander Nel'don. Again, I am sorry."

"There's no need," he said before ducking out of view. A few moments later and he was behind the gate and helping a couple members of the 4th Garrison to open it. "Come. I understand you have some trouble walking still. My assistant has a chair ready for you."

That earned a third sigh of relief and he meant it more than the other two combined. "Thank you, sir. I am a bit concerned about those stairs."

"Understandable," he replied with a slight grin. As soon as the gate opened, an aide and the promised chair almost magically appeared at his side. Spidous waited until they were yards away from the gate before continuing. "We've heard some interesting things about you. The Maiden and I both poured over your report from Toniki, and she had me dig into your time at the Academy."

"How did you do that? Those records are under lock and key."

"Hmm. You don't know much about this place, do you?"

The aid stayed behind and Spidous took charge of the wheelchair and began to push the exorcist towards a long ramp that ran alongside the westernmost stairs that was hidden in the grass. "Just that information comes here if it involves the Order, sir."

"That it does," the paladin confirmed. "We have access to the yearly training reports from the academy, as well as reports from the field."

"Oh... I had no idea."

Akaran didn't see the smile that answered him, but he did take note of the armed guards that were patrolling the stairs. There were at least four that he could see, though there were numerous men wearing Order vestments and robes standing near the smaller gateways leading up the hillside that were trying very hard to look unarmed themselves.

Trying, and failing. Not only were they casting furtive glances in his direction, they were also keeping their eyes on the soldiers from the 4th as well. As he was rolled up the ramp, he saw one pair of Order members stop and quickly frisk a man wearing a Lover's cloak – pretty much solidifying the fact that this installation was guarded much better than your typical temple (or even a garrison).

"Few that aren't assigned here do. It's not a *guarded* secret, as it were, though the Order doesn't openly shout the purpose of this shrine for all to know. Most just assume we are a training facility, or a transitory barracks," Spidous told him as he was wheeled past two of the pretending-to-not-be-guards and into the first gateway on the hillside.

Once indoors, it was a quick push down a dimly-lit and grungy-looking hallway that was in stark contrast to the beauty outside that it made him question if he was in the same building. That thought came to an abrupt end when two turns down corridors filled with man-sized recesses and slats in the walls just big enough for someone to fire an arrow through delivered him to a foyer larger than some ballrooms.

Larger, and vastly more impressive.

"Welcome to the Lower Hall," the paladin intoned. "When you stay here, this is where the meals are served. It also functions as a welcoming area for lower-status dignitaries and the like."

If this is for the nobility they don't give a shit about, you gotta wonder what's on the upper floor, he inwardly mused. The lower hall had enough banquet-sized tables to easily feed a room of two hundred, making him wonder just exactly how *big* this facility was, and why they would need this many people in it. It was also decorated with glossy marble walls and polished granite floors. There were at least four different statues dedicated to Niasmis and Her archangels, including not just the questionable Miral but also the loathed-by-everyone-outside-the-Order, Li'Orla. It also had Samia's golden visage hanging over one doorway, which was probably all the effort most of the Temple would give her.

"I will warn you that as ornate as the hall is, most of the Repository is far more utilitarian and less gaudy. While Love should never focus on the bare minimum..."

"...sometimes less is more, and our resources are better spent improving the lives around us than covering the beds in silk," the exorcist finished.

The paladin briefly looked mortified. "Oh, heavens no. All the beds have silk sheets. We aren't barbarians."

There was a long, lingering pause from Akaran before he spoke up again. "So... what I'm hearing is that moving in is an option? Is that right, sir? Please?"

"Afraid not," Spidous replied after a hearty round of laughter. "We don't have accommodations for someone in your position for extended periods. You are, of course, welcome to use this shrine as a waystation when needed, as is anyone of the Order. But you will not have as easy of a time here as you would in the Manor."

"I understand, I suppose. Something tells me that this place wasn't built with gimps in mind."

"No, it wasn't. But I'd like to know what *you* think it was built for," he asked.

Akaran blinked and looked around the hall one last time before being wheeled underneath Samia's warm, golden mask. There were diamond teardrops at the edge of her silver eyes, and rubies for her lips. She always looked sadder than she did loving, which made her place as the second of the three Archangels of Love all the more strange to him. "You want me to do what?"

Spidous wheeled him down another hallway and paused next to a wrought-iron door with green vines with tiny red flowers growing all around the frame. "Your thoughts. Initial feelings about the Repository."

"That vine isn't natural. There's not enough light for it down here."

"Not what I meant, but that's *wveld-weed* for you. Grows with torchlight or sunlight, as long as there's a steady supply of *ilmalcium* in the soil. Maiden-Templar Prostil loves it so much that you'll find it growing just about everywhere."

He wiggled his nose a little. "Where does the ilmalcium come from? Not familiar...?"

"Talk to the gardener. I focus more on cutting things than growing them."

"Fair enough."

"Now, your thoughts?"

He mulled it for a moment before turning his chair around to study the paladin as much as he had been studying the building. "I don't really have any, sir."

"Now that's not true," the paladin chided. "You've been studying the shrine since you wheeled up to the gateway."

Akaran took note of the way that he clenched his jaw when he corrected him, and watched his amber eyes glint in the torchlight. They were so pale they were almost orange. "Just trying to determine a lay of the land, sir."

"Which is exactly what I wanted to see from you," he retorted with an irritated huff. "Now, what does the land tell you?"

"That this isn't an archive for reports or a transitory station."

The paladin didn't move a muscle and just continued to stare into Akaran's good eye. "You come to that conclusion how?"

That look was beginning to get unnerving. "You've got members of the 4th Garrison standing at each entrance past the main gate, meaning that whatever is stored here is important to the Kingdom – and not just the Order. You've either got Order knights or paladins protecting the archways in, but they're not broadcasting the fact so It's hard to say which is which and I have a feeling that's what you want."

"Maybe it is. Anything else?"

The exorcist gave a quick nod. "We've gone past two different guard stations with templars at each. And that first hallway? You could hold off a small siege there alone. If the other entrances look anything remotely like that then you've planned for a pitched battle if it ever comes to it."

"This shrine was built soon after the establishment of the Reformed Order. There are a lot of reasons to want to protect against those that would do us harm."

"No offense intended, sir, but there wouldn't have been a need for a place like this after the Order adapted to the post-Hardening world. A century and a half, maybe, but nothing so soon. It was brutal for a generation, but hearts softened some soon after. To an extent. Not a great extent, but they quit hanging us in the woods."

Spidous nodded slowly, sucking in air through the corner of his mouth. "Anything else?"

Akaran pointed back the way they came. "Think I saw a Granalchi go wandering out into one of the other passages leading into that hall. If this was just an archive, there's not much we'd have here that would be of interest to the Academy. Or if there *was*, there'd be no reason to have one here. When it'd be just as easy to walk a report to the local Annex – but he looked *really* comfortable around the other people and *didn't* have an escort, which means he either works here or visits so often you don't see the need to have him under guard."

The paladin didn't say a word for the longest time, then reached over to the iron door and started to open it. "Interesting."

"Am I right?"

"You passed the test."

"What test?"

"The one that decides if you're to be kept around, or send on your way tomorrow," he said with a happy little grin.

For a jovial smile, it was anything but reassuring. "Sir? But am I right?"

The paladin thought on his reply for a minute before finally saying, "You are someone that it would be hard to keep things a secret around. Which is good... because that's what we need."

"I don't have any idea what you mean, sir."

"Prostil will explain," he replied as he opened the door then pushed Akaran into another short hallway. "I imagine you've been questioned at length by the officers at the manor, yes?"

"Yessir."

"And it probably feels repetitive to you by this point, doesn't it?"

He grunted out a response that wasn't polite enough to be heard, then followed it with, "You've no idea."

Spidous laughed again, his flushed cheeks almost bouncing with delight.

"You'll be happy to know then, at least, that we aren't as interested as to where you've been, but more for what you can do."

"Not much," Akaran retorted with a shrug.

"You'd be surprised," he returned as he pulled back a curtain hiding another door and pushed the priest inside. "Catherine? Your exorcist, as requested."

Catherine – like almost everyone else he'd seen in this glorified pothole of a city – had to have been at least thirty years his senior and had graying hair to match. It wasn't all gray (there were still streaks of chestnut brown hair in it) but it served to accentuate her dull golden-green eyes and slight wrinkles around her eyes and cheeks. "Akaran! I'm so happy to finally meet you."

And unlike most of the people he'd met so far? He believed that she actually meant the smile on her face. The fact that she hugged him right after the greeting almost stunned him silly.

When the shock wore off, he managed to meekly squeak out a simple "Maiden, it's an honor," before bowing his head to her.

"Maiden-Templar, actually," she corrected, then went on to say, "but call me Catherine, please. Spidous should have told you we don't stand much for formality here."

"He did, m'am, but..."

She gave him the warmest smile he'd ever seen before expressing profanity that he hadn't expected. "...but you've had almost a month of having to scrape around with your head bowed and lips puckered to Ridora's 'I'm-a-holier-than-thou-cantankerous-yeastroll' ass, yes?"

The paladin laughed while Akaran choked on his tongue. "Um... something like that?"

"Knowing her, I'd imagine it's more than just something," she said while he continued to cough in shock. Then she turned her attention to the paladin-commander and smiled again. "Did he pass your test?"

"Surprisingly well. He'll be suited for your request."

"That depends on the request, I think...?"

She sat down on the edge of her desk and adjusted her long, ruby-red dress as she made herself comfortable. "Let me start from the beginning, else I may not earn your trust."

"M'am, of anyone I've met in this town, you outrank me in ways that I haven't seen since the Grand Temple," he replied as he tried to figure out what, exactly, her game was. "I believe that trust is a mandatory requirement."

"Obedience, not trust," she pointed out. "I've always found that gaining trust furthers the obedience, and I like both from the souls in my service."

The way she said 'souls' made the remark far less reassuring than she had (hopefully) intended. "Yes m'am...? I don't really know what you think I can do...?"

"A great deal, judging by your jacket after the Coldstone Incident," Spidous pointed out.

"I can't do that much now."

"Not every soldier serves with a blade," she argued as she smiled knowingly. "I know it's frustrating. I've been there before, much as you. I was able to keep my grasp of magic, but, I know the touch of the unholy."

He tilted his head, still wondering where she was going with this. "You did? May I ask what happened?"

The Maiden slowly pulled the sleeve of her gown up her right arm, revealing an atrocious gash that went from her wrist up her arm and past the edge of the robe. "Gondorma. Ten years ago."

He went pale and felt his breakfast roll up into his throat. "Holy all, Maiden that looks horrific."

"I had attempted to banish it twice before it did this to me. It took exception to the third time," she lamented. "It shattered my wrist and then attempted to pull my forearm out of the skin. It was partially successful."

Breakfast started to knock on his front teeth as he clamped his hand over his mouth. When he was finally able to swallow the revulsion, he managed to say, "I can't even imagine that... that sounds..."

"I admit that I didn't stay awake for the entire experience."

"Thank the Goddess for small favors."

She nodded while Spidous cringed. Wasn't the first time he'd heard the story but he kept wishing it would be the last. "Yes, truly. We weren't near any kind of field hospital, of course, and there's only so much magic itself can repair. The Goddess saw fit to allow me enough of Her will to help me keep it together but by the time we reached a settlement the damage was too great to adequately heal with Words alone."

He shuddered again as the memory of Makolichi shattering his knee rushed back in all of its unholy glory. "I... then you can relate. I am sorry you went through that, Maiden."

"Catherine, please. I insist."

"Yes m'a... Catherine."

Blessedly, she pulled the sleeve of her gown back down to cover the scar. "After, I suffered... terrors. Nightmares, mainly, but there was a time that the smell of mushrooms or the very thought of going into a cave would..." She trailed off for a moment while looking at something that was just over his shoulder, or maybe she was looking at nothing at all. "It would invoke old feelings. Like you, I was also sent to the Manor."

"Should I guess that your issues with Ridora start there?"

"So you were told about our disagreement."

He nodded slightly. "Just that you have one. And you did just call her a cantankerous yeastroll."

"The details are not important," she said with a slight smirk. "Yes, we have one, and yes, it has made things strained between our two institutions. It's incredibly vexing, and it's part of why I asked you to come here."

That raised his curiosity even more, if such a thing was possible. "How many I serve, Mai... Catherine?"

"You've lost all ability to use magic, yes? You're unable to sense and unable to be affected?"

"Apparently I can be affected by the tangible results of magic," he clarified. "Not the magic itself. I'd rather not be used as a test subject for any more spells, if it's all the same. That mother-fisk... ahem... the *Adept* from the Academy has paid several visits and... I don't like him."

"Gorosoch?" Spidous asked.

"No, Lolron."

"You poor man," he groaned.

Catherine shook her head and patted his hand. "No, no testing. But I would like you to keep your eyes open for us, please."

"What do you mean?"

She and the paladin exchanged a glance, then she explained herself. "With the nature of men and women that make it to Ridora's doorstep, there have been occasional, shall we say, *hangers-on* of one incident or another."

Spidous went next. "Ridora isn't an exorcist herself. She's a healer and has some training in psyanistry, but she is neither an ambianist or an ether-keneticist. The Manor is never sent anyone that is believed to have an aura that is actively corrupted, though mistakes have occurred in the past."

"Yes," the Maiden said in agreement. "To build upon that, if you were suffering from possession or a poisoning of your soul, you'd have instead been placed under the watchful gaze of the Grand Temple. As your injuries aren't of an active or radiant nature..."

"...they interred me in the Manor until they don't think I'm crazy anymore. It's because of the training that goes on at the Grand Temple, isn't it? When a mind has been broken, you don't want to risk them being re-exposed to higher concentrations of magic. But you don't want someone out in the wild that might spread something. Or lash out in a fit of madness. Or worse."

"Told you I had faith in this one."

"That's it exactly," she replied. "Still, to err is human. Ridora has graciously allowed -"

Spidous interrupted her with a disgusted little grunt. "You mean she was told by Johasta."

"Ridora was *told* by Johasta to -"

"Sorry," he interrupted again, "I meant 'threatened with revocation of permissions.' That's much more accurate."

Her smile faltered for a moment and her eyes took on a steely look that could've melted a tower shield in a heartbeat. "May I continue, *Commander* Spidous?"

The paladin caught the tone (he'd have been deaf if he hadn't) and quickly corrected himself. "Ah, yes. Apologies. Can't stand the old bat any more than you can."

"She's been mandated to allow routine examinations by someone from the

Repository," Akaran interjected.

"Effectively, yes," the Maiden replied, "just as a safety precaution. There are things that strive to stay hidden in the ether."

"I can't do anything to find them."

"I know. But one thing that Ridora *won't* do is allow us access to speak to the people she hosts. We would like to, but she doesn't feel it's prudent. Thinks it is risky to press. We can study the grounds, check the wards, look for tampering of any kind. We *cannot* talk to anyone that might be affected by influences that we would find *vaguely objectionable*, should you understand my meaning."

He did, and the implications were uncomfortably staggering. "You... want me to spy on the other patients? This sounds more intense than what the templar at the gateside waypoint asked me to do."

"Ah, so you met Karaj." She nodded quickly and gave him another reassuring smile. "*Spy* is such a negative term, no matter how my assistant may have phrased it. The truth is that I don't trust Ridora's judgment, and I never will again. If you can provide regular reports when you return here, it would be appreciated. That's all."

And there was another question. He was starting to get tired of them. "When I come back? You make it sound like it's going to be a routine thing."

"It is," the paladin replied.

"It is?"

Catherine reached behind her and handed him a formal letter marked with a wax seal of the Order. "Yes. As part of an arrangement with that trying woman, to keep you active, you will study here, three times a week. Cannot let your mind dull with your body. Nel'don will be your tutor."

Spidous cleared his throat and squeezed his shoulder. "You showed a mind for deduction while untangling that mess in Weschali. Putting down a haunting that stretched across the northeastern part of the province? You deserve a great deal of credit for that. Your leg *will* eventually heal. When it does, I expect you to be taking your sword to the various necks in the Abyss — and I think an enhanced education will open many doors in your future."

The praise wasn't faint but it felt somewhat damning. "I... I see. But without magic, I can't...?"

"Even if all you are able to do is teach, a war cannot be fought without those that can impart knowledge. Every general needs advisors, every soldier needs a mentor, and even the Queen needs to have voices on the field that can speak truth in muddled times," the paladin said without a trace of doubt in his voice at all.

There may not have been any doubt, but that thought hurt worse than his knee did. "A teacher then? That's where you think I'll be?"

"*We* think that your story is far from over," Catherine countered. "While you're waiting for the next chapter, we think you will do best to arm your mind."

"I... I see," he said, feeling like the world had just been kicked out from under his chair.

She smiled again and reached for another loving hug that failed to improve his mood. "Oh, it isn't so bad. Besides, there is one truth that you should hear."

"M'am?"

"Working towards discovering your own answers may help you heal in ways that no templar or adept can manage, even if they aren't the answers you seek."

She was right about that.

Two weeks later, he'd need to start finding a slew of answers to questions that nobody wanted to ask.

VI. DEATH OF SANITY
Madis, the 10th of Riverswell, 513 QR

Albergast's Inquiry of the Lower Elements, Third Edition, Akaran decided, was the type of book written by someone that hated people in general and who sought to make sure that there was no question about the depths of his derision. Not only that, he was equally as convinced that it was the type of book you'd force someone to read if you were angry with them on an unabashedly spiritual level. The only thing that had made that revelation worse was the knowledge that it was only the second book he had been assigned to take back to the Manor to study in the two weeks since he had started his tutelage under Spidous.

It felt like a poor tiding of things to come.

The first book, the *7th School,* had been such a migraine-inducing review of the basic principles of alchemetic arts that he was *entirely* certain that old lady Hirshma had written it herself. The thought of stealing it and sending it by courier back to her at Toniki had crossed his mind more than once. So had taking it outside and burning it.

That felt like an even worse idea.

Not necessarily a wrong one, but a worse one.

As he entertained throwing the *Inquiry* into the fireplace with it – just to keep the other book company – chaos started to erupt outside his room. By the time he made it to the door to look around and see what all the shouting was about, Seline barged into his room with her carefully-tended hair hanging on her shoulders looking like a badger's nest. "Akaran! Are you alright?"

He looked up at her from the bed after pulling his eyepatch back down. "Leg hurts. Head is pounding. You need to have the chef look at that pig he fixed last night. Not gonna lie, tasted wonderful, but gave me the absolute worst -"

"I don't care about your dinner. *Are you okay?*"

"Not the first hospital that doesn't care about what people eat," he groused, "won't be the last."

She visibly relaxed against the door and he realized just how disheveled she looked. Not only was her hair an absolute mess, her dress was wrinkled and there were a few stains that looked like blood. "Then yes, you're fine. Thank the Gods."

"More like apologize to the pork."

Seline sighed and rolled her eyes. "Yes, fine, the pig was overcooked. Happy?"

"No," he said, "but it's a start."

She stepped into the room the rest of the way and pushed his door shut as she crossed her arms and glared at him. "I do *not* have time for you this morning."

Akaran pulled himself up in bed and stretched, showing her more of his scar-covered torso than she wanted to see. "Then why are you here?"

"Because," she started to say before tilting her head and staring at one of his books. "Wait. Is that the 7th *School*?"

"Unfortunately. Dryer than the pig."

"*I don't care about the damn pig!* Don't particularly care about that book either," she snapped, "but if you value your scalp then I wouldn't let Ridora see it or... or your head..." Seline went on before she let it trail off as she sagged against the door in a mix of exhaustion and defeat.

Finally, it dawned on him – it didn't look like she was bedraggled from a long night of fun. This was worse. Her eyes were bloodshot and her face was streaked with dried tears, those stains were *definitely* blood, and her hair was barely held in a loose knot on the back of her head. "Seline? What's wrong?"

Her voice fell to a tired whisper and she refused to meet his concerned stare. "It's... Livstra."

Akaran tilted his head slightly. "Just had a session with her last night. She seemed fine? What happened?"

"I can't... I can't tell you right now," she replied, with a quick brush of her fingers through her tangled hair. Once she regained composure, she cleared her throat. "Just... are you okay? Did you hear anything out of the ordinary last night? After dinner, before first meal today?"

He took a breath and thought about it for a moment before shaking his head no. "Nothing. I ate. Went to the atrium. Prayed. Came back to my room. Took my daily dose of cocasa, and tried to sleep."

"Tried?"

"Dreams."

"Still?"

"Every time I shut my eyes after dark," he said before sucking on air a little, "though weirdly, never if I nap in the day."

She ignored that and continued to press him. "But you didn't hear anything?"

"Nothing abnormal," he replied. "Whatever you did to quiet Oda down the hall, thank you."

"What do you mean?"

Akaran shrugged and gestured to his right. "He usually starts talking to the walls when the first moon comes out. Barely said a thing all night," he said as he took a moment to give a longing look at his dresser and added, "that, or whomever supplied the last batch of the root finally figured out how to cultivate a strong batch."

She pursed her lips and nodded slowly. "Oda. I didn't think he had the wherewithal to figure out the locks on his door. Worth a look."

"Worth a look for what?"

Seline ignored the question and pointed a finger at him. "I need you. Grab your cane, follow quick. Thank you for being mostly dressed this time."

He shivered and pulled the wool robe he had draped over his shoulders tight around him. "I've been getting cold."

"It's midway through spring."

"Still cold."

"Wonderful," the healer groused, "the last thing we need is for you to start getting worse."

"It could just be that it's draf..." he started, then gave up. "Anyway. Not taking my leggings off unless someone forces me to. Though we really need to talk about that pork though."

The look she gave him could've withered a forest. "*Enough!*"

Realizing that just this once, discretion might *actually* be the better part of valor, he did as instructed. A few moments later, they were marching down the hallway towards the communal dining room. It didn't take more than a few steps to realize it was more than just Seline who was out of sorts.

Several other healers and assistants were moving through the manor in a hurry, escorting patients from one room to another. He caught sight of three guards from the 4th sweeping through the building. Importantly, their hands were on their swords and they were storming so fast that their cloaks were whipping in the air behind them. You didn't have to guess that these men were anything other than pissed-off. Even though it didn't take that long to get to the dining room., the sight of them made *him* wish he had a sword, too.

Despite repeated quiet attempts to ask her what was going on, she refused to answer directly. "All you need to do right now is come watch some of the other residents. You don't need to talk to them, you don't need to entertain them, you don't need to do anything but watch them."

"What am I watching for?"

"We're short-handed right now, so you just need to keep an eye on them, make sure nobody hurts themselves, okay?"

The idea of playing shepherd for a room full of the decrepit didn't fill him with glee, so he continued to push. "I can, I guess, but... why? Truly, Seline, what's going on?"

"Ridora has the manor being turned inside out, top to bottom, every room.

You and Benjain are the only two residents with enough sense to be put in charge of watching out for the others."

He stopped in his tracks and made a face. "Benjain? Isn't he the one that drools?"

"It's just drool," she retorted before tugging at his arm until he started walking again, "he's a nice man."

"It's *distressing*."

"Yes, and it's distressing to hear your digestive emissions after *you* eat," she retorted.

Akaran glared over at her out of the corner of his eye. "That only happens when I eat the pork."

She steadied herself and fought back the urge to haul off and punch him with her hand on the dining room doorknob. "Swear to the Gods above, Akaran, I will shove a spit down your throat and let you see how the pig feels if you don't drop the subject."

"Fine, fine," he whined. "Are we looking after them together?"

"No. I have other charges to attend to," she said as she pulled the doors open. Thankfully, there were only four people and one guard present. The guard took one look at Akaran and Seline and took off out the other entrance as soon as she nodded in his direction. "We'll come for them as we get a chance. Just... stay here, watch them."

They were all sitting at different spots in the hall, and none of them looked like they had even registered their entrance, sans one. She looked like she might have been close to Ridora's age, and her amber eyes were speckled with little white flakes in the corners. It was unsettling, but it was also the mark of an adept psyanist. "Stay here and watch. I can do that. How long?"

"Until we can get to them."

"What if one of them needs to go use the restroom?"

She shook her head and turned to look him in the eye. "They'll have to hold it as best as they can. Orders from the Lady. You can't leave the room either."

Perplexed, he tilted his head. "I can't? What did I do?"

"You complained about the pork too damn much."

"But -"

Seline raised her finger and almost pressed it on the tip of his nose. "They're not going to bother you. Akaran: that's Bistra, Tanstin, Appaidene, and Divitol. You four, this is Akaran."

The only one to acknowledge their presence was the woman with the amber eyes and silver hair. She was a bit waifish, and he could see her hands shaking from across the room. "Hi... hello." It gave him hope, albeit brief, that maybe this wouldn't be so bad.

"Bistra, isn't it? Aren't you the one they call the Auraman-"

The healer quickly covered his mouth with her hand and shook her head violently. She scolded him in a hushed and hurried whisper. "No, don't. Don't call her that. Just Bistra, do you understand?"

As he tried to nod, the other woman spoke up nervously. "Ye... yes, I... I am."

Seline cleared her throat and spoke to the crowd again. "Everyone, Akaran is going to be watching over you for the next little bit. If you need anything, just ask him; if he tells you to do something, pretend he's me asking."

Bistra nodded, but the other madmen (and woman) didn't say anything. The one she called Appaidene – a pretty woman in her early thirties – just rocked back and forth with a small ratty doll in her arms, oblivious to her blonde hair cascading down over her face. Tanstin and Divitol didn't even acknowledge his presence. The former was hunched over in front of the latter, his head twitching to the side every few heartbeats as he spoke in a stream of unceasing gibberish.

As for Divitol? The oldest of the bunch, he was bald and his eyes were utterly vacant. He sat and drooled without making a sound. Though every now and again, he'd lift his right hand and make an odd symbol in the air and silently tried to mouth something. "Was that a wardmark?" Akaran whispered.

"Yes. Don't pay it any attention. He can't do anything with it."

"I really feel like I should know how he can't."

"Do you really think we'd operate a hospice that caters to the magical without precautions?" she whispered with a conspiratorial nudge.

Akaran blinked and worked his mouth a moment before he could completely formulate his thought. "You've neutered them like I am? Sel, really think that this sounds like *pertinent information* I should know about!"

There wasn't enough patience this side of eternity to keep her from rolling her eyes back with a pained sigh. "Not so much *neutered*, as you put it, as *muted*. Look at his left wrist."

He glanced at it and kicked himself for not seeing it earlier. "Wardmark," he muttered, then after staring at it, added, "*Distruvas-instada*, isn't it?"

"Yes. We use it in a few different ways. For minds that we think can be recovered, we put it on an iron bracelet. For those that can't..."

"Tattooed. Inscribing them with a counter-spell. *Distruvas* to interrupt, and *instada* to focus the effect on their person."

"Exactly. It's not perfect, but it is effective for most."

He ran the end of his tongue over his teeth. "They use the right set of spells, they could overpower it. Or just force of will it enough..."

"And if they did, we would know and could rush to them before they were able to complete their invocation. It happens from time to time, but it is the most humane method to use."

"Wouldn't having it inked into the skin worsen their dementia? It... it would have to feel like something is buzzing in their heads all the time?"

Seline shrugged sadly. "The other options are to take their hands or tongues," she explained, "and that does not feel appropriate for a place of healing."

"Point," he replied under his breath, then paused. "Why don't you have one on me?"

"Because when you're able to channel mana once more, most of our job will be done. There's no need to weigh you down with what you don't need."

It stung to hear it put that way, accurate as it was. "I really think you should've told me. It would've been reassuring to know how you're taking care of semi-wild magic after everything I've been through," he complained.

"And I really think that someone should've told me what kind of insufferable ass you are." Before he could raise his hackles and hit her with a witty retort, she quickly went on about the group. "They're not going to bother you. Probably won't even realize you're here."

From off near the fireplace, the other exorcist tried finding her voice again. "I rea... I realize... he... is he nice? He... is he?"

"No, not really," he quipped.

Bistra cringed and curled up against herself a little tighter as Seline gave him an utterly withering look. "*Goddess dammit enough*," she hissed under her breath. "Yes, I promise, he's nice. He's safe, too."

"He doesn't look safe. Not safe. Doesn't look safe."

"She's not wrong..." he muttered just loud enough for Seline and only Seline to hear.

"She's not been right about things for a very long time," she said with an almost mournful sigh. "Please, just watch over them. Don't scare them. I'll be back for them as soon as I can."

"Wish you'd tell me what's going on."

She dropped her head and then gave his hand a quick, uncharacteristic squeeze. "Wish I could. Wish I could," she repeated as she turned and quickly slipped out of the room.

Akaran leaned on his cane and looked around the room again, feeling utterly lost and as confused as everyone else there. "So.... hi," he said loud enough for all of them to hear. Bistra weakly waved a hand in his direction, but two of the other three didn't make a move. The woman with the ratty doll took a moment away from brushing out its hair to wave it at him. "Riiight. Hi to the doll, too."

"Sh... she likes... she likes it when people talk to Dina."

He looked over at the other exorcist and tilted his head in confusion. "Dina? Who's that?"

"H... her doll," she said as she pointed at the feeble blonde, "the one... one she's holding. Dina. Her... her baby."

"Oh. Her... baby?"

Bistra curled up in her chair and hugged her legs to her chest. "Uh.. huh. Not... not her real baby. It's a doll. But it's, it's her baby."

"Right. Her baby," he muttered as he walked over and sat a few chairs away from her. His cane made a dull thudding sound when he set it down on the floor and she almost jumped out of her skin. Once she relaxed slightly a little bit later, he tried to talk to her again. "Um... do you have a baby?"

Her eyes went wide and she quickly shook her head no. "Me? No, no baby. I don't need a baby. Don't want can't... no baby. No more babies."

Sore subject, he mused. "Ah, yeah... right. No babies."

"Go... good. They are... they make noise," she said to explain herself. "Too much noise. Can't take noise. Too noisy. All the time. Everything is too noisy."

"I'm not a fan of noise either, it's okay."

Bistra's eyes studied the wooden floor intently. "No. Not okay. Can't be okay. Even quiet things are noisy. Can't you hear it? *You're* noisy. Can hear it all around you."

He looked around himself and lifted his arm to try to peer behind the chair. "I'm just sitting here?"

"Not you," she replied with a wave of her hands like she was drawing a shell around him in the air. "Things *around* you. Air around you is loud. Air that can't be smelled can hear it can see it but it's loud. Doesn't belong. Noises that don't belong. They come from you."

That didn't make him feel any better. He moved his hands in a rough mimicry of hers along his sides and slowly shook his head. "I'm... sorry?"

She blinked and bit at her fingernails. "Why? Not your fault. Noise isn't yours. Noise is around you. Noise is in you. Not your noise. But noisy."

"Noisy, huh?" he said before blinking and realizing what she meant. "Oh! The ether?"

"Ye... yes. Noisy ether. Can hear it. See it too."

"That's right. You're the one that specialized in auramanc... I mean, ether-kenetics?"

Bistra visibly shuddered and nodded as she clutched her hands tight. "Ye... yes. Yes sometimes. I... they... I was called that sometimes."

He raised his hand again and lazily waved it back and forth it in the air. "You can see the ether still, can't you?"

"Can see the noise. Can... can hear the noise can... it's there. Loud when you move. Pl... please don't move?"

Abashedly, he settled down and hung his head before mumbling an apology. "Oh. Oh, I'm so sorry. I won't."

"Is o... is okay. Pro... promise."

He looked over at the other end of the room and tried to study the three madmen lost in their own thoughts. "Am I being too loud for them?"

She twitched in her chair as she followed his gaze. "The... them? N... no, no. They can't hear. Can't... can't much." She raised a shaking hand and pointed at Divitol. "He, he lost his sight. He fought... flying de... de..." she choked on the word, then tried again. "Snake. Flying snake. Not... other thing. That's what... what the healers told me."

"A flying snake?" Akaran looked closely at his face and noted a host of scars that streaked out from around his eyes, nose, lips, and ears. They were joined by smaller bits of blister-damaged tissue. "Those are feedback injuries."

Bistra smiled slightly and pulled a dirty, damaged journal out from under her hip. "Ye... yes. It was... was reflective. When... when they said what did it... I drew a sketch, see?" She opened it up and started to flip through the pages.

Finally, she turned it around and held it open for him to look at it. He was expecting a little scribble; instead, he was greeted with an *incredibly* well-drawn picture depicting a four-winged dragon-like creature. It had ten spikes that jutted out of the top of its long, lanky spine, and each of its feet had three hooked claws that were designed to grip prey and rip it to shreds. The face was the oddest part – while the body was serpentine, the head was almost as flat and wide as the top of a brick with two fish-like bugged-out eyes sitting on the upper corners.

The younger exorcist pursed his lips. *That is NOT a snake.* "That's a... oh, that's... right. That's a... *chulbak*, isn't it?" *One of the few Abyssian species considered 'native' to this side of the Veil.*

Her eyes lit up and she gave him a genuine smile. "Ye... yes. I saw one. Once. Years ago."

"Native to the Southern Grazelands of Civa, right? If I remember?" *Blessedly rare and incredibly territorial in regards to their own species. They're so close to dragon-kin that there was a dispute for decades if they were unholy or not. Took a brave idiot with a death wish to see if an exorcism would work to classify them right.*

"Yes! You know them?"

He pursed his lips and shook his head. "I've never seen one. But I studied a little. They... let me think. They have a habit of interfering with spell work and they're one of the few things that like to hunt drakes, aren't they? How'd one of our priests even manage to stumble across one?"

"He's... not Order. Hunter. He -"

Seline opened the door and called out for them, sighing loudly in relief when she realized he was still there. "Akaran? Good you're still here."

"You thought I was going to hobble off after just a few minutes?" he asked. "Besides, where am I gonna go that you wouldn't know about with guards traipsing out in the halls?"

"Guar... guards in the hall?" Bistra interrupted as the healer glared a hole into the young man's face.

"Just... leave it be," she warned before calling out to the others. "Appaidene? I need you."

From the other side of the room, she nodded and waved her doll at them. When that didn't get a response, she started to make bird-like chirping sounds. When *that* didn't get any response, she started to pout.

Seline ran her hands through her hair and lightly bounced the back of her head off of the door frame. "I don't even know why we have her here."

"She seems nice?" Akaran offered.

"She'd be better in a monastery," she retorted before calling out again. "Appaldene? Come with me sweetie. We need you."

The waif of a blonde continued to pout and started to sulk over to them with her doll in tow. "*Chi-chir-chirrup?*"

Seline didn't try to respond to the tottering young woman and turned her attention back to the exorcist. "I'll be back shortly. Keep your eyes on the rest?"

"Just one," Bistra quipped.

Seline gave her a puzzled look. "What?"

"Just one," she repeated. "He just has one eye. See?" she added as she pointed at his face. "He can't keep both eyes. Just one."

The pair of them gave each other the same pained look as he replied, "I'll keep watch."

"Please," the healer implored as she took Appaidene's hand and escorted her out of the dining hall.

That, once again, left Akaran to his own devices. Seemingly satisfied she had talked to him enough, the other exorcist plucked a piece of charcoal out from behind her ear and quickly started to sketch something out in her journal. After a few minutes of giving him furtive glances between strokes on the paper, he gave in to the uncomfortable silence and started to ask her what she was doing.

"Drawing," she said before he could even get the question out.

"What are you drawing?"

"A drawing," she explained.

When she didn't see fit to elaborate on that, he tried again. "I can see, but what are you...?"

She set the little stick down and stared up at the ceiling with an intensely confused look on her face. "What am I? I am... I am me. I don't know what else I am. I... I am... I... I'm drawing."

The priest fought the urge to tug at his hair before giving up and peering over the edge of the sketchbook, and raised his eyebrow when he saw what she was doing. "Hey. That's me."

"No, the drawing is *of* you. *You* are you. What I am is drawing," she dismissively explained as his head started to throb for no polite reason.

A second, closer look and he realized that what he had first thought were just stray marks on the paper were actually something else. She had sketched in dark tendrils of various sizes sprouting out from behind his head and down his right leg. He recognized them for exactly what they were without asking and felt his stomach fall to the bottom of his bowels.

"Um... what are those?" he asked anyway, *hoping* that it'd be anything but.

She didn't look away from her journal as she dismissed him with a little wave of her hand. "The noise around you. You can't hear it. I can tell."

"No. That's not noise," he argued with his voice almost in a growl, "I know what that is, that's not around me. I got rid of it."

Bistra put another tendril on the paper, this time near his mouth (and he was almost convinced she did it on purpose). "It's hard to quiet noise sometimes. Stays with you. There's noise around me, too. Can you see it?"

He leaned back and tried to size this strange broken priest up to no avail. There was absolutely no doubt in his mind that she had lost her mind. The bigger question was what was left behind. "No. No, I'm sorry. I can't."

"Would you like to?" she asked as she finally looked back up at him with her off-putting star-flecked eyes.

There was a moment when he thought he saw a reflection of his aura in them before she blinked and the image faded away. "I'd like nothing more. I don't know if I ever can again."

"Of course you can. It will be easier when the ice gets out of your eye. I can show you. For now. This way? This way now you can see," the other exorcist said as she started to flip through her sketchbook.

He struggled to keep his face from faltering. *Ice out of my eye? How can she possibly know...?*

Over the next few minutes, she showed him pictures she had sketched of herself. Just like the others, they were incredibly well done – you could almost describe them as insanely so without being off base. Most of them depicted her in her room, peering out her window or tucked into a corner in her room on her bed. A few of the sketches had her standing in the back of the atrium, and one just showed her face.

All of them, however, had one other thing in common. In each picture, there was a humanoid shadow in the corner. Or peering in through the window. Or in one case, wrapped all around her. In the atrium sketch, it was between her and the effigies to the Gods. In a few others, there were what looked like little fangs poking out of the top of it. "See? The noise around me." In the most recent ones, he saw that there was a round pendant or necklace of some kind in them, always just on the edges of the paper.

Akaran reached over and ran his finger across the shadow like he was tempting to bite. "What is that?"

"Noise," she said, "noise with fangs. Always. Even now. It's here."

"It's... here?" he asked as he stiffened up instinctively. If he'd been able, there were three different Words he'd utter then and now. As it was, the best he could do was scour the room with a paranoid glare as he clutched at the arms of his chair.

There wasn't a damn thing he could see, though the priestess continued to profess otherwise. "Always here. The fangs are always here."

"But there's nothing -" he started before the dining hall door swung half open and Seline stuck her head through it.

"Bistra. It's your turn sweetie."

He quickly raised his hand up between the two of them to top her from standing up just yet. "Seline? She was just saying that there's something in here."

The healer paused and gave him a tired and sad smile. "A shadow? Yes, she always sees the shadows," she said as she walked over and helped Bistra stand up. "The dark took her once. I don't think it ever let go."

That struck a little *too* close to home and he handed the other exorcist her journal back before she could walk away. "Bistra? It was... nice... talking to you."

She smiled nervously down at him and clutched the journal tight to her belly. "And you. Though loud. Too loud."

Seline raised her eyebrows, then leaned in and whispered a quiet not-really-a-request to him. "Don't. Yell. At. The. Guests."

His protests to the contrary were completely ignored.

The next fifteen, nearly twenty minutes elapsed with nothing but boredom. Tanstin moved away from his disinterested companion and began to gibber incomprehensibly at the fireplace. The priest walked over to try to see if he could get a response from the poor man, but one whiff of his putrid breath scuttled that idea on the spot. That left the quiet madman, and the atrocious scarring all over his head was enough to turn his stomach before he could bring himself to doing it.

The only thing that left him to do was to start to stretch his leg and peer into the corners of the room, half-heartedly looking for Bistra's supposed shadows. A bit later, Seline wandered back into the dining hall and collected the gray-skinned and gray-haired gibbering sap.

When she was gone, the remaining patient quietly shuffled over to the priest and sat down directly across from him. After a few uneasy minutes of staring at each other, Akaran tried to break the silence with a simple, "Um, hi?"

That didn't get any kind of reaction. Several more minutes passed where the only thing he could do was just watch a little bubble of spit in the corner of Divitol's mouth inflated and deflated with every wheezing breath the man tool. Desperately, he looked for something else to do.

And didn't find a damn thing.

After what felt like an eternity of uncomfortable silence, the borderline comatose guest spoke up. His voice was gravely and rough, and there was an uncomfortable wheeze from deep in the back of his throat. "Not a spirit."

The sudden sound made Akaran almost jump out of his seat. "What?"

Divitol steeled his fingers and turned his scarred head towards the doorway. "Not a spirit. Fangs are real. Not a dream. In dreams. But not."

Just like that, the priest focused his full attention on the madman and felt his jaw clench tight. "Have you seen it?"

The question went unanswered for several long minutes. "Once."

"Didn't you tell someone?"

"Wouldn't believe," he grunted. "Don't think I talk."

"You don't seem so chatty, no."

The blind man squinted and his scars wrinkled up disconcertingly. "Don't like talk. Hurts."

"Then why tell me?" the exorcist asked, leaning back slightly in his seat.

Divitol shrugged and subtly gestured towards the door with his shoulder. "You collect. They don't."

"Collect?"

"Trophies."

The priest stared at him, utterly puzzled. "I don't collect trophies..."

He grunted noncommittally as he pointed at his leg. "Do. You carry two. Eye. Leg."

It almost felt insulting to have the old wounds called *trophies,* but maybe for him it made sense. "They're reminders more then trophies, I guess."

"You do. Of *things,*" he said, stressing the word so hard that it made his skin crawl. He lingered with a long pause and then asked, "Guardian of Winters?"

The title said with that gravely voice was unnerving, but not as much as hearing it at all. "How... how did you know...? Did someone say something to you?"

Akaran heard someone at the door as the madman leaned in and spoke in a hushed whisper. "In the room. Under bed. Third board from moonwall. Things explained."

"What in the world? What things? What room?" Then after a moment, he added, "What's a moonwall?"

Seline gave the scarred huntsman a sad little look after walking into the room. "Won't get anything from him. He doesn't talk."

"He just told me that you guys didn't think he could."

She studied his face and then replied with the faintest of smiles. "Oh he does, does he? Did he happen to say anything else?"

Her disbelief raised his hackles for reasons he didn't quite understand, but they raised regardless. "That the fangs are real."

"Did he now," she said with that same not-quite-condescending tone. "Well. Thank you for watching over them. I'll come get you in a few minutes."

After she was gone, he sat back and glared down at his knee. "I don't collect trophies."

Before long, he'd realize how wrong he was.

Seline brought him back to the atrium a little bit later and to what amounted to an unhappy tribunal. Ridora was there, and joining the two healers was a man he'd only had the displeasure to meet in passing. Henderschott wasn't wearing his helmet this time, so his closely-shaven ash blonde hair was on full display.

As was the rest of him, in his full Glorious Army of the Dawn motif. It felt like overkill for a simple garden meeting, but who was Akaran to judge? Before they could get out a single word, he lifted his cane and interrupted Ridora before she could start. "Can you *please* tell me what's going on?"

"Unfortunately," she said, sighing into her hand, "and you're the last one to be questioned." She looked as disheveled, if not worse, than Seline. Henderschott's glare just made him look like he was ready to set the world on fire.

It was, the exorcist quickly decided, a reasonable feeling.

He frowned and sat down in one of a handful of chairs scattered about. They'd sequestered themselves in a corner and there wasn't enough sunlight splitting through the clouds above to keep them from extinguishing the torches. "About what? I haven't done anything."

"No one is saying you have," the lady of the manor reassured him.

"But you're assuming," he pointed out, "or else you wouldn't have saved me for last."

Seline's frustrated sigh returned. "You're the most lucid of any of the other guests. The sooner that we could calm the others down, the better."

"Doesn't mean you haven't done it," the guardsman grumbled under his breath.

He shook his head and lifted his cane. "All I've been doing is reading. Just reading. Can't fis -" he started before catching Ridora's glare, "- can't *focus* on anything else."

"Remains to be seen," Henderschott charged as the two women beside him rolled their eyes. "For all intents and purposes, you are one of the most dangerous of any of Ridora's guests."

"We went over this," Seline interrupted, "no he's not."

That didn't soothe the priest any, and his already-knotted shoulders took on a mind of their own. "Interested in a demonstration?" he growled at the guard.

"We might have already had one," the slightly-older and vastly-cockier soldier retorted.

Seline's sigh was matched by the lady of the manor dropping her head into her hands. "Men. Must we?"

"Yes. We must," Henderschott snapped back at her. "What were you doing last night?"

"Sleeping. Badly," he retorted. When he caught the evil eye Seline started to throw at him, he didn't bring up the why. "What were you doing last night?"

Flipping the question didn't make the commander any happier. "Sleeping. With someone."

"I'm sorry."

"What?"

Akaran looked him up and down and smirked. "If she slept through it, you must be as boring as you look."

Seline devolved into a coughing and spluttering fit that didn't win her *any* points with Henderschott. Lady Ridora choked back an un-ladylike noise of her own, then stamped her foot on the ground. "*Enough*, gentlemen. I did not bring you two here for a cock-fencing match."

"Not much of a match," the priest retorted, "apparently, he's boring," which, for some reason, made the blonde healer choke up even harder.

"AKARAN!"

Henderschott ignored her and crossed his arms over his chest. "Let him get it off his chest. I can see he's not the one we're after."

"He's just upset that your stick is bigger than his," Seline mumbled out of the corner of her mouth to the priest, with her hand over her face.

While the guardsman leaned in and started to demand her to repeat that, Akaran interjected himself back into the commentary. "Maybe if you told me what you were after, I could answer the question."

"If I thought you were capable of anything, I'd have already asked it."

This time the lady turned to him and pointed her finger at him. "HENDERSCHOTT."

The other healer lifted her face to the skies and mouthed a prayer for guidance before adding in a shout of her own. "BOYS. *ENOUGH*. This is *not* the damn time!"

"No. It is not," Ridora added, "and a poor time made all the worse with us on edge."

"I'm not on edge," he protested. "I'm *fine*. Although if you three don't quit glaring daggers at me I'm going to start feeling unwelcome. What in the pit is going on?"

When the Lieutenant-Commander finished cursing under his breath at him, he finally offered what the priest already knew. "What's going *on* is that a woman was attacked last night."

"Livstra, I heard. So why are -"

"You *heard* or you had a hand in?" he demanded.

Seline lifted her hand slightly. "I told him, Hender."

"You were told not to tell a soul until we brought them -"

"I was a bastard about getting up until she told me what was going on," Akaran interrupted in her defense. "So I'm taking a guess that you've been going through everyone to see who did it?"

Ridora nodded slowly. "While we have no reason to believe that any of our residents would, it is a sad acknowledgment that not all of them have responded well to treatments. Given past traumas... we had a list of most likely that had to be seen first."

He sat there and looked back and forth between the two of them. "Since he's calling me your most dangerous guest, that means either you *don't* think that I did it, or you were asking everyone in the rooms around me first in case they heard me do something that might point to my guilt."

"Oh? And how did you come to that conclusion?" Henderschott half-sneered.

"Because if I was assigned to watch over the last handful of their patients to be interviewed, then you obviously interviewed the ones sharing my hallway first because those four aren't on it. You *also* didn't come into my room to tell me anything was wrong until you *had* to *and* there's no chance that you considered that collection of half-wits to be threats to anything but your noses."

Ridora's left eyebrow arched up as she straightened herself up in the chair. The guardsman answered with a vaguely-impressed smirk and draped his arm over the back of his chair while the healer just put her hand on his leg. "If we *did*, the Lieutenant Commander would already have you in shackles," Seline reassured him. "Please. I know you were in your room last night reading. Did you hear anything, see anything? Did you leave your room at all?"

"No. Like I already told you: I ate. Came here and prayed. Went back to my room, chewed some root, and tried to sleep. That Goddess-damned pig had me tossing and turning more than the dreams did."

She pulled her hand off of his leg and started to hiss at him through clenched teeth. "That pig -"

"- was horrible, I agree," the lady interjected. It was nice, at least from Akaran's perspective, that someone else earned the Look of Death from the healer. Ridora didn't seem half as amused and he was fairly sure that Seline didn't have grounds to threaten her.

She did it anyway, of course. "My Lady, I swear if I hear about that roast one more time..."

The guardsman waved them both into silence. "When your stomach woke you up, did you hear anything?"

"It was quiet last night."

"So you heard nothing," he grunted out in frustration.

"That's what I mean," he said with a shake of his head, "it was *quiet*."

Henderschott pursed his lips while the two women exchanged glances. "Is that unusual?" he asked.

"Yes."

Ridora sucked lightly at her cheek and then added, "We do have some nights that are louder than others. We are a ward for those that have disturbances of the mind and body. It brings a level of disquiet that we sometimes have trouble mitigating."

"My head was pounding all night. Felt like someone was trying to squeeze it in a vise. Between that and my stomach, I was grateful for it."

"No shouts, no screams?" the guardsman pressed, "and you didn't leave your room at all?"

"No. Can someone tell me what happened? Please? Is she going to be alright?"

Hender continued to glare at him and managed to contort his face to look like even more of a condescending prick. "I thought you said you knew."

"That she was attacked," Akaran countered, "though I've kinda gotten the feeling that isn't the full truth."

Ridora shook her head and pressed him harder. "Think, please. Have you heard any of the other residents or staff say anything poorly about her? Anyone ever speak ill of her?"

"No. No, not a soul. Of course, I don't talk to much of anyone..."

That wasn't good enough for the guard. "What did *you* think of her?"

He had to stop and massage that thought a few times before answering. "Not much, though not less than others. I don't think she likes me. But she was fair. I hated what she did with my leg but -"

"So you admit you aren't fond of her," he charged half-triumphantly.

Akaran shook his head. "I'm not fond of anyone that presses on my knee," he said as he cast an apologetic look at the two healers. "Sorry, it's not personal, it's just..."

"It is reasonable," the lady replied with a sad little nod. "How is it I once heard it said? Therapy is sadism legalized by the Queen?"

"Wasn't I the one that said it?"

"You were not wrong," she quipped.

Seline, on the other hand, was not so forgiving. "There is going to be *extra* therapy later if you utter another word about my roast."

It was the first of her threats he finally decided to take seriously. "You were the chef? Oh," he said as his eye went wide a little, "sorry. Okay. So. She was attacked, I gathered. Is she going to be alright?"

"I'm not sure you should be told," Henderschott grumbled.

"You know, I haven't even really talked to you except in passing before now. Who are you to judge me?"

"He's in charge of the city garrison," Ridora replied, "and as for the specifics of what happened, the details are not so important."

"If you're going to accuse me of it, I'd say it is," he argued.

The younger healer stroked his left leg softly with her hand. "Nobody is accusing you."

"He does," he said as he shook his head and brushed her hand away. "You brought me in last to question me about it and you've gone through everyone else. I am assuming she's injured to the point she can't talk, so you can tell me at least what happened. One of the other patients get angry and hit her?"

"It's worse than 'can't talk,' Akaran," Seline managed to choke out as she cupped her hands in her own lap. "She... she was killed."

"Murdered," the guard pointed out, "cruelly."

"Oh, pits," the exorcist sighed as he slumped over and bowed his head out of respect. "I'm sorry. Sincerely, and deeply, I am. Please tell me what happened?"

Sel shook her head and tried to hide her face behind her golden locks. "I can't. I'm sorry, I..."

Dropping his hand down to his sword, the Lieutenant raised his eyebrow and attempted to stare daggers into the side of Akaran's head. "Insistent."

With a nasty look right back at him, he spat back at him angrily, "Someone gets killed. I'm assuming violently. And I don't hear a thing. Yes, I'm going to be insistent."

"Why do you assume violently?"

"Because if you gripped your sword any harder you're going to break the handle."

The guard looked down at the hilt and then slowly relaxed his grip as he peered over at Ridora out of the corner of his eyes. "Is he stable enough?"

"My leg is broken, not my mind," Akaran argued.

Seline coughed slightly between sniffles, interrupting them to add, "There's an active debate over that."

With a short nod, the lady gave her approval. Henderschott focused his gaze back on the priest, and began to explain. "She was mutilated. Her eyes were removed and her chest was ravaged," he said as the other healer bit back another tired little sobbing sound. "It appears she was forced to choke to death on her own tongue, though it could have easily been strangulation or loss of blood. Her remains are still being examined."

A touch of color faded from Akaran's cheeks as he let out a guttural, 'ooof' from the back of his throat. "That's more than just *violent*, blessed be. Nobody heard anything? "

"Nobody, even you, if you speak the truth."

"If I had, I would have said," he replied to the guardsman, going on to say, "Pits, I would've done something. Anything."

Ridora nodded gravely. "I believe you. We all do – don't we?"

"I don't think he has it in him," Seline replied.

Henderschott rubbed the heel of his boot into the ground as he sized the exorcist up for the third time since he hobbled into the garden. "I do. I think he has it in him to do that much and more."

"He does," Ridora replied with a smile that was either oddly proud or slightly heartbroken, "just only when it is deserved, isn't that right?"

"When the Gods say do, we do," Akaran replied with a tired little sigh, "no other way to argue it."

"Not with your record, no," Henderschott added.

"Seen it?"

"Heard."

"Fair enough," the exorcist replied with another sigh and a shake of his head. "If I can do something to help, tell me. I will. I may not have been fond of her but I never thought she deserved anything like you just described. The only thing that I know is what Divitol said earlier."

Tilting his head, Hender looked down at the empty chair beside him and a piece of unrolled parchment. "The mute? We couldn't get a word from the man."

That got Ridora's attention more than anything else he'd said so far. "He said something to you? Interesting. What, exactly?"

"That the 'fangs are real,' and that he doesn't think you guys believe that he can talk."

"I already told you he can't," Seline argued.

The guardsman rolled his eyes dismissed him with a wave of his hand. "More rubbish. Well. Let me assure you of one thing, exorcist: when we find out what happened to her, there will be fangs and they will be *very* real, indeed.

The healer beside him interrupted Akaran before he could say a word. "I don't think there's anything else to be said here. Akaran this... this is not a place for you to be at today. Please, go out tonight."

He looked over at her with a mix of confused surprise on his face. "You're throwing me out?"

"No, it's not that," she replied slowly, "it's that this is not a place of health today. You need a place of life."

"She is right. Those that do not need to be here for the tasks ahead of the day shouldn't if they have a choice," Ridora added, then to the guardsman, "Henderschott? Isn't the Bewedded March today?"

Akaran didn't think it would've been possible for him to look even more disgusted. He was wrong. "It is. One grand headache."

"One grand arrival," she corrected, a single finger lifting from her lap.

"Headache," he repeated. "Royals being royals and taking up my time."

The exorcist glanced back at him and flicked his tongue against his teeth. "I might like you after all."

Seline tried to brush her dress back into shape as she wiped tears from her eyes. "Go... go and watch it. Please. It would do you good."

He thought about arguing and for a change, decided that discretion might be the better part of valor. "I... I guess. I'd rather stay here and help."

"There's no way you can," she replied. "A night away from your studies and your efforts will aid your recovery."

"But... I don't know where to go to watch it at... the city gate?"

"Try the *Drunken Imperial*," Henderschott suggested, "it's an inn in Lower Naradol.

Ridora's glance at him could've made the grass behind the man whither and it's a miracle it didn't. "That district is no place for one of my charges."

"He'll fit in," he argued, "vastly easier than anywhere else if I've read him *half* as well as I think I have. Plus, it's safe enough. With the patrols out today, nobody will be out of line."

"Someone was," Seline whispered.

"They *will* be brought to task for it. I give my word, Seline. She'll be avenged."

"She will," Ridora replied soothingly, "there will be peace back in these walls. I promise. But for you, Akaran, there will be merriment. We will call for you if we need you again."

He put up a few more disgruntled objections to their deaf-turned-ears. When that didn't work, he finally took his leave and went to go find someone to tell him how to make it down there. On the way out, he couldn't help but feel like the shadows were peering at him and that ever guard he passed was giving him a *look*.

After he left, the three of them conferred for another few minutes. "He didn't have anything to do with it," Henderschott told the two of them.

"I could have told you that," Seline retorted with a sniffle.

"You did," he reminded her, "and he didn't."

Ridora relaxed in her chair and slipped the dagger she'd been sitting on out from hiding from under her hip. "You weren't so sure earlier."

"I am now," he repeated, "and I'm right about something else, too."

"You frequently are, Lieutenant. What other thing are you right about?"

He stood up and pointed at the door the priest had left through. "That kid's leg heals? There's gonna be violence. I don't know who it'll be aimed at, or what, but maybe it's a good idea to *not* patch that one up."

Seline blinked a few times and wiped her hair out of her face. "What could possibly make you think that?"

"Didn't you listen to him? *'When the Gods say we do, we do,'*" he quoted. "If that boy gets a message he thinks is from the Gods he'd kill every single one of us without thinking it over twice. I'm damn sure he's the most dangerous man here and I'm fairly sure he's the scariest motherfisker in the city. Zealots are *dangerous* and he's one good knee away from proving it."

The two women pondered him in silence as the warning made them both feel a little sicker to their stomachs. They quietly concluded the meeting without any more luck nor leads, and went back to work trying to restore the Manor to some sense of order.

He was wrong, of course.

That title, for now, wasn't owned by the exorcist.

There's a theory that says that certain buildings exist in the world only to arrange meetings between people at certain points in time. A suggestion, an idea, that a singular place only exists because a grand creator has call to make it so. That the combined efforts of masons and woodworkers and weavers and blacksmiths would all come together to create an edifice not knowing that it would hold a mark of history.

If that theory were to hold true, the *Drunken Imperial* might be one of those places. Singularly forgettable, utterly important, and for an inn that only stood a pair of stories tall in a city full of buildings that eclipsed it easily, you'd be forgiven if you forgot it existed. It wasn't as dilapidated as the other inns and taverns in Lower Naradol, a fact that Celestine 'Cel' Navarshi took a great deal of pride in.

She also took pride in being the only female inn-keep in the entirety of Basion, but took no delight in one of the two people standing along the eastern balcony on the second level. That profound lack of delight was matched and shared by the self-described bodyguard, although to be entirely fair, he didn't really like anyone. "I simply don't see the point behind this."

Lady Anais showered him with the faint praise of her pale-pink lips curling into a slight smile. "Oh, Donta, it's just a wedding. People are allowed to be happy."

"I don't see happy people."

She looked down at the throng of people lining the streets and then off in the distance where the full envoy from Clan Odinal was making their official arrival into town under torchlight, magelight, and whatever other light the locals could throw fit together. "Tsk. You barely can stand to see people."

You could've drowned half of the assembly in his navy blue eyes, and frankly, he'd enjoy every minute of it. "Chattel. Meat sacks in skin."

"Dower, even for you," she chided.

"They're beneath us."

"They may be," Anais replied, "and yet we've been beneath them."

He looked over at her and felt his lip curl as she enjoyed a mug of tea that cost more than what the inn was actually worth. "We're not now."

That damnable smile returned and made the wrinkles in her face vanish for a heartbeat. "All the more reason to be happy."

He quieted down and started to follow her as she walked across the balcony. The parade was being attended by almost every person in the city, and wound from the main gates through four different districts before it would come to an end at the Ellachurstine Chapel. "Seen more mages today than I ever want to see again," he groused.

"Mages and guards and priests. Too many of each, I happen to agree," she sighed, idly trailing a gloved finger down the edge of the balcony railing. "Can't fault them for wanting to find their happiness either. It's a feeling that is oft in short supply in this world."

"Shorter elsewhere."

She tilted her head slightly in agreement, then studied his face worriedly. "No question of that. Are you feeling alright today? You're even more irritable than the norm."

"I don't *feel* and you know it. Neither do you."

Anais wagged her finger at him so delicately she might've not even moved at all. "I feel enough. I can feel the anger radiating off of you, for one."

He grunted and didn't answer her until that *damn* smile pushed him over the edge. "Keep tripping over undesirables. Had to deal with that parchment-mage earlier, on top of it."

"Which one?"

"Ishtva," he replied, as if it explained everything.

And it did. Her smile disappeared and her lips quickly matched the sneer of disgust on his. "The Eyes of the Annex," she said, the word coming out like she had just stepped in a pile of manure. "I am so glad that you were able to get him to agree to do business with us. Get anything from him this time through?"

"A desire to hit him," Donta replied with a shake of his bald head. "There's been nothing new entering the Repository – yet."

"Yet?"

"They've been told to expect a shipment entering the city soon. The Oo-lo's have been busy ransacking that mess in the eastern mountains."

Sneer switched to concern, and concern made her straighten ever-so-slightly. "More fallout?"

"Yes," he grumbled, "Documents. Tools. Relics. Whatever the Granalchi didn't attempt to claim or outright steal from those cocksucking fools. Ishtva is equally upset and excited"

"Of course he would be. If they go past his desk the Bladebane will know more about it than anyone else the Academy could send to Toniki, I suppose."

"He couldn't have been more excited if he tried," the bodyguard replied, "but pissed that they're about to get entombed."

"Yes well, he can be as pissed as he wishes. I'm vastly more interested as to what they have been looking for in the west... or the south."

Donta's eyes narrowed. "The south? The only thing south of here is open water."

"Open but not as exposed to prying eyes as they wished the waters to be," she told him as she turned back to the cheering crowds lining the street. "The dockworkers. They are very angry about a missing ship. The one I mentioned to you earlier, that even set us in a bind?"

"Still? Ships go missing all the time."

Anais shook her head and took a long drink from her copper mug. "Not in clear weather. Nor do they always get the interest of the mote."

"Interest of the...?" he started and trailed off before grabbing her by her arm and turning her around so fast she almost dropped her drink. "He's *here*?!"

She pulled herself free of his grip and swatted his hand away when he tried to make a second, almost panicked, grab at her. "No, not now."

"But earlier. He was here," he pressed.

"Unfortunately. I grow weary of hearing from it."

The bodyguard slipped his sword into his hand and pulled it halfway out of its sheath. "You didn't tell me? What did he say? What did he want?"

"Nothing more than the usual from that vile piece of bile, and no urgent trouble for us," she assured him as she tried to project a calming aura around him that, truthfully, she didn't believe herself. "Why we're behind, why we don't know, why haven't we made a move yet."

It didn't help. "You didn't think to tell me? We promised that there'd be no secrets between us," he snapped back at her.

"There's no secret to be had," she replied with a gentle nod of her head, "so calm yourself, angry one. I only saw him hours ago and saw no reason to run after you like an upset newlywed chasing after her husband."

"Don't be insulting."

She arched an eyebrow and rubbed at her arm. "Don't be petulant and my insults won't be needed," she cautioned, then with a harsh gaze that belied anything else she was attempting to say, added, "and I believe you know how I feel about being *touched*."

Donta cringed and backed away, placated for a moment. "I... yes. Apologies."

"Accepted. It's a joyous night, after all."

The remainder of the threat left unsaid, he refused to return her gaze and instead latched his eyes on a man wandering through the throng below. "A night, yes."

Anais continued on without missing a beat. "What he *did* say was that there has been a ripple someplace there shouldn't be. That of all odd things, that ship may hold the cause of it. Our benefactor is not thrilled about it, but he may try to bend it to our interests."

"Bend it how? Has he added 'raise a ship from the sea' to his talents?" he scoffed.

She paused and took a sip from her cup. "Only to offer a reminder that pandemics loosen lips."

The bodyguard didn't say anything for the longest time before replying, "That doesn't bode well."

"No. It doesn't," she agreed. "I feel he wants to make a move on the board soon. He wants the Urn, and the mote let slip he's after some other relics. They aren't believed to be here, but in our efforts to secure that glorified chamberpot, we are asked to keep our senses attuned for leads."

"As if there isn't enough to do."

"Quite," she agreed again. "After much needling, I was able to coax it out of him. 'The Heart of the Doppelganger,' the 'Axe of Nightmares,' the 'Diamond of Skrah,' the 'Diamantic Blade,' and some book that he claims to have lost. 'The Book of the Past Dead.' Never have I met a man so, so..."

Donta chewed on his lip and continued to stare down at Akaran, who was otherwise blissfully unaware anyone had seen him, nor cared if they had. "Enticed by a flair for the dramatic?"

"Would you expect less from one such as he?"

"No. So. We're being pushed for time, given more work, and a vague threat. How quaint."

She nodded, then gravely replied with, "Best forewarned is forearmed, even from him."

"*Especially* him," he agreed, "both of them." He reached for her and stopped before actually touching her cool skin, and then gestured down to the street. "There. See that one?"

Her eyes followed his finger. "Who? The one with the stick?"

"Him. That's the sad broken priest you had me ask about."

Anais made a soft 'hm' sound as she sized him up. "Oh. Interesting. He doesn't look so... threatening. Are you sure that's the one responsible for the swirling storm of shit brewing eastward?"

"Told you he wasn't. And yes."

"Does look lost though," she mused, "I wonder if he needs to be found."

Donta stopped himself from expressing his actual opinion, and instead opted to *gingerly* caution her. "Don't get close. Don't know how broken he is."

The lady flicked her tongue against her lips and smiled slowly, more or less ignoring his tension. "True. Though, a limping exorcist that can make his way into storage is more helpful than a healthy one we can't get near. It never hurts to dabble in the waters."

"Don't drown."

"I can't see as how I could, not with you by my side," she said with that irritating as all smile aimed at the back of his head. "You're always there to pull me up when I need to swim."

He didn't bother to reply as she made her way off the balcony and down into the bar below. Akaran was leaning against the bar, cane propped up beside him, and Celestine-the-innkeep bemusedly flirting with him to earn a few crowns to an incredible lack of success. The only focus he had was making a dirty look at the ox-horned flagon in his hand and the frothing *stuff* on top of it.

Anais caught Cel's eye and glared at her until she shut her rounded jowls and went to go pester another customer. "You know, they say that the only people that drink here are ones that are trying to forget something or those that regret what they remember," she said right behind him.

"I regret the taste," he grumbled without turning around.

"That would be a thing to forget."

He sat it down and made a disgusted look. "I do not see how."

"A day like today, it is easy to see how," she purred.

He looked out the closest window and stared at the throng outside. "It's not day anymore."

"Or night," she countered, "nights can be fun at times."

Akaran sat down on a stool and shook his head. "Not from where I'm from."

"And where would that be, hm?" she pressed, joining him on the opposite stool much to his chagrin.

"Not from here," he sighed before taking a long and hard drink out of the mug. A choking gag afterward followed, coupled with a hasty wipe of the foaming mess off of his goatee. "Forgive me lady, I don't really want to talk to anyone. I'm just here because they told me to come watch."

Anais lit up with the same smile she kept trying to force on her bodyguard and somehow had even less luck than Celestine did. "You can't watch and listen at the same time? It's a skill we should all strive to master. Telling the difference between what we see and what we hear."

The exorcist shook his head and grimaced like he was about to spit some of the ale back out. "I don't think that you understand. I'm not really in the mood to chat. If you don't mind, lady...?"

"Lovic," she replied with another purr.

"Lady... Lovic. Fine I -"

"But please, do call me Anais," she interrupted.

He looked down at the mug and tried not to growl his reply. "Lady Anais Lovic," he repeated, "fine, hi. Now if you don't mind...?"

"Hello there as well. How've you been enjoying your stay in Basion... DeHawk, isn't it?"

The exorcist slowly slid his hand down from the mug and turned to face her. "How'd you know?"

"I hear things," she answered with a dismissive wave of her hand. "There's few priests in this town of your age with a cane. So, have you?"

Mollified – for the moment – he responded simply. "It's... nice. I guess it's nice."

"It's the safest place in the kingdom," she replied with a bemused smile. "Which is a truly odd thing to say. I don't know about you but the thought of living in what is essentially an open grave? It does very little for my nerves."

Akaran ground his molars together and for the life of him, he couldn't figure out why. "An open grave? We're in a basin."

Anais raised her finger and then gestured around the room with a sweep of her hand. "And what is a basin but a hole in the ground with nothing to cover it? And as we stand here, waiting for a throng of merry men and women to come prancing down the street, there are naught but walls about us – weeping on one end from the falls above, draining into a ditch at the other? The safest place in the kingdom, mayhaps, but it does say a lot for how people to be safe they prefer to hide with their head in the ground."

It wasn't the way he would've described the city, but now it was the only way he was going to think of it. "Huh. Well, could be worse."

"It could? However so?"

"We aren't dwarves," he countered, "so we, at least, can still see the sky above us. No risk of getting buried."

"Always a risk of getting buried," she said with a smile that made him feel like that was more of a threat than not, "even in the safest place in the kingdom."

"Riiight," he said with a groan and a roll of his tongue before starting to turn back to his mug. "Well then, Lady Lovic -"

"Anais, please," she interrupted.

He didn't even try to hide the roll of his eye. "Fine, Lady Anais, I've been hobbling around for the last few candlemarks and I imagine that there's other people you'd love to talk to and I'm just -"

"How have you been enjoying your studies at the Repository?" she quickly interrupted a second time.

"It's studying. It's not a thing to do for enjoyment," he replied before he could stop himself. A dirty look at the mug of ale after made it clear what he blamed for the slip, eliciting a quiet laugh from the irritating inquisitor beside him.

"Oh, of course it is! Opening a tome, reading the history of the men and women that came before us," Anais gushed, "discovering new places and worlds the likes of which we were never meant to see with our own eyes. It is a way to expand the mind and to take in such broader concepts than just a day of, well, sitting by and watching a parade."

"I like sitting by," he said as he grimaced and started to shift back and forth on his feet. "Discovering new places is why I'm walking with this damn cane."

"There will be other times, you know. Are you being well-treated, at least? For the pain?"

Akaran pushed the mug back and turned all the way around to stare at this frustrating, invasive, and far-too-chipper woman. "Okay, who are you? What do you want from me?"

She tried to slip her hand over his and missed cleanly when he jerked it away. "Just to talk," she replied, "you're an interesting person, from what I've heard. I like to meet interesting people."

"You heard wrong. I just wanted to watch the march. Do you mind, please?"

"No, I don't mind at all. It is a delightful thing to watch, don't you agree?"

"I did," he grunted.

That infernal smile lit up her face again and made his skin crawl. "And now?"

"And now..." he started to reply before letting the answer trail die unsaid. "And now, have a pleasant evening, Lady Anais. I don't like to talk to people I don't know."

"Then how do you ever get to know people?"

He pushed himself away from the bar and left the mug behind. "I've been realizing that it's better to not."

Anais shook her head and raised a dainty hand again as if that alone would be enough to stop him from going. "You'll find it's better to know than not – a word of advice. I am worth talking to, you'll find."

"I'm not," he retorted. After giving the horn of 'ale' another dirty look, he sauntered off mumbling irritated little epithets under his breath.

Once he was back on the street and safely outside of earshot, she replied to that loud enough that Donta could hear once he was standing in his place behind her. "I'd disagree."

"I wouldn't," her bodyguard grunted. "Told you he's nothing special."

"And you'd be so very wrong."

"There's plenty of places to find broken assholes, Anais."

She conceded that point with a nod and traced her fingers over his mug. "Yes – this is true. You noticed what he did, didn't you?"

"Pout?"

"He didn't notice what you feared he would," she clarified as she shot a smug little grin out the door after him. "*That* means he is useful. Watch him. I suspect we will need him soon enough."

Outside, the parade continued.

All throughout the city, merriment was had. Diplomats waved from the top of horse-drawn carriages, couriers scampered down the sides of the streets, and children ran back and forth with unbidden shouts of joy as gold and red flags fluttered behind them in their wake. Music played from seemingly everywhere and nowhere while hedgemages and warlocks made the sky shine with explosive bursts of sound and light.

As Akaran hobbled along and let himself get ever-so-briefly distracted by the flamboyant theatrics, almost everyone around him was fully committed to the celebration. Every now and again he heard nasty remarks about the 'Bastard of Odinal' and 'Whoretribes of the Midland,' from the menfolk, but for every one of those, he heard maidens (and women decidedly *not* ladies) make swooning noises and inappropriate comments about lands the groom-to-be could raid if he so wished.

There were the derisive looks from other priests of the Order of Love. Outside observers might find that a bit odd – but not if they knew how a religion built on the very concept of *love* would feel about *arranged* marriages where *Love* had little to say in the matter. That wasn't to say that they weren't having fun with the celebrations, but one can still enjoy a party even when one would be happy if the host died of dysentery.

Even the shadows found reason to rejoice, in their own way. Every shout, every laugh, every stroke of a lute raked the nerves of the things that called the safest place in the kingdom home. Under the streets and down the alleys, things began to froth and roil.

The irritation in the air emboldened them. The celebrations would bring gluttony, envy, wraith – sin. The future, immediate and long, would let them feast to their delight.

And he felt it.

Akaran felt them. Felt something he knew was there. Could smell them.

Felt the warning that the madman and madwoman had espoused earlier in the day. Knew that there was someone out there with ill-intents and a flair for bloodletting. Knew that in the festivities that there was an undercurrent of damnation waiting to find another victim.

Worse, he knew the Manor would blow him off. They'd call it paranoia. They'd call it a result of the cocasa. They would call him an addict, or insinuate that he was worse off in the mind than he cared to admit. It was hard not to even question himself, but he *knew* it and *hated* that he knew it.

With every laugh and shout of delight, he flinched. Before long, the sights and sound of the celebration forced him to risk running into the irritating woman with the unpleasantly pleasant smile back at the *Imperial*. A little bit later and a few minutes of bartering with Cel and he had a room to hide in for the night (though with no luck to hide from the nightmares).

And while people cheered, people squabbled, people bartered, and people drank – as people were so oft known to do – people watched. Their eyes sharp, their steel sharper, their spells as flashy but far more dangerous as they hovered at their fingertips. There was more than one murderer stalking the crowd tonight, and while warning of fangs still felt fresh in the exorcist's mind, another group waited.

The Hunter's Guild was out in force.

It was just a question of who was the prey.

VII. A LIBRARY OF DREAMS
The Morning of Staddis, the 13ᵗʰ of Riverswell

The three days since Livstra's death hadn't done anything to improve anyone's mood. Seline hadn't been able to bring herself to go upstairs, while the orderlies and other healers on the grounds were sullen and full of nervous glances and hushed rumors more than helpful hands and pleasant words. The patients didn't seem to notice either way, though one of them hadn't quit crying since she passed.

At all. Every day. All night.

It was quickly reaching a point for the priest that if someone didn't do something about them, he was going to have to find another place to stay. The *Imperial* hadn't been that bad for a single night, so that was always an option – as was the Repository. Either place would be fine.

Almost *any* place was better than here.

As Seline adjusted his knee and made him bend it until his leg almost touched his chest, the next thought was that anywhere else absolutely *had* to be better than here. "Fisk me, please, don't do that," he begged as his eye brimmed with tears.

She ignored him and did it again. "It has to be massaged. *You* have to work it and I *know* you're not. Not even sure you're sleeping the way your eye is so sunken." The healer stopped midway through lifting his leg again and bent down to touch his cheek. "You look fevered, but you feel cool."

"I've *been* working it. Every day. Three full candlemarks a day. I walk through Basion as much as I can getting to and from Miral," he promised through clenched teeth, "I'm trying, I swear I am."

She ran a cotton-covered finger across the cut. Keto had finally let him take the bandage off, though it still looked ugly and covered with a deep purple bruise all the way around. It didn't show signs of infection, but it still looked maddeningly inflamed. "It has to be massaged, too. That's the only way you're going to keep it from getting ruined on the inside."

"I'm trying!"

"I know, Akaran, I've watched you. You just aren't doing enough, that's all," she said with a slight sigh and another push and tug on the limb. As he did his best to keep from cursing her using every foul word he could in every language he knew, she gave him a sad little smile to go with it. "You're really fighting on the stairwall, but I am proud of you for trying. Has it gotten any better since we operated?"

"Some days. Other days, no."

That earned a frown and she tilted her head to get a better look. "I re-read Keto's report on the operation, and I do trust his work. There was just so much that had to be redone – your kneecap had to be put back together with *wires* and as ghastly as that sounds, they had to reattach a ligament with -"

"Don't," he interrupted.

"Don't? Don't what?"

He cringed and pulled away from her grip. "Tell me. Don't do it. I was there for some of it. I don't want to know everything."

"But it was your leg," she replied, flabbergasted. "Surely you want to know what they did to it?"

Akaran stretched it again on his own accord and then scooted away from her hands. "No. I don't. I woke up halfway through it, I screamed, someone shoved something awful in my mouth, I quit screaming. When I woke back up it was swollen and bloody. It hurt every fisking day before, it's hurt every fisking day after and I don't think it's getting any better."

She almost pouted as she backed away from him. "Well. It will take time. We truly did do everything possible for a man in your condition, with your... limitations."

"Limitations, huh. Suppose that's a polite way to say it."

"That will also get better. You remember what Lolron said – it will take time. Here, let's start your stretches."

He started to grumble under his breath but eventually stood up and began curling his leg with slow repetitions. "I've been researching it, over at the Repo."

"I assumed you would be. Have you found anything out? Discovered anything useful?"

"Discovered a hatred for their filing system."

"You have a hatred of a great many things, don't you? Not a good attribute for a man of Love," she chided, "or from a man in general."

The priest let the dig slide and stopped flexing his leg. "I can't find more than three cases in the last seventy years of archived notes."

Seline pursed her lips and drummed her fingers on the edge of the bed. "Well, that's just the archives there. There are other archives that the Order of Love operates, and to be fair, the Mother of Hearts is not known to keep the best notes for history that doesn't concern Her."

"Maybe," he groused, "though the scribes were pretty adamant that if it had happened to anyone else in the last century, it would be recorded in there."

"Still. Three is still more than just yourself," she said with a hint of encouragement honey-coating her words, "and that gives you hope of at least some measure, doesn't it? Were the circumstances similar?"

He grunted in pain and went back to flexing his leg. "Hope? Two of them died due to injuries sustained when they lost their power," he replied as she started to cringe. "Neither were with the Order – pair of Melian priests that were trying to end the 2nd Imperium War early back around 412. They destroyed a Temple of Illiya so violently that the feedback from the ether scoured their bodies of any trace magic."

Seline blanched and recoiled slightly. "They... blew up their ability to use magic? Did I hear that right?"

"The temple, their magic, the valley the temple was in, and a small sylverine mine," he added. "Unlike me, the Queen had healers that were able to patch them up with spellwork."

"Healed them? I thought you said they died?"

He shook his head and began doing repetitions with the other leg at her insistence. "I said 'patch.' Records indicate that you still need lungs to breathe and their sudden deficiency in that department cost them their lives a few weeks after. There's only so much good just covering up holes in somebody's ribs can do."

She cringed even harder and looked slightly ill. "Air... air is at times useful. I can see where there may be discomfort involved in the absence of being able to use it. Should I ask about the third?"

"The third was a man named Nealin the Wise," Akaran explained, "who, as it turned out, wasn't. He is, was, from the Order. Apparently he decided he wanted to explore trans-dimensional portals and was successful in opening one to the Sands."

"That's much like the wizard from Toniki was doing, wasn't it?

"Close to the same eventual result, too."

"Shall I presume the causes of his passing weren't natural?"

"Oh, it was natural," he replied with half a smirk. "He spent three years studying the nature of the worlds between the worlds, and claimed to have walked back and forth through the Veil three times. After the fourth time he walked through one of the portals, he reappeared a decade later – naked, babbling, alone – in the middle of Matheia."

The way he said it made goosebumps pop up down her arms. "I shall assume he didn't start there?"

"He had been last seen standing in his study in the capital."

"Which one?"

"Dawnfire."

Seline blinked and wiped a loose strand of hair out of her eyes. "Oh, dear."

"He was eventually repatriated back to the Kingdom. He *somehow* convinced the Holy General of the time to let him continue his work even though he couldn't work any more spells of his own."

She pursed her lips and started to massage his ankle. "Is this where the 'not wise' part comes in?"

He winced and nodded. "After he talked his way into getting someone to open up another breach, he stepped through it and stood in both worlds at once, with his last words proclaiming, '*Mortals can be one with the soul of the Origin; mortals can be in both worlds at once, mortals can touch the Gods even as we stand wrapped in flesh.*'"

"His last words?"

He slid back onto the bed and painfully lowered his leg onto the mattress. "The portal closed."

"He… he made it to the other side?" she said with a hopeful little chirp.

She should've saved her hope. "Not entirely. Half of him did. One foot in the grave, as it were. Nobody knows where the other half went, but…"

Her face fell like a brick. "Oh that's… that's horrible." Then, after a long minute, she cringed and asked, "Um… So… It just… did it cauterize the other half or…?"

"I don't know. Not reassuring, either way."

That was hard to argue, but she tried. "Just because *they* went mad or died from their injuries doesn't mean you will. You're at no risk of losing your life from your leg now, and your arm has healed."

"Doesn't mean I'm *not* going to lose my mind."

"As you've said, you're in the right place for it if you do," she replied with a little grin before she slapped her hand over her mouth and turning bright red. "I'm sorry. That was inappropriate of me to say."

Akaran gave her a little grin and leaned back against the pillows. "You're not wrong," he replied before he gingerly touched her wrist. "Seline? Are you okay?"

She jumped like she'd been shocked. "Yes? Of course I'm okay. Why wouldn't I be?"

"Because the funeral was yesterday. I heard it was a lovely service. I'm sure she felt honored."

The younger woman nodded and forced herself to relax a little. "With the blessing of Isamiael, I hope that she was already in the embrace of the Heavens."

"I'm sure she is," he replied with a faint little nod.

Neither of them spoke for the next few minutes while he nursed a piece of cocasa between his lips and she fidgeted at the end of the bed. "Akaran? No, no, I'm not alright. Can you tell me? You know. You've seen it."

Puzzled, he tilted his head and blinked. "Know what?"

"You know what… what's it like?"

"What's it like? What's what like?"

She folded her hands over her lap and looked to make sure nobody was lingering outside his room to eavesdrop. Even then, she leaned in to whisper at him. "The other side. The Mount."

He looked at her like she'd just grown a second head. "I don't know? I -"

"But you were *there*," Seline pressed. "You *crossed over*. You *experienced* it and came back."

Now it was his turn to cringe. "I was in Tundrala, I wasn't walking alongside Isamiael," he replied, "or Anyone else. Got a dirty look though, I think."

That wasn't enough to dissuade her, and after another furtive glance outside, she leaned in even closer. "No, it's not that. You got to experience the *feel* of it, the sight of it? You were in a place where no mortal gets to go and come back from."

"But mortals have," he argued, "more than a few times. The Granalchi press that limit all the time. I mean it's not an every-day thing but it's well documented that -"

"And they don't talk about it after," she replied with a sad look. "We've been looking at what happened to you; spent some time speaking with some of the priests of Stara. Your experience there is rarer than you know." Before he could try to downplay it, she interrupted him again. "You do know that if you were anyone but a Niasmis follower, there might be talk of making you a saint if we ignored the, 'and he left a demon there,' part."

The revelation was almost insulting and he cringed harder than she did at the thought of the bifurcated mage. "Me. A saint. Me a... no. Just... absolutely no."

"I'm not at all joking," she countered. "Everyone wants to know. Apparently word about you was delivered to the Ellachurstine Shrine from the Temple of Stara in Gonta."

"About me fro..." he began as the color drained from his face and the word died in his mouth. "Deboria. Goddess. No. She didn't. She *wouldn't*. There was the sealed letter and Risson said that it was to be kept quiet I didn't have anything to do with it I promise I didn't," he hastily added.

She grinned at him and decided to rub a little more salt in the wound. "Not just her. You also made an imprint on Lower Adjunct Inniat."

"Inniat? I don't know anyone by that name," he replied, then stopped and furrowed his brow. "Wait. I never *met* him, but he's Deboria's second."

"He vouched for you," he replied.

"I have absolutely no idea why."

"Well, he did. When Risson joined us at the garden yesterday, he asked me to make sure you understood that should you ever need their aid, the Shrines of Stara are to provide it and no questions are to be asked."

All he could really do was sit there and try to process that with a dumb look on his face. "I... huh. That's just completely unexpected."

"If you had been there, you'd have heard it from the man himself."

He sighed and gave her a little apologetic smile. "I know. I should've."

"Why weren't you?"

All he could do was shake his head. "I know it's no excuse, but I just got done overseeing the funerals for more than twenty people. Some I knew. Some

I didn't. Some I ordered burned."

"I suppose that you'd get tired of them but you still should have -"

He stopped her and took a ragged breath before saying, "I also had to watch someone burn alive trapped in a cage. I can still smell her skin blistering."

Seline couldn't stop herself from covering her mouth again as her eyes went wide. "You..."

"I know that funeral pyres are a necessity. I know that they are important," the priest rambled on, "and I know it is an honor. Fighting Daringol? I ordered several pyres lit without consent of families or ceremony, at that. I had to. But I just... the thought of the smell just... I couldn't bring myself to go. I'm sorry."

She felt bile bubble up in the back of her throat and stared at him like she was seeing him for the first time. "Oh, Akaran. I didn't realize. I understand now. We aim to keep the triggers of trauma at bay, and I just tried to send you into one."

"I'm just not... I'm not good at them," he admitted. "I don't know what to say. What to do. Where to stand. Sit. Where to do anything. I've never been good at them. Toniki... had too many of them. I prayed for her, if that counts for anything in your book."

Seline scooted up the bed and tenderly touched his hand while she gave him the warmest smile she could. "Of course it does. I do understand. Thank you for being honest with me."

He answered with a little non-committal sigh and worked his leg in silence for a minute before looking back at her. "Are you sure you're doing okay?"

"As okay as one can," she said honestly enough to count.

"Good," he said with a nervous little grin. "Then, ah. Let me ask you something."

"Yes?"

The priest took a deep breath and tried to rush through the question. "While I was out in the city for that grand arrival thing -"

"You mean the Bewedded March," she interrupted.

It didn't stop him for long. "- the grand arrival thing," he quickly repeated, "I heard about something called the *Danse Festistanis* that's tonight. I didn't know if you would want to go or..." he said as her mouth fell open and her cheeks turned a brilliant red.

Seline didn't respond for what felt like a month before she finally found her voice again. "Akaran? Are you... are you asking to court me?"

His eye went wide as his jaw flapped open with more force than hers had. "*Court you*?! Oh, no! No I didn't mean that, no, not at all!" he blurted out as a crimson blush spread over his cheeks in turn.

"Then why would you ask me to *that* dance, of all things? Don't you know what it is?!"

There was a brief moment, a hopeful moment, where he thought that the simplest answer might be the best one. "A chance for wine and belian-berry tarts without Ridora saying no?"

A grin blossomed on her face even as the blush persisted. "Well, yes, I suppose it is. I hadn't quite thought about it in quite those terms but yes."

"There are other terms?" he squeaked out.

All she could do was stare at him and the stupidly innocent look on his face before breaking down into a fit of giggles that somehow, someway, made him feel *so* much worse. "I can see you aren't used to celebrations of this magnitude. You serve the *Goddess of Love*. How can you not know what the Danse is?"

He let out a deeply frustrated sigh and waved his hands aimlessly in the air. "I keep telling people. I *kill things*," he whined. "I don't go out and spread cheer or arrange couples to spend their lives together. I was trained to go out and spread skulls open. I give impassioned *condemnations*, not *sermons*!"

"So you've never been to a Danse Festistanis? Truly? Ever?" she asked incredulously. "Isn't the Grand Temple of Love within a day's walk of the Queen's Capitol?"

"Never have been," he replied with an irritated little huff. "I mean if you don't want to go -"

"All the time you spent next to the Queen's Palace and you never...? They have more weddings in Mulvette than the ocean has fish!"

"People never really liked to invite me to things..." he muttered dejectedly under his breath.

She fought to keep from rolling her eyes as she replied with, "Can't possibly imagine why," before clearing her throat and sizing him up all over again. "Akaran, the... how best to say it? The Danse is a celebration of the upcoming wedding -"

"I kinda figured?"

Seline ignored him and trudged on, watching his face as the realization hit home, "- *and* you're supposed to take *your own* future betrothed to it. *Or* should you take someone that isn't, it is seen as an invitation for them to consider you as theirs."

Seeing things crystal clear for once, her reply bounced around in the hallowed hall of his head before a light shined in the dark, dreary, unsettled corners of his mind. "Oh," he said, just as that light flared with a bit of blinding brilliance that made him feel *so* much like a horrible person. "OH! Oh, Seline I, oh!"

"Yes, *oh*," she replied with a mirthful grin, "and as much as I am truly honored to be considered as your -"

"Noooo! It's not. Not that," he interrupted, straining the 'no' to the point it could've broken in the air. "I'm sorry. You're very nice but, no."

"Oh? Quick to dismiss me?" she quipped back at him as her grin grew from ear to ear.

"*What?* You're the one that said no about being -"

"So you *did* know."

Flustered, embarrassed, and feeling like a cornered rat, he tucked his arms around his body and shook his head so hard it hurt. "Wait, no. No, you're twisting this. I mean there's someone else that I have that, well, no, I don't have but I -"

The healer grinned and carefully tied her hair into a bun as she watched him squirm. "So I'm not good enough to supplant this other woman you have your heart on, am I?"

"What? No!"

"So I am? Then your heart mustn't be set on her that firmly."

He planted his face firmly in his hands and almost sobbed in tired frustration. "What? No. Okay, you're just twisting my words now and it's not funny."

"I don't know," she said with a brilliant grin that made the dimple in her cheek dance in the daylight. "I'm finding it quite delightful."

The groan from his throat was so pained she checked to make sure she hadn't leaned against his leg somehow. "No, listen, you have been very nice and... sorta kind to me while I've been here. And yes, please do not take this part the wrong way, but you are *incredibly* lovely and *very* intriguing."

"However, there is a very large 'but' there," she said as the dimple flexed at him like it was mocking him for daring to open his mouth

"Yes. There is," he replied before quickly adding, "but not yours."

She made a show of looking over her shoulder and down at her backside. "I don't have a large butt? Is that a requirement for your interests?"

If he didn't have firsthand knowledge, he'd have been willing to be that this, this right here, was the pit. "Oh Goddess. No, I am *not* answering that question."

"I think you should. It's making you turn red in the face."

He looked at her between his fingers and gave her a pleading stare. "Goddess... just... there's a girl. From Toniki."

"Is she more shapely than I?" Seline needled.

"I am *not* answering that," he retorted. "She's... really nice. I like her."

Her smile shifted from a tormenting bit of mischief to one that was warm and wholesome. "Does she like you?"

The first thing he flashed back to was the kiss she'd planted on him right as he took his leave from the village. The second thing was the dozens of insults, dirty looks, and the fact that she had drugged him at one point. Granted, he'd returned that favor later, but there it was. "I really don't know."

"Have you tried to write her since you arrived?"

He slipped his head away from his hands and stared at her dumbly. "Write her? You mean a letter?"

Her little chuckle felt like she'd just cut him with a knife. "That *is* the way most young soldiers keep in touch with the girls that do not follow them to war."

"But I'm not at war.."

"You are with yourself, and she did not follow you. True?"

"True, I guess," he replied with a little defeated sigh. "No, I haven't."

Seline's smile crumbled slightly, but she continued to pounce on this new revelation. "But you have been thinking of her? And you feel she has hips that are easier to bear children than I do?"

The way he jumped back in bed and quickly hugged his pillow for support was almost comical. "Bear chil… WHAT?! Oh, *Goddess*, I don't know I never… She's *nice* okay? And I want to see her again and maybe…"

"Maybe take her to this dance you're asking to take me," she finished.

He finally answered with a grumbled, "Can't happen but yes."

She chuckled a little again, though it wasn't as happily. "So you ask me with the love of your heart aimed elsewhere? A woman could find that offensive, and think less of a man that would do such a thing."

"Oh, *Goddess*," he groaned, dragging the title out for an entire breath. "*No.* I just thought that… I thought that you could use a chance to get out of the manor and clear your head after everything."

"And that's all? No secret attempts to court me? No dastardly plans to land me in your bed?"

If her intention had been to make him blush again, it worked. "No. No plans. Of any kind. I don't even want to but…"

"…but?"

Akaran cleared his throat and tried to explain himself as best as he could and he prayed it would be enough to get him out of this mess. "You've been trying to help me and I've seen enough people die lately so I thought maybe you might enjoy a chance of fresh air. And hopefully someplace where people laugh. And not like Folia does, upstairs."

The little blonde healer studied his face for a moment and reluctantly gave him a little nod. "Her giggle gets annoying, doesn't it?"

"I'd really rather go stab walking corpses than listen to it."

She pursed her lips and agreed, and then nodded at him. "Okay. I'll go. I suppose it couldn't hurt."

He let out a little nervous breath. "Okay. Then… okay. That's… okay."

"You don't sound so sure."

"I wasn't expecting you to say yes," he admitted.

Her eyebrow raised up, and for the first time, he noticed that she had eyes the sweetest shade of brown with just a few hints of grass-green streaks along the edges. "Should I say no?"

He winced and looked a little wounded at the idea. "No, stay with the yes. It's tonight, I think they said after the sun sets?"

"That seems the norm, yes."

"Okay. I'm supposed to go see Prostil today. I can meet you at the Danse?"

She nodded again and stood up, straightening her dress and smiling down at him. "That seems fair. Where is it?"

"Comstead Hall? West Giffil," he replied, "though I'm going to admit I have no idea where that is. I'll figure it out."

Seline pursed her lips and nodded slowly. "Hmm. Comstead? That's not far from the Annex. Yes; I will go and meet you there." Then she sized him up again with that damnable mirthful grin she'd been tormenting him with. "Please do your best to be on time? The Danse is not a safe place for a single maiden. We tend to be hunted by young suitors searching for a happier life and a warmer bed."

"I'll do that."

"*You* be careful as well," she *sternly* warned him. "Plenty of bored noblewomen – single and otherwise – that will be out and about looking for the trouble only a young man can provide."

"Do you *really* think that's going to be a problem for me?" he said as he held up his cane. "I'm not exactly a winner."

She shook her head and rolled her shiny brown eyes. "No, you're something far worse. You're a *project*."

Dumbfounded (again), he looked up at her with a blank and dull face. "A project? What's that supposed to mean?"

"Oh, you poor naive boy," Seline sighed. "You'll know... you'll know."

And for the next half hour all he did was sit there, and continued to have absolutely no idea what she possibly could've meant.

The bowels of the Repository were larger than anyone on the outside world gave them credit for. Most people would assume that there might be a few bunk rooms, a kitchen, a dining hall. Then it'd be likely that they'd assume that there was some kind of vault buried deep underground to justify the sheer number of guards stationed outside.

You'd be forgiven for thinking that.

Once inside though, if you were lucky enough to make it the Hall of Studies, you'd realize that this wasn't just a cave stuffed into the ground. In order to make it inside, you had to go through at least one guard post (inside the mountain), through the lower receiving hall, past a second guard post. After you did that, then you'd have to wander through the living quarters – and in almost every single hallway, have to pass under the eternally watchful eyes of either Miral himself or the Goddess he protected.

The study chamber itself was fascinating edifice in and of itself that would be welcome in any castle that had an interest in maintaining a library. The crux was that this part *wasn't* a library, or at least, wasn't the only one. Even with two levels, eight massive bookcases and a handful of scroll racks, this was where people who had permission to bring things up from the lower vaults came to read.

Which was what he was doing when it all started to go wrong.

S.K. Addlerbatt's *Shattered Ruby: The End of A'Twol* had been sitting out on the desk when he first made it into the hall from down in the vaults. Who had left it there or why was a good question. The priest that oversaw this area – Brother Levathil Pilatti – had a very strict rule about leaving books unattended:

treat them as you'd treat yourself. Should you leave a book out, you could also expect to be left out; likely in the rain, overnight, mostly naked, and chained to the stairs for the evening.

It was an effective threat that typically ensured people put things away.

This book hadn't been on the list of planned studies to work on. Per request from Spidous, he was *supposed* to be muddling through *All the God's Un-Men*, a tome written by some elder priest in the Order of Love and another, probably-just-as-old Adept in the Granalchi Academy. From what he had been told, the book was supposed to be an incomplete listing of all known extra-planar entities that inhabited the various Worlds Beyond Worlds.

Which, in his freely-admitted lack of experience, would have to be an exercise in bullshit. The creations of the Gods were believed to be infinite in their own realms. The very idea that a pair of mortal men could even begin to comprehend that was in and of itself either insane or so self-aggrandizing that it needed to be dismissed outright.

After expressing those concerns, the Paladin-Commander had made it clear that he was to read it anyway. "There are more damned and not-unholy-but-hungry monstrosities in this world that are the result of the worlds of Others than many would believe. You are suffering from a curse from one of those beings; it may give you some insight to study the nature of things similar."

By the time he found a copy of the *Un-Men* and brought it back up from the Library of the Discordant – halfway down the stairwell filled guts of the facility – the *End of A'Twol* was sitting there like it was waiting for him. Aside from the fact that it hadn't been there when he had walked through the study hall an hour prior (and that he hadn't seen anyone else removing books from anywhere in the lower levels), it was odd for more than just its unannounced arrival. Not only was it laying out, it was laying out and open. Not only that, there was a chain attached to the spine, suggesting that it had come from one of the secure vaults buried deeper underground than most of the other rooms.

It was also opened to a page written in both Queen's Common and some odd chicken-scratch that made his eye throb to look at it. The Common was simply, "*This is the truth of A'Twol. This is not the truth of the Dunesires, the Animators, or the Marshals. This is the truth of what is and what has happened. Spoken as truth, and uttered to paper. Paper then uttered to tomes, and tomes made multitudes. Should the harsh sands will it, the truth will find a home where it is safe to be said.*"

As preambles to musty old books went, that was about on par with the rest of them he'd run into. Once he settled in and set down the other book in his hand, he took a glance at the other text. The only thing *that* did was make his eye throb even harder. When that ache settled after a hearty yawn and a few minutes of looking away, he tried turning the pages.

He didn't make it before a little line in purgalaito at the very bottom took his attention. The first rule of spellcasting was to never, *ever* read an invocation out loud without knowing what it did. The second rule of spellcasting was to never, *ever* invoke a God or Goddess you weren't already comfortable with. The third rule was a reiteration of the first, and in his surprise to even see the words there – not to mention his general cocasa-influenced befuddlement – he promptly forgot all three of them.

"*Eberenth, aiy covax proshadi; Eberenth, aiy covax stensavi; Eberenth aiy covax mastadi ya al zalbat?*" he read aloud, frowning as each word seemingly struggled to pull itself off of his tongue. Nothing happened.

At first.

At second, a wellspring of pain stabbed him in the back of his good eye and caused him to pitch face down onto the table. When his vision came back, the room had gone dim. Most of the torches lighting up the study along the sides had gone out, casting bookshelves and tables alike into shadows. The fountain in the middle of the room still bubbled, but nothing but puffs of black fog trickled out.

A brief flurry of movement on the other side of the table took his instant attention, and he nearly fell out of his chair when he saw her sitting there. Except he couldn't; his legs wouldn't move and his arms felt like they were weighted down. "You can't be here."

"*Of course I can,*" she said, "*you're here.*"

"But *you* can't be. This isn't real. *Can't* be real."

Rmaci gave him the best smile she could. The way her lower lip had melted to her gums made a mockery of the very idea of what a smile should be. "*You're real. I'm real because you're real.*"

He tried to look anywhere else but at her naked, ruined body. Since the last time he had dreamed of her, she'd developed even more pulsing sores and gouges in her charred flesh that exposed yellowing ribs and blackened lungs under them. "This is consecrated ground. *You* can't be here."

"*You brought me here,*" she countered with another attempt at an alluring smile that *might* have worked if her eyes weren't completely hollow and her upper lip as chewed and bloody as her lower lip was just a mass of scars and fat.

"No. You're not here," he repeated as the room pulsed around her like he was staring at her through a glass of water. "You're burning in the Abyss."

"*I burned in the mortal world,*" she corrected, "*I'm freezing in the pit.*"

"The Goddess prevents you from being here. This is just a dream."

She slid her hands out over the table and left a bloody smear in her wake. "*Dreams are real.*"

Repulsed, he continued to try to stand up and simply couldn't move no matter what he did. His heart started to pound in his chest and he felt a steady pounding in the back of his head start to roar in displeasure. "No, they're not."

"*Seek counsel with Nia'valth if you do not believe dreams are a realm unto their own,*" the shade suggested, "*or seek counsel with Her followers if you aren't man enough to seek Her yourself.*"

He swallowed hard and watched her broken fingers creep ever closer to his hands. "This isn't a curse from the Nightmarion. It's me. It's just me, it's in my head."

Rmaci tilted her head to the side and a bloody mess started to trickle out of a hole in her cheek. *"Maybe. A lot of things can be found in a head. None of the things you need will be found in that book,"* she said, pointing down at it.

He followed her finger down and realized that the pages he had been staring at had gone blank. "I was just reading...."

"You were, but you shouldn't," the damned soul warned.

The priest managed to force his fingers to move enough to flip through the old crusty pages. Everything was gone; not even a single smudge of ink remained at all. "That spell...? Did I...? Did I just use magic?!"

"I don't know spells; but I have learned more of the Gods. You don't know the wealth of knowledge that is offered to the damned. So much we know – it's a curse," she wistfully sighed as steam out of her ruined ribs. *"To learn so much and have no way no power to do anything with it. The secrets of the universe. All of the universes. They're mixed in with the suffering. It's a torment."*

"That didn't... you didn't answer the question."

Rmaci laughed – or at least, that's what he thought the gravely grinding sound that she made was. *"Why would I answer your questions? What have you done for me that would make me want to do for you? No, no you didn't summon me with that spell. I may not know spells but I know failure; your failure. You couldn't invoke a God to make a flea jump; you think that you could invoke a curse to bring me forth?"*

He pushed the book away and painfully pulled his arms closer to his chest. *If I can just reach my cane I can end this with one swing...* "Then why are you -"

"There's no help for you there," she said a dismissive wave of her hand, *"suffering is in that tome. Suffering is why I am here. You're suffering – not enough – but the suffering that book brings is not the suffering you are to endure."*

His desire to refute her overcame whatever paralysis that she had cursed him with and he managed to shake his head in an angry 'no' that was matched by an equally angry retort from the migraine rampaging through his skull. "You're *here* because I'm having another one of these damned bad dreams."

"Are you sure?" she purred with that terrible, hollow voice of hers, *"How can it be a dream when you're awake?"*

"What?"

"Look," Rmaci instructed with a gesture overhead. He slowly craned his neck up and saw three people milling around on the balcony overhead. They were talking to each other like nothing in the world was wrong at all and were seemingly ignoring him. Then she waved her hand off to the side, flinging bits of ash and scorched skin across the room. A few other priests and students had entered the hall and were working on sorting books and scrolls. *"Are you asleep? If you were, would you be able to see so clear? Hear them? They see you, and do not care."*

Akaran tried to call out for them, but nothing happened. He tried to force himself up again, and couldn't move. His hands suddenly felt glued to the tabletop and it took all of his strength to even make his finger twitch. He just barely managed to whisper out a call for help that couldn't be heard over the din. She stood up and sauntered over to him just in time for him to be able to whisper, "What did you do to me, damn you?"

"*Nothing worse than what you've done to me,*" the shade said as she took a disgusting mockery of a luxurious, erotic stretch that showed off every gaping hole and every twisted lump of flesh that made up the woman she was in death.

"Stop this, dammit!" he half-begged and half-commanded. Out of the corner of his eye, he saw that there was a glowing white aura around the head of the statue of Miral across the room and shouted at it. "GUARDIAN! HELP ME! PLEASE!"

Rmaci chortled and placed her hands on either side of the back of his chair as she leaned in over him. "*He won't. He's already burned a hole in the back of my head just looking at me. A common turn of phrase for most. For the dead, we mean it. See?*" she asked as she reached behind her skull and pushed forward until her fingers impossibly began to wiggle through the holes where her eyes had been.

Akaran tried to recoil and pull away even as she laughed at him and then her face began to expand impossibly wide. Her head vanished as her mouth swallowed it up, and then as her throat expanded like a man-sized tunnel as she moved in to swallow him whole.

While he screamed in terror, three people watched him from the balcony. "He's asleep," one of them remarked, "in the study. The boy is *asleep* in the *Hall of Studies.*" The speaker may have been wearing a hooded robe that obscured their face, but you could *feel* the raw contempt radiating off of her.

"Come now, Karaj, there's no cause for the angst," Catherine scolded, "he's young, and in pain. It is more trying for him to hunt for his materials than it is for any of us. The fact that he's managed to stay so focused on his research is itself worthy of some leeway."

"But he's *asleep* in the *study hall,*" her assistant repeated, quickly turning away from the offensive sight of it. "And dare I suggest it is *less* from the effort he's putting in than it is the weed I saw him chewing on in the library. Chewing cocasa! In the *library!*"

Feeling just as annoyed by it, Spidous grunted a minor agreement. "I happen to agree. I'll speak to him about appropriate times to consume that garbage. I also repeat my objection to letting him anywhere *near* that book."

"You saw the same report I did," the Maiden replied, "you know what your comrade-in-rank reported. *Who* he reported. If *that* monster is going to rear his head again, and *if* he is preparing to stalk that boy, he needs to know."

"Paladin-Commander Steelhom trained him. I prefer to respect the wishes of the exorcist's mentor and not fill his head with thoughts of a fictional boogeyman cooked up by the madmen of Sycio."

Catherine arched her eyebrows and crossed her arms over the bodice of her flowing red dress. "I would daresay that there are a few dead soldiers and a half-blind young lady in Toniki that would like to debate how fictional he is."

He shook his head and grunted in continued annoyance. "Someone claims to be capable of murdering an entire city, and we're willing to accept it without proof? It's easier to believe that he truly did walk in Istalla's realm than that."

"Well, my friend, it is safe to say that there are others that believe in him more than you. That particular book was stored away in the vault for a reason, and stored there under specific instruction from the Holy General."

"One must also be warned. If it is as Steelhom suggested that this so-called Man of the Red Death is walking in the borders of the Kingdom, I should note that he is rumored to have acolytes everywhere. A cult, of some kind. A secret society, maybe. Wouldn't be the first to blight the world, and it would be wise of us to show caution," Karaj added.

"Said in a book written by a man whom went mad and died soon after copies of it began to spread," Spidous retorted, "copies that, may I add, were hunted down and burned by Sycian agents for how poorly of a light that it cast the Jewels of Sycio in."

"A king wrote it, you mean. Not merely a man," Catherine disputed.

That didn't impress him any, and he quickly shifted topics as Karaj stood there in silence. "If you wanted him to work on a task, there's another that badly needs someone with his outlook — tethered to the magic of this world or not," he curtly replied.

"Oh? What?" Catherine curiously asked.

"You heard of the murder in the Manor, yes?"

"Yes, of course. Horrific."

"Surprised it doesn't happen more often, given the people that call that place home," her aid muttered half under her breath.

He nodded at both of them and added, "It's not the only one."

The Maiden blinked and relaxed her arms. "It isn't? What do you mean?"

Spidous started to explain the circumstances of Adept Odern several weeks ago, highlighting the brutality and the lack of any credible suspects that anyone had managed to find. He even managed to touch on a concern that it might have been somehow related to the arrival of Clan Odinal, but quickly shot that down as, "Mere political hand-wringing," and, "An excuse to give the nobility something new to talk about."

"Par for the course these days," Karaj agreed.

Just when they thought he was done, he dropped a revelation that they liked even less. "While not often, there have been rumors that other poor souls have gone missing. Vagrants, mostly. Nobody that would be missed."

"How long has this been going on?" Catherine asked with a distressed frown suddenly on her.

"Souls go missing all the time in a city, m'lady," he replied, "so it's hard to say. One year. Maybe two. Maybe longer."

The frown turned to fury. "Nobody has found this to be unusual? Worth investigating?"

He barely shook his head as he dismissed the sudden concern. "Of course they have. Henderschott is a busy man though, and it's hard to seek for those that were never officially within the city to begin with."

After a moment, she started to rub her chin. Unhappily, but thoughtfully. "This disturbs me, Spidous. I should have heard of this well before now."

"It's only since the Guild began searching for clues about Adept Odern that anyone's taken notice."

"Which makes this is a shame. No, it's worse than shame. This is an embarrassment," she decided. "Admitting it or not, they are all children of Niasmis. None should be left out in the cold so carelessly that they are not even noticed if they are gone."

Karaj pulled a small bound notebook free of her rope belt and started to quickly flip through the pages. "I would agree with you, m'lady."

"You think that he could handle it?" the Maiden asked, peering down to watch as a priest in the hall finally found the courage to try to rouse the exorcist up

"Are you serious?" the woman in white asked, nearly dropping her notebook. "The boy is addicted to cocasa. Haven't you seen how his hands shake? Or the way his eye is chronically twitching?"

A muffled shout and a thud below made all three of them look down as Akaran began offering a stream of hurried apologies to the priest that was inexplicably holding his jaw and laying down on the floor. "Yes, I am aware. Who better to search for a murderer than someone that's already paranoid?"

"Quite literally anyone, m'lady," Karaj replied.

"Maybe. Maybe not. Send him to my office when he finishes making amends to..." she peered down over the edge of the railing and shrugged nonchalantly. "...isn't that Adept Ishtva?"

Her aid looked down and nodded. "It is," then after a long pause, added, "maybe he's not as useless as I assumed."

Catherine was nursing a cup of tea when Akaran limped into her office a short bit later. "So I see you've had an interesting afternoon so far. Care to tell me why you felt it necessary to introduce the concepts of gravity and blunt trauma to Ishtva?"

"A nightmare," he admitted sheepishly, "and I can't begin to apologize enough."

"Oh, you can. Do you know who that was?"

He looked down at the thin, bloody bandages lightly wrapped around his knuckles and shook his head. "Someone with a thick jaw?"

"Thick head," she idly remarked, "and one that belongs to the Granalchi Annex. His name is Ishtva – one of two men we part-employ part-tolerate from outside the Order. He serves as a liaison to the Headmaster-Adept. You haven't had the pleasure to meet Ledger Philanus either, have you?"

"Philanus?" he replied quizzically. "No, I don't think I have."

She nodded curtly. "If you had, you'd know. He's from the Guild."

"The Guild and the Academy? If you don't mind my asking, why...?"

"Why do we have someone from the Academy poking around in our hallowed halls?" she guessed. When he nodded, the Maiden went on to explain. "He's a mattanist. The Academy taught him how to copy ink on parchment."

Akaran blinked and stared at her dumbfounded. "Copy the ink? Like... a doppelganger?"

She covered her mouth and chuckled mirthfully. "Oh, of course. The first thing you'd think of *would* be a shapeshifter, wouldn't it? No, not quite. He's able to look at a scroll or a journal and then use a few different spells to make an instant copy of the text on a blank piece of parchment."

"So... he doesn't have to sit down and just... transcribe it?"

"Not at all. I've seen the man take a pile of scrolls as tall as you and make a perfect copy of it in less than a trio of days," she replied with a hint of admiration in her voice. "He's quite frankly worth his weight in gold."

The younger priest cursed under his breath and rubbed his hand a little harder, almost like he was trying to hurt himself on purpose. "Then please, I owe you an apolo-"

Catherine interrupted him and smiled smugly as she laced her hands behind her head and stretched before she stood up and motioned for him to follow her out to her balcony. "Ah, no. He's worth his weight in gold, but he's as dense as lead."

"Oh. Okay?"

"No," she sighed as her smile faltered just a little, "but I'm not going to yell at you for it. Oh, and as far as Philanus goes? The Guild has a very bad habit of running into old artifacts and monstrosities that would be better off in our hands than theirs. We share information with them, to an extent, in the right circumstances," she added as they made it outside. Once they were, she took a minute to take in the view. For a moment, so did he, but it didn't look like they were looking at the same thing.

"That makes sense. They're always sticking their heads where it doesn't belong," he agreed.

From their vantage point, they could see that the city was wide awake and in full swing – another happy, productive day in the Kingdom. It was almost a shame to risk upsetting that balance. "Well, it's not like they're all bad. They do help clean up our messes, just as much as we help clean up theirs. Speaking of messes... Ridora still hasn't solved the mystery of Livstra's death, has she?"

From where he was standing, all he could do was wonder what chaos was brewing out there. She smiled; he glared. When her question registered in the back of his head, it jostled him out of his miserable reverie. It set him back a little that she'd even ask. "No. Or if they have, they haven't told me."

"If they had, that sanctimonious wench that runs the Manor would've bragged about it to the city," she gloomily muttered. "That's what I need you to look at for me."

Akaran stretched his neck and groaned painfully as he did. "You want me to try to look into her death...? I don't know what good I can get done that the orderlies haven't already."

"It's not the orderlies that should be trying to sort it out to begin with," she complained. "It's a job for the guard – and by extension, us. That's why I want you to cast your eye to this situation, and look from out to within."

"I'm afraid I don't understand," he replied, befuddled (again – a state of mind he was getting utterly tired of). "You want me to investigate the murder of someone at the manor, but not *at* the manor."

"Yes, that's right," she said before taking a deep breath. With a wave of her fingers and a Word he didn't recognize, she willed a shimmer of pale gold light to manifest and wrap around them in a sparkling dome. He could see through clearly, but he had a sinking suspicion that nobody would be able to see or hear them from the outside. "What have you heard about the murder of Adept Odern?"

"Murder of an Adept? One of the Granalchi?"

"Yes, the one and the same."

He chewed on the air for a moment and wracked his brain before coming up empty. "Nothing?"

She looked away from the city and gave him a slightly distressed frown. "Really? Then let me be the bearer of bad news."

"Seems to be a common job with our profession."

"Yes, that it does," she agreed. "Almost five weeks ago, Instructor Odern, an Adept with a specialty in defensive and combative magics, was found murdered."

He pursed his lips and whistled slowly. "That's strange all of itself."

"Very. Among other things, he was skinned and beheaded."

Akaran cringed and fought what was left of his stomach to keep it still. "Hopefully the skinning was after."

"I don't have much hope for it," she said with a cringe of her own, "given that his heart was found stuffed in his throat."

"Blessed be," he replied with a wince. "Someone was trying to send a message."

She nodded her head in total agreement. "It would seem so. While I realize that Livstra wasn't skinned, the rest of the murder was equally as distressing."

"You think that the butcherings are related."

"Even if not related, maybe events that aren't self-contained with each other," she suggested. "There have been reports of people going missing, to make matters worse."

Akaran bit his lip and tried to gauge how serious this might be from the look on her face. "How many?"

"More than a handful, less than a city."

"Who?"

"The unwashed and easily forgotten, sadly," she bemoaned.

He felt the hair on the back of his neck start to lift and tingle. "For how long?"

"Too long," she replied, "and it has taken too long for anyone to care enough to notice."

A steady sinking feeling took hold of his stomach. "So... people have been going missing for... what? Months now?"

She gave him a sad little nod. "Years, we've come to think. At least two. What I was able to find out on my own is very rough and not at all reliable."

"People have been going missing for months, possibly years, and nobody's looked into it before now?" he asked again, unsure if he should be disgusted more than worried.

"You know it as well as I how easy it is for certain souls to fall between the cracks."

"Those cracks are why people like us do the work we do," he deftly pointed out.

She had to give him that one. "That's so incredibly true. What's worse is that I fear without the recent killings, these disappearances would have continued to have gone unnoticed until they numbered in the legions."

Akaran shuddered and looked out over the city. "I don't like how you just said 'legions,' so you know. Has the Guard had any luck? They answer to some stiff prick named Hender, right?"

"Yes, that's him," the Maiden confirmed. "Lieutenant-Commander Randic Henderschott. He's overseen the security for Basion for almost four years now."

"So for half the time he's been in charge people have been going missing," he groused. "Doesn't look like he's doing a decent job at his post."

"An issue that will be taken up with him directly in the near future, should your investigation bear fruit," she returned before going silent for a moment. "The truth is? Nobody has had any luck solving any of these murders or disappearances to the best we can tell. Even the Guild has had little luck."

"The Hunters are drawing a blank on this? That's strange."

She followed his gaze and sighed in vague annoyance. "Most unlike them, I agree. They are normally quite skilled at ferreting out their quarry. I give them some leeway with this mess, however."

"Eh? Why?"

She pointed at a two story building with a sloped roof in the distance. "Elsith, their Huntsmatron? She's had her hands tied by Maiden Esterveen's Betrothed and the Merchant-Master. All of her men are busy being held to older writs of protection and the like."

"But it's literally their entire job," he argued. "If *they* can't figure anything out, what makes you think I can? They've got more resources available to them than I do right now."

"No, they have *magic*," she pointed out. "That is not the same as resources."

"Really fail to see the difference there," he retorted.

Prostil rubbed at the side of her temple. "Of course you do. But consider: now that you are without magic, you're going to have to become inventive. If you never regain the use of spells again, being *inventive* is how you'll survive through the rest of your life. And if you *do* regain it, you'll have one more skill in your repertoire."

He stood there and debated calling her the dumbest person he'd met in the city so far before deciding against it. "So you're sending me on a murder-turned-missing-person investigation to help me learn to live without the boons of the Goddess? Really?"

"Even without magic right now, you know what to look for in cases of demonic attack. Since the mundanes and the monster hunters haven't had any luck with it, perhaps it's time to ask someone with an eye for the afterlife to poke around," she countered.

That didn't help. "So you suspect demons."

"I don't know what to suspect," she admitted, "which bothers me worse, and greatly so. This shrine, this library? There is all matter of object stored here that agents of the Abyss would love to lay hand and claw upon. If there *is* evidence of the damned working against the inhabitants of Basion, it needs to be found post-haste."

"Found, then rooted out."

"Yes," she agreed. "And yet, *my* hands are tied, before you even ask. This damnable wedding has tensions in the Province so high that Esterveen, Hannock, and every other sod with the Queen's permissions to rule are going about telling everybody else that nobody can do so much as shit without being told where and how to do it. That includes the military, and by extension, *me*. Otherwise I'd have already sent Spidous to the Manor and forced him to pour over it with a dozen of the archivists to root for clues."

"So... you need a guy like me that's not officially currently with normal permissions to act like he has them. Ideally permissions granted by someone that isn't you?"

Catherine pursed her lips and gave him a nod. "For those reasons and others," she admitted. "There is not a priest or a handler or a soldier or a scribe in this building that has not been seen in every district tending to the masses over the years. We're *known*. We'd be *recognized*. Our ability to look *quietly* is hampered by our own reputation," she went on to explain in an attempt to cut his next argument off at the knees.

Or at least, knee. "So even though I'm walking around with the emblem of the Order around my neck and it feels like every other priest in this city knows who I am to see me..."

"...you are largely unknown by the city proper, for all the time you spend in either your room or your studies," she finished.

"Damn," he sighed as he saw exactly where this was headed.

"So, will you?"

He ran his hands through his hair and quietly adjusted his eye patch before giving her the only answer that he could. "I can't really ignore it now even if I wanted to. If you think they're related, then anyone in the manor could be next."

"Or here in the Repository, or elsewhere," she added, "even the Guild itself could be a target. Goddess help us if the wedding is targeted in any way."

"Everything you've just said is awful," he pointed out with a mutter. "Yes, I'll do it."

That earned the first smile she'd had since learning of Seline's hungover fate. "Good. Then one very strong request: please be discrete. You still have rank and permissions granted to an exorcist of the Order, but without your magic..."

He saw where that was going, too. "Without it, it's going to be hard for people to take me seriously. Same with the cane."

"Same with your penchant for cocasa," she pointed out.

"I need it for the pain," he shot back, "it won't stop and won't go away. Without it... no. Wish it'd do something for this damnable headache, but no luck there either."

Prostil tilted his head up with a finger on his chin to carefully study his bloodshot eye. "Without it, you develop the shakes, vomiting, and bloody piss – yes?"

He absolutely refused to answer that last part. "Without it, my knee hurts so much I can't walk even with this blasted stick."

"Either or, that alone will open doors for you in some parts of the city. It is much easier for the wayward of the Pantheon's flock to feel comfortable around a man that echoes their own sins."

That felt far more insulting than she meant it. Or at least, than he hoped she meant it. "It's not a sin. It's a medication."

Her response didn't make it any easier to tell. "One man's medicine is another man's downfall. Yours too, should you not be careful."

"Really don't need a lecture," he groused back. "I don't like taking it, but I take it. If I don't take it, I suffer. It's fairly straightforward."

"Many of the wayward you're soon to see will feel the same way," Catherine cautioned. "Either way, it will help."

For a few moments, he thought about arguing with her. Poking around town was the last thing he really wanted to do, and working underneath Ridora's nose seemed like heartburn in the making. *However*, he decided, *it might just keep me out of the library...* That, he felt, was all the incentive he needed. "I'll be as gentle and polite as I can, Maiden-Templar."

Her eyes went wide and she emphatically shook her head. "No, Akaran."

"No? But you just -"

"Please," she begged, "*please* be better than that."

VIII. DANSE MACABRE
The Evening of Staddis, the 13th of Riverswell

"You look absolutely terrible. Are you okay... and... and are those bandages on your hand? WHY are there bandages on your hand?" she asked incredulously.

"Papercut?"

He saw Seline standing half a block away from the gloriously-built Comstead Hall when she caught sight of him and waved him over. Now that he was closer, she wished he wasn't. "What happened?"

"I need to talk to Lolron. I had an... incident... at the Repository."

"What kind of *incident*?" she seethed, the glimmer in her eyes sending fresh chills down his spine. All threats aside, she looked stunning. While she was only a couple of years his senior and he'd never seen her in anything other than a peasant's dress, tonight she looked as regal as any of the ladies-in-waiting from the capital. In fact, between the expertly wrapped bun she had her hair laced into, the silver necklace adorned with carnelians and a single sapphire, and the dress... if he didn't know any better, he'd have pegged her for royalty on the spot.

And for a brief moment, he wondered if he really did know better.

"The bad kind," he offered sheepishly.

"*Well?*" she hissed again, a decidedly un-regal growl rumbling from deep in the back of her throat to punctuate it.

He took a deep breath and quickly explained what happened. The longer he talked, the more her anger faded. That it was replaced with a look of pity and concern didn't make him feel any better. "I asked about the spell. It couldn't have caused anything like that to manifest."

"Are you sure?"

"Positive," he said with a slow nod, "it was invoked with Eberenth, and She doesn't deal in the dead. Knowledge of the dead, but not the dead themselves."

She pursed her lips and straightened her moss-green gown across her shoulders. The dark brown trim along the ends of the bell-sleeves and down the (admittedly distracting) plunging neckline made him think of the old bat of an alchemist from Toniki, but, she looked so beautiful in it that he couldn't really concentrate on what she was asking him. "What was it supposed to do, exactly?"

"Oh, um," he started to reply as he began to stumble nervously over his words, "it's a revealing spell, of sorts. It's a call to ask Her to see, hear, and understand." Akaran stopped cold and bit his lip before continuing with, "I suppose in the context of a book, it might make it possible to read *sycidac*."

"Syicdac?"

"Native tongue in Sycio. Must have been some kind of translation spell."

She thought about it for a minute and adjusted the bundle in her arms. "I don't dabble in much magic but no, that doesn't sound like something that should summon the damned, even under the best... well, worst of circumstances."

"That's my feeling, too," he said with a pained sigh.

"How bad was it?"

The exorcist quickly shook his head from side to side. "The worst one since I left Toniki. I'm not going to talk about it."

"You really should. What happened, exactly? It might be pertinent," she pressed as she handed him the lumpy pile of clothes in her arms, "and here, put this on."

Akaran narrowed his eye as he looked at the rolled-up pile of fabric and struggled to hold it and his cane at the same time. "What's this?"

"I know you would not have thought to bring appropriate attire yourself. Put it on. It'll fit over your tunic," Seline replied with a little huff, then reiterated, "What was the dream about?"

Akaran wasn't sure if he should be offended or appreciative, and decided that saying nothing about the offer may be better than saying anything. "Fine," he grumbled as he leaned against a nearby wall and started to slide the offered coat over his shoulders. "You know how typically I dream of Frosel?"

She nodded slowly and helped brace him upright as he changed. "I do. We wish you'd be able to focus on someplace else."

"Your wish was granted. After she swallowed me she... I... it wasn't Frosel. I think it was the Bog. Faegoli's Bog."

"Faegoli's...?" He struggled into the long black coat and buttoned it up as tight as he could. Seline gave him a warm and encouraging smile, then quickly started to brush her fingers through his hair to tidy him up. "I don't know where that is?"

The exorcist gave a little indignant whimper as she did something that felt horribly obscene yet strangely enjoyable to his ponytail. "Faegoli's Bog," he replied with a little yelp of pain, "Neph'kor's realm."

"The Rotbringer?"

"The one and the same."

"I don't remember you saying you saw it in your report...? So how do you know it was that, and not just a figment of your imagination?"

He shuddered as a glimpse of the Bog popped into his mind's eye. A field of vibrant, glowing yellow and green mold that engulfed him midway to his chest. An oily cavern roof overhead where countless bodies had been impaled and left wiggling on coal-black stalactites. A constant rain of bloody piss and pus misting over the mold. A rolling mound of obscene fat thrashing in agony as dozens of *shiriak* consumed its flesh.

He'd never know it, but those little demons deserved every bite they took, and so did the monster they feasted on. Failing the Rotbringer brought repercussions. The shiriak found a way to gain revenge for being consumed in life, and the glutton? The punishment was fitting. (Yet, the shiriak themselves would never know anything but starvation no matter how much they fed – Neph'kor's condemnation was being spread equally all the way around.)

Akaran slapped himself across the face and pushed away from the healer. "Because it sure as *all* wasn't the Mount," he groused, "and it was so much worse than Frosel. I am *not* talking about it," he repeated, "and you *don't* want to know."

"You know Ridora is going to want to ask you -"

"She doesn't want to know either. I'll tell Lolron, but only because of what triggered it."

Seline gave up asking with a sigh, then went back to straightening up his new formal robe. "It's a bit old and doesn't quite fight right. Couldn't let you walk into the Danse without you making the *attempt* to look like you belonged."

He looked down at the thigh-length coat and had to admit that it was pretty nice. Silver embroidery ran up the length of the middle and its old copper buttons glinted in the moonlight. The sleeves were long enough to almost cover his wrists, and the pair of gloves she'd included took care of the rest. "This is... this isn't bad," he admitted.

"You almost look like you clean up well," she replied with a hint of a self-satisfied smile. "I've done worse."

"Henderschott?" he guessed with a nasty little grin.

The healer cringed and turned away, coughing uncomfortably. "Much worse."

When she didn't reply to his wicked little chortle, he offered his arm to her. Accepting it with a tiny surprised smile and a remark of "Yes, there may be hope for you yet," they started their approach to the Hall. "Just be warned," she cautioned as they approached the gate, "I had a moment to look at the guest list before you arrived. Half of the people here have more money than you'd find in the coffers of the Temple of Stara, and the other half are holy men *from* the Temple. This is not a crowd to be loose of tongue with."

She wasn't kidding.

Once they made it past the pair of servants working to make sure that only people of *acceptable* status were allowed into the Danse, the inside of the Hall came just short of taking his breath away. For an impressive building on the outside, the interior looked absolutely incredible. While the wooden ribbed ceiling wasn't anything to write home about, the solid marble walls were impressive. It wasn't until he looked really closely that it became obvious that they were large pieces of tile instead of just one massive piece (credit, he decided, worth being offered to the Mason's Guild).

No, what made it so impressive was the mix of lights and decorations. It was the best-lit building he'd been in since leaving the Queen's Capitol itself, and considering that he'd seen several different temples since then – that was worth noting. There were no less than twenty sconces lining both walls and each of the four massive dining tables at the east end were covered in additional candelabras. That was to say nothing of the five glass chandeliers dangling from the ceiling, too.

What made his head hurt was that there wasn't a single stray wisp of smoke to be seen anywhere. None of the lights even emitted the faintest puff of a cloud. He'd have understood if it was magelight of some kind but a curious touch of one of the candles resulted in a slightly scorched fingertip (not to mention a rolling of Seline's eyes).

The experiment with fire was quickly ended when his lovely companion pulled him away from the walls and towards the center of the room. Along the way, he had time to take stock of who might be who, made a little easier by the way everyone was dressed. More than half of them were wearing thin cotton robes that were entirely red or gold, or at least, with gold trim. She recited a quick list of names confirming that, yes, most of the ones wearing the colors of the Dawnfire flag were actually members of Dawnfire nobility.

Not all of them, of course. Some merely wanted to look the part. There also were a few people with all white or white and gray robes (local priests that he recognized even without Seline pointing it out) and a few folk that wore outfits in greens and browns. "Merchant-Master Hannock made it clear that anyone representing the Queen had best be wearing her colors for these events," she explained, "just to show the wastelanders that we are united under one banner."

"Then why aren't we?" he whispered back in the same tone she was using.

"Because we aren't representing the kingdom. Well, no, that's not entirely true. I mean that we are, we're just -"

"- not getting paid to do it?" he interrupted and finished for her.

She started to scold him for that, then reluctantly nodded her head without giving him the pleasure of hearing her agree. Not that it would have changed anything; the reds and golds made it easy to pick out who took a cut from the Queen's coffers, but the midlander delegation didn't leave anything to question either. They stood out just as starkly as the nobility; you could even make the argument that they were more-so.

Despite the (thankful) death of winter more than a month and a half ago, most of the Odinal men wore brown or black fur coats with iron plates sewn into the fabric across their chests. Some of them weren't taking well to the sudden arrival of a heatwave (or, as Akaran called it, false-summer) and a couple of them looked so miserable that the exorcist honestly felt sorry for them.

Their women, on the other hand? That was an entirely different issue to address. Every single one of them, regardless of age, wore thick cotton dresses with belts made of looped copper rings. He only spotted two of them wearing anything on their heads, and both of them were wearing elegant brown scarves that draped around their necks and down their backs. Intriguingly, they also all wore elbow-length gloves on their right hands – and just the right. Most of them were leather, but a few were silk (including the ones wearing the scarves).

Before he could ask his not-a-date about it, Seline stopped suddenly and put her hand on his shoulder. "Okay. How'd you do it."

"Do what?"

"Get us in here," she whispered just loud enough for just him to hear, "I *saw* that guest list. I'm *seeing* the people in the room. *What did you do* to get us in here?"

"Oh, that, nothing major, I promise."

She faced him and lifted both of her eyebrows incredulously. "I know you're down one eye but you *do* see who all is in this room, right? I'm not entirely sure that we shouldn't be out caring for their horses."

Akaran grinned and pointed off in the corner where an old friend was standing. "I have no idea who almost any of these people are, honestly. But you see the battlemage over there?"

The healer followed his finger and couldn't tell which of the soldiers in the pack he was gesturing at he was talking about. "No?" There were at least six different men (four of them Dawnfire troops and two of them midlanders) along with three different women all clustered together, laughing and happily drinking the night away.

"The one with the flagon and the beard. The big flagon... and bigger beard. Standing next to that woman in the black dress," he replied. "Specialist-Major Badin. He's the guy that escorted me to the city."

"Badin... okay but... I know that I'm a little rusty on my ranks in the military, but I am fairly sure that a random mageblade can't get us in here..."

He shrugged and pointed at the woman beside him. "He met someone. Apparently, she has clout. Ran into him the other day. He told me he could get me on the guest list and anyone I wanted to bring with me."

"Has... clout?" she started to whisper before she squeezed his shoulder so hard her fingers went white. "*DO YOU KNOW WHO THAT IS*?!"

"No? But to be fair you didn't know who he was and -"

"I swear to the *Gods* I don't think it's safe to take you anywhere," she sighed as she let go and steepled her fingers in front of her face. "Don't talk to her. She's a headache you do *not* need."

"Who is it?"

Seline took a breath and then stopped herself "No. You know what? No.

I'm not telling you. If I tell you, you may go try to talk to her. So, I'm not." He stood there looking wounded and insulted, and then gave up and started walking towards the banquet table and a steaming pile of fresh pies. "I honestly wasn't sure you were going to make it. You were running so late..."

"I'm sorry," he replied with a little shrug, "but after that nightmare, I found some interesting stuff in the library."

"Anything new that can help you?"

"Me, yes, leg, no, magic, no. Do you remember the girl I mentioned? The one I... miss?"

There was a brief pause and an indignant little huff from the healer before she replied, slowly and in an irritated low tone, "Yes."

Oblivious, he didn't reply until he was staring at the golden-crusted pie sitting there on the table, with little tufts of steam floating from the cuts on top like a siren call for his soul... or at least, his nose. "The village was attacked while I was dealing with... *stuff*... at the end. A few people died. She lost her eye in the fight."

"Oh... oh that's horrible," she replied with a slightly aghast and vaguely apologetic look.

"Yeah... lost a friend and... I wasn't even there to try to save them," he lamented.

"I'm sure you did all you could," Seline replied softly.

He ignored the utterly vile look a serving girl gave him as he started to cut into the pie, although the healer didn't try to stop him even after she caught the same disgusted stare. "I found a description of the bastard that did it. Unrelated tome to my research," he went on as he put the first piece on a simple ceramic plate and handed it to her, "which is good, but confusing. However, it's a start."

She had a mouthful tucked between her cheeks before she thought to ask, "Good? Why?"

The way his eye went cold and his lips curled into a faint mockery of a smile almost made her choke on a piece of baked peach. "Because when I'm healed I'm going to hunt him. I'm going to find him, I'm going to hold him down, and I am going to gouge out his eye for her and feed it to him before I break his neck," he promised.

She *did* choke hearing that and nearly dropped her plate. "You -"

He didn't wait for a reply from her before looking around the room and tilting his head slightly in mild confusion. "So... there's a lot more people here than I expected."

Seline managed to finish chewing as she awed how fast he went from *ready to murder* back to *just wanna have fun* and tried (desperately) to not show it. "Oh? More than you expected? We've had dignitaries filling the city now for more than a month and you're shocked that there are this many bodies present for the first city-wide meet and greet?"

"Well... yes," he answered with an utterly stupid look on his face.

"You really aren't one for ceremonies like this, are you?"

"It's shiny?" Akaran replied with all the innocence of a three-year-old holding his first gold coin.

The healer gave up trying to deal with how utterly absurd he was and broke down into a peal of laughter that caught the eye of a few people around them, including someone that she vaguely wished hadn't. That, of course, was the someone that broke away from the pack and strode over in their general direction.

Most men (and some women) would've noticed that she was taller than your average man (let alone your average woman), or they would've noticed how shiny her toffee-blonde hair was (short as it was), or possibly even her pale-pink eyes. Others would've had their breaths taken away by her shoulderless white gown with gray and silver lace running around the edges.

Most would've.

For a fleeting second, Akaran wished he was most.

What he noticed instead wasn't the pink sash around her waist, or that she was the only person in the room wearing sandals instead of boots of some kind. He noticed the braided copper circlet around her forehead, and the faintly glowing piece of multi-faceted clear crystal anchored in the center of it. "Seline! Of all the souls I was expecting today, you were not one of them," she said as she stretched her arms out to wrap the younger woman up in a tight hug before turning her eyes towards Akaran. "And I see you brought a guest. He looks of better class than the last."

"*I'm* of better class than your last?" he asked the healer as she started to turn a brilliant shade of red as the older woman held her head almost directly on her bodice. "Should I be worried about you?"

"Oh, heavens, no," she quickly denied. "Th... this is Akaran, he's one of our newest residents at the manor."

"A patient?" she asked with her beautiful eyes going wide as she sized him up and realized that he was walking with a cane. "You know that there are people that could find that concerning. Though... you'd not be the first nurse to wish to spend *extra* time with a man in her care."

Seline's blush was turning into a thing of legend as she backed away from the hug and shook her head so fast part of her bun became undone. "Oh, Goddesses. No, priestess. It's nothing like that. I'm sure."

"Oh, I am *quite* sure," the taller woman contested as Akaran just stood there with a grin. "So let's have a look at this patient you brought to the dance."

"He brought me..." she muttered.

"I'm not so sure that makes it better, you know."

"Priestess!"

Figuring that there was only so long he could enjoy her discomfort, the exorcist cleared his throat and interrupted their exchange. "She's telling the truth, actually. I'm not here as her um... *interest*. I'm just here to watch."

"I can see you're not here to dance, unless you are more talented with that stick than I think you are," she replied as he started to turn a little red himself. "She said your name is... Akaran, wasn't it? You wouldn't be the same one that Deboria Ult spoke so highly of, would you be? The one that Risson worked on a few days back?"

He nodded a short response, then admitted he had no idea what praise she was referring to. "I don't know why she would."

She made a show of counting on her fingers as she replied to him. "You stopped a demon from rampaging through Gonta and prevented all-out war from erupting on the northern border. You punished the Order of Frost in a way that managed to both irritate those frozen little watchmen and provide a necessary service to the Gods as a whole. You also arranged for Deboria to meet the man she says is the new love of her life, blessed be her heart and hopeful union."

The last one on her list nearly made him drop his pie. "I did WHAT? She... Steelhom and... they WHAT?"

"I'd say that's worthy of being spoken for."

"Did they get... did they...?"

"Get married?" she asked. "No, no, he's still in the courtship phase. I've known the woman for years and she wrote more about *him* in the letter she sent *about* you than she actually did about *you*. I'd say you did well on all accounts."

He tried to work his mouth and eventually ended up swallowing loudly enough for the two of them to hear before replying, "I don't know about that and I don't think I want to know. For the rest, a job is a job," he said with a slow shrug. "I go where the Goddess sends."

"Do you feel She sent you here?"

"Command did. I assume it's the same thing."

"Not an unwise deduction, though, much as the commanders of most militaries do, I assume that they confuse themselves with the Gods more often than not," she replied as she winked over at the younger woman. "Seline, I like this one. If you ever *do* decide to take an interest in him, I'd do it quickly. He might not last long on his own."

"I might not... what?" Akaran managed to choke out with a troubled look and suddenly felt even *more* trouble when she looked back at him with a distressingly large grin. "I'm just here to get my leg taken care of. That's it. Leg, then gone."

The priestess answered with a chuckle from deep within her chest. "Well, you should be warned. Many an eligible maiden are taking a shine to the idea of wedlock these days. The streets are just full of women on the prowl." He froze as she touched his hand (and Seline felt the hackles on her neck rising all over again for no reason she wanted to consider), before she added, "and one that has connections with the crown by rank? One that so *obviously* could use a woman's touch to help him return to glory? Oh, my boy. I'd not walk down an alley alone were I you."

"Yes, yes, well, his studies at the Repository take precedence," the healer interrupted quickly, "and his efforts at the Manor to recover are far more important than going out and prowling for eligible and unattended ladies."

"So he's interested only in the ineligible ones. Is that why he brought you here?"

He coughed and carefully extracted his hand from her grip. "No, I... truth is? We needed to get out of the manor. The house hasn't been... relaxing... lately."

"Oh," the priestess replied with a sad little nod. "Oh, yes. So this truly isn't an excuse to convince the young lady to provide *extra* care? She has truly done worse in her life before, you know."

"It's only an excuse to drink honey mead and eat berry tarts, priestess," he answered with his eye briefly cast up to the gem in her circlet. "My word to the Goddess."

She smiled in response and practically brightened up the room. "Then you may be a better man than what I've heard – and I've heard much."

"Do I want to know?"

"Mostly good things," she replied with a twinkle to her eye and a glimmer from the stone.

Seline coughed and tried to interrupt before he could put his foot in his mouth. "Akaran? If she's quite done trying to make us both feel immensely uncomfortable – behavior ill-befitting a woman of her stature, I may add for good measure – this is Priestess Lexcanna Jealions, of the Ellachurstine Shrine."

The exorcist quickly bent his knee as much as he could and bowed his head. "Priestess. I'm sorry, I didn't realize. I assumed Stara, but not -"

"- that I am the caretaker of the local temple?" she finished for him, then gave him a forgiving little nod and smile. "Oh it's quite alright; I know how little work your Order does with mine."

"We don't always get along well, no..." he replied with a half-mutter.

"That isn't what I've heard about you, though," she quickly returned as she looked over her shoulder, searching for someone. "I actually came with Risson. He's down at the other end of the hall right now. It's a painstaking job, but we've been meeting and greeting everyone that's come in from Midan."

"Midan?" Akaran asked with a slight frown.

She flicked her fingers in the general direction of a cluster of the Odinal delegation and answered simply, "Them."

"Midan is one of the city-states along the Midland wastes, Akaran," Seline explained, "and is where Clan Odinal makes their home."

"Oh," he said with a little nod, "that makes sense. Meet anyone interesting?"

Lexcanna grinned and turned her attention back square to him. "Oh, quite a few actually. Everyone from the Tessamirches themselves to Merchant-Master Hannock and Betrothed Tyreening," she said before she brought her hand up to the side of her mouth and whispered, "Tyreening is already half-drunk. Sanlian would *kill* him if she knew."

"Sanlian? Akaran asked.

"Sorry. Most only know her as 'Maiden Esterveen.' Sanlian is her first name," Lexcanna corrected.

"A gossip as always, priestess," Seline sighed under her breath.

She didn't even try to deny it. "Ah, we all have our vices. Spending one's days in the Chapel administering to the misbegotten that want grace and the rich that *need* it gives a woman ample opportunities to hear things," she said as she started to grin a bit more. "Besides, it's a matter of practicality."

"How so?" the younger girl asked.

"Knowing who's who and what secrets are who's secrets helps ensure a steady supply of donations to the chapel coffers."

Akaran grunted off to the side and gave her a second, more thoughtful look. "Knowledge is always power. So you've met the Odinals?"

"I have. Very interesting. You notice their women are all wearing gloves on their right hands?"

Considering that it had been bothering him since the first time he'd laid his eye on them, he replied quickly. "I did. Fashion choice or other?"

"Other, it seems. One hand always ready to show love, the other always ready to fight for it. Every single one of them is armed, at that." The priestess pursed her lips for a moment and then thoughtfully asked, "Doesn't your Order have a saying about that?"

He smirked with his response. "A velvet glove or a gauntleted fist, know which She wants us to be."

"That's the one," she quipped, "you know, you might have much in common with them."

Akaran casually swiped another pastry off of the table and stuffed it into his mouth. "Doubt it," he mumbled through the flaky crust, "the wartribes didn't welcome my people any more than the Civans did after the Hardening."

"Times change, and influences do too," she counseled.

"Not that much."

Seline made a 'tsk' sound with her tongue and lightly slapped his hand away from the tray when he made a move for another innocent confection. "Oh, come now. How many times has anyone in this city given you grief for who you follow?"

"Not often," he admitted, "but there's also more of the Lovers here than there are in most other places in Dawnfire, shy Mulvette proper."

It almost pained her to admit it, but Lex gave him a little vote of support. "He is right. In my own travels through the kingdom, the reception for those that bear their hearts on their sleeves is not warm. I can only imagine how much the idea of this wedding is frustrating you."

What was starting to feel like his default expression popped back on his face as he gave her a blank look. "It's a wedding? Why would it frustrate me?"

"Your people are none to fond of arranged weddings, aren't you?"

"No, we... oh," he said as it dawned on him. Akaran took a long look around the room and suddenly looked completely deflated. "Political, not true? I never considered that it was anything but heartfelt?"

She rolled her left hand through the air even as she ducked the right back into the sleeves of her white gown. "True enough for any couple, I suppose, but yes, it is more politics than it is of tenderness. It's why so many people are upset over it."

"People let themselves be upset over such silly things," Seline chimed in. "A wedding is a wedding. Houses need to be aligned at times. It's been done in such ways for thousands of years, and thousands more to come."

"Doesn't mean it's tasteless," he spat with a deepening frown.

"That's true," the priestess agreed, "but the Golden Baronessa being cajoled into going to bed with one of the barbarians of the midlands? Oh, you have *no* idea how upset people are."

Seline coughed and covered her mouth with her hand. "You forgot the best part of that."

"Oh, yes," Lexcanna replied with a rolling of her eyes. "How dare I: the mother of the groom is from Civa."

Akaran looked back and forth between the two of them and then stared over at the largest gathering of midlanders as his eye narrowed into an annoyed little slit. "Arranged marriage from one of the midland tribes with someone that's adored in Dawnfire, and his mother is a Civan."

"That's right," the healer replied.

He looked over at her and asked, completely seriously, "Was someone drunk when they came up with that idea?"

The priestess bit back a little giggle. "I do believe you've managed to completely eclipse the idea in one simple question."

"There's a few other complications, of course," Seline added.

"Oh, of course," he replied sardonically, rolling his eye over the gossip.

Lexcanna wagged a finger at him and shushed him with a 'tsk' of her own. "Don't be so quick to dismiss. The *why* the alliance is being broached is as equal importance as the disdain for it. The woman right over there – do you see her?" she asked as she pointed to a noble several feet away.

She was wearing a dark cloak with a green leather vest under it. Even though the room was feeling more hot and stuffy than not, she was wearing a pair of thick chainmail gloves and carried herself like she had on a lot more than that underneath. "Impossible to miss. Think I've seen that huntress before."

"*The* Huntress," she told him, "That's Huntsmatron Elsith. She manages the Guild Hall for Kettering. Notice she looks a bit irritated?"

Irritated was an understatement. Ignoring the fact that she was openly armed (in her defense, about a third of the room was) she was one of a very few openly armored, too, and from the look on her face, she was about to carry out a writ on the spot if one was even suggested. "She looks like she's ready to trigger the end of days."

"Not quite that bad, but yes, she's tense," Lexcanna admitted. "The bride-to-be's half-brother is a man named Kee Tessamirch... he's in here somewhere. He is the sole commander and shareholder of the Advensi of Massadine, an otherwise unremarkable mercenary outfit formed after the last Imperium War."

"Mercenaries, hm? I'm listening."

"Interested in being a soldier of fortune?" Seline gently chided.

Missing the joke, he shook his head. "No, it's not that. But mercenaries get hired to do things that either result in more dead and defiled that we have to go clean up, or, sometimes we have to hire them when *we* have to clean up a mess and other people in the area don't want us around," he admitted. "Always nice to know who's on tap where."

"Once a soldier always a soldier, I see," the priestess interjected.

"Knowing where the swords are keeps you alive."

She had to nod her head and accept that for what it was. "A fair observation. Still, the reason why Elsith looks as if she's recently swallowed a roach is because Kee plans to use Hylene's marriage to secure new contracts leading to and from the midland – contracts that the Hunter's Guild used to have sole access to."

The exorcist cringed and suddenly felt really, really bad for her. "And she's on the hook for losing access to what, I presume, is a wealthy market for the Guild."

"Very."

That pang of pity redoubled as he tried to imagine how much trouble she was in. "Well, if the Advensi are just a new group, then it surely can't matter as much to the Guild to completely shaft them, can it?"

"There will *always* be contracts for the Guild, make no mistake," she cautioned. "However, it is safe to say that upper management has not been looking down on her fondly over it."

"Doesn't sound like it's her fault."

"Oh it's not, but since when has that ever stopped people above from yelling at the people below them?"

Seline nodded knowingly. "Is that not one of the grandest truths stated in one breath?" Her not-a-date looked over at her and she shrugged at the unasked question. "I provide care for a manor full of mentally and physically ill. Do you think I'd somehow be immune to the irritation of the Lady myself?"

Before he could reply, Lexcanna barged right back into the conversation. "So. What of you two? I've talked your ears off by this point. Anything new? Anything entertaining, worth mentioning? I heard about Livstra. I can only offer my most sincere apologies. Were they able to find the culprit?"

The healer looked pained at the casual question and Akaran replied before she had to. "No. They've narrowed it down to a couple of the patients but the staff has been cleared," he explained as she looked at him in thankful relief. "Seline needed to get away from everything tonight. That's why we're here," he said, repeating himself from earlier as he narrowed his eye at the older, taller, woman, "to get away from it."

She took the hint and quickly agreed. "Of course. It's a night of celebration, after all. Well. I won't keep the two of you any longer. Please do feel free to talk to me any time you wish, *Sir* exorcist," she replied, stressing the 'sir' a little too much for his comfort. "I would love to get to know you if you're not otherwise attached to anyone."

"Thank you, priestess," Seline returned with a warm smile. "May Isamiael keep you in good health, always."

"And Love with your heart," he added.

"And may the Pantheon look favorably upon you both," she said before she slipped back into the crowd proper.

After she was gone, Akaran sagged down against his cane and let out a breath he didn't realize he'd been holding. "Is it me or did we just get run over by a herd of cattle wearing a priestess disguise?"

She grinned at him and raised her finger. "Remember my advisory about noblewomen that would be interested in unattended young men?"

"I do..."

"She knows you're unattended now," she warned, "and a wise man would find a way to run."

He grimaced and braced himself for an inevitable headache later. "A wiser man wouldn't have broken his leg."

"Just be careful," she repeated, "as there are some things that certain women carry that are easy for a man to catch, and hard to be rid with or *without* magic."

The exorcist's blank look returned and he chewed on the air before finally going, "Is that a polite way of saying -"

"It is how I will say I need to go speak with Tidesinger Quinchecco by the minstrels," she interrupted. "I haven't seen the man in months, and I'd be remiss if I didn't."

"Riiight. I'll be -" he started to say before seeing a larger banquet table with something very large, very meaty, and very delicious staring at him. "- there. I'll be there."

Seline followed his gaze to the sight of the roasted ox and the pile of pastries laying around it and rolled her eyes as she walked away. After she made her exit, he hobbled over as fast as he possibly could and tried to ignore the steady clacking sound the end of his cane made on the floor with every step he took. Once he was firmly entrenched beside the roast, he let himself listen to the soft tunes coming from a band of minstrels playing in the corner.

While they worked their magic with a pair of lutes, a flute, and some strange horn that he'd never seen (or heard) before, he tried to pick out what he could from the conversations around him. It didn't take long to realize that Lexcanna had been very, very right – people *weren't* happy about the wedding. He'd written off the grousing of the commoners at the parade as just commoners being common. In here though? In this throng of the rich, the powerful, the egotistical, and the stuffy?

They were just as divided, if not worse. Quite a few liked it, but the ones that didn't? They struck him as having no compulsion against using coins to express their displeasure. Or coins for trade, coins for bribes, and coins for blood.

Still, there were enough that were cheerful that made him hope that this wouldn't be as bad as the priestess had suggested. Not only that, but more than a few people were talking about ways to make even more money off of it.

That included the woman that had accosted him the other night. As soon as he caught sight of her, he did his best to make sure that she didn't catch sight of him. While she was out of earshot, he did his best to take note of everyone standing anywhere close to her – and two of them stuck out like a sore toe. The first was the sergeant-at-arms from the manor, though he'd kept a really low profile recently, and only popped his head up when the Lady requested his presence directly.

Akaran privately assumed it was because he had expected the manor to just be one of those 'show up get paid go drink' jobs, and now someone was forcing him to *work*. Now though, seeing him having an apparently meaningful (if not hushed) conversation with that strange woman? That didn't sit well. The only thing that set less well wasn't who was talking to her – but who was watching Anais off from the side.

Donta, he recalled, discretely staring at the only man wearing a hat in the entire Hall. *Has to be her bodyguard. Extortionist, too, and at her command*, he mused as he thought back to the incident he'd witnessed at the docks near the northern stairwall. *I don't want to get on his bad side, nor hers...*

With that tidbit of knowledge firmly in check, the next sight that took his attention was a lively discussion between two women against the far wall. One was a short, brown-haired lady with more curves than not who was wearing a fox-tail lined vest over her shoulders and a white robe, and the other could've been her sister. Her dress was a shade of pebble gray, and her face was oddly familiar. Whatever they were fighting over didn't stop until Ladjunct Risson hurried over and pulled them apart. It wasn't until they were separated that he realized that brunette was Ridora's assistant Raechil – and was trying *far* too hard to look *much* older than she actually was.

That made him wonder how she managed to get into the dance, and wonder even harder why she was picking a fight with someone wearing the mark of a Melian Deconstructionist. *A haughty name for a priestess if I ever heard one*, he grumbled disapprovingly to himself. *'We break things' is not a religion. I don't care how well many people worship Her or even if Melia IS the Matron Goddess of the Kingdom.*

Despite his best efforts, he couldn't overhear them. However, as he strained, he continued to make himself at home with more than a few tarts and sweet rolls. That changed when a very short, very irritated, very foul-mouthed old woman came over and told him exactly where and how he could eat the next slice of cake that he was staring at on his third pass through the pastry line.

Nor did she care that he was just a wounded soldier trying to find comfort. She made it clear that he could find his comforts outside and in the company of the finest goat in the city if he didn't mind first his mouth and then his fingers. It had the effect she wanted and he slunk off into the celebrants with a mumbled apology for taking more than his fair share.

Neither one of them believed it, but it was enough to convince her to let him stay. He almost decided to go see what was happening when Risson threw his hands into the air and stomped off, letting the two of them squabble all by themselves. His attempt to do so ended when he overheard someone being *much* more interesting and *much* more incorrect a few feet away.

"All I am saying is that we shouldn't invite the Order that was responsible for the 3rd Imperium War to have say over the wedding," the first said in what may have been *the* most condescending tone of anyone in the entire hall. "It is a celebration of joining houses. Alliances. Peace. We don't need *them* to have *any* kind of say in the matter."

"Yes, but that was a long time ago," the woman beside him argued in a futile attempt to convince the blowhard that it was okay, "and it would truly do all of well if the Lovers offered their blessing."

"The blessing of the Harlot's servants doesn't matter," he countered, staring down his crooked nose at the beautiful woman stuck putting up with his shit. "They are a failing organization that is only tolerated because of how they suckle the Queen's tits. *You* stayed in our father's loving arms while *I* fought on the front line of the war that *they* started."

That was all Akaran could take. The sound of his voice alone was enough to make him grind his teeth together, but hearing this idiot slander the temple? If the bounty of pastries had dried up, there was less reason to play nice. "That's not even close to the truth," he said loud enough to interrupt them before the beautiful, violet-eyed woman beside the blowhard could reply.

The interruption didn't come without earning a dirty look from a dirty-looking man in his late thirties, maybe early forties. Hey had a beaked, crooked nose that was almost impossible not to stare at and the longer the exorcist did, the harder it was to keep from laughing at him. "Excuse me?" he demanded with a haughty little sneer.

"That's not true," Akaran repeated. "The Order of Love had nothing to do with the start of the 3rd."

"Oh? And how do you know? Were you there?"

"No, but I studied it. It was an important matter for the temple and it was mandatory to read into it in our training."

That earned another sneer, which oddly seemed to fit the tall, square-faced nobleman quite well. "Well, I was actually there," he huffed.

He tilted his head slightly and narrowed his eye. "In the war or actually at the Concords of Woulofon when the war started?"

"I served in the 3rd under Maiden Dreanna Allav. I answered directly to her Consort-Blade," he retorted back. "As her Consort was directly involved with the Concords, I know exactly what I speak of."

Akaran sucked a little air through his lips and leaned against his cane, utterly unimpressed. "Dreanna never had her forces get through Anthor's Pass, did she? She was tasked to stay behind and guard Anthor from 489 until 501," he returned, adding, "she didn't really see any notable action until the Underwars forced the Kak'kal'kak orcs out right into the middle of the Midland theater?"

"Yes... yes, that's correct," he replied slowly, tensing up as he tried to make sense of this interloper. "A student of history, I see."

The exorcist didn't let up. "Were you assigned to Maiden Allav at the start of the war?"

"Yes, what of it? It bears no meaning to the conversation at hand."

He grinned haughtily while the woman looked on bemused with a tinkle in her eyes. "But if you served for Dreanna's Consort-Blade, then you never left *that* battlefront either. In fact, you'd have been stationed near Ginsgmeg when the Concords turned into a riot and the war started," he eyed him up and wrote him off as a soldier-with-ego and not much more. "And, in truth, unless you're a *lot* older than you look, you're too young to have been actually *serving* in the army when the war broke out."

His lady companion stifled a dainty laugh behind her hand and quickly clarified, "My dear stepbrother means he was a squire to the Consort as part of an arrangement with our father. He didn't actually take up arms until just before the deployment to Anthor."

"And he would've been almost in diapers when the Concords happened," Akaran pointed out.

"My *age* is irrelevant," he snapped, "and you're far too young yourself to be casting aspersions on what I have thus-far done with my life or where I was at when I grew up."

"It is when you're wrong," he contested. "The Order was specifically forbidden from having *anyone* representing us at the Concords. It was before Johasta was appointed to the rank of Holy General, and the Order was relegated to keeping our heads down and mouth shut in all matters of state."

"But the Order was still responsible."

The exorcist ignored him as he bit his lip and worked through memories of old musty tomes and an even mustier history lesson. "In *fact*, not only was the Order not present, one of the sticking points before the Concords fell apart was the request from the High Flame of Civa to have the Grand Temple razed to the ground and the soil salted."

His verbose opponent cleared his throat and smiled like he'd just won something. "So you admit that there was a motive for your wretched people to see the talks fall apart. Tens of thousands of good men died because of you."

"Tens of thousands of good men died because a stupid little boy chased his cat through the Castle Woulofon stables and knocked over a torch," he retorted. "The resulting fire is what caused the death of Princess Aveve and everything else went downhill from there."

The argumentative idiot waved his hand and dismissed him with a sneer. "That pathetic story. No. Mark my words – the Order of Love was responsible for those talks failing. Not some silly cat."

Akaran just rolled his eyes. "I marked your words. They just happen to be wrong. The cat wasn't silly. The *kid* was stupid. I'd run too if a little boy was chasing me and trying to pull my tail."

"A feeling more women are inclined to agree with than I think that you would realize," the beautiful woman beside him replied with a snicker.

He'd have guessed that there wasn't any way for the noble to look even more scandalized at being called out for being an idiot. He was wrong. "Hylene! He speaks as if he was there. What would such a low-born priest even deign to know about the nature of war? Let alone the causes of it."

THAT'S the Golden Baronessa? The bride-to-be of this... pretentious... shindig? he marveled to himself before following up the thought with an equally poignant, *Well, shit.*

"There are a great many of priests of his cloth that call this place home, Kee, my brother," she pointed out with a smile and a respectful bow of her head towards the priest. "I have heard that they teach their scribes well, even at a young age. If he swears the Lovers had no hand in the outbreak of the war, who are we to question?"

"Oh, not a scribe," he clarified quickly. "Exorcist. I don't enjoy studying as much as I'm told to."

And now he looked even *more* embarrassed. It was almost starting to get funny. "Gah! You'd side with one of *them* over me?"

"You are a student of the blade, more than you are the scroll," she returned before turning her focus back to Akaran. "What of you? If you're an exorcist, you must take up arms, but I have heard that the studies you are subjected to would rival that of most men in my father's court. Or my brother's employ."

Her brother's jaw dropped and he quickly tugged his bright blue vest straight. "The Advensi employ numerous -"

Akaran ignored him and focused on the Golden Baronessa instead. "I hate spending time sitting down and pouring over musty tomes. I'd much rather be out fighting. But... history is where you find dead things."

"Where you find dead things...?" Kee replied with his mouth agape. "See? There's no reason to believe a man that has no desire to touch a book. At least *I* appreciate the efforts of an author."

"*But* wars bring dreadful things to light," the exorcist pointed out. "Creatures that the dark spawns because of the conflict, or creatures that exist to take advantage of it. Like I said: it's where you find dead things," he said with a shrug. "Say what you will about the Order, it's groups like yours that help keep people like me busy."

Kee growled under his breath and pointed down at the exorcist's cane. "Yes. Busy. As busy as a lame man can be, I presume. While you talk about things you don't know, my men are happy to help ensure peace between noble houses in our own fashion."

"Peaceful for your employer. The dead would disagree"

"Peace is peace," he snapped back.

Hylene cleared her throat and gave the priest a fresh smile. "So. What is it that brings a man of the cloth such as yourself to our Danse?"

"Pastries," he deadpanned. "That woman with the dark hair and the tan dress made me stop eating them."

She hid her giggle behind her hand as her eyes glittered in amusement. "And funny to boot! Isn't he just marvelous, Kee?"

"Wonderfully delightful," he replied as he rolled his eyes to the ceiling.

A passing servant stopped and put her hand on top of Akaran's. "If Madam Comstead herself is the one to shoo you away," she leaned in to interrupt and whisper, "you'd best not even look back towards them." She let the touch linger on his hand and slowly winked at him before adding a, "If you're here by yourself, maybe we can talk later?"

He flushed and Kee made a disapproving growl in the back of his throat that chased the maid away. "Does *no one* have manners in this party tonight?"

The Baronessa, however, giggled and agreed with the warning. "Yes, she's quite right. I'm afraid I've known her all my life. Not an unkind woman but she does have a preference for how things are to be."

"Good to know," he grumbled with a defeated little sigh. "Then if those are gone... I do hope you'll have a pleasant night. May the Goddess keep your hearts warm."

"Oh, no," the nobleman growled at him as he pointed his finger at Akaran's face. "Since you found it necessary to inject yourself in a conversation that didn't involve you, perhaps you can answer a question."

"You were spreading li... ah, I mean, expressing *incorrect opinions* about the history of my Order," he started – and clarified – with a little smirk of his own. "I'd hate to think that someone so well respected such as *you* wouldn't want to know the truth of the world."

Kee let it slide but glared darkly as he started to ask his question. "I understand that your Order holds marriage in exceptionally high esteem, as an institution."

"We do," he replied with a short nod. "Nothing is greater than the joining of hearts together. Were there more love in this world, we might all suffer much less."

"Yes, well. As you are well aware, not every marriage is done for such an antiquated expression. It seems that half the city is up in arms over my beloved sister's desire to settle in the Midlands. What say you?"

The exorcist pursed his lips and looked back and forth between them. "You want my opinion on your sister's marriage?"

"I believe that's what I asked for, yes," the mercenary responded.

Hylene templed her hands and bowed her head slightly in a gesture of respect. "What he left out is that we've been thus-far unable to secure an audience with Maiden Prostil and earn her blessing. She is the one woman that has been unwilling to speak to us about it."

That was a red flag if there ever was one. "Do you have any idea why?"

"Oo-lo is Oo-lo," Kee replied with a little dismissive snarl. "The desire to be flippant in the face of their betters is one of the reasons that so few of us give a care for what they think."

"But you do."

"*I* do, Sir Priest," his sister interjected. "With so many angry, it is enough to make a mind wonder if I have been cursed by the Gods for her choice of whom to wed. The Order of Stara has offered their voice of support but I feel that they would offer it for anyone that makes suitable donations to the church coffers."

Kee grunted and shot a glare off in the direction of Priestess Lexcanna on the other side of the room. "And those donations *are* made."

"Somehow I don't doubt that," Akaran replied with a little grin. After he took a drink and chewed on the best way to phrase it, he waded in as delicately as he could. "I don't speak for the Maiden. I don't speak for the Order. I don't have that right."

"Though you are a member of it, isn't that right?" the contemptuous merc retorted. "Or does prancing around with a cane somehow forbid you from being able to speak for the others that follow your *supposed* Lady?"

"Supposed?" he snapped as he gripped his cane tighter and gave him a withering look. "If you asked me for an opinion on how to best keep a wraith from pestering your house, I could give it on behalf of the Order. Since you're asking for an interpretation of holy edicts and the Voice of Love, then at best, I can just give you my personal."

"And why not an official?" Hylene asked.

Akaran gave her a bit more leeway and tried to temper his tone. "Baronessa, I'm a priest. But I'm not the nice kind. Like I've told everyone else: I'm not someone who was taught to convert souls. That's not my job."

Her brother looked down his crooked nose and for the first time, looked moderately interested in the younger man. "And what, pray-tell, *is* your job, then?"

"To cull them. I have been taught, and trained, and had my body broken by one simple edict: to deliver the word of my Goddess."

"You just said -" he started to retort before he was shut down.

"That word is *begone*," the exorcist finished. "So. I can give you my *interpretation*, but I can't speak on behalf of those that know Her true feelings on such matters."

For some reason, that seemed to resonate a little bit with Kee and he backed off (if just barely). "Interpret away."

Akaran turned to Hylene and looked her dead in her violet-laced eyes. "Do you love him?"

It should've been the question she expected.

Of course, that meant it wasn't. "I'm sorry?"

"The man you're about to marry," he clarified. "Do you love him?"

She stood there like a doe that just realized it had been spotted by a dragon. "I... I don't know, really. I mean we haven't spent a great deal of time together or the like. He's always been fairly polite... for a midlander."

"Then if you don't know then I don't approve."

"Even though it stands to bring countless riches to the family?" Kee asked. "Once to her family, the entire city shall benefit. Surely that makes it worth it, does it not?"

The exorcist took another drink and forced himself not to give that the response it actually deserved. "With all due respect, the only time a city benefits from someone getting richer is when they get arrested and their assets seized by the crown. Your company – your family – earning money only benefits you, and I sincerely doubt the people that work for you will share in it with extra stipends added to their pay?"

A few feet behind him the maid from earlier had to cover her mouth to keep from unleashing a peel of laughter. The mercenary turned red with anger, and his sister looked genuinely hurt. "You don't feel that it is the duty of the daughter of one of the great houses to ensure the success of her family?"

"I do," he replied with a little shrug.

"Then you understand why I do it. With or without love," she replied with a ladylike sigh of resignation.

"I do," Akaran repeated before deciding to throw caution to the wind. "But may I be frank, Lady?"

"I see no reason for you to stop now," she said with a hint of an indignant huff.

The exorcist took a deep breath and laid it out as simply as he could. "If you love him, then by all means, marry him. If you think you can love him, then by all means and blessing, take his hand in yours. Be fruitful. Be successful. Be blessed. I *wasn't* kidding. This world needs more love in it. Both as the Goddess and Her very nature, and as kindness shown between people. If we had more of it, maybe we'd need fewer people like him," he said, gesturing to Kee, "and fewer people that get hurt like *me*."

"Oh, I see," her brother snarled, "so your interest isn't in a matter of faith, but in a matter of cowardice. You feel that if more people did things our of the goodness of their hearts, there'd be less cause for men to prove themselves on the battlefield. Or worse, like you – to prove themselves and be found wanting."

He shook his head no. "It's not even that. Lady Tessamirch?"

"Yes?"

"You want to ensure the success of your family – that's why you agreed to this wedding?"

With a hint of nervousness to her smile, she answered honestly. "Yes, it is. I never gave much thought of it until my brother introduced the two of us."

Akaran paused and gave careful thought to how he phrased it. "This world is changing. Women are being more successful, day in and day out, with their lot in life. So much of the Kingdom is controlled by women of power – the Holy General, the Maidens, the Huntsmatron of Basion even, and so many more. Wouldn't you rather be successful in the way that they are? Wouldn't you rather do more with your position than just..." he explained before his voice trailed off as polite words failed him.

Intrigued, she leaned in a little with her eyebrow lifting. "Than just...?"

"Well, I mean. If love isn't why you're interested in marrying him, then couldn't you find another way to secure your family's place in the world? Rather than debase yourself?"

She caught his meaning as plain as day as her brother stood there dumbly. "Debase myself? *Debase* myself? Marriage is a way of securing assets, of binding houses together. Our children will be citizens of both the Kingdom and the western midlands. Our family's reach will transcend borders because of it."

"That's *exactly* what I mean," he replied. "You don't have to secure an alliance that way. You can seek out riches and fame in your own right. You don't have to do it on your back."

The maid choked and Hylene's voice went up a dozen octaves. "ON MY BACK?!"

Kee, on the other hand, was so incensed that he drew his knife halfway from its sheath. "Are you DARING to insinuate my sister is a common whore!?"

"No," he quickly denied as he tried to find a way to backpedal out of this. "All I'm attempting to tell you, both of you, is that if she doesn't love this Odinal fellow, then maybe there's a different way for her to secure your family's future. If you were so sure of it yourself, you'd lead your company off to victory instead of relying on your sister to make the contracts for you," he charged.

Tried to backpedal being the operative phrase. What he did was piss Kee off so much that he finished drawing his blade and pointed the ceremonial dagger at Akaran's neck. "That is EXACTLY what you are suggesting! That my sister is a whore!"

He backed up slightly and raised his finger and pressed it to the tip of the blade. "You said *common*," he argued. "Offering her body to a strange man for her for business contracts takes her a few shades over the ones that sit on the street corner," he went on before bowing his head towards the Baronessa. "No offense intended, my lady, of course."

"NO OFFENSE!?" she screeched and advanced on him like a furious banshee. "I'm to be married in a matter of weeks, and you, YOU, a *priest*, dare stand here and tell me that not only will you provide no blessing but you think I little better than a street corner slu- ?!"

The first shout had caught Seline's attention. The screeching had convinced her to run. "NO! No, no, of course not, no!" she hastily interrupted. The suggestion that he had just called the Golden Baronessa of Basion City a whore caused her to slam her hand over Akaran's mouth and stand between them. "What he means, what he... ah, what he means is that he's able to *understand* why some people are upset. I mean, you're quite the darling of the city."

"He stood there and claimed that I'd be signing contracts in bed!" Hylene countered as her hands shook with rage.

Akaran glared at her and managed to mumble out a retort, despite Sel's best efforts. "I said that your brother would sign them after sending you there."

"Oh you have crossed a line, peasant!" Kee snarled, lowering his sword *only* because the healer was in the path. "First you come and insult my intelligence and now you insult my sister?! How *dare* you!"

The exorcist pushed Seline's hand away from his face and did a surprisingly good job at keeping his tone level. "You stood there and lied about the Order and then bragged about how you arranged for your sister to hold suckling children against her tits with a man she doesn't love. How would *you* describe it?"

"I would describe it as -"

"I think we *all* would describe it as a way that ensures the success of your family and provides for theirs," Seline quickly interjected, "and an arrangement that helps strengthen the bonds between nations so that peace can be ensured to last even longer between our peoples."

"There have to be other ways than to do it by trapping a woman in a loveless marriage!" Akaran protested.

She shook her head and cuffed the back of his head. "There doesn't have to be *anything* as long as everyone is pleased with the result."

"Doesn't seem like anyone is," he grunted.

"*Most* people can't claim to have the heritage or education that House Tessamirch has, boy," Hylene's brother snarled. "Surely not some lowborn from a despised order like *yours.*"

"At least we don't tell our sisters what cocks they -"

Seline lost every ounce of color in her face and quickly positioned herself between him and his impending broken jaw. "AKARAN! Why don't you go and find something else to eat?"

"Lady Comstead told me no," he petulantly whined.

"You don't go back home to Lady Comstead," she warned, the raw, furious look in her eyes almost enough to set the air on fire. "Why don't you go somewhere else. Eat something else. Talk to someone else. *Now.*"

"Yes. Before you find yourself in need of more than one cane," Kee warned.

Akaran peered over his (hopefully still a) friend's shoulder and shot the mercenary a vile look of his own. "Is that a threat to an officer of the crown?"

"A friendly warning from one soldier to another," he snapped back. "Unless you're willing to find out how hard it is to *fight* on your back, I'd find somewhere else to be."

The priest glared fresh daggers at him and started to storm off. But not before, much to Seline's dismay, grumbling a retort just loud enough for the three of them to hear. "If what I hear about the midlands are true, you'll be able to ask your sister."

As Hylene started to make a sound that could've given a passerby the idea that wild hogs were rutting within earshot, a pig of a man was in the process of having a conversation with a lady. Or two pigs, depending on how you felt about Maiden Esterveen's Betrothed. The unabashed pig of a man next to him was a larger-than-life type sort, and the first thing to note about the big man from Sycio was that he was a rarity in the local courts of nobility due to his profession. "The stance of the Dunesires is that balance must be struck, nonetheless," he told the three poor souls stuck listening to him.

While the Sycian was a big bastard (literally and figuratively), Paverilak Tyreening was a tall one. "Yet to allow the open communion with demons? With the dead?" He also wasn't impressed with the shiverdine, and was managing to express his distaste of the slaver from Sycio in a way that would've made Kee jealous on the other side of the hall.

"Ah, but you speak of such things as if you do not do them yourselves. Everywhere one looks in this city you find a temple or a priest who seek to speak to the dead, do you not?"

"Yes," the Maiden's betrothed argued, "but there is a difference between the dead and the tortured and those blessed with life eternal, Se'daulif."

The slaver shook his round head and the movement made his chest-length beard drag through the fine goblet in his pudgy hands. "Is not the life after life eternal, regardless of which of the Gods one finds themselves serving?"

Paverilak narrowed his slightly-jaundiced eyes and looked at him in disbelief. "But it's known that the places where the Fallen work Their will are places of darkness and suffering."

"How is it known?" the other man challenged. "Who is it that makes these claims?"

"The Orders of the Pantheon, of course."

"And you believe them?" he scoffed. "It is preached by followers of Covorn that His realm is an eternally rolling field of quiet and peace. A garden where no grief can be found in the grass. It is said that the Palace of Avaritsha offers pleasures of all kinds to no end for eons upon eons, pleasures that none can deny – does that sound like a place of darkness and suffering?"

The comment earned an uncharacteristic flinch from the third person in their conversation, and Anais cleared her throat with a nervous cough. "Ah... yes. But who is it that can trust those that preach a lack of restraint?"

"This is where the Dunesires see things in such a different way!" Se'daulif crowed. "To *them*, we do see evidence of the divine in every day. We speak with them as they walk down the streets alongside us. In giving life to those passed, it is to commune with the next world every moment of our lives. We are but short of breath. Theirs is inexhaustible through time. Thus, it is no sin to speak to the things of eternity, and thus, we lose nothing by entertaining them."

"I have seen some of those things walk before though, shiverdine," she countered. "It it not easy to consider that the places where the Fallen hold sway are places of purity and beauty."

He flashed a toothy smile through pudgy lips at her as his pale red eyes lit with the very idea of it. "Ah! But dear one, purity is such a boredom! How few pleasures can there be if one is not willing to allow oneself moments of debasement?"

Anais covered her mouth to hide a sudden rush of revulsion as Paverilak spoke up. "Any a drunken fool will tell you as much. Easier to think that one'd be spending the afterlife with a head in a bucket from enjoying those excesses."

"Let it never be hard to imagine. Excesses do not bring salvation from the Gods," the lady cautioned again, despite the deaf ears it fell on.

"So again say the priests of the so-called light," the slaver retorted. "They are men that speak to beings that choose to see us as below Them, whereas the Gods you say are 'fallen' are the ones that seek to send Their emissaries to us to spread Their words and knowledge. One just must ask Them and be given what one deserves. Tell me, do you gain the same from the lofty Ones that claim to be the good in the world?"

"Yes, one does oft get what one deserves, be it good or -," she started before she saw someone new enter the hall. Her eyes lit up and she lost the thread of conversation for a brief moment before finishing and excusing herself. "- ill. Gentlemen, I will leave you to this rousing debate. A woman must always keep her eyes focused on the businesses at hand, of course."

"Oh but Anais, it is a party!" the betrothed argued, almost desperately, to try to keep her there. "Let the business of the day come to an end."

"If only that one could, one would. Gentlemen," she said with a smile as she quickly left the pair behind and slid effortlessly across the floor. When she reached her goal, any false humor she had went up in flames. "*You* are *exceptionally* late," she hissed at the much younger, albeit slightly taller and distressingly thin man that hadn't seen her coming.

"Circumstances beyond my control, I give my promise," he replied with a respectful bow of his head, "and one I am grateful to have resolved."

Anais looked down her nose and crossed her arms. "One I resolved for you. I hope you haven't forgotten that."

"Oh, no, not at all! Of course I owe you my way here, but again, it truly was outside of my control. I had to -"

"Were I you I'd find ways to quickly discover *how* to control your circumstances," she warned. "And now what are you doing *here*?"

He blinked his pale-brown eyes and looked utterly confused. "Completing our agreement? I mean you wanted me here and -"

Anais grabbed him by his shoulder and pulled him close to keep her voice at a whisper. "I can tell you don't have it on you. Tell me you didn't just leave it with your horse outside, Ettaquis."

"I can't say that it's my wish to be here," he answered with a hushed whisper as he looked around the party. "I was waiting for you at your room at Thesd Villa when your *associate* ordered me to find you here. It took far more effort than I wish to admit to bribe my way into this party."

She stood perfectly still for a moment and let her gaze travel towards her bodyguard. "Donta has been with me all evening..."

"Not him," he replied, "never got a look at him. Spoke with a strange cadence, sounded like he was in the rafters."

"Oh, that one," Anais sighed as her face drooped, crestfallen. "I see. I assume that he didn't leave you with any room to debate his request?"

"None. Very strange man, I -"

"I'll have words with him about it," she interrupted again with another pained sigh. "I assume that you have Moira somewhere safe?"

That earned a quick nod and a relieved smile. "Yes. I made sure that your package is safely stored away."

She took a quick look around the room and beckoned Donta closer. "There is no safety to have it stored away if it is outside of your immediate sight. You should at least have delivered it to my manservant."

Ettaquis took a deep breath and gave her an encouraging smile. "Be calm, lady. This is not the first thing I have carried for you."

"You don't understand its importance," Anais snapped, "nor where it came from."

"It's that you named it 'Moira.' It's just a -"

She shut him up with a glare. "It is what it is and what it is is both important and dangerous. Take Donta to it, right now. There's work to be done." He nodded and then she quickly added, "Oh, and make sure he knows who talked to you earlier."

As soon as he was back within earshot, she gave the two of them a series of quick instructions and waved them out the door. Her intention was to follow them after taking a chance to go poke at a few additional people – just to keep up appearances. However, the moment that Donta and the courier were safely outside, a third party decided to intervene instead. "I was wondering if I'd ever get a chance to speak to you."

Anais felt her skin go cold as she recognized who spoke to her. "Huntsmatron Elsith," she replied slowly, "I wasn't aware that the Guild possessed formal attire. It looks lovely on you."

Elsith ran her hands down the length of the turtle-green and cinnamon-brown dress she wore, a positively condescending smile on her lips appearing as she adjusted the green cloak around her shoulders. "Lady Anais Lovic. I would offer my thanks, but my time is short. You are a surprisingly well-connected woman for not having any holdings in the city."

"I simply have a way of making friends," she slowly replied

"You have a way of making more than that – or at least, so says the *Uob*," she replied, the 'u' sounding more like a 'y'.

Anais's face crumbled for a moment before she went on the defensive. "The Uob doesn't speak unless given permission. I'll assume then that you merely imagine what I own."

The Huntsmatron slid up beside her and casually tucked her hands under her cloak as they talked. "You would be surprised at what I know, *Lady* Lovic. The Guild keeps tabs on all of our clients, past, present, and ideally, future."

"You must have a long list of clients then, Huntsmatron," she replied. "Now if you excuse me, I must -"

"I think you should stay a few minutes longer," the other woman interrupted as she went on to say, "I need to speak with you. We have business to see to."

Anais feigned her shock, though it wasn't entirely a facade. "Now? But now is a time for celebration, not of dealing with writs and worse. Nor do I have any current contracts with the Guild. Your organization does not... suit my needs."

"That hasn't always been the truth, now has it?"

"I have no outstanding writs with the Guild, Huntsmatron, and the one I had in the past was sufficiently fulfilled," the lady replied as she slowly looked around the room, checking for any other unwelcome guests that may be inclined to join the two of them "On the other hand, if you had a writ for me, you'd not attempt to claim it in a place like this, would you?"

"What could possibly make you think I have a writ against you, Lady Lovic?" Elsith pressed, her condescending smile turning into one that was far more predatory. "I just came to talk."

Anais turned slightly to look the younger woman in the eyes. "Because blood is your language, and writs are your voice. Whereas I dabble in contracts and shipping; arrangements and assignments. I trade information to make sure that my clients leave the table happy and their coin-purses well-fed. Our interests do not intersect."

She didn't so much as even flinch under her gaze. "Oh I wouldn't be so sure. You *do* deal in information – in secrets, in contraband, in backroom deals and smoke-filled alleyways."

"I did not come to this party to have my honor questioned."

"I'm not, Lady. I'm exposing it," she retorted, "and in the *privacy* of public before the *public* of public, should you understand what I mean."

Anais took a step back, fighting to keep her composure still. "If I do deal in such things, then is it really in the best interests of anyone to press about them?"

"One might say that this is why I waited for your man to leave."

"A lack of manners and a spine coated in cowardice? You act below your station, Huntsmatron."

Elsith nudged her cloak open and made sure that the hilt of the ornate blade fastened to her waist flashed in the candlelight for Anais's benefit. "One does not work for the Guild without understanding how low our stations must be at times."

"I think that your accusation of speaking falsely could well be flipped to you now, were I of such a mind," she retorted.

"Maybe, maybe," she agreed, "but now we understand where we each stand and that's important when opening a contract. Wouldn't you concur?"

Anais tilted her head and blinked a few times in confusion. "Entering a contract? After every lofty insult you've proffered?"

"I know who you are, Anais," the other woman retorted. "What you do. How you do it."

"I *sincerely* doubt that."

Elsith ignored the vehemence in her reply and affixed her with a steady gaze. "I know that recently you've been digging into the Order of Love and you have your eye on something that they have buried away inside that blight on the wall."

The lady huffed in annoyance and dismissed her suggestion offhandedly. "I dare say you could name more than two handfuls of parties in this very room that wouldn't have their eyes interested in one thing or another in that blight, as you say. Your husband being chief on that list."

"He has his hobbies," she agreed, "and you, yours, even if the *why* is questionable."

"If you have to question it then you don't know what I do or how I do it."

"But I know that you want access, and I can help with that. I won't condone theft, of course, as a contracted agent of the Crown," she said as she tilted her head off towards a gathering of Oo-lo priests and priestesses standing several yards away, "even if it would inconvenience those smug Harlot-worshiping shits. *However*, if you really are just someone that deals in information, then I have something to offer in trade."

"You've done very little to convince me that you're worth my time," Anais said with a slight growl to the tone of her voice. "However, in the *interest* of not developing a feud neither of us will enjoy, I'll listen. What is it you want, hmm?"

"Let me cut to the chase: we have a suspect in the death of Instructor Odern," Elsith answered as she leaned in close enough to speak in a whisper.

"Who?"

She sighed and rolled her eyes. "Oh, don't play coy, Lovic. It is beneath you."

Anais looked up at the slightly taller woman and frowned. "Not to hear you say it. So you have a suspect — at long last, I might add. He's been dead now for how many weeks? Seven?"

"Six."

Her eyebrows lifted in surprise. "I would have expected the Guild or the guard to have hung the man responsible by now. Especially given the connections the Granalchi have in this lovely little depression of a city."

"Our investigation was slowed when his murderer was done the same," the Huntsmatron grumbled.

"Done the same?"

"Again, Lovic, don't play coy."

"No, in this, I truly don't know what you're talking about. I have no interest in the affairs of the Granalchi and unlike *you*, I have no taste for death," the lady replied without a hint of dishonesty. "The only interest I have in the dead is what they leave behind with their estates, or when they were supposed to deliver something that failed to make it to its destination, and matters such as that. None of the recently departed that I've had arrangements with might have had ones with Odern."

Elsith shrugged and replied with a simple shrug. "Rob graves all you wish, I won't stop you. We believe that he was killed by someone he owed a great deal of money to."

One shrug begat another. "Not an uncommon fate. Still surprising that it would happen in such a grisly fashion."

"A common fate for an uncommon man done with a nearly-unique flair, I grant. And this is why I come to you: the woman we believe killed him was found dead three days ago. And, oddly, in much the same fashion. You heard of the woman slain at Medias Manor?"

"I had heard that story, yes."

The Huntsmatron nodded. "They're related."

Anais lifted her eyebrow and sized up the shorter woman. "You think that one of the aids of the Manor had or... actually did... kill a Granalchi? That's an interesting theory. I suppose you've reasons for it?"

"Many," she admitted, "and none of them explain who would have taken her life as well."

"If it was done the same manner, then wouldn't the obvious question be that... what was her name? Liv? Wouldn't the question be that she hired one of your green-cloaked goons to murder him, and then the assassin turned their blade on her? Or a goon of a similar bent as the Guild? Though I can think of few that could. The Advensi, maybe, if they are as skilled as rumor has it."

The Huntsmatron nodded. "It would be obvious, yes. Her full name was Livstra Oliana. She no longer lives up to the abbreviation, rather amusingly. And no, the Advensi couldn't cut their way out of a tent."

Anais retorted with a disgusted look at the comment. "If that's how cavalierly you treat her passing, I am not in the least bit shocked that you've found no leads."

"Oh, we *found* leads," Elsith replied, "just none that make sense. That's why I am here."

"You mean there's a reason for you to continually insult me? I'm shocked."

"I know enough about your work in the city to have you suffer more than a *shock*," she shot back. "However, I have a proposition for you."

Anais rolled her eyes and took another step back away to force the other woman to speak up. "I really don't have any desire to listen to it, but go on."

She didn't give her the satisfaction and crept back in close again. "As much as it would be that I would prefer that you're right – and that it is merely a case of one of my 'green-cloaked goons' has gone into business for themselves, I don't believe that's the case."

"And that brings you to me… why?"

"Because you know people, because you have connections, and because I have heard your name more than once in recent dealings with both the underground and the upper echelons."

"I do not entertain the likes of assassins and murderers in my circle," she retorted, "and I am at a loss to think of why you would assume that *my* connections, as short-lived as they are, would outnumber *yours*."

"You entertain at least one," Elsith pointed out. "You don't have to look at your bodyguard more than once to understand what he's capable of."

Anais's eyes narrowed down into tight little slits. "Huntsmatron? I would be *very* careful of what you understand his capabilities to be."

"That aside," she replied with a dismissive wave of her hand, "Lady Lovic, allow me to speak clearly: I've hit a wall. I have no idea who executed Livstra, who she hired to murder Odern, and the *why* is questionable at best. She would know that doing so would put her operation at risk and it's not in agreement with the arrangements she had made within the city to be otherwise ignored. I *need* information and that is why I come to you."

She gave up all pretense at pretending not to be confused by anything, and everything, that the younger woman was rambling on about. "First you say she had an Adept murdered, now you say that she has some kind of operation in the city? You make it sound like you actually suspect an aide to the feeble-minded of doing something improper? I was being flippant when I suggested as much."

"Because I do, and because she does."

"Even still. I know nothing about it, and I've had no dealings with anyone from that dreadful manor. Nor have I made any efforts to secure a standing within the underworld of this town."

Elsith shook her head. "One of those is a lie, though I respect why you claim it. I *know* what you do, Anais. Saying that you've made no connections to the Fleetfinger's Guild – and others – to operate in the borders of this province isn't a way to be truthful."

"They will deny it as strongly as I. I trade in *contracts, shipping, mercantile arrangements*, and *assignments*. Nothing more, *nothing* less," she argued with a hateful little hiss.

"Save the indignity, *Lady* Lovic. I speak plainly because I've no time for bullshit," she groused before giving the older woman a pleading look. "I need your help."

"You have a *very* strange way of asking," Anais retorted. "You want me to use my contacts with the elite of the city to find someone that even the Guild cannot? Is this to be done out of the goodness of my heart, or ?"

"It would be a way for you to gain allies," she offered.

The information broker dismissed that outright with a wave of her hand. "I *have* allies. While it is important to make new ones every day, I am content with the ones I have now."

"But if you had *us* as an ally, you'd also earn the ear of my husband."

Anais stopped protesting for a moment and then let her lips turn into the faintest possible hint of a smile. "I see. So in short, you believe that I have eyes and ears that you need, and you believe you have eyes and ears that *I* want."

"Need, not want," the Huntsmatron argued. "Otherwise, yes. That's the truth of it. We have an agreement?"

"We have an agreement that I will listen to you telling me more about it, on the condition that you mind your tongue from this point forward. We will work out the specifics after."

Elsith took the rebuke in stride and replied with a slow nod. "If you help us find the bastard that did this, you might end up with more friends than you know what to do with."

"A lady like myself is *never* without ways to put her friends to work, Huntsmatron," she returned with a huff. "Be careful what it is, exactly, you wish for."

"Well, for now, I wish that you tell me what you know of the Gambling Mind."

"That it is a terrible way to lose one's coin," she shot back.

"Not the personality," Elsith replied, "the person – or I should say, the title. And why, exactly, a woman with her unspoken reputation would have even wanted to kill Odern to begin with; you can't collect coin from a dead man, and nobody seems to treat it as a message being sent in debt to her enterprise."

Anais frowned and brought her hand up to her pale lips in surprise. "A healer has an enterprise?"

The Huntsmatron nodded slowly and gave a scowling glare to the room in general. "Not just *an* enterprise, I'm afraid. *The* enterprise. Lady in Waiting to Ridora Medias, chief healer of Medias Manor, Livstra Oliana. Also known as Liona Reanage, the Gambling Mind."

Lady Lovic's jaw dropped. "I *know* that name."

"You would, if anyone would."

"She's an agent of the Fleetfinger's Guild?"

"She *ran* the Fleetfingers in Basion," Elsith corrected, "and it's a bad thing that she doesn't anymore for a variety of reasons despite how well-behaved her former underlings are playing together for now. Now do you see why I need you?"

Elsewhere, Akaran continued to fume into an apple he had smuggled off of an unattended plate right out from under Lady Comstead's nose. "If you don't want people to eat the damn rolls don't put the damn rolls out," he muttered under his breath, pouting as he stood in a corner.

A familiar chuckle interrupted his grumbles, and followed it with a, "Yeah but they're damn good, aren't they?"

He nodded in quick agreement. "Have you tried the tarts? They are delicious."

"They don't even compare with what I've been eating," Badin quipped back. "Haven't seen you in a while. Really glad that you got my letter."

"Came at a great time, too," the exorcist admitted. "I thought you had shipped back out though. Your 'staying for a couple of weeks' has gone on a lot longer than I figured it would."

"Well, like I said... the tarts don't compare," he returned with a wicked smile that made Akaran raise an eyebrow. "Remember I said I had connections?"

His friend nodded and took another bite from his apple. "Something like that, yeah. End up signing up with Henderschott? Impress the 4th enough that they let you change alignments?"

The battlemage shook his head and gestured to the other side of the hall, and then cast a loving look into the corner. For the first time since he'd met the man, Badin was actually *glowing*. "Over there. See her? Black dress?"

"Half of the women in this hall are wearing black dresses... oh. *Oh*." He looked up from his stolen meal and nearly choked on it. Seline hadn't been wrong about the fairer sex stalking the dance so far, and the nobility of Basion had seemingly made a deal with the damned for beauty. His friend's conquest was enough to take his breath away with the smoldering look in her dark brown eyes (let alone the look of the rest of her). "Who. Is. *That*?!" he exclaimed, accentuating every word in the question.

"My new posting."

"Got a feeling it's more than that, the way you're grinning," Akaran said, needling at him.

"More than one way to hold a post," the mage admitted with another grin.

"Okay, but, speak truthfully. Who is she?"

Badin slowly pulled his eyes away from her and smiled from ear to ear. "You're not going to believe this, but that's the Mother Eclipsian. Her name is Erine. And, thanks to you, I'm assigned to her for the duration of the wedding celebration."

The exorcist felt his jaw drop. "Start that over from the top. First, the Mother Eclipsian? What's a Lethandria cultist doing out in the open?"

"They're not that bad," his friend chided, "truthfully, she's reasonably respected in town. She and Lexcanna have a good arrangement: the Temple of Stara offers solace and aid for those in the light, and the Eclipsian helps guide those that otherwise feel too ashamed of themselves to be around the more devout types. To hear the two of them talk, it helps keep a form of balance in the city."

Akaran pursed his lips and made a soft, 'huh' sound in his throat. "So, Lexcanna and the Order of Stara helps people clear of conscience, while Erine and the Order of the Cloaked provides aid to...?"

"...those that don't think they're worth salvation, but who don't look forward to damnation," the mage finished. "City is home to a lot of men of the sword, my friend, and not a lot of them think that they've got a lot of hope to get to the Mount."

"I had no idea you were one to think about matters of the soul," the priest pointed out between bites of the apple.

"Yeah well," Badin said with a slight cough, "she made a compelling argument."

The younger man looked back at the beauty and then after a moment, gave his friend a *look* that spoke volumes. "*She* did or her *bodice* did?"

"I decline to answer that," the coal-haired mage replied, "but I'll say some things helped to hold my attention." Before Akaran could make another witty remark, he continued on. "*Either way*, the Midlanders aren't exactly thrilled about her. Something to do with the Sun God or the War God. Something. So, she requested security for the duration of the wedding, and was clear that she wanted a b-mage."

"And you got the job? How?"

Badin gestured at another cluster of people. "That prick over there – the tall one in the yellow? - that's Paverilak. Guess when he showed up in town he demanded all of the Specialist-Majors that serve here to be his personal escort. So, the local Commander remembered seeing me when I dropped you off at the Manor."

"And I bet he had a terrible time convincing you, didn't he?"

"Not after I laid eyes on her," Badin admitted.

Again, Akaran couldn't blame him in the least. "She make you happy?"

He nodded with another sheepish smile. "You know? I haven't had anything harder than an ale in a month. She's... she's wonderful."

"Then that's amazing, my friend. You may be the only man here that understands what a relationship should be built on."

"So says the follower of Love, eh?"

Akaran chuckled and genuinely smiled for the first time since walking into the hall. "Yes, so says."

"How about you? Any luck on that front?" Badin asked with a bit of a completely uncharacteristic glow to his cheeks.

The priest snorted. "Not trying."

"You're not?" Badin asked, amazed. "Boy, just *look* at this room. If that lass you came here with isn't up to your tastes then -"

"I'm *not*," Akaran repeated firmly. "I miss Mariah."

"Yes and she isn't *here*. She had the chance to follow you and she didn't," he retorted. "You're young, my boy, so go spread your wings. Or, better yet, go spread someone's -"

The priest shook his head and interrupted him a second time. "She could've, she didn't. Even if I *was* interested, there's nothing I have to offer anyone. I live in a madhouse, for the sake of all, so. No," he sighed, "just no."

"Well. Eh. All I'm gonna say is that with *this* crowd? If I wasn't going back home with Erine, I'd be going home with *someone*. It wouldn't hurt you to mingle."

"I'm fine with mingling with the pastries."

"My way isn't as fattening," Badin quipped, "but to each their own, I suppose. OH. Speaking of m'lady, I have something for you."

Akaran furrowed his brow a little as he tried to find his sack of cocasa for another mouthful. "What in the world would a priestess of the Goddess of *Night* want with *me*?"

"That, I don't actually know," the mage replied as he handed him a rolled-up scroll. "When I told her I'd given you an invite, she asked me to make sure you got this."

"Read it?"

The mage snorted. "You think I'm dumb enough to read the private correspondence between two priests? Not a *chance*."

He tucked it down in his belt before looking at it. "Fair, and probably for the best. I'll look it over later. Say, you in a hurry to get back to her?"

"Always," Badin replied, "but I can wait for a few. Something on your mind?"

"You could say that," Akaran answered. Then, without warning, he launched into the story that the Maiden-Templar had given him earlier in the day. To his credit, the mage listened intently and asked questions at all the right times.

When the priest finished explaining the situation, his friend pursed his lips and idly flicked a small stray spark of lightning into the air. "Well. Shit. I thought the wedding was the worst thing going on."

Akaran just nodded his head. "I figure that if you're going to be in charge of protecting one of the local heavyweights, you should know."

"No, you're right, I should. The people going missing are exactly the kind that Erine ministers to. Thank you. I'll keep my eyes and ears open."

"All I can ask. Thank you, my friend."

"Don't think anything of it – but you *can* pay me back."

"How?"

Badin reached over and gingerly lifted the Order of Love sigil dangling on Akaran's neck with one finger. "When we first got to the city, you gave that templar some numbers. I've been trying to figure out what they mean and honestly, I don't have a clue."

He blinked a couple of times as he tried to remember what the mage was talking about. "Oh. Five-one-one and six-three-nine?"

"Yeah, that."

"Oh," he replied, "you could've asked then."

"Didn't want to pry in front of your Order. It's just been bugging me."

Akaran nodded, then flipped the sigil over. Five-one-one was etched across the top, and the other three numbers were carved into the bottom. "I graduated from the Grand Temple in 511 QR," he explained, "and I am the six-hundred and thirty-ninth exorcist to be assigned to serve the Goddess since the Reformed Order was founded in 296."

The mage felt his eyes widen. "There's only been six hundred of you in the last two hundred years? That seems... low?"

"It's a calling," the younger man admitted, "that doesn't call to many. I shared a class with ten other students. Average time it takes to train is between five and fifteen years."

"Huh," Badin replied. "I had no idea..."

"It's complicated," Akaran added, "though they train us with other Followers of the Goddess, depending on the lessons. The Order basically borders down to the Lovers, the Healers, and the Fighters. Lovers spread the teachings of Love, aid the poor, serve the Temple as caretakers and preachers."

His smitten friend nodded along, though he'd gone back to staring longingly over at Erine. The priest, on the other hand? He was so caught up in the explanation that he didn't even notice he'd lost his attention. "Okay..."

"Then the Healers, well, that's a given. They heal. Sometimes with magic, sometimes without. They're blessed with the ability to channel Her divine will to help soothe hearts and mend bodies... they start as healers, then later, if they're any good at it, become titled Clerics and eventually, if they're truly blessed, Templars. Not everyone goes all the way up, kinda like in the army. Sometimes a private is just gonna be a private, or sometimes they get to become a general."

"Right..."

"And then you've got my branch, and we... well. You know what we do. Exorcists hunt for small things and fix those problems. Inquisitors are sent to root out more entrenched heretics and to aid the Kingdom purge undesirables, while Paladins and Paladin-Commanders..." he slowed down as he realized that he had utterly lost Badin's attention, "...help the Kingdom track down roving bands of kitten marauders and wage war to keep them away from the Queen's coveted stockpile of cream and cheese..."

"Right, kittens, the worst..." his friend replied as he watched Erine start to dance with the same woman that Akaran had seen arguing with Raechil earlier. "...wait, what?"

Akaran shook his head and covered a laugh with the back of his hand. "My friend, go see to your lady. I need to get some fresh air."

The battlemage ducked his head sheepishly. "I'm sorry. I just can't take my eyes off of her."

"I'll never fault a soul for being in love," the exorcist chuckled as he slapped the mage on his shoulder before he went wandering towards the nearest door.

Whatever Badin said in response was lost in the background chatter.

A few minutes later and he found a porch balcony overlooking Avagerona's Rest at the back of the grand hall. "This was a horrible idea," he muttered to himself.

That, of course, took the attention of another guest of Comstead Hall. This time, instead of a woman of nobility or a mercenary of questionable ethics, he was greeted by what he could only describe as a man-shaped granite wall who towered over him by several inches and muscles in places he didn't think were actual places. "Not your type of party either, eh?" the mountain of a man asked as he sucked on small piece of rolled, burning cloth. There was a particularly foul odor that wafted away from him, though it almost smelled like burnt cocasa.

It gave him ideas for later. "I don't party," he grunted.

"I do. Not like this, but I do," the midlander commiserated. "Always hated this kind of... thing. Father used to make me attend every special function from the time I could crawl until the year past."

"Ah. I'm sorry you lost him."

"Oh, didn't lose him," he replied as he took a drag off of the makeshift pipe. "Just was finally able to tell the codger that I had outgrown the need to go piss about with old men that wouldn't know how to pick a fight if their swords were already bloody."

Akaran caught himself snickering and gave the stranger an askance grin. "Now that... that is a sentiment I can agree with. Give me a straight round in the field over all the backstabbing in there."

"At least the food's a bit better here than there. Beats the shit outta rations."

"It ain't rations, that's for damn sure," the priest agreed.

The other man nodded and looked him over. "Eaten your fair share, huh?"

He shook his head and looked down at the waves. "Not as many as most. Not as few as some."

"Can tell that it looks like you were in a fight," he replied. "Other guy bigger than you or faster?"

"Both," Akaran answered as he took a bite of cheese. "Demon."

The other man gave him a quick respectful bow of his head. "Ah. I congratulate you on winning."

"How do you know I won?"

"You fought a demon," the other man replied. "You walk with a stick, but you're still walking. Sometimes living means winning."

Akaran grunted and looked down at the water below. "Doesn't feel like it. Feels like the bastard took more from me than I did him, to be honest."

"Eh," he wordlessly replied before offering his thoughts. "Wounds heal. Now you've got a stick to go with it."

The priest looked down at the chunk of wood and sighed. "Yes. A *stick*. I am ever so fisking grateful to be blessed with having a *stick*."

The midlander laughed just a little, but it was so jovial it forced a smile from Akaran. "Oh, 'course you are. Swords are nice and all but a stick? Now that's an all-around fine weapon."

"You realize I can't tell if you're joking."

"Who makes jokes about sticks?"

The first answer he had didn't seem to be the one that the stranger was expecting, so he flipped the conversation. "I'm... I'm sensing you're not from Dawnfire. Odinal?"

"Fresh from," he replied with a stretch. "Lived much my life up there. Ain't always an easy thing. Fair though. Treat the land right, she treats you. You don't, she won't. It weeds out the strong from the soft."

There was a brief period of silence as he remembered a few of the lectures that Hirshma had offered up in the mountains about the ways of nature. "So I've heard."

"Ever make it that far?"

"Just as far as the eastern Equalin," he answered, "think about three, four weeks south of Hovoth's Strait."

The midlander nodded and flicked the burning roll out into the dark. "Ah. Now can't say I've been that far myself, not east. This is as far as I've ever been from home. Been an experience, opens one's eyes."

"Gonna be honest with you," Akaran started, "I didn't think the Midlands *had* nobility. Didn't expect to see so many... many..."

"...old fiskers and pretty little prizes dangling off their arms?" he finished.

"More or less."

His guttural laugh forced the priest to grin again. "We don't do it like you folk down here. Each one of those men are warlords in their own right, and their prizes have all been fought for. Not a one was just given or taken."

"Then explain this damn wedding," Akaran grunted. "To hear the brother of the bride say it, it's a unification of houses more than anything else. Doesn't sound like a fight for a prize, if you don't mind my saying." Then, quickly realizing what he had just said, he looked over and raised a hand up defensively. "And I really hope you don't mind me saying."

"You know Kee then?"

"Just met," he said as he took another bite. "Didn't know he was Hylene's kin until I told him what I thought of it."

"Ohhh. You didn't happen to say that in front of her, did you?"

"I'm standing outside looking at the moon instead of standing inside looking at the lady that accompanied me," he retorted. "So you tell me."

His eyes lit up as he started to rub his hands together eagerly. "Ohhh. Mind if I ask exactly what you said?"

Akaran took a *long* breath before admitting to it. "That a marriage without love is just a way to get people to fisk for money."

The midlander sputtered a horrified protest and then bent over, howling from laughter. "AND SHE HEARD YOU?!"

"Only time I've ever seen someone turn that shade of purple was when one of my instructors overheard me saying that the Holy General smelled like a shithouse rat."

"Were you as right then as you are now?"

After a moment, the priest shrugged. "Think so. Stand by it."

That only made him laugh even harder. "Oh you poor man! I can only imagine. Oh God above, I don't think I wanna go back inside now. At all. Maybe ever. You really didn't suggest she was a whore, did you?"

Akaran finished off the last bite of his stolen dairy and shrugged again. "Kee didn't seem to like being equated to a pimp, for what it's worth."

His new friend gripped the edge of the balcony as tears of joy flowed down his face. "Well, least I can tell you honestly know the man. Pompous asshole doesn't even come close, does it?"

"Goddess *no*," he agreed. "Though pissed as she got, can't help but feel sorry for her husband-to-be. Hope the old codger is up to it."

"Should've hit him with the stick," he suggested. "Shuts him up quick."

The priest stared dumbly down at the gnarled limb. "It's just a stick."

"Naw! Now that much I'm gonna have to disagree with you on. *You* see it as a stick, *we* see it as a *brawl*."

"A brawl...?" the exorcist asked, completely confused. "Not sure I follow. A walking stick is a walking stick. What am I going to do – smack someone on the head with it?"

The other man nodded his head emphatically. "Absolutely! Best part of having a stick. 'specially one that you don't need two hands for, like one of those fancy quarterstaffs I hear that some of your people use. Civans, too."

"It doesn't cut and it doesn't bludgeon as effectively as a mace. I don't think there's anywhere safe to stick a bladed edge on it to use as a glorified axe. My mentor uses a weighted staff, but it doubles as a halberd. I'm not sure anyone would trust me with anything with sharp edges on it right now."

"Then you should know the damage it can do," his new friend chided.

"Well, yes," Akaran reluctantly admitted. "But he always backs it up with magic. I just assumed he enhanced it more than relied on it for what it is."

"Ah, but it's lighter. Mind if I...?" he asked as he reached for it. Akaran shrugged, tossed it over to him, and leaned back to watch. The midlander caught it with one hand and began to quickly spin it around in a circle over his head. "Lighter, quicker, just as hard if you hit it right," he added as he scooped up an unattended goblet with his other hand and tossed it into the air.

Akaran caught the glimmering gold sigil on it and tried to interrupt the stranger to no avail. "Uh, wait, that cup is -"

He twisted the cane and connected firmly on the mug in mid-air, launching it out over the Rest and out of sight. "You put your wrist behind it and a good brawler will knock a head so far back that they won't know why they're looking up at the stars until after they bleed out."

"A good sword will punch through armor," he replied as he tried to guess where the cup – Merchant-Master's gold sigil – would've landed.

"A bad one'll get stuck in it," the other man retorted. "A good stick will take a man's breath or break his bones so he can't *stand* to swing his sword anymore. 'Sides. Back home, we always made sure to dress up our brawls. Give them added punch."

"...are you trying to sell me on the idea of a spiked club?"

"A spiked or studded club that's weighted for the wielder and able to break armor and bones in the same swing. You absolutely should consider it sometime," he said as he tossed the cane back to the priest. "Just a thought for the next time you get into a fight with another demon. Or some daft noble."

He caught it and wondered if the stranger might actually have a point. "If there is one," he lamented.

"Aw now. Don't mope. Like I said. Wounds heal. You'll be back and ready to fight before you know it," he said with a hopeful little grin. "Say, you wouldn't happen to know how long back you pissed Hy off, would you?"

"Um. I don't know. Half a candle-mark, maybe more. Probably more."

The taller, slightly older, and far-better-built man groaned like a little boy. "Piss. So she's been fuming alongside Kee for that long?"

"Not *that* terribly long. Maybe it was sooner..."

"You don't know her like I do," the midlander replied with a shake of his head. "Suppose I'd best get back in there. Talk her out of having the governor skin you."

Akaran cringed and looked at him anew. "Oh, you know her? I really am sorry..."

He shook his head again and waved the priest into silence. "Nah, you're right. Love's damn important to a wedding. Wouldn't have asked her if it wasn't."

"You wouldn't..." he started to reply as he felt what color that he left in his face drain away. "You're her fiancée. Malik Odinal, aren't you?"

"Aw now, don't be surprised," the warlord said with a chuckle. "Truth be, you aren't wrong. Kee'd pimp out his mother *and* hers to a pack of trolls if he thought he could make a pile of coin about it. Fact that someone finally called him on his shit is just about the best thing that's happened this entire trip."

He took a nervous little breath and tried to look anywhere but at the big man. "Just so we're clear, um, what I said isn't indicative of the rest of the Order and what everyone else thinks. I'm just a guy with a sword... well... stick. I don't do..."

"...diplomacy?" he guessed. When Akaran nodded, he grinned from ear to ear. "Trust me. That's a good thing. Diplomats are useful, but so's a man that'll say what he means, too. You gonna be stuck with that stick for much longer?"

"Don't know. Hoping not, but..."

The head of the Odinal delegation nodded in understanding. "Sometimes the stick tells us how long we're keeping it, not us how long we keep the stick. I get it. I get it," he said as he looked out at the lake. "Tell you a true thing. When you can walk better, find me. I know a few things about how to use a stick you might want to learn."

"Pretty sure if I show up anywhere near you, Hylene'll beat me to death with one," Akaran retorted, "even *if* I'm even allowed to get near you again."

"Nah. She won't."

"Wouldn't be so sure. I mean I did imply a few things."

Malik shook his head and gave the younger man another shit-eating-grin. "Ah, I mean it. She gets cloudy and all that, who doesn't? It'll pass. She really is a sweet woman. And her brother? Let me guess: he was off extolin' the virtues of that band of twat-necked ruffians that call themselves warriors?"

"He was," the priest answered, "when he wasn't taking shots at the Goddess. So exceedingly happy with all the new contracts he expects to get from your people."

The big man grunted and let his gaze wander to a pair of young women that were frolicking down the shores a few dozen yards away. "Won't happen."

"Oh?"

"Nope, not gonna happen," he repeated. "See, Hylene don't think much of them herself, and I surely don't. Haven't met a one of them yet that's able to keep up with any of the men my father trained. If they can't keep up with m'father's men, how is he gonna keep up with the bandits from the other clans?"

Akaran thought about it for a moment and offered his opinion. "He really seems to think that you marrying his sister is going to change that."

Malik dismissed it immediately. "Worst that's gonna change is that the Guild will work harder to keep contracts that I've already put ink to. If he can get some bodies down here guarding caravans before they reach the Dawn borders, then power to him – but he won't get any contracts with what he has now up where we're from."

"For some reason, that makes me smile."

"Because he's a jackass with more lady parts than man bits and you want to see the egotistical fisker land on his face?" he asked with that same mischievous grin.

"Something like that."

The clansman laughed again. "Best part is, his sister knows."

Akaran tilted his head and gave him a quizzical look. "But she was bragging about how it'll help her family?"

"How it'll help *her*," he clarified. "I love her, don't get me wrong. Thing is, she stands to gain a great deal once we're wedded, and her line after many a golden thing. But Kee? Dick and shit."

"That... yeah. That makes me smile."

"Thought it might," he chortled. "Take that off to bed with you. In the meantime... I gotta go see to her to make sure I *have* a bed to get to. See you soon, I hope."

"Hope so too," the priest replied with the first genuine smile he'd felt all night. "G'luck Malik. I'm... honestly, I'm glad you love her. Love is worth more than most people know. For what it's worth, you've got my blessing."

The midlander laughed again with his smile going from ear to ear. He walked past and slapped Akaran on his back as he wandered off in search of his bride, leaving the priest all alone for the first time all day. As the band played in the hall behind him, he leaned against the balcony, shut his eye, and just focused on the fresh air wafting up from the lake below.

He was still doing that when Seline found him a bit later.

"Well, whatever you said to Malik worked wonders. The Odinal clansmen *love* you. Not just him, but *all* of them," she said as soon as she was confident he wasn't asleep standing up. "Although I'd stay clear of anyone with the flag of the Advensi. You made a *lot* of enemies tonight."

"I'm sorry," he sighed. "They asked for my opinion."

"You were *not* obligated to give it," she retorted as she stood next to him. When he didn't rise to the bait, she shook her head tiredly but then rain her fingers through his hair. "Accurate as it may be, you didn't have to *give* it," she ever-so-firmly repeated.

He felt himself melting under her touch before he realized it. "I'll keep that in mind for the future."

"The future?" she asked with a snort. "Pull something like this again and you won't have one. If I had any say in it, you wouldn't, but."

"But? What's wrong?"

"It looks like you will," she replied. "I had a courier from Prostil find me. You're being summoned back to the Repository tomorrow. Daybreak. The note says you already know what it's about?"

Akaran nodded grimly. "I do. Seline, do you trust me?"

She looked back into the hall. "After that stunt? No. I sense you're about to say I should though, aren't you?"

The exorcist nodded slowly and stared down into the small lake. "Please."

"Then it's best you come get some sleep," she warned after a long moment of silence. "I sense you're going to need it. Just…"

"Just?"

She reached over and gave him a quick, chaste hug that she'd deny giving to anyone that asked her about it (and he'd deny enjoying). "Just be careful. Please."

IX. A QUESTIONABLE PARANOIA
Zundis, the 14ᵗʰ of Riverswell, 513 QR

By edict of the Queen, or at least, *a* Queen (it was hard to remember which one did what over history), cities with a population greater than four-thousand souls were mandated to have a Garrison Office representing whatever troop was assigned to monitor a given province or region (if more than one garrison was required). This could be anything from a hut that barely had room for a table, desk, and chamber-pot, or, it could be built like a full-scale outright "Fortress of Doom" encampment which seemed to be a popular motif around parts of the northern border.

The actual Garrison Command Office for the province would be more castle than outpost. Those could typically be found in the provincial capitol, although in this case, that wasn't the way it worked. While Basion is the capitol for Kettering Province, it didn't hold the actual G. C. O. (or 'gecko,' as disgruntled guardsmen called it when out of range of the local Knight-or-Garrison Commander, depending).

No, instead, that honor was relegated to Port Cableture to the south, since it was the home base of the 2ⁿᵈ Naval Fleet. That said, the 4ᵗʰ Garrison Office in Basion edged closer to 'Fortress of Doom' levels than it did 'barn closet,' and in defense of the Lieutenant-Commander that supervised it, managed to look powerful and important without being imposing or gaudy.

In fact, not only did the G. C. O. in the Akkador East district look more like an estate than a fortress, it even felt downright comfortable. Covered in flags, rugs, and assorted wall-hangings all bearing the crest of the Dawnfire Army, the office was one giant red and gold beacon of lawfulness and far more couches than you'd expect to see in a military base.

Even with that being said, weapon racks adorned half of the hallways he passed through and shields were placed at regular intervals on the walls. The three-story-building was also covered in ramparts, loopholes, and other defensive augmentations. From what he could tell upon entering, the first level was reserved for eating, training, and he could hear a blacksmith pounding away outside. That left the second level for the city barracks, and the third for the local commander's needs.

Which meant stairs.

Lots, and lots, of stairs.

He was right about the second floor. While the first had varied civilians walking about and non-uniformed guards lounging here and there, the second was a full barracks with handfuls of militia getting ready to go on shift and or were winding down from whatever patrol they'd just been on. The only non-guard he saw was a big, thick, bruiser of a huntsman arguing with a sergeant over some old bounty or other.

By the time that Akaran made it up to Henderschott's office, almost every third utterance from his mouth was a borderline blasphemy. Every second one *was* with no question to be had about it. When he stumbled into the office, his eye was brimming with tears – which didn't exactly help win the soldier over. "Oh," he grumbled, "it's *you*. What do you want?"

"Much more than you can offer," he quipped before saying, "I've got a few questions."

The soldier looked up at him from an exorbitantly large pile of papers, journals, and scrolls that made for a disaster of a mess on his desk and casually flung a quill down into the middle of them. "Oh do you? This should be good."

"Good would be an improvement."

"Usually is. Get on with it."

Akaran sat down on a chair that was one of five in the entire outpost that didn't have padding with a grimace. "Prostil sent me. She's asked me to look into the murders of Odern and Livstra. Same with some reported peasants that have gone missing lately. Figured here would be the best place to start."

The other man leaned back in his seat and held his face in his left hand, curling his fingers around his chin. "That's neither her job nor yours. What's her interest?"

"Not entirely sure," he half-lied. "She took offense to someone being murdered at the Manor, I know that much."

"She has no control over the manor and their murders don't have any apparent relation other than how violent they were. Since she doesn't have any say in it, neither do you."

"She's a Maiden of the Queen," Akaran pointed out. "She has say in anything she wishes."

The soldier shook his head. "No, she oversees a musty library that costs my office more in salary to defend it than it could possibly be worth."

"Knowledge is power. There's a lot of power in that building."

"There's a power in many buildings, starting with this one."

It was the exorcist's turn to be dismissive. "No, there's a garrison in this building. That's not power, that's force."

"Force about to be used to throw you out of here," Hender retorted as he leaned forward and glared at the priest. "Even *if* she had any kind of authority over it, *you* don't."

Akaran bristled and reached into his gray coat. "I'm an exorcist in the -"

"Save the dramatics of pulling out your sigil," the garrison's commander interrupted. "What you *are* is a patient in Ridora's menagerie of lost souls."

"I never had my commission revoked," he shot back, "so I still have authority over the Queen's men."

"Do you now?" Henderschott asked. "Would Ridora say the same thing if I asked her?"

"I'd hope so."

"Hope's a dangerous thing."

The priest let his lips curl into a nasty little smirk. "So is getting between a fight with two Maidens."

"What makes you think that will happen?"

He looked the commander dead in his brown eyes. "Well," he began, "if Ridora tells you that I don't have authority, then Prostil tells you that I *do*, you'll have to pick which of the two you'll have to listen to. That kind of argument will put you on the path of explaining to the Provincial Maiden why you felt the need to interfere in a lawful request from an exorcist – who outranks you by Queen's order – and then one of her other Maidens, who *assuredly* outranks you. You don't want to go through all that, do you?"

Henderschott sat in total silence as he chewed on his lower lip. Finally, after a longer pause than anyone needed to suffer through, he spoke back up. "You don't play well with others, do you?"

"Not so I've been told," the exorcist agreed. "Help me out with this and I'll get out of your hair."

The other man went silent for a few more moments and then sighed brokenly. "Fine. We're laying some ground rules first."

"Not one for playing by the rules either."

"Learn."

The ferocity behind the snap set him back slightly and he decided not to press the edict. "What are they?"

"Don't waste my time," he started, "and don't come here with half-baked ideas. If you don't have solid proof of something, I don't want to hear it. Don't bother my men. Don't interrupt them. Unless it's an emergency I don't want to see your face in this office."

Akaran had to reluctantly give his agreement but made it clear he wasn't happy about it with a dirty look of his own. "If I find anything, I will make sure you know first. I'm not here to pick a fight with the garrison," he replied reassuringly. "And, let's be honest: if I find something, someone's going to either *be* dead or *need* to be dead and I'm not in the shape to do the latter even if I want to and *you'll* need to deal with former."

"The jury is still out on that," the guardsman cautioned, "I do *not* like the idea of a *suspect* in one of those deaths looking into the other."

"You said you didn't think I did it."

"I don't think I can *prove* it," he countered. "Speaking of being honest, let's be clear on this too: it's not that you're here to pick a fight. No, you're here because you're bored and you need something to do. We both know it."

It was Akaran's turn to lean back in his chair and shrug. "Be lying if I said that wasn't partially the case. I really don't like that there have been people going missing and nobody's done anything about it yet. That's almost enough to make someone think there's corruption behind the scenes."

Henderschott clenched his teeth so hard that it made his jaw twitch. "Suggesting someone is getting paid off to look the other way, are you?"

"I don't know. Are you?"

The guard bristled up and then relaxed with a slow smirk. "Maybe you're not as boring as I had first thought. Fair enough, what do you want to know?"

"How come you haven't been investigating the missing people rumors?"

"I did," he replied. "We didn't find anything substantial to back them up. Yes, people went missing, but that happens. In all honesty, the most interesting thing that's happened since Liv's death was the *accidental* maiming of one of my men," he said as he made little air-quotes with his fingers around the word.

"Accidental maiming?"

"He had a bit too much to drink at the Danse," he clarified. "One of the maids *accidentally* knocked him into the path of a horse-drawn carriage after it was over. We have her in custody now. Believe it or not, she's the sister of one of the girls assigned to work in that damned manor of yours."

I wonder if that's the woman that Raechil was arguing with last night? he mused to himself. "What makes it questionable?"

"He had attempted to make the celebrations an evening the both of them wouldn't forget an hour prior," Henderschott replied. "It would seem he was right, albeit not in the intended fashion."

"Good reason to question it," the younger man agreed, "but not related to missing people."

"No, but it's more interesting," he retorted. "Random vagrants deciding to move away from the city without telling anyone else? It's hardly worth our time, let alone the Maiden's."

Akaran shook his head no and decided to be a bit argumentative about it. "People don't just vanish. Not without a great deal of training and magical aptitude."

"Vagrants do. The unfed do," he countered. "It can be hard to make a living in the city. Those that can't tend to try their luck out in the Fel'achir."

"But I assume there's some record of people that come and go through the city gates."

"Some record, but it's not perfect," the other man disputed. "I wouldn't be able to give you a full census on the population of the city on the best of days, and this wedding headache has not made this the best of days."

Akaran pursed his lips. "How many people have been reported?"

"You mean you don't know?"

"No, I have no accurate idea. Prostil said it was 'more than a handful,' but didn't have much more to offer than that."

Henderschott sighed in annoyance and started to tidy up the pile of papers on his desk to little avail. "My office routinely gets complaints about the missing and the lost. Most of the time they turn up on their own. Sadly, a lot of rumors have been abounding lately."

"Enough rumors and you start getting a pattern," the priest pointed out.

"True enough," he agreed. "Patterns themselves can be problematic. Best as I can say, from what I remember the last I looked – and it was a goodly while ago – about fourteen different people were never accounted for dating as far back as two years ago. And a little more than a dozen in a city this size is nothing to lose sleep over."

"Unless you're one of the dozen-plus."

"Unless you are, of course," he had to reluctantly admit. "In all truth, Akaran, nobody ever stays missing. They come, they get what they need from Basion, then they go. They come back or they don't. It's no different than any other city, or village, or port, or rural outcropping."

He leaned back against the hard back of his chair and blinked in surprise at his attitude over it. "That is an *insanely* caviler response, don't you think?"

"No less an accurate one," he replied. "Of them, in the last year, there was only one instance where the disappearance seemed to be legitimate. We never were able to find the person and there was no evidence of foul play."

That was something he felt like he could finally work with. "Who was it?"

"To be completely honest with you, I don't have any idea," the commander replied with a little shrug. "His... no, her... name is on a report in here somewhere."

"Somewhere is a start. Want help looking for it?"

"Ah, no," Hender replied with a faintly nervous shudder at the thought of anyone else playing with his records. "There's nothing to find at this point. It was almost a full year back. Some claymaker from the Lowmarsh."

It was better than nothing. Not much, but better. "Remember anything specific about her?"

The lieutenant-commander gave it a moment's thought and started to dig through a different pile of papers to his far aside. "Just that she left in the middle of the night and her children never saw her again. Wasn't anything more to know outside of that."

"Except for her children," Akaran grunted.

"Except for," he agreed. "We really did look, you know. It's how we started hearing the rumors about the other supposed disappearances. I had my men look into it several times. There was nothing *to* find."

"Except for a missing mother," the priest reiterated.

The older soldier grunted noncommittally and gave up hunting through the paperwork. "Not everyone is a saint, exorcist, you should know. Sometimes a mother will abandon her children."

"All the more reason to find her."

"Some truth to that, I suppose," he sighed. "If I can find her name, will you get out of my hair? Please?"

Lying felt like it'd be more fun, but... "No, but it'll be a start. I need something else, too."

You could almost see the groan that Henderschott made. "What?"

"The murder of Adept Odern," Akaran started, "tell me about it. The Maiden didn't have much to give me."

Groan met grimace met a very unhappy shuffling of papers until he worked some down into a thin stack with a black wax seal stamped on the top of the pile. "I wish *I* did. Instructor-Adept Odern Merrington. Teaches – *taught* – magic at the Basion City Annex, under the hand of Headmaster-Adept Telburn Gorosoch."

"Defense instructor, right? What school?"

"Don't know, not a mage."

He thought about pushing, but couldn't fault the commander for that one. "Alright, go on."

Hender lifted an eyebrow and gave him a bemused smirk. "Oh I can go on, can I? Thank you," he mocked. "Middle of the city, sometime between the second and third bell. No witnesses."

The priest took it in stride and looked up at a map of the city on the south wall. They were in Akkador East, against the eastern wall of the basin, and south of the Repository in Chiadon. "Which district?"

"Piapat," he said, "and we believe he was finished elsewhere after being disabled." That area was practically in the middle of the city, a large district bordered by both Upper and Lower Naradol, West Akkador, and West Giffil. While there was only one neighborhood in it that was up against the Avagerona River, the southern edge of the district was flush to Orshia Overflow. "A tanner found him nailed to the back of her shop in an alley, through the feet, upside down."

Akaran cringed and assumed that it was down in the southern part of Piapat and closer to the lake. "The Maiden said it wasn't a clean death...?"

"I've rarely seen worse," he replied with a sad shake of his head. "His torso was flayed and his heart was stuffed in his throat."

"Blessed be," the priest whispered. "That sounds a lot like -"

"- a lot like what happened to Livstra? Yes," he agreed. "though that's a topic that hasn't been spread far and wide either, and it would be much appreciated if you didn't."

"Noted. That doesn't need to get spread around. I imagine the rumor mill is churning it out as it is, though."

Henderschott snorted in disgust. "More than you'd know. But. There's *rumor* and then there's *officially quoted* rumor."

"Fair," he agreed. "Still. Nobody at the Manor could have done that."

"Oh, several people *could* have. I don't think you know the type of people you share bunk space with. We just haven't had any luck tying one to the other," he replied as he leaned back in his chair. "Your leg is the only reason you aren't sitting in a cell. Odern's death happened just before you arrived, too," he said as he pushed the pile towards the exorcist, "though I had the guards quizzed to make sure you came to town when you said you did."

Akaran started to read over it and swallowed back a disgusted wave of bile. "I wouldn't do anything like this." The first wave was joined by a second as a sudden pang of more cocasa hit his system and he felt his stomach start to churn.

The lieutenant must've noticed the sheen of sweat appear his forehead and confused it for a sign of a guilty conscience. "You're in a mental ward. It's hard to say you even know what you'd do," the commander pointed out. "Same with the rest of them. There's only four more patients there that have the same permissions you do to come and go, and she employs ten aids to watch plus her other staff. That list includes her three physicians, and another seven priests representing the Pantheon that assist her. It doesn't give a large pool of suspects."

"Yet big enough that you haven't been able to pin the murder on anyone in particular," he countered.

Hender grunted in annoyance. "Yet big enough, yes. If it wasn't someone that lives or works in the manor, it had to be someone from outside. Those are the two options. Guess which one I like more?"

That earned a sigh and an under-his-breath curse from the priest. "Well, it's not like I wouldn't hope for a patient if I were in your shoes. Any kind of evidence left behind with Odern, even if not Liv?"

"We're pretty certain that he didn't die there," he replied as his hands started to tremble a little. "For one, he had no business anyone can make sense of in that area of the city – for another, there wasn't enough blood at the scene to account for the manner of death."

"Lovely," Akaran retorted as he sifted through the reports. "I can see why you're running into a wall. Has the Guild had any luck scrounging up information?"

"No. Or if they have, they haven't been sharing," he grumbled. "If that's the case, then I'll have their certification to work in Basion rescinded."

"Do you know what they've already looked into?"

The soldier shook his head again. "They tore apart the Annex and everything near Piapat. They seem to be leaning towards someone from the Odinal clan."

With a frown, Akaran looked up and tried to figure out if he was serious. "Any idea why? They seemed nice."

"Between us? Because those mercs don't like the work that Odinal is getting ready to do with the Advensi. So if they end up discrediting the delegation, it won't sting as much when Elsith has to go tell her bosses at the regional office that they don't want to work with them anyway."

He briefly flashed back to what Malik had told him about the way the contracts were actually heading, and for a brief moment of greater-than-usual wisdom, opted to keep that to himself for now. "Of any group, you'd think that the Guild would understand that the brutality of men knows no nationality," he deflected.

Hender leaned in and grinned. "You have to admit, some people are more inclined to acts of violence than others."

Akaran went utterly stoic and then very slowly, lifted his head back up and stared the older soldier right in the eyes. "Some people are," he replied as a second wave of nauseating *need* wracked his gut.

The threat worked better than expected. The lieutenant commander flinched and scooted back slightly under his brutal glare and shook his head. "I wish I had more to go on. I really do. Even if it was where the murder actually occurred. That alone would help."

"It would," the priest agreed with an annoyed sigh. "Alright, so, at least I know where to start at. What about the homeless? Where have they been going missing from?"

"Naradol, mainly."

Trekking to the other side of the city sounded like an utterly lousy thing to do, but it was the only real option available. "I'll head there next. Start asking around."

Hender stopped him before he could even reach for his cane. "Oh, you won't find them there now."

"I won't? Why?"

He cleared his throat and pointed over at the map and a rough circle someone had drawn on it outside the city proper. "Per the request of Betrothed Tyreening and Merchant-Master Hannock, they were encouraged to leave the city while the wedding celebrations were undertaken."

The priest blinked and stared at the wooded area on the map in confusion. "What? Really? You expelled them? How many?"

"Less than a hundred."

"It's not that warm out there!"

"It's also not midwinter," Henderschott argued. "My personal understanding is that a tent city of sorts was set up outside the walls out in the woods. There's game and wild food enough. I've heard that some of them are even doing better than they were begging for scraps on the street."

Akaran chewed on that for a moment before shaking his head. "I'm disgusted but somehow not surprised. Fine, where is their camp?"

"I'm not entirely sure. You can talk to the gate captain. He should know."

The priest took another minute to look at the map before he sighed in utter frustration – both from Henderschott's uselessness and the urgent need to rip into his pouch and stuff his mouth full of painkillers. The latter, he assumed, would be a bad idea in the middle of the Garrison barracks. "I will. Thank you,

Commander."

"*Lieutenant* Commander," he corrected with a tone that was more smug than he actually deserved to use.

The priest stood up and leaned on his cane, but didn't make any effort to leave. "One last thing."

Henderschott looked up and frowned. "What now?"

"I vaguely remember you and Livstra arguing when I first got to the manor," he said before asking, "What was it about?"

"Oh. That was you in the cart?"

"It was. What was it about?" he repeated.

His left eye twitched and his right hand tensed up. "Nothing important. Just an old gambling debt."

Akaran narrowed his eye and stared at him a little more intently. "That could be important. You roll the dice often?"

"I'm doing it now with you," he returned.

"You could do worse."

"To be seen," he groused. "Oh, and Akaran?"

"Yes?"

Henderschott started to stand up but settled on leaning halfway out of his chair. "I don't really like you, and I really don't trust you. Don't make me regret this, and whatever you do, keep your head down. The city is on edge with this damn wedding and we do *not* need a panic."

"Same, same, I'll try not to, and no. A panic won't help anyone."

Once he was out of the garrison, there was only one other thing he was sure of: he was being followed. For a change, it wasn't paranoia; he couldn't lay his eye on the man, but he just *knew* that the hunter that he had spied in the barracks was now spying on him...

His first look at the Basion City Annex had admittedly taken his breath away. During training with the Order, they'd run him past a couple – and you couldn't walk into the Kingdom's seat of power without seeing the Annex of Mulvette staring down at you from its vantage point overlooking half of the entire city. Even though most Annexes had a similar build to each other, whenever you got close to one, it took your breath away.

For the first time in his life, he could dismiss the idea that it was some enchantment that the cocky bastards had cast to instill the viewer with a sense of awe and wonderment. It also meant that he was going to go back to the Manor and pen a letter to a couple of old friends to win an outstanding bet on the very same subject. With a sigh, he looked up at the massive set of towers and decided to celebrate that victory, however small it was.

The happy thought aside, this was the *one* place he did *not* want to go. Unfortunately, with Henderschott's instructions to the vagrant camp leading all the way outside the city and south of the Manor, stopping by the Annex on the way felt like the second-wisest course of action. The first being to not go there at all, but even in his cocasa-fogged mind, at some point it felt like he might have been complaining a bit too much.

It didn't take him more than five minutes to come under the scrutiny of no less than three different mages once he was on Annex grounds and another five to have a flock of students trying to discretely follow his movements. The only reason he didn't thwart their attempts to stay hidden (he'd seen actual shambling corpses do it better) was because he had absolutely no idea where to go.

"Find the shiniest and tallest building," ended up not just being simple, but accurate directions. Actually finding the reception of the marble tower was a different story entirely. When he finally did find someone that was more interested in helping him than studying him – if for no other reason than to shut him up and get him to whine somewhere else – the response was to make him rush to an antechamber.

Then wait.

In the future, an appointment *would* be needed.

Or at least, that's what two different white-robe wearing scribes told him while staring so far down their noses that he suddenly understood how dwarves must feel. The next problem was, as he figured the moment he saw the damnable tower, was even more damnable stairs. The school went up four stories straight into the air, so *of course* there were stairs.

But at least there's no snow, he kept repeating as he trudged up one flight to another. *Never snow. Never again am I going to see snow, never am I –* he chanted until he made it halfway up the second floor and looked into an open classroom. Two Adepts and a handful of novices were busy throwing hastily-formed balls of ice back and forth at each other while frozen little white flakes descended freely from the ceiling.

They never did figure out who punched a hole in the wall by the door.

Once he made it to the third floor he was greeted with the knowledge that he wouldn't have to ascend to the fourth – which was great. The less-great side of that coin was that by the time he made it up there, Gorosoch had gone all the way back down to the reception hall. "Oh, he knew of your injury and didn't want you to injure yourself any further," the smug little prick of a scribe had told him. "I commend you for making it this far, but I am most afraid you'll have to go back down."

They never figured out where the dent in the stairwell came from, either.

By the time he made it back downstairs, not only had Gorosoch wandered off to a different tower entirely, his leg was screaming at him in what felt like three different languages and none of them belonged to beings of the mortal world. Thankfully, Lolron (of all people), happened to see him wandering around like an agonized idiot and offered him a quiet storeroom to sit in away from the main annex until he could catch his breath until the Headmaster could be found.

When Gorosoch turned up a bit later, Akaran was half asleep and utterly exhausted. Sleep that was, as usual, being plagued with visions of the damned that made him feel like the campus was as much a mausoleum as a library. When the Headmaster's page woke him up, he was all-too grateful for it. "Exorcist? This is Headmaster Telburn Gorosoch. Headmaster Gorosoch this is -"

"Akaran DeHawk!" he exclaimed, his slightly sunken navy blue eyes glimmering like all the diamonds in the world, "Finally! It's an absolute pleasure to meet you."

"Headmaster," he repeated with a bow of his head. "I didn't realize you knew me."

"Knew you? Of course I do. We all know you."

Akaran tilted his head slightly and blinked. "We?"

"The Headmasters," he clarified, "you have created *quite* a stir."

For a minute, he entertained the fleeting hope that there was somehow more than one at the Annex. "Headmast...*ers*?"

Telburn adjusted his tan robe and smiled like a young boy with a brand new toy at the Celebration of the Origin. "Well, yes! Any of us with any interest in elemental magic, at the very least. And conjuration. And ulta. Ether, too."

He slowly stood up and scratched nervously at the back of his head (and started to wish that there was more than one exit... and that the mage wasn't standing in the way). "I'm not sure why?"

"Because of the coldstone, of course. Every Annex in Dawnfire has been provided a copy of the report on it."

Akaran nearly dropped his cane. His jaw, however, fell like a rock. "Excuse me, what? A report on it? What kind of report? What have you been told?"

"Not as much as we'd like," he admitted. "The nature of the stone, yes. We have no idea on how to make another one. Your Order has gone to great lengths to stonewall us, you know. We've been desperately trying to figure out *why*. In fact, they haven't even let us come and talk to you about it. Threatened censure in the Queen's Court if we did." His eyes started to shine even brighter as he walked over and took him by his left hand. "They said absolutely *nothing* about you coming to us about it, however!"

"Ah, respectfully," he replied as he pulled his hand free and straightened his own vestments, "no."

The Headmaster did something that Akaran absolutely did not expect to see him do: he pouted. "No? Okay, then at least you can explain why everyone from the General down to the janitor has locked down everything but the most basic of nuggets of study from us?"

Akaran coughed into his shoulder and picked the most diplomatic way to phrase the 'no' and took a shot at it. "Because I had to cleanup a mess caused by a wizard the Academy expelled. Because his work almost triggered a new Imperium War. Because his work could have, and did, let legions of the damned loose."

"All things the Academy would carefully control if given the opportunity."

"All due respect, Headmaster, my Order has to put down rogue experiments that break free of the Academy's control on a regular basis," he pointed out.

Telburn waved both of his hands dismissively and kept the smile on his face. "We are perfectly capable of cleaning up our own messes. We can handle anything that could possibly come up as a result of errant accidents with -"

The priest gave him a disbelieving half-glare. "Is that why the Granalchi holds the second-largest retainer on record with the Hunter's Guild?"

"Mistakes do happen from time to time," he conceded.

"I'm well aware," Akaran grunted. "Listen: Usaic violated a rule I can't believe has to be a rule. He opened breaches. You know that's a forbidden research and before you ask how *I* know, remember that we get taught about the rules that the Academy and the Order of Light – let alone the Order of Love – have agreed to."

"Breaches? Whatever do you mean?" he asked, feigning innocence.

"You know what I mean. Gateways. He made the stone by opening doors – *plural*. Doors that went to places that *shouldn't ever be opened* and then the fool *left them open*. Things *came out* of those doors."

Light both simultaneously went off in his eyes and dimmed to a bare spark. "I... see," he said, slowly rolling the reply out of his mouth. "Yes, I imagine that your Temple would have issue with that. You did say he was rogue? You should know that a certified adept would never leave such gates open in our own research."

"Doesn't matter," he pointed out. "Start cracking open holes, certified or not, and Johasta would order an inquisition into the Granalchi. It'd be an all-out war. Our Goddess, your knowledge."

For the first time in their talk, the smile vanished. "You'd never be allowed. The tolerance the Queen shows your Order only goes so far. She can't be without our magic."

"To keep the doors to the Abyss shut? Wouldn't push it," Akaran argued. "Say what you will about humanity as a whole, but most of us learned the lesson that Agromah presented."

"Most of us, except those in Sycio," he mused.

"I can say a few things about *them*, too," Akaran groused.

The Bladebane smirked. "I've no doubt. So by your words, I shall assume he opened a door to Frosel. Interesting."

"On second thought, I'm leaving," he shot back as he came to the quick conclusion that nothing he said would satisfy the older man – and that anything he said might well come back to bite him on the ass.

Telburn quickly stepped in his path and raised his hands up in surrender. "No, don't, please. You have to understand. What we've been told about the coldstone is one of the greatest discoveries in the last decade," he implored, adding, "you must realize that it would be so intriguing for me to learn more about. Would you oppose being interviewed?"

"Yes. I would."

"Correct me if I'm wrong but aren't we providing you personal assistance with your current situation? Lack of magical aptitude at current, and all that?" His eyes lit up again as he started to look the exorcist up and down. "I'd love to study *that* more, too. If it's a function that can be replicated it -"

The priest rapped the end of his cane against the cold stone floor and balled his other hand up in a tight fist. "I will *not* let you use me as a weapon."

"But you are an exorcist of Love," he argued. "One would say you already *are* a weapon."

"*Her* weapon, not *your* weapon," Akaran retorted. "Headmaster, I... yes. I would love your help, *more* help than what Lolron provided, to be able to use magic again."

Telburn's smile faded again, slowly but knowingly. "One does not have to have skills in psyanistry to know the intent of what you're about to say."

"I can't trade my knowledge of the coldstone for that help though," he sighed. "I would be breaking oaths to the Order, no matter how much I want it."

The mage gingerly took Akaran's hand in his again and nodded understandingly. "I do hope you don't blame me for trying. I am sympathetic to your problem, of course. As Lolron offered, I am willing to help personally."

"It's just that all things have a price," he lamented.

"A little studying surely can't hurt anyone."

"You'd be surprised," he sighed again. "I'm here to help you, actually. Maybe we can work something out this way instead."

Gorosoch blinked and squeezed his hand a little tighter before letting go. "Me? And what kind of help are you here to provide?"

The exorcist cleared his throat before finally getting to the statement he'd prepared. "On behalf of both the Order of Love and in the interests of the Queen's Law, I've opened an inquest into Odern Merrington's passing. He died in a way that was similar to one of the attendants at Medias' Manor."

He stepped back and looked at the priest like it was the first time he was really seeing *him* and not just *research*. "Oh, yes. I heard she had passed. I wasn't aware of the circumstances."

"They were bad," he deadpanned.

"I see. You think there's a connection?"

Akaran shrugged. "I think the worst of everything. It's what I do."

That earned a slight smile. "I suppose it is."

He slowly sat back down and pulled a worn leather-bound journal and a piece of charcoal off of his belt and looked up at the Headmaster. "The garrison didn't have much to give me to go on. Is there anything you might...? Does he have any enemies, did he ever dilly the wrong dally? Was he on the outs with the Academy?"

"No, nothing of the sort," Gorosoch replied as he put his mind to it. "Nor was he working on any kind of controversial research. I am afraid that there is absolutely nobody that should have had any reason at all to kill the man."

"That's not true," he argued, "at least one person did."

"Yes, that is apparent and obvious now, in hindsight."

He checked a few marks off in his booklet and started to go down the list of questions he'd prepared. "What type of research was he doing before he died?"

"Nothing out of the ordinary. He was less a 'researcher' and more a 'teacher.' Combative magics."

"A battlemage and a caretaker don't have much in common."

Telburn shook his head. "Oh, he wasn't a battlemage. Well, maybe in the widest sense of the word," he clarified. "No, his focus was on defensive magics. Girding the mind, protecting the body, training his students to see past illusions. Wards, shields, redirection – things of that sort. A bit of a pacifist."

Akaran made a show of writing that down and added a few 'hmm' sounds for effect. "Any chance I could look at his notes? Read some of his most recent efforts?"

"You could, though I doubt it will do any good for you," he cautioned. "My understanding of your Order is that you primarily focus on magics of ambianistry and psyanistry. His was much more mattanic and elementalism."

"Not going to look at it to learn how to do it," he replied, "though we like to study anything that'll help keep us upright. I'm interested more to see if I can find a motive."

"You won't find one, but yes, if it will ease your mind, then be my guest."

He nodded and looked up from his book. "Thank you. Do you know if he had any bad habits? Women, theater, drinking?"

"You assume theater is a bad habit?" he asked, puzzled. "Is there some kind of link your Order places with the Abyss and entertainment of that nature...?"

Akaran cringed slightly. "No... it's... well. The Grand Temple had a yearly re-enactment of the *Rise of Queen Dannivette*, performed by children aged five to nine years. They made us watch. Every year. It's horrible."

"That's a lovely play though, surely you can't dislike it?"

"It was performed by *children*," he stressed, "*every* year. And they *made* us watch. Do you have any idea what that's like? Not a single one of them could carry a tune in a bucket."

"Ah," the Headmaster replied with a little noise of derision. "Well... well, fair enough. No to theater. No to drinking. He had an eye for games of chance, but between us, I think it was because he liked to test himself against the charlatans."

The priest sucked on air for a heartbeat and quickly jotted that down. "That's a good reason to murder someone. If you're a charlatan, that is."

"Suppose so," Telburn admitted, "though I find it difficult to imagine that he could be killed by some common thug though, not like that."

"Hit someone in the head hard enough when they aren't looking, and you can do a lot to them before they wake up," Akaran pointed out.

The mage shuddered at the thought. "True. Grisly, but true. I'll have one of my students deliver his most recent work to your room at the Manor. I'd offer to let you root around in his dormitory, but everything he had has been packed up and moved into storage elsewhere."

"Any chance I can get into that storage?"

"No. That, I will have to draw a line against. For one, the most base of his belongings is stored with private materials belonging to the other instructors. For another, his actual work is stored outside of this reality."

It was his turn to look like an idiot again and he gave Telburn a vacant stare. "Outside of...?"

"In a pocket in the Veil," he said. "It cuts down on clutter. Also provides more protection than just having something locked up in a building – like they do at the Repository."

Akaran continued to stare like a bewildered fool. "That can't possibly be safe."

"Oh you find that the Granalchi have ways to ensure safety of many things," the mage smugly replied.

"I really don't... I've had my fill of... of..."

"Trans-dimensional travel and planar shifts into dimensions that humans aren't capable of experiencing without assistance from entities divine or other?"

He nodded a little too vehemently. "All of that. Yes."

After a moment, the Headmaster shrugged. "Quite reasonable."

"As to Odern, and his replacement," Akaran quickly replied, desperately trying to move back to his somewhat-prepared line of questioning, "does it usually take a while to get someone new to a position?"

"It can."

"Who's in line to take his spot?"

"Nobody from Basion, if you're wondering."

Akaran scribbled that into his notebook. "I am, actually. Did his replacement ever meet him before his death?"

Gorosoch crossed his arms and defensively straightened up to his full height. "No, I can end that line of thought for you in the here and now. Someone from the Grand Library will be assigned to take his place. I trust all of the students of this Annex, but they are just that; students."

"Going to be a long-shot to ask, but have you had any visitors from out of town that might have been in line for the position?"

"Not a one, I am sorry to say. Again, there is no chance that that could have been a motive."

"Wonderful," he grunted. "Why do I feel like I have even less of an idea where to look?"

"Ah, but that isn't so. You're closer now than you were," Telburn replied with that irritating glimmer back to his eyes.

"Oh?"

"Of course!" he exclaimed. "Now you know where *not* to look. When your clues eventually begin to arise, you won't be distracted by the maybes that simply cannot be."

Akaran looked down at his journal and muttered a reply of, "Known knowns, known unknowns, and unknown unknowns."

That made the mage smile even wider. "Yes, exactly. At you can at least consider this: you know that whomever did it can't be the type of monster your profession normally hunts."

"What possibly makes you think that?"

"This is Basion city," he replied, "the safest place in the kingdom."

"Apparently it isn't," he countered with a faint smile of his own. "Do you know what they say about 'safe' places back at the temple?"

Gorosoch gave him a puzzled little look. "Hm? No?"

"Safe places are areas where nobody looks for monsters," he answered before giving the Headmaster a cold, serious stare, "which is *exactly* how they like it."

His tone – and the haunted look in his blue-gray eye – made the mage flinch and almost take an involuntary step back. "Well noted. Let me get that research to you. If there's anything else you can think of, don't hesitate to ask."

Akaran wagged the charcoal stick towards him before he could leave "Do you know where he liked to play his games at?"

The question seemingly caught the Headmaster off-guard and that itself made the priest make another note. "Hmm. No, I don't. I'll ask around."

"Please," he urged. "I've been given a broad brush on where to look – and to make sure that the two deaths *aren't* related. Or the disappearances."

Gorosoch tilted his head again and scratched at a little patch of unshaven stubble on his chin. "Disappearances? In Basion?"

Akaran nodded and then gave the mage a rundown of his conversations with Henderschott and Catherine both. "Something is wrong. I can feel it. It's in my bones."

"All this and the wedding," he mused. "Forgive me for saying this but would it be wrong of me to hope that the person behind it is one of those uncultured barbarians from up north?"

"If the people vanishing hadn't been going on for more than a year, I'd say anyone is a suspect for all of it. They may well be for the murders, though but I doubt the rest." *If I can even prove the rest*, he grumbled to himself.

"Well, not anyone, I assume," Telburn replied with a faint smile.

"Well, the Temple isn't," he agreed.

The Headmaster's brows raised again as he took stock of the priest for a third time. "But I am?"

"No offense intended," Akaran began, "but you're a mage. And a powerful one at that. One of only a few people in the city that could easily overpower another Adept, break into the Manor and butcher a woman without leaving evidence behind, and vanish random citizenry without a trace."

He mulled it over for a moment before having to reluctantly nod in understanding. "And of course, I want something from you," he added. "Several things. I imagine that's making you wish to trust me even less."

"Right now I don't trust anyone," the exorcist admitted.

"Not an unwise decision," Gorosoch replied with a knowing little nod of his head. "I will say, however, that I had nothing to do with the death. I'm the one that contracted the Guild to look into it."

"Yet they haven't found anything of note so far, a month later," Akaran pointed out. "That's either an indictment against them or praise for the culprit."

Telburn's smile grew warmer but there was something less friendly in his eyes when he replied. "You're wise beyond your years, exorcist."

"I'm in pain and I want to find who did it so I can go back to bed."

"And driven," the mage replied with a chuckle. "I'll get what you need and we'll see each other soon. That offer to truly work on you is still on the table. I don't know if I can fix it, but I would like to find out more about... well, all of it."

Akaran sighed and looked down at his throbbing knee. "If it turns out I can trust you, then we'll talk."

"An entirely reasonable stance to take," he replied as the exorcist put his notes away and stood up to go. "Oh, there is one thing I should mention now that I think of it."

"Hm?"

The Headmaster casually wrapped his fingers around the copper disk hanging from his neck. "When they found his... it's hard to justify calling it a body, but his remains... his sigil was missing. You've seen them before, yes?"

The exorcist gave him a little nod and a puzzled frown. "Circular disk, copper, right?"

"Yes, with circles etched within it, and various gemstones on each orbit. As a rule, we try to avoid losing them and I can honestly say that I've never seen the man without his. If you find one loose, do let me know?"

"I will," he replied. "If I'm not mistaken, each — what'd you call it, orbit? - denotes a school that the mage is fluent in, right?"

"That's correct," Telburn confirmed, "and if you find one you think belongs to Odern, check it over. His will have a triangle made of gold in the center. The second orbit will have an opaline gem, the third a pearl. The fourth will have a moonstone and a chunk of pyrite; the fifth, a piece of amethyst. The center is to designate his rank as an instructor, while the other three -"

"Ambianist, psyanist, ether-keneticist, and a mattanist, right?" he interrupted.

The mage didn't bother to hide the pleasant surprise that Akaran made him feel. "I'm impressed! Not many that do not seek knowledge at the Academy know what the orbits mean."

"No offense, again, Headmaster, but -"

"- but, the Temple does occasionally have to clean up our messes from time to time and knowing which of us is doing what helps you gird your loins for battle, or somesuch?"

Just this once, the exorcist looked like someone took the wind right out of his sails. "Well. Yes."

Telburn just laughed at him. "Do you know the significance of the stones themselves, however?"

"The stones? No."

He dangled his sigil and ran his fingers over the various ones decorating the disc. "While each orbit designates a school, each school has various specialties within. Each specialization, a stone. While you can say and be quite right that Odern had a mastery of those four schools – he was an instructor, after all – his line of study was more precise."

Akaran settled back down and dug his notebook back out, scribbling away. "Go on. It can't hurt to learn more about him. Gives me an idea of what to look for."

"How so?"

"Knowing what he was good at shows me what his weaknesses might've been. I mean, if he were a hydromancer, I'd not expect him to burn to death in a fire."

"Or drown, I imagine. You've a valid point, so yes, let me explain," he thoughtfully agreed. "I was going to anyway, you know. Habit of being a teacher." Before Akaran could comment on *that*, he went on and explained. "In ambianistry, Odern was an auramancer. His research into psyanistry gave him ways of understanding magic of illusions, while his efforts in the Fourth School allowed him to teach classes in both raw ether manipulation and para-psiphonic."

His impromptu student frowned and tried to spell that particular word twice before giving up. "Okay, that's a new one to me. Parpsi...?"

"*Para-psiphonic*. In layman's terms, parasitic manipulation of magic. The magic of transferring ether from one person or object to another."

"That sounds borderline evil," he muttered.

"In the wrong hands, it is – but can't all things be turned into tools of the cruel? In the right ones, it might be what you need to research for your own problem, based on what Lolron has told me," he pointed out. "That being said, he also had above-normal levels of skill with physical object manipulation. Making things float, for example."

Akaran kept his head down and tried to write as much of that out as he could. "So you're telling me he could make illusions, manipulate ether, manipulate objects, and read auras." When Telburn gave him a nod of agreement, he sat back and blanched. "He wouldn't have been easy to kill."

The mage nodded again. "This is why he was a teacher in *defensive magics*," he stressed. "It would do his students no good if he was an easy fight."

There's people in this world I'd love to punch out, he thought quietly, *but this bastard wouldn't've been one of them. Whomever put him down didn't do it in a fair fight. Or if they did... if they took him head-on there would HAVE to be witnesses. It would've sounded like a thunderstorm.* "That... all of that actually helps. Thank you, Headmaster. I'll do what I can to bring his murderer to justice," he said with a smile that was a few degrees warmer than he felt. *Though more accurately, going to have to bring justice to the killer. Possibly with a garrison's worth of help...*

"It is always a pleasure to help a man of the Temple when the cause is just," Telburn replied. "Let me know when you're ready to discuss your personal matters."

Akaran replied with shrinking niceties as he stood up and made his way back to his horse outside. *Have a feeling if I talked to that man about anything, he'd be just as happy to leave me hanging somewhere as Example A in one of his classes...*

The Headmaster watched him go with a smile that stayed on his lips until the second that the priest's back was turned. When his page showed up a few moments later and began to hand him an armful of scrolls, the poor kid didn't notice the intense scowl the mage was sporting. "As requested, sir, all of the documents relating to -"

Gorosoch interrupted him and pushed the papers back into the young boy's hands. "Now that I've met the man I want two things, and I want them right now."

The lowly assistant's face crumbled as he felt his day turn inexorably worse for no apparent fault of his own. "Yes, Headmaster?"

"Get Lolron into my office, for one."

"I think he's in the middle of a class -"

"It's canceled," he snapped. "Get word to Ishtva, too. He is to use *all* methods available to get the final report that the Lovers filed about the coldstone. *And* Philanus. If Ishtva can't, then the Ledger can. *Every* method, *any* cost. I do not care *who* he has to bribe or with what, but I want it *right now,*" he demanded with a growl.

The page took a nervous step back. "Of course, Headmaster. Let me just -"

"One more thing," he added. "Send someone to find my wife."

A feeling that was not disputed by the Hunter outside, trailing the priest every step of the way.

Flynn's Landing was *not* part of the tour that he'd been given. Any tour. By anyone. Not even the city guard knew exactly where it was – or if they *did,* they weren't inclined to *say* no matter how much he waved his sigil at them.

The sun was almost gone by the time that he found someone that knew where to find the mythical camp outside the city, and oddly, it wasn't one of the local homeless that had his answer. All *they* wanted were alms, coins, and at least one toothless hag had offered to help him root through his clothes to find cocasa that she could smoke. At least, that was what he *hoped* she had asked for, but it was hard to tell.

No, help for him came from a well-meaning *undlajunct* from the Order of Light that had assumed since he was out busy talking to the homeless, that he himself must also be destitute. It took nearly ten minutes before he could convince her that no, he wasn't mad, no, he didn't need to go back to his own Order for help, no, he didn't need to find faith with one of the other Divine. It finally took two crowns to convince the twit that he needed directions and not salvation.

Though, in her defense, she did stumble into him while his mouth was full of painkillers... and right after he'd fallen into a puddle of mud. It hadn't left for a grand first impression. Neither, as it turned out, did he get to leave one when he ran into the Landing.

More stairs were the first thing that greeted him. The camp was somewhere south-west of the manor, and that meant either going up the northern wall or using a rarely-traveled set of stairs near the Overflow to make it up into the Fel'achir. The steps closest to the Overflow won the battle, and by the time he got over them, they had about won the entire war.

They were so utterly frustrating that he had left his horse at the Manor.

Not even halfway down the stairs, and he wished he was there with her.

The next task was to find the roughly-traveled and barely-maintained path that took him on a wandering path out of Basion and into the dense overgrowth that the Fel was known for. It didn't take long at all to realize why nobody had tried to settle in this particular stretch of woods and he had almost given up all hope on finding the camp before the sun settled to nothing.

Of course, once he got close enough, the smell was enough to let him know he was on the right track. By the time his eyes found the first traces of torchlight, the air was full of the scents of wet dog, feces, and smoldering ash. He could only imagine how much worse it would be once he was in the camp proper, and before he knew it, he was.

An old chunk of tree bark had been pegged to a tree and the words "Welcome to Flynn's Landing" were carved onto it. A second, closer look showed that 'Flynn's Landing' had been written into the wood over a different name – Asio – which was a who/why/when/where question for the future. For now though, the only thing that mattered was that nobody wanted to come forth with information.

Or even so much as a hello.

After the third attempt to get the attention of the unwanted and the unwashed, a kid just slightly younger than the exorcist finally poked his regally-shaped nose out of a ramshackle hut to glare at him. "Whatever you want, go away."

"I want to help."

"I want to eat this rat, and you're making a ruckus," he snapped back.

Akaran blanched and felt his stomach flop just a little. "Rat? Did you at least coat it with honey?"

The kid stepped out of his(?) house and stuffed his hands into his pockets (pockets that just happened to be right next to a strange knife, the type of which he'd never seen before). "Do I look like the kind of guy that can afford to get *honey* for his *rat* that he caught today?"

He looked thin, but also strong enough to put up a fight in the right circumstances. A jagged scar across his throat gave the impression that he could hold his own, and the irritated glare he was giving made the priest feel like he might just like the brown-haired scrapper. "You look like the kind of guy that shouldn't turn away help."

"Nobody offers to help, so I don't think that's what you're here to do."

"It's close."

"There's either help or not help, there is no 'it's close' to it," the boy countered, "so which is it? I want to eat my dinner."

Akaran started to point his finger at him and counter with something heated and profound, then slowly stopped, bit his finger instead, and gave the kid a bit of a nod. "That's fair. I get the impression not a lot of people like to be of service for anything up here."

"Nothing new there," he agreed before sneering at the priest. "So. What. Come to tell us we're too close to the city proper? Yell at us for violating another horsecock of an ordinance? Remind us we ain't shit in the eyes of the Queen?"

A crowd had started to form around the arguably-equally-irritated duo and a few of them had large and very blunt objects in their hands, which did nothing for his feelings of anxiety and general paranoia. "No, no, and no, though that's part of the problem," Akaran replied. "I'm not here to give you any grief. Any at all," he repeated.

"You'll forgive me if I don't believe that."

"I will, but I'm not. I promise. Just a priest trying to do the right thing."

The kid pointed at the sigil on Akaran's neck and let his hand drop down to the blade at his waist. "No, you're an *exorcist* and that means the *right* thing isn't the thing that brings a happy ending."

He blinked and quietly applauded the boy for realizing it. "You know, you're the first person today that understands that. Most people see the Order sigil and think that I'm supposed to be some paragon of virtue," and then before he could reply, he slowly tucked the pendant back under his vestment and lowered his head, "but it also means that you've met people like me before. So. Let me reiterate: I'm here to help, and I bring no intent of harm to you or yours."

"Paragon of something," the kid grunted as he leaned against the hut. "What do you want?"

"Trying to find some missing people. I heard that this was the place to look," he said as he studied the way some in the crowd were looking at them. "Was hoping to talk to the camp leader. I'm guessing you're him...?"

A shadow of disgust and sudden anger rolled over his face. "I am. Leamer Flynn," he spat back, "and if this is your idea of a joke, you're a sick son of a bitch."

"I'm not joking, Flynn, I swear to the Goddess. I'm here about it."

Leamer looked around the grumbling crowd and pointed at the priest. "Y'all hear that? We have someone here *looking for* our missing."

An old crone cackled back at him. "Now that he's seen it he can leave!"

A kid more than half as young as any of them flung a small rock at the exorcist, shouting obscenities as he did. "Only people you care about missing are *us* from the city! You ain't givin' no shit about us otherwise!"

"Okay, hold on. I'm not here to bring grief!"

The crone shouted at him again. "You're doing a damn good job of it if not!"

He turned to her and gestured wildly. "All I did was say I'm here to help!"

"Like the garrison did when they threw us out?" the little boy beside her shouted back. "Fisk them, fisk you!"

Akaran turned and gave Flynn a pleading look. "Okay. Seriously. Whatever's happened between you and the 4th, I haven't had any hand in it. I'm here to help. That's all."

"I got some ideas for how you can help, boy," the crone cackled as she made a lewd gesture with her tongue at him. "Why don't you grab your stick and come over here, help an old lady out."

The priest looked over at her and then quickly back at the camp leader. "What in the pits is with these people?"

"These people? You mean my people?" he scoffed.

"I mean *all* of you," Akaran retorted. "I came here offering to *help*."

Flynn crossed his arms over his chest and managed to look down his nose at the exorcist – an impressive feat for being shorter than him. "You came here to feel better about yourself at our expense. Go tell your bosses you came and waved your hands and everything is going to be fine and get outta here."

"How about no? I came here with questions."

"The answers are 'fisk' and 'you," he offered.

Akaran clenched his jaw and looked at what was turning into an angry mob and went for plan 'B'. "So I'm guessing that there *haven't* been any disappearances and I'm wasting my time. *Fine.*"

The camp's boss made a big show of hocking up something nasty in his throat before spitting it into the dirt. "Oh there have. Plenty of them. An' every time we go off an' talk about them, we get the same line from Henderschott and the other ass-licking sword-jockeys. People come, people leave, get over it."

"That was about the same shit I got from him too," he replied with an understanding nod. "It's why I'm out here now. Because people *do* come and they *do* go, but communities matter. Six or seven people going missing a year for a couple of years and -"

Leamer bent over with laughter as the crone rolled her eyes and started to shuffle her way to his side. "In a year? SIX? Is that what they said?"

"Yeah, that it was only around six or seven. Around fourteen, fifteen in total. Why?"

"Priest, someone's been lying to you," he replied with a tear in his eye – and it was hard to say if it was from laughing or 'other.' "You wanna know how many it actually has been?"

"More or less than six?"

"One."

"That's less," he said with a brief moment of hopefulness.

The crone covered her mouth as she cut loose with a ragged, hacking cough. "A month," she corrected, "an' sometimes we lose more."

The only part of Akaran that moved was a subtle twitch along the edge of his eye. "That's more. How long?"

"More than a year, year and a half," Leamer replied.

He stood there silent as he studied the crowd and quickly counted off how many people nodded or otherwise expressed agreement. When the numbers tilted towards Flynn's favor, he looked him in the eye and felt steel firm up in his voice. "That's insane. People have been going missing for that long and nobody's done anything?"

"Oh they did things alright," he replied with an angry wave of his hand towards the city. "They said they were gonna look. Said they were gonna search. Said they were gonna take care of us. What'd they actually do? First chance they got an excuse to round us up and throw us out, that's what they did."

"Made us an offer," the crone added. "Said as long as we kept our trash out of the city while that fancy muckup is going on then they'd grant us land out here, long as we shut up and don't bother them no more about it."

"They? Which they?"

"Paverilak Tyreening," Flynn replied, "of all fisking people. Guess his Maiden really wants the wedding to go off without a hitch."

Akaran grunted and shook his head. "No wedding has ever gone off without a hitch. It's a wedding."

The crone belted out more of her awful, fingernails-on-glass laugh. "Says a man that's been married before!"

His eye went wide and he nearly dropped his cane as he tried to distance himself from *that* suggestion. "Me? Married? No. *Goddess* no."

She just kept laughing as Flynn went on about their situation. "Married or not, that was the deal. We shut up we move out they grant us a chunk of land for all of us to call our own."

Akaran shook his head again and glared at nobody in particular. "Let me guess: you did your part, you're not getting assistance from the garrison, you're being left to fend for yourselves, and you're responsible for your own well-being."

"That's right."

"Which doesn't solve your problem with people vanishing, just makes it go away. Which, ironically..."

"Which is all those bastards Hannock and Henderschott want," he agreed.

He rolled the names back and forth on his tongue and tapped his fingers on the head of his stick. "Win-win for everyone but you. Quaint."

"Right," the teenager confirmed. "So we don't matter, but if we stop droppin' off the face of the planet, we get a place to call our own."

Something about the way he said it managed to piss the priest off even more. "Well, you *do* matter, and I'm here to *tell* you that *you matter,*" he said, almost growling as he uttered the words.

Flynn snorted and rolled his baby-blue eyes up to the stars. "Forgive me if I ain't believing you none."

"Well, that I can't help," Akaran sighed. "Tell me about the people going missing? Anything that stands out, anything they have in common with each other?"

"In common? Aside from being piss broke and homeless?"

"Aside from," he repeated. "Same family? Children only? Adults and children? Women only? Men and women?" He stood there and thought on it for a moment and added, "Any of them known for drinking more than they should or using the wrong kind of herbs?"

"Like the kind you're usin', boy?" the crone asked.

He glanced over and twitched a little at the accusation. "Or worse."

"I can't say as I've ever thought about any of that," Flynn admitted. "No kids, none I can remember. Just adults. Well, no little kids." He stopped and looked Akaran over again, eyes wary. "You're serious an' all about this?"

"People do come and go all the time. Nobody needs a reason or owes an explanation about why they decide to up and leave," he replied, then slowly pointed at the crowd. "My heart is saying that you wouldn't be pissed about it if you didn't think there wasn't a real reason to be concerned. Would you be? Would any of you be?"

Their leader straightened up and let his jaw dangle open for a moment. "You really are serious. You really do care."

"Yes."

The crone quickly grabbed him by his wrist and shook her head. "Flynn? He means it. Be scared."

"You don't need to be scared," Akaran said with a (failed) attempt at sounding reassuring. In truth, finding out how much worse this was making his stomach churn and he knew the tremor in his voice was giving it away.

"Yer a holy man on a mission," she shot back with a dismissive grimace. "*Everyone* should be fiskin' scared. *You* know that better than *any* of us."

Flynn ignored her – or if he listened, he decided to go with it anyway. "I'll tell you what I know. Much as I know."

The priest let out a little breath that he didn't know he was holding. "Okay, good. Start with this: when was the last time anyone vanished?"

He checked off weeks on his fingers. "Hm. Now let me think. Probably been a bit more than a month since anyone did. Bit more, bit less. Hard to say; we got kicked out thenabouts too."

"Two months, okay," he replied, and honestly, it was as far from okay as okay could possibly get. "Interesting. But nobody since then?"

He chewed on his lip for a minute and started to nervously play with the knife at his hip. "We've had a bunch of people decide they don't like waiting for the assholes in charge to live by their word. Lot of folks just up and took off so I don' know if anyone's gone missing or not from that bunch."

Akaran tilted his head slightly and looked puzzled. "Why'd they go? You got offered free land."

"Free land if we left the only place we've ever called home so that the high and mighty wouldn't have to see us underfoot," Flynn clarified. "How'd you feel if there was that going on, and nobody cared about what was happening to you?"

"Oh, if you've ever heard of the Hardening, you know exactly how my Order feels about that," he pointed out. "Know what direction they went?"

"Scattered about the wind."

Akaran pursed his lips and dug for his notebook. "Tell me everything you know about the ones that went missing. I'm gonna pray that most of them went off on their own but I wouldn't get your hopes up."

"We gave up hope for the best ages ago. You should know that."

"Then hope for retribution," he suggested.

Something in the crone's old gray eyes lit up and the corner of her lips turned up into a wicked smile. "Ohhhh. Flynn, I like him. We keep him."

Flynn bowed his head slightly and opened the door to his hut a bit wider and gestured for him to follow. "Come with me, sir priest. I'll tell you what I can."

The Landing, unfortunately, wasn't equipped for Akaran to bed down at night. Not that they didn't begrudgingly open their homes for him, but more that there weren't enough beds for him to have one (and a decided lack of sanitary rooms with seats). When he asked about the possibility of simply working his way through the woods back to the Manor, he was instead mocked out of his shoes for even daring to suggest it. When he remarked on how much of a pain it was to even get to their camp to begin with, Flynn had responded, quite bluntly:

"That's the point."

Somewhat defeated but exhausted and hurting a lot worse than he was going to admit to people that *weren't* receiving any kind of medical care, he excused himself after an extensive period of questions and answers. Answers, unfortunately, that gave birth to more questions – and a solid guarantee that if Henderschott had been paying attention, something would've been done about this before now. *Lazy son of a bitch*, he grumbled as he worked his way back down the ruined stairwall.

Leamer had given up a surprising amount of information, even if most of it was bad. The only bit of good news came with the knowledge that kids weren't being taken. Adults and older teenagers, yes. Anyone below the age of fourteen years, no. It was still *bad* but at least the children seemed to be as safe as children stuck in a vagrant camp in the woods could be considered *safe*.

Of the missing, nobody had vanished in the last two months that fit the bill. A full family unit had departed without word, and some children had vanished through the cracks, as had a younger girl or two – but as ghastly as that was, it wasn't out of the norm. Unfortunately, if the disappearances really did follow the pattern that the camp leader had suggested, that meant that there was an indirect link between the disappearances and the murders.

It was a stretch, and he knew it was a stretch. Even if the city guard would throw him out on his cane if he even suggested it right now... it was a stretch he couldn't ignore. A stretch that he'd submit to Henderschott's office anyway, albeit by letter and through at least two couriers.

There was more to go about with it, too. Of the people that had vanished, around half of them had left their personal belongings behind. The other half had taken them with them on their way into whatever unknown awaited them. That wasn't to say that the vagrants had *much* but people who can't afford replacement cups weren't known to typically leave them (and whatever bedrolls or clothing they claimed to own) behind.

The numbers started to match up in a host of unpleasant ways. Someone had been plucking people off the street and into the shadows for nearly two years, with an average of one 'unknown' disappearance every six to ten weeks. It was going to be impossible to narrow that down to a finer point, and would probably remain so until he could figure out the why.

Also the where.

There were three scenarios that he could come up with to explain the disappearances. The first option was that someone was grabbing them and then shuttling them off elsewhere in the kingdom for one less-than-pleasant reason or another. Then again, as long as there were Lords and Ladies, there'd be no shortage in demand for indentured servitude (at best) and bald-faced slavery (at worse).

As awful as that was, it almost seemed like the *best* option. The second possibility was that someone was keeping a stable of human cattle somewhere for 'reasons.' There was, he quickly decided, absolutely no *good* reasons for someone to keep a stockpile of vagrants. This left the *bad* reasons, and it made his stomach flip. Unfortunately, it also meant that this wasn't implausible – he'd seen dogs destroy a sheep's leg in a month from butcher shop to chewtoy – and if someone was playing with their toys a too hard, they'd need to restock them every few weeks. There was a complication to this option that didn't sit well, and it was matched with the third choice.

If they were keeping them local, there would be some evidence of some kind. Witnesses. Cries from a house. A 'sack of grain' kicking in a cart.

If they weren't keeping them, be other evidence too. Bad smells. A questing dog with a habit for digging holes would've dug up a skull. Probably more screaming. But doing either without leaving a trace meant that someone had a disposal system setup to avoid being caught – and that was really bad.

That's assuming that they found a place in the city where the ground wasn't half-rock to drop the bodies in without leaving a massive mound behind. That effectively ruled out Yittl Canyon, and if someone just casually dropped them into any of the rivers, lakes, or streams? Well, the corpses would've turned up by now.

They're being destroyed. But how? People aren't so stupid to ignore the smell of burning flesh. Could they be pitching them into the local Pyre when nobody noticed? That's... I mean it's not impossible...?

The third option, and just as likely as the second idea, was that someone was doing more than just *keeping* them around. They were abducting them, using them for something, and then either sending them out of the city without a 'return to sender' option, or putting the remains on a cart off to the wilds. Maybe they were bribing a guard to look the other way while shuttling them off? *Could be worth finding out who runs the local Fleetfinger's Guild. See if they'd be willing to help keep a less-than-ethical business running smoothly.*

It almost felt a little more likely than the first or second options because while slavery was one thing... burying the dead was another. And that was a damn disturbing idea. Made worse when you asked a very important followup question: how do you hide that many bodies? And more importantly, where?

Who else would benefit from a steady supply of corpses? If there's any Uoom followers around... but, no, the God of Death doesn't encourage people to add to His ledger. This town is rife with physicians. Maybe someone's worked out an arrangement to study leftovers? Would Keto know anyone that's up to no good?

That doesn't answer ANYTHING about Liv or Odern though. Why go to so much trouble hiding abductees but making sure that everyone sees what happened to two semi-prominent members of the city? Why would you try to drag attention... unless you wanted it?

And much more importantly – this many missing under circumstances this dark?

Why aren't there pissed-of wraiths roaming the streets at night? Violent deaths don't always spit out the damned, that's a given. Thankfully. But one a month for a couple of years?

The damned should be up in arms.

With that thought hanging off of his neck like a millstone, the next stop was a trip back to the *Drunken Imperial*. Cel took one look at his pained limp and sagging shoulders and got him a room with no questions asked. She even threw in an extra blanket and a spot on the ground floor. It helped, but by morning, that didn't make much of a difference.

"I've been waiting for this," Rmaci whispered in his ear. *"No priests, no spells, nothing but you, me, and a bit of privacy..."*

Akaran twitched and tried to look up at her, but he couldn't. Someone was holding his arms tight behind his back, and his feet were mired in a pool of black gore. "Please, woman. I just want some rest."

"Rest? Rest is the thing we all want. All of us where we are. The thing you took from me. Wasn't my life, wasn't my soul. It was rest you took from me.

There's no slumber here. There's no escape from the horror of our eternity."

He struggled for a moment as more of the room came into sight. He was in some kind of dungeon, from the looks of it, with rusting chains and cuffs dangling from the walls. A lone torch offered light, though it had blue-green flame and an acrid smell. "Just... what is it you want from me?"

"*I want you.*"

He quit struggling and sagged in the grip of the person holding him hostage. Metal bars started to manifest in front of him as the room took on a clearer, sharper tone. "For what? Torture? Drive me mad? What do you *want* from me?"

His tormentor finally came into view. For the first time since she'd began haunting him, she was completely clothed. It was odd though; her outfit looked strikingly familiar. She had a white cotton tunic that hung below her waist, and a leather belt across her sash. She had on thick black gloves and a symbol was trying to appear on the center of it — but the stitching kept fading in and out and twisted as it tried to take hold. It was almost like it was trying to reject itself from appearing. "*To feel what I felt. To know what I know. To understand why I want you this way.*"

"Then *tell me*!" he demanded with a scream so hard that it made his captor let go of his arms. Akaran lunged forward and grabbed the bars of the cell and pulled at them even as the metal burned his hands. "*Tell me* what you want and we can *do something* about this!" he shouted. "Or fisking *kill me* and get it over with!"

Rmaci covered her disfigured mouth with her hand and laughed throatily. "*KILL YOU? And send you to a reward? You... you know that, yes? You judged me, set me aflame, condemned me, and scattered my ashes. Cast them from cell to the frozen seas below and the oceans above! And you shall be REWARDED!*" she replied, her voice rising to a crescendo that stabbed into his head like daggers.

"YOU WERE CORRUPTED! I didn't have a CHOICE!" he shouted back as he dropped to his knees — and screamed in pain the second that he hit the cold stone floor below as his knee erupted in burning agony. "You fell to Zell's realm because of what YOU DID! Not ME. Your ashes were given the same respect as your victims — and buried with more honor than you deserved!"

"*Is that what you think?*" she asked, mocking him. "*That I was buried with honor? Respect? That my bones found a haven?*" Rmaci demanded to know. "*OH. OH YOU DO! HOW PRICELESS! LET ME SHOW YOU WHAT HAPPENED!*"

Another voice chimed in — calm, firm, almost (but not) quite sultry. It rolled over Akaran's ears like smooth velvet. "I would advise that you let the child rest," it intoned.

The charred corpse twisted her head around as her cloudy eyes widened in surprise. "*Who are you to intrude in my domain?!*"

"Your domain?" the new arrival replied as she stepped out of the shadows.

No, Akaran realized, *she's stepping with the shadows...*

She – it was *absolutely* a she – continued addressing his tormentor without pause. "That's an interesting choice of words. You stole truths and you stole lives in life; you are being treated accordingly. Do you wish to add theft of realms to your ledger in death – or even wish to sin further with lies and clouded words?"

"*I am in his body! His mind! I CLAIM IT AS MINE!*"

"That much is true; but *this* is not *there* and this is *not* your domain," the other woman scolded from the shadows. "Out with you now; I've no patience for this and I need to speak with him," she said as she pointed a pale finger at the exorcist, "as he has decided that he can't be bothered to read my letter."

Read her letter? *What*? He had time to think before Rmaci screeched in anger. The stranger shot her hand out and wrapped it around his torturer's throat. With a flick of her wrist, the night-garbed interloper simply *flung* the former spy out of the room, and the room followed suit like it was tied to her neck.

Reality snapped back with a crashing thud that all-but punched the priest in the face as he shot straight up in the crappy, barely-a-bed that he'd been sleeping in. "What the... what in the *fisking* inferno is going *on* tonight," he groaned before another bolt of pain between his eyes made him roll to the side of the bed and promptly throw up all over the floor. "That's new. Vomiting is new," he groaned to himself. "Don't like it. Bad new. Not a good new."

"And decidedly unsightly. Please do tell me you'll assist Celeste by cleaning it up before you leave in the morning?"

The voice belonged to the same woman from the nightmare, and when he twisted around to see the speaker, he realized that yes, she was real. Worse, she wasn't alone. Much worse?

He recognized her.

"You... Mother Eclipsian? What are you...? WHY are you?"

"Why am I? A question we all must ask, from time to time, I suppose. Why am I here? A better one," she replied with a smile from her lovely full lips. Her dark brown eyes twinkled in the soft candlelight and her flowing velvet black gown seemingly flowed over the arms of the chair she had claimed and pooled at her feet.

Any other day and he'd have been delighted to have her in his room.

"A more apt one is why you are not offering to extinguish that candle or groveling at her feet," her companion snapped. That particular voice belonged to a taller, less-elegant woman that was in her early twenties, but possibly younger. Unlike the Mother Eclipsian, she was also armed with two silver-bladed daggers dangling at her waist. "She rescued you from that cacophony in your mind – the *least* you can do is offer your thanks."

"No offense intended, but I'm not offering *anything* until someone tells me what just happened," he grumbled.

That earned him a hateful stare from Erine's bodyguard. Before she could retort, the priestess intervened. "To be true, that's a valid question. You have a problem with nightmares, child, and it's beginning to cause headaches for those of us that can hear them."

"Not doing me any bloody favors either," he muttered as he reached over to the candle. "Forgive my manors. I know that we work on opposite sides of the coin, but..."

"No forgiveness needed," Erine replied, "as your nature is to wage war with the shadows, Kiasta's is to protect them. She forgets that at times, we must cross paths for one reason or another; though this time it is only paths we cross – and not swords."

He let out a breath he didn't realize he'd been holding. "Still... just... what happened? Please? I feel like someone just tried to fire a cannon out of the back of my head."

Kiasta touched her patroness's shoulder and answered his question in her stead. This time, at least, her tone had been mollified. "You are aware of the nature of Lethandria, yes?"

"The Goddess of Night, Darkness, and Shadows? Impossible to not be, given what I do..."

"Then you know Who it is that calls Lethandria 'mother,' don't you?"

Akaran frowned and slowly nodded. "Among other things? Nia'valth."

"Correct," the bodyguard replied. "The Twins of One. Do you know Her titles?"

"Titles?" the exorcist asked, confusion starting to make his headache worse. "I hope you mean the common ones. She's called the Goddess of Dreams. Nia, The Daysteed and Valth, the Nightmarion."

Erine nodded in satisfaction and interrupted her aid. "Yes. So then – what it is you see when your eyes close? Most assume that dreams are nothing more than what a mind does as it decompresses the events of the day. This is true, in a fashion, but dreams themselves are connected to Lethandria's daughter. The Dreamscape is both in and out of the realm of mortal man; it exists in this plane and outside of it. When you have a nightmare, Valth is the soul that directs and channels the essence of your slumbering torment – for what reasons are not of ours to say."

He frowned and took a drink of stale water from a cup at his bedside. "I can't particularly say I'm a fan."

"I'd reconsider that," the Eclipsian responded with an understanding smile. "Your soul, my soul, Kiasta's soul; *all* souls may be intrinsically linked to the Dreamscape, but it is because of Nia'valth's control over that realm that we do not suffer the scars from our rest in our physical flesh when we return from our slumbers."

"But She could stop them entirely."

"She could. Maybe. It isn't ours to assume that She could; She, like us, was made by the Origin and set to the tasks we must undertake in our lives. Why did He link us in such a way? Why did He feel the need for mortals to dream as we do? Why were we cursed with nightmares and not just pleasant daydreams?" Erine shrugged and her gown rippled with the subtle movement. "Why must we cough? Why must we eat? Why must we breed with each other; why must our unions be both pleasurable and at times painful? Why is it that we find food enjoyable – but we are not entranced with the way that it leaves our bodies?"

"If you can call that food," her bodyguard added as she caught a whiff of the puddle of Akaran's indigestion. "You poor boy; what did you *eat*?"

"Life's a wonder and the Gods work in mysterious ways," he muttered in resignation. "That's Them though. What ways are you working in, Eclipsian?"

Erine smiled and shimmied a little in her seat. "The question I was waiting for. In short? Your nightmares are of your own making, but they are not of your mind's design. There's some... *consternation*... about them. You've earned our interest."

The exorcist frowned again and tried to sit up straighter. "Consternation?"

"Yes," she repeated. "It's not uncommon for people to be cursed with vileness in their sleep, and it isn't uncommon for those that have earned a connection with the next world to find their sleep modified in an unpleasant manner. Yet the ripples that your dreams are having in the ether mark them as unusual. Unlike what they should be. I *felt* it radiating from you at the Danse; it's why I had Badin ask you to speak to me."

"All the same, Eclipsian, I don't know how kindly my Order would take it if I sought help from yours," Akaran quietly pointed out. "I'm sorry that you feel like your involvement is necessary and worse that whatever is going on with me is causing issues with you and yours..."

Kiasta's eyes went wide. "You're refusing aid from our Lady? Are you mad? After what my sister has said about you, I'd think that -"

"OH!" he exclaimed, "I THOUGHT you looked familiar. You're Raechil's sister, aren't you?"

"Unfortunately," she retorted, "it is a complicated relationship between us."

"No, I don't think he's refusing the help," Erine clarified, "merely that he needs to see if he's allowed to accept it at first. Yes?"

Akaran nodded and yawned. "I am. I'd love nothing more than to say, 'please, find a solution so I can sleep,' but..."

"...but while our efforts are at times conjoined in battle to maintain the balance of light and dark, other times they are not," the priestess replied with a knowing smile. "You are a wise one, aren't you?"

He snorted and rubbed at his throbbing knee. "If I was, do you think I'd be in this situation?"

"Even the wise are given to fits of impropriety," she countered, "though I hope you are able to understand why we are here."

"Honestly? I don't have a clue, Eclipsian. You've offered some vague promises to help and pulled me out of that nightmare – which I'm *exceptionally grateful* for, please don't take me wrong – but I don't know why you're here. Now. At whatever Goddess-damned time of the night it is."

"There's more in the shadows of this city than my Lady wishes, and the things within the dark are not as friendly with each other as they should be," Erine replied with a sudden frown that showed off wrinkles in her youthful face he didn't realize she could've possessed. "Thus, I come speak with you to caution you of their existence – and to ask that when you act, you do so with the understanding that there is a balance that should be had here."

He couldn't stop the muscles in his shoulders from tensing up if he wanted to. "Respectfully, Eclipsian, you didn't need to barge in my room at this time of night to tell me that bad things lurk in the dark."

She couldn't stop her giggle even if she had wanted, although it unnerved him – and her bodyguard at the same time. "No, no, that I do not. I came to offer warning; not just of your dreams." Erine paused and frowned a little again. "Though I must say, that woman was decidedly repulsive. That odor of... saltwater and sulfur? It's almost like I can smell it even now, even interacting with her in the plane of your mind."

"You get used to it," he grunted. "Don't eat anything for an hour."

The priestess nodded and made a disgusted face. "Gain permission from your Order to speak with me. Sooner, the better, I think. I imagine that they'd like you to stop screaming in the Manor as much as I'd like to stop hearing it in the ether. Fair?"

Akaran didn't even bother putting up a fight. "Fair. The darkness is not a friend to those of us that walk in the light, but fair."

"Except you *don't* walk in the light, child," she deftly pointed out, "you *hide* in the light when you need rest, but you *live* in the dark."

"Don't try to argue," Kiasta warned, "I've seen her confound people smarter than the two of us put together. It's... it's not worth it."

He took the warning for what it was even as Erine cast her assistant a smug little smile. "So. You had two warnings?"

"I did," she replied slowly, "and ask that you take this next one seriously. There are no shortages of times that the light and the dark argue over the necessity of balance, and I imagine that you and I have opposing feelings. The dark is a haven for some, a curse for others; it is a realm in which monsters reign, but a place where innocents may find solace if they need. Can we come to an agreement on that much, yes?"

"Reluctantly," he admitted, "though there's an argument to be made as to which is better."

"Were that argument to hold true at all times, men of your nature would not need to exist."

Akaran bit his tongue and simply nodded.

"Balance be spoken of, this city is no different. There are terrible people who live in this place; terrible people who do terrible things. Then there are others that simply live in the shadows because they have no other choice."

"Not everyone is lucky to live in the light, I know. Have you seen the people that frequent this inn?"

"Aside from yourself?" her bodyguard asked.

"Including myself."

Erine coughed into her hand and the bickering pair quieted down. "I am aware that you are hunting something in the dark."

The exorcist felt his eye narrow and his neck tense up even harder. "I only started asking around yesterday..."

"Oh, child," she scolded. "In truth? It wouldn't matter if it was you, or one of the pompous ones from the Repository – when a warrior of the light arrives, I watch. I knew you would find reason to hunt *something* once given the opportunity – those in that giant vault are too busy keeping their own dark locked away to bother with me and mine. *You* are not, regardless of *when* you began to ask."

"So this is less an offer to help and more of a warning to keep my nose clean in your yard?" he challenged after a brief moment.

She blinked in surprise as her aid finally cracked a smile. "Oh. No, no, please – do not presume to think that I bring a threat. As I said, there are things in Lethandria's domain that are horrid. I bear no ill to one that seeks to drag abominations that threaten the peace kicking and screaming from the shadows to where they may be unmasked by the light. With my blessing; please. I have *seen* how such things act. Do not think that all monsters are granted haven – they may call the darkness home, but not all that do are welcome."

Kiasta cleared her throat. "Before you look confused? The Goddess offers a haven for everyone. Unfortunately, sometimes a guest shits on the rug. Feel free to rub their noses in it."

"Yes... shitting on a rug. That is... a way to describe it," Erine grumbled. "Whatever it is you're hunting? It's doing more than merely *shitting* on my rug. It's not playing nice with the other things in the dark. It's not native to our area – nor is it native to the areas below."

That brought the exorcist's line of thought to a complete halt. "I'm not sure I understand you correctly. Are you saying that whomever has been killing and disappearing people isn't Abyssian?"

"I don't know *what* it is, Akaran, and that is where the concern lies. The normal places that a man of your ilk would hunt? I would not waste your time looking in them now. My eyes have been opened in the dark for a great deal longer than yours," she said as she stood up, "and I have heard the cries of those whom have been forgotten. All that I can say is that it is not a soul that is native to this realm, nor do I feel that it is one of those abominations that Lethandria gives reign to dwell in Her abode."

"So you admit that the Goddess of Night lets the dark run rampant," he charged. "That doesn't make you entirely believable."

"Oh, child," Erine softly scolded as she made her way to the door, "you say that as if the Gods of the Pantheon do not let monsters garbed in light roam freely in the streets in Their own realms." She flicked him another smile just before they left. "Of anyone to know that – you should."

After he cleaned his mess off of the floor, it was another hour before he could get back to sleep with *that* strange comment romping around in his head. Not that he'd get to rest for long — though thankfully, it wasn't Rmaci that returned to haunt him.

Though an argument could be made that the next visitor was worse.

Waking up to an angry blonde woman sitting at the end of his bed was going to be a recurring theme later in his life. In fact, counting a few episodes in training, this wasn't even the first. That didn't make it any better, but at least not the first. He recognized her from the dance right away — though between the brooch on her cloak and her armor, he would've figured her for the Guild regardless. "Not a social call?"

"Not a social call," Elsith repeated.

"Shit." Akaran sighed and rubbed at the back of his neck. "You know, you're the third woman that's woken me up this morning like this. Wouldn't be so bad if someone offered to hug me. Or gave me a drink. Something."

The Huntsmatron reached over to his table and carefully started to hand him his cup of water. Before he could take it, she flung it up into his face. "Water offered."

He flung his covers off and tried to slap her, but she dodged it easily. "Get the fisk out of my room. *Now.*"

"You're an injured neophyte priest that's spent the last day looking into the death of Adept Odern and making noise in places that should be quiet. Why?"

"Because I don't have much else to do with my time," he offered with a shrug.

Her eyes narrowed down into tighter slits (somehow) as her hand slid under her cloak. It didn't take much of a guess to know what she was reaching for. "That answer isn't good enough."

"Lower your expectations," he retorted. "It's the answer you're getting."

"You've also been spending time at the Landing and talking to any and every asshole, shithead, and degenerate between the Repo and Overflow. Why?"

He matched her glare for glare. "Because I get bored looking at books."

If flashing her dagger at him was meant to intimidate, it didn't work. "Your tongue won't win you any favors right now. You're interfering with Guild business and I want to know why."

Akaran rolled his shoulders, cracked his neck, and shook his head. "No, I'm investigating murders and the missing."

"It's Guild business," she snapped. "We have active writs regarding -"

"And I have authority to open an independent investigation in the name of the Public Good," he bluntly interrupted. "What's the problem?

She huffed at him and crossed her arms. "The problem is that if priests are going to start poking around and asking questions, it's going to make my job that much harder. People are going to stop thinking that it's just some idiot with a knife and something harder to understand."

He ignored her arms, and slowly laced his fingers behind his head as he stretched and pressed into the bed away from her. "With all due respect, you haven't been doing your job that well."

Elsith's eyes flashed with red lightning at his insolence. "Excuse me?"

"My understanding is that you've had the writ to find Odern's killer since he was dropped. Doesn't say much for you or the guard," he growled. "*Speaking of*," he added before she could give an indignant reply of her own, "Henderschott hasn't taken the homeless disappearances seriously. From what I've heard, neither is anyone else. People are being hurt and obviously nobody in charge of Basion has given a damn. Now someone does. You're sitting here pissed off about it and I'm wondering why."

"Someone's been taking *all of it* seriously and if you start pushing people around then I'm not going to be able to collect on the writ. Go back home and leave this to the professionals."

"I *am* a professional," he spat. "Back home has a dead body too. This isn't just about a Granalchi."

She leaned back a little and bit the end of her tongue. "You think that the dead woman at the Manor is related, do you?"

"Her name is Livstra. She's not just a dead woman. She had friends, family."

"None that worry enough about her to hire us to look into her death," she replied, as if that was all that mattered.

If the circumstances of the conversation were different, he might even be a little understanding. "If you did a better job finding Odern's killer, they might. Or if you had done a better job already, maybe she'd still be alive."

She didn't even try to hide her angry hiss. "Are you accusing the Guild of her death?"

"No, just saying that if you had cared about the missing homeless, then maybe Odern and Livstra would both be alive. Shit doesn't happen in a void. Prostil suggested that this mess might be linked and I'm fairly sure she's right."

"We aren't paid to care about the missing homeless."

"If you weren't paid to care about Odern, you wouldn't be in my room."

Elsith gave him a disgusted look. "No I wouldn't be. Leave the damn matter alone."

"Can't do that," he retorted. "Won't, even if I could."

Her face went cold as she clenched her jaw so tight you could've made a diamond in her mouth. "Yes, you can. It would be in your best interests."

"No, it wouldn't," he countered as he tried to pull the bedsheets out from under her. "Yes, I do think that Livstra and Odern are tied together Their deaths were too similar. I have a feeling that a few of the vagrants are too."

"Then go home and let the people that can still walk deal with it," she snapped back with a huff.

"I can't do that. Livstra may not have been one of Niasmis', but she gave comfort to those of us that are. Her death is an insult to the Goddess."

She slammed her fist down on the bed and leaned in so close he could guess at her breakfast. "Oh is that what it is? The ego of the Order of Love has gotten bruised?"

"No."

"Then why say it?"

Akaran shoved her back and sat swung his legs out from under her with a grimace. "Because it gives me all the excuse I need to keep working on this and to tell you to shove your attitude up your ass."

She jumped back with a bemused bit of shock in her eyes. "You're playing a very stupid game. You're going to cause our quarry to go to ground just by talking about it."

"It already has. If it was still out and active, you'd have found it by now."

She adjusted her cloak to show off the other weapons in her arsenal in another attempt to intimidate, and it failed just as miserably. "And what happens if you find the person that did it, hm? You can't fight, you can't use magic, and you can't walk."

"I can walk just fine."

"No, you can't Do you want to know why?"

He looked her in the eyes and snorted in disgust. "Because someone scarier than you broke my knee?"

Elsith smirked at him. "Because someone like me is going to break it again," she said before she hauled off and delivered a closed-fist punch to the side of his leg. He pitched forward screaming, clutching at his knee like it was coming apart. "The Guild has a writ on this. You piss around and you're going to cost both us *and* the Granalchi money. Consider this your *one* warning – stay the *fisk* out of it."

"You fisking bitch!" he howled. "FISK! I will do whatever the FISK I want to do and YOU can't stop me!"

"Oh, I have ways," she mocked as she stood up. Before he could do anything to stop her, she grabs his cane and chucks it into the fireplace. By the time he managed to crawl off the bed and pull the burning stick free, she was long gone.

On the other side of Basion, a less contentious – but just as dour – conversation was taking place in a villa much nicer than even the best lodgings that you'd ever dream of finding in Lower Naradol. No, Thesd Estate in East Giffil was anything but low class. It was almost a demand from the owners that you were in finery from sun up to sunset, regardless of the circumstances.

Which made it all the more concerning when Anais's bodyguard walked in looking like a bedraggled rat and interrupted her efforts to pour through a pile of contracts. "Donta? Are you unwell?"

"It's nothing," he grumbled, "except I have news."

"No, I would say it's something," she said as she smoothed out the wide sleeves of her pale white gown. "You look positively ghastly."

He glowered at her and sat down on the other side of her round, polished oak table. "There has been need for excessive care today. Someone has stirred the guard and the Guild. It has been... taxing... using all of my skills to avoid them. Made all the worse with that new job you stuck me with. I spent all night checking for tunnels and worse in the cliffs."

Anais stacked the contracts tight and orderly as she frowned down at them. "What roused the sleeping giants from their slumber, I wonder?"

"Some fool thought it wise to set loose that exorcist you've had your eyes on. He's been asking anyone that will listen about those murders and about some pathetic wretches that have gone missing."

That made her stomach flutter a little and in all the wrong ways. "Let's hope that someone has him kept on a short leash then. He may be lame himself, but... the rest of his Order is sadly not under his metaphysical constraints. We'll have to be even more careful," she sighed with an extra curse as she crumpled the top letter on her pile and threw it to the floor, "unfortunately. Damnation be unto all."

To say that he was taken aback by her response was an understatement. "Now *you're* the one sounding distressed. Is there a problem?"

"One could say that, yes," she sighed. "The speaker of the Union of Bankers has decided to run his mouth as of late and I've had to place objects in motion to discourage him from doing so in the future. That, and I've had to deal with some issues around Moira. It has been... as you said, *taxing*."

"I thought Moira was a completed deal?" he asked. "Although the Uob... I'd be happy to speak to them on your behalf."

She let the thought leave her with an uncharacteristic smirk before turning him down. "The Uob should be dealt with now. If their mouthpiece continues to speak out of turn then yes, your involvement will become necessary. We'll need a hastily-appointed successor to fill his seat, if it comes to that, though it will not make me cry if it does."

The waxy-skinned brawler almost... pouted. "Fine. But the artifact...?"

"Well. We knew that there would be risks. The issue should be resolved, or at least, buried. I found a place to bind the offending aspect so mitigate its influence for now."

His pout turned to a concerned frown. "I should have done that. What if someone had seen you?"

"*You* should not be near Moira and you *know* why," she pointed out as he glowered even harder. "Have you had any luck finding an ally in the Guild yet, or have you been too busy dodging them?"

"Other than the one that accosted you?"

"Other than," she agreed. "I don't trust her."

His eye twitched. "Shouldn't trust any of them. But. Huntsman B'tril. Sycian native. Some skill. Psyanistry. Ambiantics."

Anais pursed her lips and thought about how she could put that to use. "What makes him viable? Simply someone that can be bought or...?"

"Whoremonger with... specific... tastes," he said as her nose flared and her lips curled in disgust. "It won't be hard to leverage him."

"Detestable," the well-to-do broker shook her head and fought back a fresh wave of revulsion. "I will let you deal with him as you see fit. My hands will remain clean."

Her bodyguard didn't even try to cover up his cold mocking laugh. "They'll never be. Neither of ours."

She folded her hands up and studied her silken gloves for a few wistful moments. "As clean as one can be, I'll say then. I am happy to say I found the other pathway, at last."

"A priest to bribe? How novel."

"No, I doubt that I will need to do anything so expensive," Anais replied with more relaxed smile as she discussed her newest conquest. "Her name is Faldine. She's been assigned to escort a duchess for the foreseeable future. By all accounts, she utterly detests it — it's a punishment from the Oo-lo general in charge of their Order."

He laughed again, a bit more of a chuckle than anything else. "Find a soul that hates their job and they are eager to do favors if it means they can be released from it."

"That is exactly how I feel," she agreed.

"How *we* feel," he pointed out.

The lady couldn't disagree. "I had opportunity to enjoy her company last night and we spoke over a glass of red *thravstil*."

"Your special blend?"

Her eyes flickered over to a large box stashed in the corner of her room. "It felt prudent. She is an Oo-lo, and a paladin at that."

That didn't earn a laugh. That earned him slamming his hands down on the table as his navy-blue eyes went wide. "*A paladin*?! Have you lost your mind?!"

She picked up her goblet of wine before another outburst would risk knocking it over. "We've had no luck playing carefully, Donta. It's time for us to take risks or else we risk more of our benefactor's *impatience*."

It didn't do much to soothe the savage beast. "The alternative could be worse."

"Worse than our benefactor's irritation? Do you really think so?"

"There have to be other ways," he gloomily argued. "We can't afford to be found out."

She looked at him as her eyelids started to droop tiredly. "Afraid of what the Order would do if they did?"

Donta scoffed at that. "Of the priests? They are welcome to try. Of *him*? Yes."

Tired or not, she forced another smile onto her lips. "Come now, Donta. There's always a way out, you and I have both made sure that we won't be caught in the cold if things go poorly. Regardless of that — this paladin will be of use to get Moira into the hands of the Repository."

"Simply plan to just hand it over to her?"

Anais took a dainty drink out of her goblet before correcting him. "No, I plan on helping her find it. It shouldn't take much effort to befriend her further, and no effort at all to let it slip that I had heard about contraband. She's so desperate for a change in her fate that it will be easy to convince her to take a risk of her own and investigate it."

Another scoff, this time with a ragged cough. "You expect her to walk down an alley and find it and not question where it came from?"

"Nothing of the sort," she replied. "A proper scapegoat will be provided. Someone that will have reason to have it. I have someone in mind but I am open to reconsidering."

He grumbled again and leaned back in his chair with an unhappy utterance. "Fine. If it works, it works, but if it looks like they are taking an interest in us, we are leaving this pox on the landscape."

She took that for as much of a win as she could get. "Say, do tell: why exactly is the Guild and Guard stirred? More than just one wayward priest, surely?"

Donta ran down the fairly impressive list of people he'd heard grumbling on the streets. "He's been pushing people for information in almost every district so far. It's setting people on edge. The Guard wants it to just go away – and the Guild is afraid someone is going to steal their contract."

"Interesting," she mused. "So if we can find a way to solve his problem, it may get rid of him from our hair?"

He shook his head vehemently no. "Working with a paladin is bad enough, Anais. Working with a paladin *and* an exorcist is a recipe for disaster."

"Not if we can offer a plausible way to mix them together," she pointed out. "It may be time for me to speak to the forgotten."

"That's even riskier. We agreed you'd not do that."

"Times, and plans, change. I have another task for you now."

Donta groaned and sagged down in his seat, a dreadful feeling of exhaustion starting to sink into his bones. "You've already put me to work hunting for some murderer. And Miral's secrets. And enforcing your contracts. What *more*?"

"Delve into the habits of the shiverdine. I need to know as much of his moral and merchantile entanglements as you possibly can provide."

X. INSANITY'S RESPITE…
Wundis, the 15ᵗʰ of Riverswell, 513QR

Embers snapped in the air around Akaran's head as the smell of acrid smoke wafted to his nostrils. A hot breeze blew past him, banishing what chill remained in his bones but causing little flickers of pain as ash danced on his forearms. Shapes started to move in the center of the smoke; fingers first, then hands. Eyes and full faces followed.

The fire spat a lone spark out towards him, and he watched it land in a sea of dark brown fur at his feet. It struggled to find life in the carpet, but it gained nothing but an unsatisfying end to a short miserable existence a few heartbeats later. One of the faces in the flame started to laugh, mocking what brief life it had lived. A voice broke through his gloomy reverie with a sharp note of disapproval. "So was it me that you came to see, or were you here just for the fireplace?"

He shook it off and looked over at Lady Ridora as she sat with her hands steepled at her desk. "Sorry, Lady. I thought I saw… something."

"Another one of those visions?"

"Yeah."

She unfolded her arms and started to make a note in an open journal at her side. "They have been occurring with more frequency, haven't they? And intensity?"

"Not much more," he lied.

Not that she believed him. "I'm concerned. They should be getting better, not worse," she said with a frustrated sigh. "What exactly have you been reading while you've spent your time over at the Repository?"

Another lie fit the bill. "History, mainly."

"That's enough to terrorize anyone," she mused, "of course, I hear you've been finding other ways to keep busy."

From anyone else, it would've sounded like an innocent remark. From her, it felt like an accusation. "I have. That's why I'm here."

She pointed one of her long nails at him and matched her accusatory tone with an equally condemning frown. "You are here because your inquisitive mind pushed you to poor decisions. Much the same as it's doing right now, I will assume. How *did* you hurt your leg anew, exactly?"

"Poor decisions," he muttered under his breath.

"I assumed as much.," she said as he shifted back and forth in his chair.

"The Guild doesn't want me looking into the murders," he returned. "They picked a heavy-handed way to get the point across."

Ridora set her pen down and pursed her lips. "Is that what you've been doing recently? No wonder you're experiencing nightmares," she mused, and then surprisingly went on to say, "though I think their methods for expressing their displeasure were more intense than needed."

He nodded in grumpy agreement as he rubbed at his upper thigh. "So that's why I'm here. I don't know how much more I can do without a chance to look in Livstra's room and where she was killed."

That didn't get him anywhere. "You've said you're doing it but you haven't said why nor on what authority. I've heard, of course, that it's under the instruction of Prostil."

"It is."

"Then the answer is no," she replied without hesitation.

That was expected. Unwelcome, but expected. "No? Why?"

She shook her head. "I don't need to explain myself to you. There is absolutely no reason for you to be spending time looking into the matter, for any reason. Had I been consulted, you wouldn't have started."

"I'd disagree," he argued. "So far I've been able to determine that Hender hasn't given much of a damn about the people of the city, that while there's little motive for anyone wanting both Odern and Livstra dead together, there's an interesting bit of timing between their deaths. Oh, and that there's been a lot more than just a handful of people going missing."

For a change, she actually listened. "Missing? What are you talking about?"

Akaran took a deep breath and then quickly related everything he had heard from Leamer, the 4th, the Bladebane, and all of the random souls he'd run into on the streets. To her credit, she hung onto every word and even made a few notes on a spare piece of parchment as he rambled. Oddly, she gave more attention to the bits about the Granalchi than she did the rest. However, when he began to describe the conditions at Flynn's Landing, she started to look distressed.

"You're acting like you're overly-trusting of what the vagrants said."

He nodded slowly. "I do. Leamer has had interactions with an exorcist before."

"Do you know the circumstances?"

"No," he admitted, "but he made it clear that he knows us."

Ridora pursed her lips. "Fair enough. It is a truth that those that are forced to call upon the aid of that branch of the Order learn to not withhold secrets."

"Willingly calling upon our aid or otherwise," he agreed. "So. The moment that the homeless get pushed out into the woods, they stop having people vanish – and we end up with two dead bodies," he said as he reached his finish, "which *almost* makes me think that at least one of them was killed because nobody else was handy. But targeting an Adept because there wasn't anyone else to murder does *not* sit well with me if that's the case."

"You said that their leader admitted that people have been leaving since they were relocated," she pointed out. "What's to say that the ones missing aren't ones that have been just leaving?"

"Absolutely nothing," he agreed. "It's going to be impossible to determine if someone is actually missing or just moved on if we can't figure out where they went to. Neither of which I expect to be granted permission to search buildings and alleys at random."

"Absence of evidence is not necessarily evidence of absence."

"No, Lady, but it's coincidental enough that it's hard to ignore," he countered. "These weren't just random muggings."

"If they were related, the ones that went missing would have been found in shapes as horrid as what happened to Odern and Livstra, wouldn't they?"

A light flashed in the back of his mind and left him with an even worse thought. "Unless we were intended to find them."

It must've dawned on her at the same time, because her eyes were going wide before he even finished the thought. "Excuse me?"

"What if the two of them were about to find something out that the killer didn't want to have known?"

She started to shift uncomfortably and looked a little nauseated. "You have any proof of that?"

"No," he admitted.

"Then why broach it as an option?"

Akaran scratched at his chin and gave her a somber look. "Because you haven't found anyone here in the Manor that could've done it. Because the Guild and the Guard haven't found anyone that might've done in Odern. Because I don't have proof of anything else. These were too graphic to be accidents."

"Which means that either the killer is cocky..." she began.

"...or it's a statement," the exorcist finished. "Which is what I need know. That's why I'm here. We need to figure out which it is, and I'm going to say that we need to do it quickly."

"I'm not at all sure that your reasoning isn't cyclical," she lightly scolded. "You've still yet to give any proof that any of these are related."

"Hopefully they aren't. Or hopefully they are."

The lady of the manor frowned at him. Again. He was beginning to wonder if that was a permanent state of her being, or a trait just reserved for him. "You can't hope for both."

"Sure I can," he said with a little shrug. "I'm doing it right now."

It was all she could do from flinging her hands open and giving him an exasperated sigh, and on some level, he knew it. "Explain...?"

"If they're not related, we have two murderers that have been able to cover their tracks plus a kidnapper who's doing Gods-know-what. I'm going to hope for that, because three bad guys is better than one."

"The cocasa is playing games with your mind again if that's how you believe numbers work."

The longer he talked, the less she liked it, and the more intense the exorcist grew with gestures and little taps of his fingers on her desk. "Well, if they *are* related, then we have just one *really* powerful person out there. One with a *plan* and that just makes me feel *bad* in general."

"These were murders, not acts of intense magnitude," she countered.

"Oh?" he asked as he arched an eyebrow. "If it's all being done by one person, then that person had the ability to murder someone that should've been capable of turning an assailant into a smoldering crater on the street. That implies strength and magical aptitude."

"Or it would if there had been evidence of a struggle at the spot where his body was found. There wasn't, was there?"

This time he shook his head and drew an arrow on her desk with his fingertip and the misplaced assumption she could follow along with it. "No, his body was moved. Which actually leads me to think it IS just one bad guy. The same person broke into this house of healing and murdered Liv without anyone noticing – which implies even more magic. A *lot* more to bypass the protections you have on the campus. You do have protections, right?"

She held back a scoff at the thought, though just barely. "Of course we have protections. Our charges are the weak and vulnerable to outside influences."

"Which means you can't ignore an outside actor of significant ability doing it since it's less and less likely by the day that it was one of the patients. Or it was someone that works here," he replied with a look on his face that was far more *smug* than he deserved to have. "or both... someone that works here that's hiding their power from you. Either or, it's bad."

"Of course it's *bad*," she sighed. "Do you think that I'm not taking her death seriously? That her murder wasn't just an attack on her, but an attack on this entire institution?"

"Of course I do. Had you considered that it was related to the Adept?"

She thought about it for a moment and pursed her lips. "Briefly, but there was no evidence linking them we could find."

He jumped on the decision and tried to drive the point home again. "So a man that specialized in breaking illusions gets killed by someone that almost *had* to have been using illusory magic of some kind to hide their attack?"

"Of course not, why would there..." Ridora started to protest before the words died on her lips. "We weren't told that he specialized in illusion magic."

"He doesn't. It was a hobby of his."

She let a short sigh of relief escape her lips before collecting herself. "You are truly stretching these supposed connections."

Akaran tapped his finger on her desk again. "At least I've been looking for them."

The lady grit her teeth and brought her hands back together. "No, what you've been doing is indulging your paranoia. Paranoia, I may add, that is being compounded by your nightmares and the cocasa. You'll forgive me if I doubt the existence of these so-called missing persons, at that."

"Rid, I mean, Lady," he said before catching himself, "let me explain. I've thought about this and nothing but this the last few days. On the surface, everything is tidy."

"Tidy?" she huffed. "What a poor choice of words."

He ignored her and tried to outline it again. "People start going missing. Nobody cares. You don't care, the garrison doesn't care. Only people that care right now seem to be Maiden Prostil and myself."

"Do not take my disagreement over their importance to the matters at hand for me not caring over their fate," she snapped back. "I simply doubt that they are as real or as numerous as described."

"Fine," he grumbled. "Prostil and I are the only ones in the government that *believe*. Better?"

Her teeth started to grate again. "Marginally, though I dislike your tone."

The warning noted, he went on. "So, that's why I want to look where she was killed. For one, it's the only place where we *know* it happened. For two, when you did your investigation, you didn't consider that whomever behind it was either a mage or somehow preternatural, did you?"

"No, we didn't," Ridora reluctantly admitted. "Though I can see why you're thinking in that direction. Mages are hard to best in combat, as is their nature. If the same person that took our beloved Livstra is also behind Odern..."

"...then instead of a killer on the loose in the Manor, you have a killer on the loose *in the city* that's able to strike with impunity," he stressed. "Even on the *best* of days I can't imagine that the Overseer would be happy about that."

"Nor are these the best of days," she finally agreed after a few moments of playing with his utterly awful idea. "Let me ask you a question first. A pair of them, to be precise."

Akaran rubbed at his aching temple as he tried to guess what she was going to hammer him over now. "Yes, Lady?"

She drummed her fingers on her desk as she spoke. "Firstly, if your supposed abductor-at-large was assaulting the lowest of the lowborn, why would he or she move up the ranks to a man of Odern's stature... and later Livstra's? Why not simply target a less-born, or not pray upon them in the woods? One would assume it would be a much easier way to carry about their business."

"I don't know," he admitted with a shrug. "Maybe the assho... the abductor tried, but Odern saw him? Maybe it was a crime of necessity, instead of opportunity? I really don't have an answer for that."

"You have answers for very few things," she pointed out.

"To be fair, I've only started asking."

She thought about offering a retort, but after biting her tongue, she let it slide. "The other question: how do I know that you're not using these dreadful incidents as a way for you to grant yourself some sense of self-importance or to otherwise deflect your attention from your current malady? That you're not seeking to capitalize on Livstra's death in a misguided attempt to satisfy a misplaced desire to show to others that you aren't as worthless as you feel you are in the eyes of our Goddess?"

Every word she uttered felt like a slap, and the final line was a punch in the gut. "Ouch," he muttered with a pained wince. "That's... harsh."

"Truth often is," she replied with a serious look in her pale blue eyes. "And if it isn't a question you can answer, then I cannot grant you permission to poke around."

"Well, I..." he started, then after catching the way she raised her eyebrow, stopped and slumped back into his chair. "Fine. You're right. I feel broken. I feel worthless. I feel like all I'm doing is sitting around and shitting into a bucket."

"Truth is also no reason for language, and -"

He lifted a finger and cut her off with a shake of his head. "No, listen. You're right. I'm broken and I know I'm broken and I need to do *something*. I spent my life being trained to do *something*. I spent my life being taught to look for bad things in good places and to not give up even if it was unpleasant or painful. And *trust me* this is. I can *feel* it. I know I've had next to no time in the field compared to others in the Order but sitting around and doing *nothing* is driving me up the damned wall. I'm not going to deny that."

Ridora, to her credit, took that in without flinching. "I sense there's more than that though. Speak it."

"Prostil ordered me to do this," he replied earnestly, "and it's given me something to think about other than my knee. I *really* think that something here is *very* wrong and I think it's going to get worse. I also think that between the Guard, the Guild, the Granalchi, and you? If you four haven't figured out what's going on yet maybe let one of us delve into it. If not me, then someone else. Another Lover. An exorcist or otherwise. Doesn't matter. But the fact that I *am* broken and lame means that I can talk to people and get better responses than what others would who are in full control of themselves – like Flynn, for example."

The lady of the manor sat in silence, studying him for a long time with her fingers constantly drumming against the top of her desk as she mulled it over. Finally, she spoke up with a slow, menacing tone to her voice. "Fine. You may go look, under one condition."

He perked up – and then sagged back down in the chair. "Yes, Lady?"

"I don't expect you to find anything," she replied with more steel to her voice than in the barracks. "If you *do*, I am to be the first person you tell. The 4th didn't look for a magical cause to her death and I am ashamed now to admit that I didn't either. Looked for traces of magic, to be sure, but only in the way that one would look for footprints in the mud. I... admit... that it was an oversight."

"Why would you? You run a house of the mad. Simple explanations are usually the best," he replied as he tried to soothe her ruffled feathers, "when you can explain things at all. Sometimes things just *are* without reason."

It didn't work, but she at least acknowledged the effort. "I would join you in this foolish errand, but I am late for a meeting with the very Overseer you just mentioned."

"Thank you, Lady. If I find anything, I will tell you. One additional request?"

The look in her eye darkened... again. "You've already started treading on thin ice; I would choose the weight of your words carefully."

A few brief visions of Tundrala flashed in his mind and he immediately wished the phrase would be dropped from the global lexicon entirely. "Don't tell anyone what I'm doing."

"Given the number of questions you seem to have been asking of anyone that moves, I imagine that the city already knows," she retorted.

"There's knowing I'm asking and knowing *why* I'm asking. Don't give these details to Henderschott or the Overseer yet. If I'm right and they're all related... whomever is doing it is almost certainly someone in power. You don't just *hide* power that you use for malicious intent. You use it to better yourself in the process."

Ridora pursed her lips again and had to agree with that, too. "Now that, at least, I can respect. You've got a poor opinion of the world we live in, Akaran. I think it does you better than anyone else I've ever met, although that is *not* a compliment," she said as she stood up and straightened her dress out. "Now, with that said. Once you're done looking in her room, you are to go to the garden. I want you to spend the rest of the day in prayer and meditation."

He looked slightly alarmed and suddenly felt like he was being grounded. "But I -"

"There are no 'buts' to be had over it," she said matter-of-factually. "You need to spend less time indulging your worries and more time indulging the Gods. You won't find recovery in some misguided attempt to find a murderer. You will *only* find it in the grace of the Gods above."

He was right; he was being grounded like a little kid. Unlike a little kid, he knew better than to argue with an adult (this time). "Yes, Lady. I have your permission then to look over -"

She leaned down over the desk and looked him right in the eye as she slid a piece of metal into his hand. "You have my permission to look in the room where we found her, and *begrudgingly* you may look through her effects. I do not expect you to find anything that Adept Lolron, the guards, or myself did not already find. This is your *one and only* opportunity to waste your time on this — and when you speak to Prostil again, you will *remind* her that her minions are not welcome to skulk on these grounds."

"Why do I sense that I'm being included in that list?"

"Conditions for your residency can be revoked at my discretion," she warned. "You would do yourself a kindness to remember that."

It didn't feel like it would be prudent to push her any further, and so he saw himself out as she finished getting ready for whatever business she had elsewhere. Ten minutes later, and Seline found him grumbling as he tried to work a key to get past the lock and into her room. "Didn't think to wait for me, hm?"

"She didn't say you were going to help."

She crossed her arms over her lovely pink tunic and rolled her eyes. "Do you think she'd let you do it on your own?"

"Hope springs eternal?" he quipped.

"This isn't a good idea," she said with a sad shake of her head. "And, Akaran. I'm not happy you're doing this. I appreciate it but I am not happy about it. I understand, though, that you're under orders."

"I am, and I'm sorry," he sincerely apologized. "I'm not doing this to upset you. Or anyone else. But your people haven't found out -"

"I know," Seline interrupted. "It just feels wrong to let one of our patients look around."

He shrugged and went back to work on the door. "Henderschott thinks that I did it still."

"I'm sure he does. I don't. I just... it feels wrong. I'm sorry."

Akaran leaned against the door and lowered his eyes, almost embarrassed to be in this mess. "Look. I may be half-blind and muted to magic, but even the blind can still feel their way around in the dark."

She sighed again and took the key from his hand. "I don't know what to do with you."

"Let me work?" he begged. "*Without* giving me a stress headache?"

"With all the cocasa you're taking, surprised you can even have one."

He ignored that and looked into the room once the way was clear. "You could've done something about the stains."

"We've been trying. This old wood it... we'd use lemons and vinegar but there's been a shortage," she replied. "Lady Ridora has a contract with the Woodmason's Guild to replace the floor..."

With an understanding nod, the exorcist went to work – and immediately understood that there wasn't going to be much to work with. After Seline lit a pair of candles in the room, the first thing he noticed was the blood. You *had* to notice it. Someone (or several someones) had made a valiant effort to clean it up, but it hadn't worked out as intended. There was still a huge red stain on the wood floor, and dark blotches across the ceiling and on some of the walls.

He had to give a quiet thanks to the Goddess for his decision to skip breakfast. It wasn't just that though. There was an odd feeling in there, like walking into a fog. He could *see* fine but there was just something intangible outside of his sight that started to nag at him the second he stepped through the threshold. Whatever it was, one glance at the healer made him realize that she seemed to be just fine as she strode in like she owned the place.

Once he got past the sheer number of splotches, he was able to pay attention to the room for what it was. This apparently wasn't her bedroom; just a workspace. There were two large bookshelves on the wall to his left, a table and a lectern next to a window across from them, and a pair of chairs next to an empty fireplace.

The books took his attention first and foremost; in part because they looked interesting, and in part because there wasn't much else to look at. Most of the titles seemed to be the typical academic rot – *Hemdin's Hunts of Overly-Scaled Beasts*, *The Peacemaster's Cures for Babbling Tongues*, *Journal of Successful Manipulations of Empathic Disease,* and others in the same vein. He did spy one entitled *Against the Odds* that didn't fit in, but the healer interrupted him before he could reach for it. "It's almost fitting that this is where she passed," Seline mused. "She spent more time in this room than anywhere else."

"What was this room used for?"

"Research, mainly. Medical texts. References from the Order of the Hand. Patient records, too," she explained. "She loved to make notes of everything she possibly could."

"Notes can be useful," he mused aloud. "Was Livstra responsible for all of it or did other people come in here too?"

"Mostly just herself," she replied. "Every now and again she'd have Raechil or someone come here to grab something."

Akaran nodded to himself and started to run his fingers over the spines of the varied books and around the dusty edges of their bindings. "Interesting," he mused, "and odd, too. There's a lot of books missing."

She blanched and looked away. "They were damaged when she…"

"Damaged how?"

The healer gestured to the stains on the floor without saying anything.

"That'd do it," he grunted with a sympathetic wince. "What was done with them? Were they destroyed or…?"

The healer looked wounded at the thought. "After how long it took to write them you think we'd destroy them? No. Heavens no. What tomes weren't related to patient logs themselves were sent to the Annex to be treated and repaired. The ones that were saved were delivered to the Repository for now."

That was worth making a mental note about. "How many in all?"

"I couldn't say," she admitted. "As I said: I didn't come in here often. No reason."

"Who had access to the room?"

"All of us," she answered, "Ridora felt that no knowledge of the mind should be kept from the caretakers, wanted it or not."

He looked askance at her and tapped mindlessly at the bookshelves. "So you were allowed?"

"Why wouldn't I be? I simply had no reason to. I do not enjoy reading as much as some of the others. I enjoy speaking, talking, learning what plagues the downtrodden in their own words."

That wasn't what he was hoping to hear. "So you wouldn't know if any of these scrolls or books were specifically targeted."

She frowned and stopped looking around. "The books? Why would they be?"

"Because if we don't know why she was attacked, maybe one of the tomes did. It's a question, and without knowing which one was where... damn. After you found the body, what all did you look for?"

For a change, he felt like he wasn't being the dense one. "What do you mean? We looked for who did it."

"I mean what kind of evidence did you look for? What things were done?"

Seline started to think on it and finally came up with an answer that took care of his question and provided no real information at all. Impressive, really. "Well, we... we looked for footprints, of course, any sign of who could have done it."

"What else?" he asked. "Did you look for magic, did you look for clawmarks? Did you look for anyone with odd new marks or scars on them? Did you just look for footprints? Details would be helpful."

She shrugged and spread her arms wide. "I don't know everything that the Guard looked for. I know they looked over everyone for blood or bloody clothes in their rooms."

Akaran blinked. "Even mine?"

"Even yours."

He felt his shoulders tense up and his stomach flip over. "They were in my room? They rooted through my belongings? They did it again?"

"Through *everyone's*," she replied, "mine, too."

"And I wasn't told? Why?"

Seline pointed at him and wagged her finger. "You didn't notice."

He crossed his arms and huffed in annoyance. "Yes I did. I thought it was Clarissa. That nosy old hag pokes in my drawers every time she comes to gather laundry."

"Well, it wasn't," she replied. "That time."

He shot her a dirty look and grumbled under his breath in lieu of a direct answer. "Fine. So they looked for bloody clothes and rags and didn't find anything."

"No, nothing."

"Whomever did couldn't have left clean."

"No... they couldn't have," the blonde-haired healer agreed. "You can see why we're stumped.

He started to pace between the bookcase and the fireplace, looking up at the ceiling as he did. "And you're confident she was killed here?"

Seline gave him a withering look like she couldn't believe he was so stupid to even ask. "With as much of a mess the room is in? You tell me."

A little sigh of frustration escaped his lips. "Had to have been someone that came here did it and left. No tracks anywhere in the Manor?"

"None, Akaran. I promise I'm telling you what we found. Didn't find."

The only other option for him to look at was the window, and he had a feeling there wasn't going to be anything there to find. After he ran his hands over and under the sill and checked the glass for cracks, he had to admit that he was right about nothing being there. "Ridora mentioned that they only looked for aura traces, nothing more. Is that right?"

"We had Lolron come look," she replied. "I don't know if that's what he looked for, but that's all he could find. But he said -"

He gave her a quick glance. "I'm willing to bet he said that ripples in the ether occur naturally in a death like this."

"He did."

"Remind me his specialty? Ulta-kenetic?" he asked as his eye caught sight of a small book laying behind one of the bookcases.

Seline nodded. "I... I think so? I... I should know but the words escape me."

He had to use his cane to fish the book out, but it worked and after a few moments of muttered cursing, he had it in his hands. "Did you have any ambianists or psyanists look at it?" he asked as he read the title to himself. *Auramancer's Exile, Compiled by Livstra Oliana. Written about Bistra, I guess?*

"Lady Ridora did," she replied. "She is a psyanist."

"No ambianists? Any priests of anyone?"

She nervously shifted back and forth on the balls of her feet. "Well, there were priests in the room, of course. Followers of Isamiael, followers of the Pantheon in general, to come tend to the body. Why?"

At this point, he felt like he'd ruled out everything else. So with a deep breath, he went for it and hoped she wouldn't lock him away in his room for even suggesting it. "Any of them look for anything Abyssian or defiled?"

It didn't get him locked up, but it did get him an exasperated look. "No? Why would they? There are wards that protect this building," she replied. "You can't possibly be suggesting that some kind of *demon* attacked her, surely."

"Well no," he admitted with a shrug before something she said clicked. "Has anyone looked at them recently? The wards?"

"Recently? I cannot say. They've been set since the... the problem... about three years ago. The Lady has forbid any more exorcists or paladins from the Order from setting foot on Manor grounds since, unless they are a patient."

"That's a really stupid order," he grunted. "What kind of problem?"

She continued to fidget and looked more and more uncomfortable by the heartbeat. "I don't know. There's not a lot I..."

He set the book down and sighed in pained frustration. "Everything. Please. I don't think anyone else will. You've ruled out the likely and the bad. Let me rule out the awful."

Seline sighed and settled down in one of the chairs. "We had a patient a few years ago. Not one of our usuals. A Makaral priest."

"The Warmongers don't usually have priests. Not in the conventional sense."

"No, they don't," she agreed, "and it was a disaster. He didn't come in through proper channels and wasn't effectively vetted. We didn't know, couldn't know, that he had been partially... infected... by a spirit."

He pursed his lips and tried to imagine how bad it could've possibly gone. "Know what kind? Might be important."

"No, I don't. I know who does though."

"Who? Ridora?"

Seline shook her head. "Catherine. She's the one that handled the exorcism. It's why she and the Lady don't get along. Well, the other reason. It went... it did not go well. People died."

For some reason, it didn't come as a surprise. Exorcisms weren't exactly a science, and his knee was example enough of what happened when you didn't condemn something right the first time around. "Oh. Piss. When you say people...?"

"Three," she corrected. "Two patients and one of our aids. That's why this... this hits even harder. We've seen it bad before but then it had reason and now it doesn't..."

That made unfortunate sense. "Was it destroyed, banished, or contained?"

"Is there a difference?"

"A big one," he explained. "Contain a damned soul, and you lock it up in something, someone, or somewhere in this world. Banish it, you cast it out of this plane and to somewhere less welcoming – with the hope it'll never come back. Destroy it, and it's gone for good in all realms, or at least de-powered and sent back to the Abyss. The Great Warden *hates* escapees from the pit, so... once gone it *stays* gone." Before she could even ask, he went on to say, "Depending on what you're facing, it depends on which one you try. Some of the damned are borderline invincible, and containing or banishing them are the only ways to put them back in their place."

To her credit, Seline actually understood him and didn't pick at his reasoning. "I don't know. I wasn't privy to the full circumstances."

That was something, at least. "I'll get the details from Maiden Prostil then."

"It would be best from her than anyone else by far."

"So what happened after? Wards were installed, I gather?"

She nodded at him. "Yes. Protections from Pristi, Isamiael, and Niasmis."

Akaran scratched at his goatee and felt his brow furrow. "I'm struggling to understand why you'd start up a hospital with the intention of treating those maddened by the damned without having wards in place to begin with."

"Before the incident, anyone sent to us was screened by the Temple of Light or the Order of Love," she pointed out. "There was no need."

He shook his head in irritation. "Forgive me, Seline, but that's idiotic."

Of all the replies she was expecting, one that blunt wasn't it. "Excuse me...? If they are found clear but hold corruption, then it isn't our fault."

"It's not that," he argued. "You realize where you are, what you're living in, right?"

She frowned and tilted her head slightly to the side. "A hospital. A sanctuary."

The exorcist shook his head again and sighed in not-so-vague annoyance. "You're sleeping in a building that has had innumerable maddened souls come through here. Some of them have gotten better, some of them not, some of them moved on to other parts of the world, and some of them have died. I imagine the ether here doesn't just *ripple* as much as it *froths*."

"We *do* care for them though," she argued. "This is a place of peace and sanctuary. It's been blessed by Isamiael, Niasmis, Pristi, and Solinal."

"Medicine, Love, Purity, and Peace," he noted. "Each of Whom no doubt have Their own ways to bring salvation to the weary that come through these doors. But have you ever considered Who *lives* here?"

"I don't understand what you're getting at."

He ran his fingers through his hair and gave the window another look over. There was something that was just slightly off about it, but *damn* if he could figure out what. "It's a shrine to Pi," he replied with a mutter under his breath.

Seline stared at him like he had just grown a second head. "Pi? You don't mean...?"

"That the Manor is a shrine to the Goddess of Madness, yes," he repeated. "No matter what kind of flowery exterior you put on it, no matter how many lace-covered pillowcases you stick in our rooms, no matter Whom on the Pantheon you ask to bless the grounds, Pi *owns* this place."

She continued to stare at him, utterly aghast. "How could you possibly even come to such an idea?"

"Because," he replied as he found a pair of grooves in the sill, "you *literally have Her people living here*. Every single one of the maddened souls bedding down in this building are either hopelessly disoriented, their minds enfeebled, their thoughts steeped in swirling chaos that they can't even begin to comprehend, or *other*, or *all* of the above." He looked over his shoulder at her and shrugged before adding, quite simply, "Not that I'm much of an exception, but what would you call a place where large numbers of a Goddess's followers congregate?"

"I... I never thought of it that way," she whispered before another realization hit her. "Is that what you've thought of this place all along?"

"*Yes*," he replied to – and a second, softer 'yesss' as he managed to work a finger under one of the windowsill grooves enough to pop the glass pane loose from the frame – bypassing the lock completely. *And here's what they missed*, he crowed to himself before faltering and giving it another look. *But... how? It's sticking out plain as day...?* "Only reason I've been able to fall asleep without expecting a visit from one of Her more mixed-world minions is that I assumed you have this place covered in wards and other spells that would piss Her off enough to keep Her from trying."

The healer looked like she was torn between being sick or rushing over to hug him. "It must... it must be horrible, knowing the things you know. If that's the way you see a house of health and worship... as... as a shrine to one of the Fallen!" She shuddered a second time and continued to stare at him in horror. "No wonder you can't relax!"

"Horrible aside," he replied as he turned away from the window and rubbed his chin some more. "When was the last time they were checked?"

"The wards? What would you check them for?"

"To make sure that they still work?" he slowly answered as he wondered when exactly she had turned into an idiot, or if she'd been like this the entire time. "You know? To make sure they haven't been interfered with?"

Seline put her hand over her mouth and tried to come up with an answer that wouldn't irritate him any more than she already had. "As far as I am aware, Ridora examines them monthly, and the ladjunct checks them for potency a few times a year."

He nodded and turned his attention back to the bookcase. That one book – *Against the Odds* – caught his eye again. But before he could grab it, he pushed her a little more. "Did Ridora set the ward?"

That wasn't the question she'd expected, and her response showed as much with a simple, "Hm?"

"Did she set the ward, or did Catherine?" he clarified, again wondering if she might've hit her head on the doorway coming in here. *Or maybe something here in the room. Feels like someone is squeezing my head in a clamp. Just won't stop. Maybe something they used to try to clean the blood up...?*

"Maiden Prostil did, I assume," she replied with a little shrug.

"So Ridora is checking wards that Catherine set," he grunted. "Why not let her come do it herself?"

Another sigh slipped past her lips. "As I said earlier. The exorcism went poorly, and Ridora decided that the violence of that side of the Order has no room in this place of healing."

"I am starting to bet that it will at one point or another," he warned with a dangerously serious tone to his voice. "I need to see those wards. I also need to see her quarters. Please tell me you haven't tossed her stuff out yet."

"We donated some of her items to the poor," Seline admitted, "though most are still there. Ridora hasn't yet had the stomach to sort through them in their entirety. Which do you want to see first?"

"The wards," he answered after giving it a lot of intense, albeit brief, thought. "They'll tell me more than anything else."

They did.

Just not what he wanted to hear.

But before he left the room, there was one last thing to do. While Seline had her back turned, he 'left his cane inside' and ducked back into Liv's study. Quickly, and very carefully, he went to work on a spot behind the bookshelves where nobody'd see it unless they were looking. When he finished and joined her out in the hallway, he had a little cut above a rune-tattoo on his left forearm, and a bloody wardmark hidden in the room to mark his passing.

As they walked away, they didn't notice the woman that had been watching them intently and they didn't lock the door to Livstra's former room. The moment that they were safely out of the hallway, Bistra slipped inside. She strode into the room slowly, cautiously, and stood in silence with her eyes closed for a long moment.

"Shadows?" she whispered.

No reply came forth.

"My shadows," she repeated. "You... you listen. Do... do you see? See his shadows? They won't like you. They don't like him, but they *won't* like you," the broken woman stated — a little firmer, a little more resolute. "I'd... I'd run. I'd run while you can."

As soon as she said it, she took her own advice and bolted back to the relative safety of her own room. Nothing responded to her, and nobody seemed to hear her. But in the corner, pressed against the ceiling, where nobody had thought to look...

...one of the shadows *twitched*.

As they walked through the manor, he didn't shut up, much to her chagrin. "Anything new catch her interest lately?"

"She only had time for the patients here at the Manor. There wasn't much else she cared about."

"Then was she working with anyone in particular recently?"

"In particular?" she repeated thoughtfully. "Hm. No, nobody that could cause her harm."

"Not what I asked."

Seline bit back her first response and rolled her eyes. "She had been spending a lot of time with Appaidene. You met her the other day."

The one with the doll, he remembered. "Was she getting anywhere with her? She didn't seem really... stable."

She rolled her eyes at him again as they started their way down the south stairs. "It's a mental hospital, Akaran. Stability is not the norm. But, no. I don't believe that she was."

Akaran stared down at the steps like a man approaching the gallows. "What brought her here?"

"She wandered into some fortress with her belly open and unable to speak," she replied. "I'm told it was a miracle that she was even able to walk."

He stopped and blanched, his own stomach flopping at the thought. "Belly... open? Anyone know what happened?"

"Nobody," she said with a shrug. "We didn't even have her name until she started repeating it over and over again after we admitted her."

Confused, horrified, and somewhat disgusted, he went ahead with more questions. "Why here? This place is only for magical trauma, isn't it?"

It was her turn to cringe. "Someone carved the Scriptures of Geshalda into her back."

The blanch returned. That name was one not known to many, and for good cause. They were a shortened version of the so-called *Affirmations of the Covetous*, the so-called 'holy' text written to appease the Soul of Envy Herself. "Oh, Goddess..."

"Lady Ridora believes that she had been with child, and that someone made a pact with the Unfulfilled to steal it. It's hard to imagine that what she suffered wasn't magical in some fashion."

"Not if she was able to get up and move around after," he agreed as he covered his mouth with his hand and shuddered in disgust. "That is absolutely *horrible*. I had heard greed will kill you but..."

"In all truth, Akaran, I do not know if the poor woman even has the capacity to wish for death," she answered with a morose tremble to her voice. "There's little left in her mind."

"Let me guess. Her fixation on the doll is probably...?"

She gave a sad little nod as they got closer to the atrium. "It's why she calls it her baby, we think. Ridora takes a great deal of pity on her. She is one of the most vulnerable residents we have."

Akaran had to agree with her assessment. "Why was Livstra focusing on her?"

"I am not at all sure," she admitted freely. "I know that Appa is obsessed with getting out of her room after dark as of late. It has been difficult to manage, honestly. If I had to assume a reason, it would likely be trying to work with her about it."

He sucked a little on the air and tried to guess why. "How long has it been going on?"

"A few years now."

"Nothing recent?"

"No, I am afraid not."

That earned a little nod and an unintelligible sound as he pondered what it could mean. "Is that all Liv was doing, or...?"

The healer opened the door to the atrium and ushered him inside. "She had cut her workload down to Appa and Bistra before she was killed."

"Bistra Enil?" he asked as he kept his grumbling opinion on one final set of stairs to himself. "The Auramancer Exorcist, right?"

"Yes, that's her," she replied before stopping and pondering something over for a minute. "You know what? She *did* say that there was more to Bistra than we understood. She never gave up hope that he poor woman could have a recovery. *In fact*, she said that there was no reason that she should still be as she is."

That wasn't something he expected to hear. "Really? Even I know enough about shock to know that it can ruin a person for life."

"That's the odd thing," she replied as they made their way to the center of the garden. It was still light enough to see without lighting the torches, thankfully. The braziers, however, were still lit and happily burning away. "Miss Enil had never shown signs of being affected by the things she faced in the shadows before a sudden break in her psyche one day. Her last assignment was nothing out of the ordinary for an exorcist of her rank – or so Liv told me."

He stopped and tilted his head a little to the side. "You have access to her reports?"

"Me? No," she said before correcting herself. "Well, yes. They're stored in the Repository. Liv could order anything that might help her heal our residents brought over from time to time. I haven't seen them, but my understanding is that the last encounter she had before she had to come here was to root out some Circle cultists in Lowmarsh."

He *immediately* bristled up, and so suddenly that it nearly made her take a step back in surprise. "The Circle isn't to be underestimated. I can see them causing someone to land here. *I* did."

She whipped her head around so fast that her ponytail slid over her shoulder. "Your fight was with the Circle? I thought it was with an escapee from Frosel...?"

"Both and more."

"Oh! I didn't... I didn't realize."

"It's fine," the exorcist replied as he forced his shoulders to unclench. "It was a convoluted mess. It was more Neph directly than it was just His cult."

Seline shook her head again and quickly wrapped her hand over his and the top of his cane. "No, there is fault. It is my job to understand the situations you were in to help aid you in your recovery. If you had run-ins with the Plaguelord's followers, then -"

"*A* follower," he corrected, "and less *follower* and more 'asshole that made a deal and didn't follow through which pissed Rot off.' The rest of it was just... unexpected corruption."

"Still," she said with an apologetic smile. "I will have to ask for your file again. The one that has *not* been redacted so excessively."

He arched an eyebrow at her and slipped out of her grip. "You could just ask."

"How forthcoming would you be if I did?"

"Not as much as you'd like," he admitted as he pointed at the few people currently in prayer at the statues. "Do you mind...?

It took a few moments to get a couple of residents and their helpers to go shuffle off elsewhere to give some privacy to the two would-be investigators. When one of the aids gave the two of them *a look* for suggesting they needed privacy, the little blonde woman's face flushed almost purple. Akaran, on the other hand, was too oblivious to care. Instead, as she tried to do some sort of damage control for her social life, he stared up at the amber, silver, and gold eyes of the assembled trio.

The statues seemed disinterested in him, which he took as a good thing. *Life gets weird when stone edifices start moving on their own*, he mused. Then again, the throbbing headache he'd had in Livstra's room got worse the closer to the three he stood. Weirder, the throbbing in his knee almost started to twitch under the skin.

After a tired, vaguely frustrated sigh at the thought of figuring out someone else's spellwork, he buckled down and got to it. "Well, let's see what they did here and if there's any chance I can make sense of it."

"Aren't all divine spells written the same way?"

"Are all cookbooks?" She paused and started to speak before he cut her off with an unhappy grumble. "Oh, they would've written these in purgalaito, of fisking course..."

Seline ignored the curse and took a few steps back as he began to jot stuff down in his notebook. "I still can't believe I let you talk me into looking at these up close."

He looked over his shoulder at her and frowned. "Why not? Atrium is open for all of us."

"Well, yes," she agreed, "but that doesn't mean the patients are encouraged to play with the magic words."

"I'm not playing," he countered. "I'm reading. Examining."

The difference didn't work to assuage her feelings any. "You know I have to tell Ridora everything you do here, right? Questioning her work isn't going to win her over. She *does* have significantly more experience than you, you know."

"I'm not questioning her work, just her reasoning," he argued. A moment later he picked up a nearby stick and lit it in one of the braziers, which had the unintended consequence of making the healer sputter in surprise and irritation. "What? It's just fire."

"That was the Holy Brazier of Eternal Light and Purity!"

He shrugged at her and brought the light closer to the writing inscribed on the front of Solinal's statue. "Then it can purify this branch while I use it to read this crap. Let's see... *Lord of Peace and Washer of Soles*... why would the God of Peace care about fee... oh, *Souls*. I see. *Washer of Souls*," he began to recite before he looked back over at his companion. "That's an odd title, isn't it? Washer of Souls? Was Scrubber of Sinful Bunions taken?"

The look on her face was worth it. "Oh blessed all," she groaned. Her eyes went up and she looked at the edifice's face and quietly whispered, "Peacebringer, he doesn't mean the disrespect."

"Wouldn't go that far," Akaran muttered back. "*Washer of Souls, may Your breath calm the turbulent, may Your touch soothe the chaos of the mind.* Okay, not bad. Have no idea what that's supposed to *do* but it sounds pretty."

"I thought you said warding magic was your specialty...?"

"Well it is, but you can imply a lot of things with a spell," he said before expounding on the subject. "It's more the feeling you get from it unless you're familiar with it. For example, see those four marks there?" he asked as he pointed down at three squiggly lines and then over at a round circle with two dots in it. "Those are more the spell than the inscription. The runemarks are where the power actually lies."

She peered down at it and couldn't begin to make any kind of sense from the scribbles. "But you can't read them? After all the fuss to see it?"

"I didn't say I couldn't," he argued. "Just that I don't know what it's supposed to do – exactly. See? Listen to it, literally translated: *Solindal, Solindal, Solindal, Breath* doesn't get the point across without the added inscription. And who wants to take the time to do that?"

"Oh… no, no I guess it doesn't. What does it mean?"

"That this was done by a lazy priest. Ridora didn't do this one. Who did?"

She pursed her lips and gave it a long, hard thought before shrugging her shoulders in surrender. "I truthfully don't remember. I'm sorry. I imagine it was either the ladjunct from Stara or one of his helpers."

He grunted something impolite and moved on to Isamiael's statue. "Alright. I should talk to them later about what it actually does. At least this one makes sense: *Lady of Healing, Mender of Flesh, Salve of the Injured, cast Your will into sundered souls and let their essence heal from within.* Those marks," he said as he pointed at a lemniscate nestled into a triangle under a semi-circle, "are for a spell that is supposed to heal cracks in your etheric aura and heal your soul, if it's been damaged. The second set of runes below it? See those right there? Those will warn the person that set the blessing if the energy in the spell is facing resistance. The stiffer the resistance the stronger the warning."

Lost as she was, he gave her credit for at least bothering to look at it with him. "Oh. I… um. I see? So if the spell starts working on someone, the person that placed it will hear about it? Sorta like a guard yelling for help?"

"Exactly," he replied. "If it was being taxed at all, the priest in question would feel it."

Seline idly played with the end of her ponytail and frowned. "If that's the case then it isn't being used is it? Which means that magic can't have been what killed Livstra, right?"

The priest thought about that for a minute before he could come up with a satisfactory answer as he moved to the third and final set of wards. "Or at least it's magic that isn't offending Isamiael. If a fire mage starts to light people on fire, a ward invoking Aqualla to keep the heat away would get twitchy. But if an ice mage started to make crystal daggers and hurled them at people? It isn't hydrokenesis, but the God of Water is the father of the Queen of Ice. So, what do you think would happen with the ward?"

"The Tidesinger wouldn't mind?"

"Not at first, unless it was specifically written otherwise," he agreed.

"But she died and was… well… you saw it and…"

Akaran nodded and rubbed his hands together. "I can build something with a hammer, or I can break it. Magic can be used to cause harm, and there's a lot of spells designed to do just that – but unless it's a Circle cultist, Isamiael probably wouldn't notice. I don't know. I don't know much about how the

Goddess of Health actually works."

She crouched down beside him and helped him brush away a little bit of overgrowth that had crowded the Goddess' stone feet. "What about the inscription on this one?"

"Simple and to the point," Akaran replied as he traced the words with a gloved finger. "*Love the ones that are hurt, for they are the ones that may know Love the least.*"

"That almost sounds like it's condemning people that don't follow Her."

He nodded and started to read the second inscription below it. "Maaaybe…. that spell though? That's odd."

"What is it?"

"It's not a ward against the damned," he said as he started to gnaw on his lip, "so much as it is a promise."

She blinked and cutely tilted her head again. "A promise? What in the world…?"

"*Trespass against the lost and Love will trespass against you,*" he read aloud.

Seline swallowed nervously as she felt a sudden lump form in her throat. "That's um… Yes. That's fairly ominous. Not at all loving."

He couldn't help but agree. "Yes. Yes it is. That's… really intimidating. She's not known to be gentle when Her people are threatened. I imagine that's the point. Just reading it is making me want to run away and I'm not doing anything that would piss Her off," he observed, though a little voice in the back of his mind added a quiet, *I think. I hope.* "Would hate to think how it would feel around something that's attuned against Her brand of divinity…"

"I suppose then the next question is if you see anything wrong with the spells?"

"No, I don't. The one for my Lady is incredibly direct – it's a purge."

"A purge?" she said, the lump growing larger.

Akaran shrugged and started to stand up with a muttered profanity. "We don't deal in flowery words. She says what She means."

"And purge means…?" she asked with her eyes slightly wide.

He quietly read it again and shrugged. "Fisk you and fisk everyone around you."

She clamped her hand over her mouth. A *little* profanity was one thing, but so loudly? "AKARAN! Language! Right in front of the Gods, even!"

"I assume They hear me when I'm not right in front of Them, too," he pointed out.

Not that it stopped her protests. "But *still!* Show Them some respect!"

"At least to one of 'Em," he grunted. He looked up at his Goddess and then solemnly – albeit quickly – bowed his head. It was not a gesture he repeated towards the other two edifices, but while he was looking down, a little glint in the torchlight caught his eye again. "Hey, what's this?"

"What's what?"

"This... necklace?" he asked as he spotted a long chain near the back corner of Isamiael's statue. "It looks... Seline?"

"Yes?"

He started to reach for it and began to lose his balance. "It's a Granalchi sigil of -" he started to say. As he spoke, the healer brushed up against him and the little purchase he had gave way, which sent him tumbling.

She tried catching him as he toppled onto his side and managed only to tear his cloak. He hit the ground with a thud and an extended bout of cursing as his knee reminded him it existed all over again. "Oh! Oh no, Akaran, I'm so sorry."

"It's fine, it's... fisk. Ow, yeah, it's fine, things happen," he muttered as he reached over to the closest statue to help push himself up. When his hand touched the inscription on Solinal's statue...

...things *happened.*

He froze where he stood, only just barely managing to open his mouth to make a sudden, "*Oh,*" sound before an icy blue aura began to emanate all around him. It pulsed out of his skin and flashed in the air, leaving behind streamers of energy that drifted up and down his arm. The wave rushed through him, down to his feet, and then shot back up out of his mouth and into the statue.

He didn't make a noise, but the air suddenly reverberated with the sound of shattering ice and pounding sleet. Solinal's edifice started to glow with the same blue light as freezing water began to trickle out of the previously-empty basin in its hands. The ground under him turned white and frosted over while he laid there paralyzed.

When he didn't answer Seline's scream for him to move, she did the only thing she could think to do; she pushed. When she did, she knocked his hand free of the Peacemaker's statue and inadvertently rolled him flat against Isamiael's.

The blue light around him vanished the moment that his hand lost contact from Solinal – but a red blotch erupted along the side of his leg as he rolled on the ground. He screamed and grabbed at it, a reaction that lasted all of ten heartbeats before the Healer's rune kicked in. Hard.

Angry white light ripped out of the side of his knee, his arm, and his empty eye, which forced a second scream up from of his lungs. Where icy streamers had wafted out of him moments before, clouds of white smoke began to roll off of his skin and burned his flesh.

He screamed anew and shoved himself away from the Goddess of Medicine. He rolled on the ground in pain until he heard a voice in his head – or maybe it was a whisper in the wind – that said, simply, "*[To me!]*"

To Her he went.

As Seline tried to grab him and hold him still, he thrust his hands out and wrapped them around Niasmis's stone legs. The steam stopped pouring off of him, and the leftover streamers of snow stopped billowing around his head. For a moment, the pain ended. His body was set awash with warmth and tenderness and a surge of *comfort* that even Seline could feel.

At first.

When the whisper returned to the wind a moment later, it was less on a wind and more on a gust; and less a whisper and more an indignant snarl. Akaran tensed up as he felt it coming. The woman next to him jerked back like she'd been slapped across the face. The other two statues seemingly shrunk on the outside of his peripheral vision.

"*[Loathsome. You... loathsome... creature.]*"

He felt his body go cold as his stomach fell. He shook as he looked up at Her statue and felt a wave of panic unlike anything he'd *ever* felt before. "Goddess I'm... I'm loathsome? I'm... I've...?!"

"*[I see you,]*" the wind whispered. "*[Look at Me.]*"

Akaran struggled and tried to look up into the statue's eyes and he swore he saw them peer back down at him. "I'm looking! Please! I'm, I -"

Then he *screamed* as his leg *rippled* from the inside out and a fresh spurt of blood sprayed out through his clothes and onto the ground. A small handful of black, foggy tentacles slithered out through his leggings and tore into the grass. He stared down in horror as a single eye peered up from the center and blinked at the furious idol that towered over its host before it ducked back into his body.

The gust became a gale.

The snarl became a shout.

And the whisper on the wind became a Word under his skin.

"*[TRESPASSER!]*"

The *only* thing that he could do was to grab Her legs tighter.

"*[PURGE.]*"

The jolt that shot through him finally gave his exhausted soul a respite.

XI. …BRIEF AS IT MAY BE.
Madis, the 17ˢᵗ of Riverswell, 513 QR

The tunnel system behind the Wall of Gardens and the Orshia Falls was both an open secret and a source of unceasing irritation for the city guard. While there were some enterprising souls who had purchased rights to use some of the caves and pathways for one business venture or other (it made for great storage of crops from the farms, if you ignored the propensity to mildew that they suffered), not everyone was so legally-minded. It was hard to say how deep the tunnels went, or if they even surfaced outside of the city. Nobody had ever considered them enough of a risk to map, and the only person that had done any deep delves in it had kept that information between himself and his God.

One would assume, however, that the God of the Undertunnels would know even if his priest hadn't included it in regular informational prayers. One would also assume that for having such an intense interest in them, Oldstone Altund – a disgusting slug of a man he was – would have had a better understanding of the people living there. He was, after all, so eager to get his hands on the quarry left behind by Bendolynn Gavasti that he had no real qualms about getting into business with Anais.

Business that he hoped would be booming.

Business that wasn't. In fact, it was booming so poorly that he had decided to renege on his deal with the broker. That decision was equally as poor, although in different ways. Donta's arrival to serve as her collection agent had neither gone well nor peacefully, and while in most times it would be considered ill-form to beat up the priest that was providing you with a blessing, desperate times often called for desperate measures.

Although, with luck, the geomancer would be able to craft a few new teeth from whatever gems he could dig up from under the city. Donta smiled down at the fresh stains of blood on his gloves, and shook the box in his hands enough to make it rattle. The box was a 'gift' to show 'good faith,' after he had a shorter conversation with the priest about the amulet and the blessing within it.

"I like to keep favor of my God," the mercenary had told the prone and blubbering sloth, "and He won't like me playing with the Stonehewn's toys."

"Surely it won't cause consternation if you're not keeping and you're just, just delivering it -!"

A solid kick to the kidneys punctuated his retort. "He gets jealous."

Soon after, the box was gifted. There were threats before he left with it, of course, and promises that he didn't know what kind of fight he was picking. Warnings that Altund controlled the powers of the very rock at Donta's feet itself.

A drawn knife and a few threats of his own convinced the Oldstone to let the rocks stay where they were supposed to stay – and to stay as far out of his way as they possibly could. "Iron comes from stones," he had retorted with a snarl, "and I can stab before you can throw."

Shame, he mused a short bit after, *fat fisk could've had other uses. Anais isn't going to be happy about this.* Which itself was very true, though knowing her, it was hard to say if she'd be more pissed over losing a potential contact or that the quarry wasn't performing as expected. *Not my fault. Let her have all of it*, he grunted.

He continued to entertain dark thoughts and muttered curses until he reached the end of the caves and had the thundering sounds of Orshia's Falls drowning them out. Or it did until he heard the sound of jingling armor and panting breath behind him. A green-cloaked huntsman half-charged/half-stumbled into him, his breath ragged as he panted for air as he clutched his swords like they were the only thing saving him from certain death.

"Move!" he ordered between gasps, "Now!"

Donta stayed right where he was, and firmly grabbed the hunter by both of his shoulders. "Why?"

"Dammit I said move!" the huntsman ordered, lording over the other man by nearly half a foot. Tall as he was, and no matter how hard he shook, he couldn't get free. "And let go of me! You don't know what's back there!"

"I know you're making noise," Anais' bodyguard replied in his typically flat, monotone voice that made the hunter sink back on himself, "but don't know you. Your name?"

He struggled again and Donta eventually let him go after he sheathed his sword. "Cassanol. Now get out of my damn way. I've got to get back to Elsith. She's gotta know!"

"Know what?" he asked with a cold little smile. "Maybe I can help."

Cassanol looked down at him and shook his head impatiently. "No, not even both of us. I found... listen. I found this," he said as he pulled an odd clump of vegetation out of his cloak, "and started to track where it was coming from and then saw... saw them. I don't know if they saw me. If they did we have to run, have to get to a temple. Come on!"

The bodyguard looked down at the pile of desiccated, shriveled, white moss and tried to make some kind of sense out of it. "What is it?"

"You wouldn't unless you knew... see, they're not uncommon in the south, the far south, in Matheia. They... I don't know why," he admitted, "just they like it there. So you see one or two now and again. Wherever they go, life... it drains. That's what it does. When they move in. Birds and bugs go away. Plants? They do this. See?" the hunter repeated as he shoved the white mass of moss at Anais's goon.

"Plants die?"

"Not just die! Look, they've been *drained*," he stressed. "See? We get... it's what the Guild gets execution writs for more than not. They don't, they never come up here, they don't..."

Donta prodded the pile of ashen plantlife and affixed Cassanol with a deathly stare. "*What?*"

The huntsman shook his head wildly and looked back over his shoulder. "You wouldn't believe me even if I told you. Doesn't matter. We have to go, we have to go right now, Elsith will know what -" he babbled until Anais' minion decided he'd had quite enough of his prattle. He was so quick, the huntsman didn't see it coming.

For that matter, he barely felt it. And before his eyes could even notice the jutting spike that was suddenly sticking out of Donta's palm – and buried in his forehead – they rolled back into his skull. "Let's see."

Cassanol's memories briefly flooded the bodyguard's mind as he absorbed the most recent ones. An odd feeling of relief and nausea poured into him and a silent cry of pain echoed through his head. It didn't matter; it would pass as quickly as the visions would.

Cavern walls. Deep into the tunnels. A trail of dead vines, rotten moss, and the occasional ashen root started to appear along the rock walls, and it only got worse the further he went. A growing feeling of panic. The torch in his hands flickered, casting odd shadows everywhere he looked. A sound started to echo from up ahead – laughing. Laughing mixed with whimpers of pain. He tossed the torch aside and drew both of his blades. A briefly uttered spell brought the darkness into clarity. He kept skulking through the cave, hunting for the source of the sound...

The hunter started to twitch and fell hard to his knees. It took Donta grabbing him by his throat with supernatural strength to keep him from falling over and breaking the connection entirely. The dying man began to gurgle pointless words from his throat. "Not... not here..."

The laughter. It kept going. It was delighted, amused. Sadistic. A man's voice. A woman's, too. Laughing and... and wet noises. Wet crunching. Crunching like someone eating a roast. But there wasn't the smell of a fire. Nothing burning. No light. Nothing that made sense.

"...can't be..."

Donta ignored him and focused, pushed harder, pushed faster. The memory was blurring around the edges of his mental vision. A few more moments and the hunter would be dead, and his secrets buried with him. *There!* the bodyguard crowed to himself.

Cassanol ducked down a recessed hall and wasn't in a cave anymore. He was in a room with... mirrors? His reflection bounced back at him everywhere he looked. His reflection, and a young woman wearing what was left of a tattered tan robe. Her brown hair was soaked with blood and her hazel eyes were staring at nothing and everything at once. Thick gashes down her arms and legs exposed muscle and bone. A gaping hole in her throat let blood bubble freely before it vanished into thin air.

In the mirror, it looked like she was being held upright by an invisible force. Like there was something in the air that was devouring her. As if her body was being consumed by the void.

But she wasn't.

Her killers didn't have a reflection.

Cassanol's eyes traveled to the center of the room and saw the pair of gore-soaked murderers holding her. Feasting on her. Laughing as they did. Giggling as an otherwise flawless, marble-skinned man with pointed ears and a single good eye licked his lips and flashed a smile that would haunt the hunter for the rest of his life.

Though to be fair, he'd expected that life to last longer.

Donta let the hunter fall with a thud and a snarl. A wave of horrific nausea swept over him – not from the murder, but from what had done it. He stared down at the corpse while his claw slid back into his hand, panting in a mix of exertion and disgust.

"Oh," he finally managed to croak out, "I see." He gave the corpse a kick and rolled the huntsman over so he could look down in his vacant eyes. "No. Nobody can know." he told the dead man with a disgusted grunt.

Not Anais, he sighed inwardly. *If she knew? No. She can't know.*

Not about vampires.

In her room at Thesd Villa, Anais had other problems.

Like always, the son of a bitch showed up when she was asleep. That, or when she wasn't there. Those were the only two times he ever bothered to make an appearance. What pissed her off so much was that going to sleep wasn't as easy for her as it was for other people.

There were rituals to be done, offerings to be made. Prayers every night to several different deities in the hope that one of Them would eventually find her worth favor. Things to be done that made rest – as hard as it was – all the more important.

One of Them other than the One who had claimed her once already.

To be interrupted once it finally came was a frustration to say the least. To be interrupted by *him* was worse. That, for no other reason, than because there was nothing she could do about it when her benefactor ordered it to come deliver word.

Anais roused up from her fitful slumber at the sound of his arrival. It was like hearing someone rip paper and cut it with a hundred sword strokes in the air. A rush of wind joined it, and it pulled her out of her dreams.

Dreams full of memories. Dreams full of monstrosities. Dreams that nobody should ever have to suffer through. Realities that should never be experienced, but were.

And ones that had been.

His appearance, as hated as it was, was almost a relief. "You. Our Master's favored acolyte. What are you doing here *now*?" she demanded as she stared at him with her eyes half-opened.

"[Master makes his move/Pause your failing efforts.]"

"My efforts aren't failing."

The creature laughed at her from the end of her bed. It was *not* a pretty thing – it was nothing more than a small gray mote with four legs, ruby eyes, and a mouth full of corkscrewed teeth. "[Master seeks an audience with the sea/The drowned will offer grief in song.]"

"An audience with the sea?" she asked as she tried to focus on his flickering form. "He's... he's moving against the Aquallans? What possible reason *why*? And why bother me? The closest Hall of Tide's Song is days away."

It chittered at her and dug all four sets of his claws into the bedframe. "[His move will anger/Orders will be wary.]"

"So you're here to tell me that he's planning on making a mess that might stir the locals up?" she growled as she sat up. "How quaint. What is it he plans to do?"

"[No details are important/Only what happens after.]"

That set her back a moment as irritation gave way to concern on her face. "Of course it matters! I need to know to protect my interests. If he's sent you to warn me, then every action he's hinting at is important, you rhyme-speaking abhorrence."

"[You will hear/If you listen.]"

"I *am* listening, damn you."

"[Not to me/To the others.]"

"WHAT OTHERS?" she demanded.

"[Our Master has found a creature/to aid all of your efforts.]"

Anais glowered at the mote and crossed her arms. "This city is awash in uncultured beasts. Haven't you seen the midlanders?"

He hopped from the end of the bed to her leg before she swatted him away. He landed on the floor and huffed in irritation. "[A ship in search of vessels/it will draw away attention.]"

Her face crumbled from irritation to outright confusion. "Even considering the riddles you speak in, this is a new low. Could you, oh please, speak *clearly*?"

"[Warning is simple and warning is clear/Do not be the warmth it seeks,]" the little beast replied. "[Second warning to be said/of equal concern and truth.]"

"Don't be the warmth... what in the name of the Gods are you yammering about?"

Rishnobia, favored acolyte of the Man of the Red Death, looked down the flat mess that passed for his nose at her and chittered eagerly. "[Panic and pandemic/always opens lips.]"

Her stomach fell as the beast vanished into thin air.

"Pandemic? That's twice you've warned me about that." When no other response was forthcoming, she shouted it at the empty air. "WHAT PANDEMIC?"

"Wake up, Akaran..." she crooned. A second, more impassioned call followed with, *"Please... you're needed..."*

Rmaci's voice didn't get him to open his eye.

The sound of bodies slamming against one another didn't convince him to open them. The sound of a man groaning in triumphant climax only made Akaran's eye water from the strain of holding them closed. The sound of her screams echoed in his memory and set his blood on fire. His eye opened and he bucked against the chains holding him against the wall.

He'd been here before, only now he was anchored across the cell, the up close and personal view that he'd missed the first time. With a scream of his own, the rusted iron manacles that held him disintegrated in the face of his fury, setting him free. He didn't take the time to examine whether that fury was aimed at or himself for not saving her in time, or her for making him relive this.

It was part of a memory. Only it wasn't just his.

The scene replayed itself over again as it had in Gonta. He broke into Rmaci's cell and tackled the guard that had assaulted her. He fought him; he shoved him into a wall. He bent down to check on her, and the jailer grabbed him by his shoulders and slammed him back into the wrought iron bars.

He turned and punched the bastard in his mouth. The guard recoiled as tentacles sprouted from between his teeth. They continued to trade blows; the guard moved slowly and stilted, like a marionette being controlled by a drunk puppeteer. Akaran moved smoothly and delivered each righteous blow like he was born to do nothing else.

When the jailer shoved him against a wall and started to choke him to death, he couldn't get voice enough for a Word. So he did the next best thing – the servant of Niasmis pulled a flaming sconce from the wall and bashed part of his face in.

It didn't stop the fight. Akaran used magic to cause his attacker – to cause Rmaci's rapist – to glow with a blazing light that showed the mass of shadows and tentacles that had wrapped around and through him. The priest snarled and fought harder, bashing and battering the guard into a broken heap.

The jailer's death was swift, but wasn't painless. Akaran made sure of that. He took the sconce, forced the guard's head back, and slammed it into his bloodied mouth. He drove it down, deeper, harder, and thrust it so deep that the guard couldn't straighten his head up.

With a snarl, the exorcist finally found a sword and cleaved the guard's head from his shoulders. He swung so hard he took it off in a single swipe; the sword cut through skin, muscle, sinew, and even the end of the sconce with righteous ease. The only satisfaction to be had was in the wet 'thunk' when his head bounced off of the floor. The priest stood there and seethed at the lifeless corpse. He watched as Daringol's tentacles faded into nothing and felt his anger ebb as blood poured all over the floor.

He'd been trying to bury the memory since it happened.

Not because of the guard – but because of what happened next.

What was happening *now* what wasn't happened *then*. Part of him felt like he deserved it. Rmaci seemed to agree. The room twisted around him. The walls shifted, melted, reformed. Reversed. Suddenly the Civan spy wasn't in the cell anymore; he was. The door wasn't open anymore. It was closed. When the world settled, he was the one on the floor of the dungeon.

It was Rmaci that stood outside of it, flanked on her sides by the headless guard on her left – and a swirling mass of blackened faces and bodies on her right. "*I need you to feel this,*" she hissed. "*You thought that saved me? You thought that burning me would set me free?*"

He was almost too disoriented to respond to her. "I didn't... I wasn't the one that set the fire!"

"*BUT YOU DIDN'T TRY TO PUT IT OUT!*" she screeched. Her ratty dress was gone, and instead, she was wearing his clothes. His vestments. His gloves, his cloak. "*YOU LET ME BURN AND TOLD THEM TO STOKE THE FLAMES UNTIL I WAS ASH!*" The only thing that wasn't *his* was the symbol on the chest; the icon of the Order of Love simply refused to manifest. Instead, he saw the story of her life unwind again and again – every murder she carried out, every lie she told, every tragedy that fell on her shoulders or act of sin carried out by her hands.

With every screamed word she flung, bits of skin and blood sloughed off of her ruined face and stained the white tunic she was wearing. "YOU WERE DEAD! The wraith HAD to be contained!"

"*YOU SWORE IT WAS GONE!*" she shouted back as she grabbed the bars of the cell and shook them so hard that the stones beneath them cracked. "*I DID NOT DESERVE TO BE SET ON FIRE – AND I DIDN'T DESERVE TO BE REBORN IN THAT MADNESS!*"

The scene repeated itself on her tunic. She lifted it up and held it proudly before him and forced him to watch. *The Commander of the 13 asked him if Daringol had been destroyed, and if Rmaci was clear of the influence. Akaran watched as he told her the truth: "The one in the guard was the one that was in her."*

When the Commander asked if she could be turned over for trial, he had replied, "In her shape...? No. I'll need time to make sure that Daringol is gone for good. I'm certain it is but..."

"THAT!" she screeched. "*YOU TOLD ME, YOU SAID!*"

"I DIDN'T KILL YOU! I TRIED TO STOP IT!"

Rmaci reached through the bars and shoved his face into her bloody stomach and rubbed his eye against the memory. *"DEATH IS DEATH,"* she argued at the top of her scorched lungs, *"IT'S WHAT YOU DID AFTER!"*

The scene repeated again, but went longer. *The Commander of the 13th flung a torch into the spy's oil-soaked cell. Rmaci got out one more coherent scream before the flames raced up her blanket. "AKARAN NO YOU -!" The next scream was of pure agony. Fire blossomed on her skin. What was left of her clothes had soaked up some of the oil, and even more had gotten in her hair. She was immolated within moments, screaming and slapping at the flames as they coursed over her skin.*

Akaran and the Commander argued as she screeched and tried to extinguish the blaze. He shouted at Rmaci's executioner, but didn't try – not even once – to stop the blaze. As they traded barbs about who had authority to do what, Rmaci burned.

By the time Commander left, the woman was already, mercifully, dead. Or so he had thought. The inferno-wreathed woman heard his edict as he left the room, and carried it with her as she descended into the darkness that awaited her soul. "Let it burn," he had told another jailer, "until it's nothing but ash."

Her spirit grabbed him by his throat and dangled him over the floor by one hand. *"YOU SAW THAT, YOU DID THAT,"* she accused. As he tried to protest, she shut him down with a question that was also a condemnation. *"And you never, ever, looked to see what happened after, did you."*

"You died. I had to deal with the rest of Daringol! The other wraiths and that *damned* Makolichi!" he retorted. "You were *dead* and to be sent to the... the Pyre of Everburning Flame. WHAT ELSE WAS I SUPPOSED TO DO?!"

"You were supposed to make sure I was purified! The wraith is still in you and you know it," Rmaci charged, then asked him the *one* question he hadn't thought of the entire time. *"I DIED WITHOUT THE WRAITH IN MY SOUL, SO HOW AM I DOING THIS!? HOW AM I IN YOUR HEAD?!"*

Akaran went slack and his eye went wide. "I... I don't know... I thought you weren't..." he slid out of her arms and slumped against the side of the cell. "I just... I thought... I knew Daringol still... but you? I thought... just... my mind playing tricks and..."

"You should've listened to that Mother-bitch," his tormentor spat. *"Let me show you what you missed."*

This time, the entire dream shifted again as places he *hadn't* been and things he *hadn't* seen started to appear one after another. He watched a couple of men scrape her blackened bones and ashes into a barrel. He saw them throw the corpse of the wraith-infested rapist on top of her. He watched as tendrils he missed, things he hadn't caught, seeped from one body into the other.

He watched the barrel be spat in. Saw someone pour a tankard of water into it to extinguish a few loose smoldering embers that had made her skull start to burn again. He watched as they laughed and mocked her corpse; he watched as they unceremoniously hauled her remains out of the dungeon and carried them off to the Pyre of Everburning Flame.

Their corpses were supposed to be thrown into the pyre where their bodies would've been blessed and purified and cleansed. Where any last vestiges of Daringol's influence would've been eradicated and their souls would have lost any remaining anchor to the mortal world. That was the point of the Pyres; to ensure that the dead never returned, that corruption within them would never translate to corruption out.

The idiots that delivered their bodies?

They dumped them in the pan of ashes beneath the pyre, and simply covered them up. They refused to give them the basic dignity offered to all men, all women, all children in the Kingdom no matter the sin. They desecrated their corpses, befouled the Pyre, defied the law, and let the bodies smolder.

He watched time leap forward. Saw people come and go without noticing what had happened or checking on the odd lump in the middle of the ashes. Saw people grieve for the fallen. Saw the wife of the jailer come offer curses and hatred.

Hatred that only fueled the last remaining wisps of the wraith.

Curses that helped give it life again.

Then he saw where she gained new life, and the moment that part of her essence was pulled back from damnation – and how it was absorbed by the wraith once more. He watched as a disgusting rat of a man sulked into the Pyre's plaza and scooped up ashes of the fallen. He made sure to take pieces from the only two relatively 'intact' corpses; Rmaci and the jailer both.

He watched as the wretch invoked the aura and will of the God of Rot to infuse the ashes and the scorched bits of flesh he had scavenged. Akaran watched as the remains were drenched in the blood of a lesser demon. He watched as this new aspect of Daringol was twisted and turned from its original purpose in death to serve as some kind of poison. To turn it into the start of a plague.

The priest was able to see the poison be placed upon a ship.

He watched as crewmen drank it.

He watched as the nesting wraith, once born as a way to absorb magic to hide the deeds of a wizard, be turned into a weapon with the intent of bringing untold suffering to the Kingdom. He watched it as it shuddered and screamed and suddenly lost nearly all the strength it possessed – a moment in time he assumed came when he banished the core spirit back into the open eternities – but it didn't get rid of all of it.

It didn't get rid of the parts that had formed from Rmaci's soul.

But for every soul it had absorbed, wherever it had absorbed them, those souls became part of the wraith's collective. It didn't matter if they died in Toniki, or died in Gonta, or died in places between, a soul marked by the wraith became part of the wraith. He saw the shadow begin to rise over a ship lost adrift in the sea, and in the middle of the wraith, he saw Rmaci's face. Just as lost, and screaming as loud as she had when the flames consumed her body.

"*You banished Daringol,*" she seethed, "*but you didn't get it out of you. Did you believe the episturine did when it cast you from Tundrala? Or didn't you realize that part of your punishment was to carry one of the beasts you pulled into the heavens back out with you? Hm? It's as locked away as your magic – locked inside your body. An unwilling guest rewarded to someone that was an unwelcome visitor where he should not have gone.*"

In his bed in the Manor, he thrashed and twisted. He already had an audience; the incident in the garden had brought them out of the woodwork. When he started screaming, Seline rushed to his side and tried to soothe him with calming words. Ridora helped tie him down so that he wouldn't hurt himself. Catherine soon followed and offered a prayer. It might have helped his flesh.

It did nothing for his mind. "It can't... NO. I BANISHED IT!"

"*No, you idiot child,*" she swore as she picked up a torch from the wall, "*you banished the soul that had bound it together.*"

"IT'S NOT POSSIBLE!"

"*Let me show you what's possible,*" Rmaci replied as she flung the blazing stick into the cell. "*because you didn't destroy it.*"

Flames raced through the room and surged up his body. He screamed in agony as the fire boiled his blood, blackened his skin, and roasted his bones. "RMACI PLEASE DON'T DO THIS STOP PLEASE!"

She watched him burn with a delighted smile on her melted lips.

"*You didn't destroy Daringol. All you did was let me take over.*"

EPILOGUE
Lithdis, the 18ᵗʰ of Riverswell, 513 QR

Dawn had yet to crest over the safest city in the kingdom.

It would not be a good day. A couple madly in love frolicked under the cover of night on the shores of Avagerona's Rest, doing what young couples often did in the dark on sandy shores. It was the only time that Malik and Hylene could get away from their handlers. Their cries of passion would soon become cries of terror and indignant anger when a head would float up next to them.

Just a head.

The body would sink. Weighed down by weapons and armor, it didn't stand a chance of making it to the beach. The head would do to send a message, Donta decided. *You were seen*, it would say, *and you are known, but you have an ally*. That was the message. Or at least, he hoped.

If not, it was another way to sow discord in the city. Discord made it easier to get people to talk. It always did. When people feel threatened, they often developed loose lips if they thought if what they had to say would keep them protected.

And who knows? It might. People are foolish when afraid.

But it wasn't the only message. Just the first.

One of Henderschott's men would pound on the door to Medias's manor. He held a message of his own; a letter direct from the Lieutenant-Commander himself. An arrest will have been made in the death of Livstra, Adept Odern, and a few other unnamed and too-insignificant to mention vagabonds. A plot had been uncovered, the letter would claim, and another body had been found.

The guard would give Lady Ridora the news that Priestess Lexcanna Jealions had been murdered in the same manner as Livstra and Odern – her head crushed and her body mangled beyond hope. There were additional injuries and wounds, too. Wounds magical in nature, and ones that would have been enough to kill her on her own.

As Ridora would listen in horror, Seline would wander by. She would hear the soldier continue to explain that they had found someone hunched over her body. A drunk. A soldier himself, a battlemage on leave from the 13th. He'd been arrested and charged, and had spent the last hour begging for one of Ridora's residents to come help him.

He'd claim he was his friend.

A claimed that would largely be ignored.

The guard would continue to explain that they had found evidence linking the Mother Eclipsian to the death, and that the battlemage was her newest consort. She was missing, and since one of Ridora's servants had a sister in Erine's little cult, maybe she knew where to find her? Or knew where Raechil herself was, so they could find her sister? She'd been released from custody a day prior, and now she was missing.

A search later would result in even more panic – Raechil was missing, too. They'd find was blood in her room. A lot of it.

The third message sent that night was written in the same. While Cassanol's head sent the first, his body was the spark that lit the third. The currents in the lake sent his weighted corpse tumbling towards the statue of Aqualla in the bay.

A sunken box tied to one of the tendrils below the water by a piece of old iron chain started to pulsate as his body floated near. A small cloud of bloody mist brushed against it as fish and crabs began to enjoy their new feast.

As the blood touched it, a word began to glow. A name. Moira.

Moments later, the Mace of Insanity's Rapture began to do the same.

It wasn't in the city that the worst part of the day was to be had.

It wouldn't even be had by the living.

Far off of Dawnfire's prosperous shores, far past the horizon, the *Q.R.W. Hullbreaker* floated aimlessly in the Alenic Ocean. The deck was barren, quiet; no crew left standing to man the rigging, the helm, or even to gaze upon the starry sky above. Nor was there a single bird to be seen for miles around. As unnaturally quiet as it was outside, what was below deck defied imagination.

There, however, it was anything but quiet – if you knew how to listen.

The bodies were still, covered in blisters and sores. Their skin had begun to rot weeks past; the saltwater in the air had done little to help keep them fresh. A seagull's corpse languished on one of the bodies, the same malady that had ruined the sailors having done the same to the bird. For most, there was only the sound of creaking boards and loosely-rolling heads.

But if you knew how to listen, you could hear the crying.

You could hear the cry for warmth.

You could hear the cry for help.

You could hear the cry as a multitude of souls that acted as one thrashed in the ether above the bodies. You could hear them as they tried to understand why they couldn't *leave*, why they couldn't go *home*, why they couldn't find *warmth*, why they didn't feel *complete* like part of them had been utterly *broken* and why they felt like other parts had been scattered to the wind. Why the part of them that should have been holding them together was far away and they knew where to go but they couldn't *get* there.

They were *there* and they could *feel* the lost parts but those parts were *trapped* somewhere and *these parts* were trapped on this ship with these empty bodies. They couldn't make the shells *move* and they couldn't make them *warm* no matter how much they thrashed inside the rotting flesh.

They couldn't understand that when they lost their core, they had lost their power. They could poison. They could kill. They could rot. They could bring ruin.

But they couldn't move and they couldn't find warmth.

And they couldn't *understand* why they were trapped in this *nightmare*.

This *nightmare* where they kept hearing *his* voice. The voice of the man that *hurt* them so much. They heard *him* scream and they screamed back at *him* and they felt *him* writhe in pain in *his* nightmares. They heard one of *their* voices taunting and talking to him but they couldn't let her know they were *here* either.

Their only solace was knowing he suffered too.

They were trapped in rotting shells, on a rotting boat, waiting to be sunk to the bottom of the sea, where it would spend eternity. They knew it, too. They didn't *understand* but they *knew* that they were screaming without hope that anyone would hear.

Except for the man that did.

The man that stepped onto the deck from a sizzling crack in the air.

The man that had heard, that had listened, and that had decided the best use of this ship of the damned wasn't to spread a plague of souls. That was the intent of the feeble-minded fools that had cursed them – to spread them like a plague. To honor his God and infect people, innocent people, with a disease that couldn't be treated by modern medicine.

By one fool, the intent was to spread them through the people. Undermine the Kingdom of Dawnfire. Hurt people in the name of the Civan Empire. To use it as a weapon to sow discord. To get revenge for the death of a spy in the City of Mud. By the other, it was just a cruelty that would be a cause of celebration at the feet of the Rotbringer.

Instead, the men that had schemed had failed to do more than condemn a ship of sailors to a madness that everyone thought was already put to rest. Except he'd done something worse. It was fate. Or luck. Or a random occurrence.

But it was still worse.

The screaming drew the notice of someone that knew how to listen. The someone that stood on the bow of the ship and heard them. He made a decision quickly. The *Hullbreaker* wouldn't be used to spread a plague.

It was going to be used to draw attention. The souls trapped below would still be trapped, though trapped in service instead of trapped under the waves. It was going to be used to draw attention away from his interests. It would be used to make life easier on Anais and Donta – if they paid attention. It would be a change in fate.

A fate different than the one that these damned souls deserved.

A fate that one could argue was worse.

His work wouldn't take long. The souls were going to be bound to his will. The ship was going to be given direction. A sailor would be *somewhat* resurrected and given a posthumous promotion to captain. They would be given instructions. They would be put on Moria's scent to guide them where they needed to go.

The ship would have direction. The souls would have purpose.

His purpose. If they succeeded? He'd release them to do what they wanted to do. He knew *whom* held their lost leader. From the sound of their cries, he assumed it was in the same general direction.

They wanted to go somewhere; that was how he heard them. That's why he paid attention. They wanted to go to the coast, and he had interests near the coast. The wraiths were simple in thought and base in desire, and did not resist his promises that they could get what they wanted if only they listened.

They agreed.

When he was done, he would step back into the crack in the air. He would gather the creatures he needed to gather. He would collect his most favored acolyte. He would go and offer a simple deal to the Hall of Tide's Song at the village of Mardux. He would continue his trip that he had planned before being interrupted by the screaming fit in the ether. If nothing else, this would make them shut up.

They might have gotten there anyway. Their frustrated screams and constant thrashing would've slowly but surely darkened the aura around the ship. It would've slowly but surely started to turn the ether. It would have slowly but surely encouraged them to travel. Or maybe the parts of the spirit that were elsewhere would find a way to them. Anyone corrupted by it would be *compelled* to rejoin the bulk of the mass. They would have to travel, and they would seek it out, and they would congregate.

Eventually. Maybe sooner, maybe later. It was a promise.

Anyone bearing Daringol's corruption *would* be attracted to other hosts.

All of that said, there was another truth. One that the necromancer realized without any disbelief. The other truth was that he knew his brother would let their arrival go unpunished. That was fine. Silence them, and put them to work at the same time. Test his brother by blood; see how long it took the one-eyed idiot to cast them back to the pit where they belonged.

Maybe even give the half-blind fool something to do. Otherwise, it was hard to say if he might show up while the man wearing the blood-red robe worked his other interests and engaged in a planned *discussion* with the Aquallans. It even saved him from ordering his indentured employees from having to put an eye on the priest. This made it was a win all the way around. If you knew him, that wasn't uncommon.

The Man of the Red Death would get what he wanted.

Because he always did.

As for the *Hullbreaker*? It now had a part to play. One critical, but short. Basion City. The safest place in the Kingdom, as it has been said.

Port Cableture, however, has *no* such reputation.

End:
Saga of the Dead Men Walking
Insanity's Respite

Next:
Saga of the Dead Men Walking:
Insanity's Rapture

COMPENDIUM OF THE DAMNED, THE DIVINE, AND ALL THINGS IN-BETWEEN

2nd Naval Fleet/Armada
The 2nd Naval Armada serves as the backbone for the Kingdom's defense of her southern shores and assists the 1st and 3rd Naval Armadas with anti-pirate activities that threaten trade between the Kingdom, Ogibus, and western Matheia.

3rd Imperium War
481 – 497 QR. The third major all-out conflict between the Kingdom of Dawnfire and the Civan Empire. By far, the bloodiest of the three. The war begins over the accidental death of Princess Aveve of Civa at the Concords of Woulofon, and only ends when the City of A'Twol is destroyed in Sycio in an unrelated series of horrible incidents.

4th Garrison
The 4th Garrison is assigned to the safety of Kettering Province. The actual 4th Garrison Outpost is located in Cableture. Inside Basion City, the local control is under Lieutenant-Commander Henderschott.

(The) Abyss
The last stop. The end. The lower part of eternity, and the last place you want to be.

(The) Auramancer Exorcist, Bistra Enil
Admitted to Medias Manor in 510 QR, Bistra has suffered a collapse of her mind, and full recovery has seemed to be completely impossible. Prior, she was one of the most exalted Exorcists in the Order of Love.

Annamelia's Leather and Waving
A tannery near the Grand Temple of Love, and the primary source for leathers used by the Order.

Aquallans
Followers of Aqualla, the God of Water.

Avagerona's Rest
A small lake at the base of the Orshia-Avagerona Falls.

Avagerona Shallows
An area in the north-east of Basion City where the Avagerona River spreads out into a localized floodplain before pouring down into Yittl Canyon.

Baronessa Hylene Tessamirch, the Golden Baronessa
Beloved by everyone, Hylene is adored above and beyond any of the other nobility of Basion, and above and beyond most nobility in Kettering Province as a whole.

Basion Annex Rune Vault
The Rune Vault holds a plethora of runes, gem, and other magical items designed to provide some kind of magical influence on an object, area, person, or other.

Basion City
The provincial capital for the Kettering Provincial Region, Basion City is often referred to as the "Safest Place in the Kingdom." Boasting a population of more than thirty-thousand souls, it is the largest city in Kettering by far. Despite being in a natural basin, the natural flow of the Orshia-Avagerona River and Yittl Canyon allow for flooding to stay at a minimum, while the basin provides extra protection. In the last three-hundred years, no war has ever managed to breach her upper lip, nor scale down the two-hundred some-odd foot drop from the edges of the basin.

Basin City is broken up into several different districts. Akkador East covers the main gateway to the city and houses the local Guard barracks and hosts several mercenary groups (including the Hunter's Guild). Akkador West is the main line of merchants and the main trading hub to the outside world.

Piapat District is the center-most, and here you will find most of the tradesmen's guilds and where almost all of the local city industry is worked. Along the southwestern wall, you'll find Orshia Overflow and Lower Naradol District where the poor gather and the city slums in general. Upper Naradol isn't much better, but it's more middle-class than not – and it's also the starting point for the Wall of Gardens.

Along the northernmost wall, the Orshia-Avagerona River flows into the city and Avagerona's Rest before it flows through the city. West and East Giffil Districts hold the merchant-masters and city officials (respectively) while West Giffil is home to the Granalchi Annex.

On the eastern wall, between East Giffil and Akkador East, the Chiadon District is another residential region that caters to the priestly minded. Here you can find the Repository of Miral, the Ellachurstine Chapel, and the local Temple of Stara.

Bearer's Guild
A loose affiliation of transporter companies that handle shipments and transports inside and outside of Basion City. Their influence doesn't expand past Kettering Province. There's a rumor that they employ trolls...

Betrothed
A Maiden's Betrothed oversees the entirety of the civilian governance in a province. They serve as the chief judiciary officer, they confirm any Merchant-Masters or Overseers, they are responsible for ensuring that taxes are collected, and other infrastructure tasks. They can be overruled by the Provincial Maiden, but are generally left to their own devices. Contrary to their title, they are not necessarily married to their Maidens, and the title is one more of reverence and statehood than it is countryside-faithful.

Castle Woulofon
Located in Imaii Province, it was once a grand spectacle to behold. After an unfortunate fire, and the war the fire sparked, it has become little more than a haunted ruin.

Celebration of the Origin
A celebration of the new year, and it occurs the first week of the spring season, typically on the 1st of Firstgrow.

(The) Cherished Atonement
A tavern in West Giffil, known for entertaining priests, pages, and those with more of a holy bent than other crowds.

City Overseer
A duty sometimes shared with the local Merchant-Master, the Overseer acts as a local Governor for the city they're installed in.

Cocasa

A plant with medicinal properties. It can dull pain and soothe the mind, but it is also incredibly addictive. Users report having less control over magic, an increase of feelings of paranoia, anxiety, and oddly, slightly increased strength.

Collectors
When the Granalchi make a mess, Collectors clean it up. Using any, and usually every, means possible.

Commander of the 13th Garrison's
The 13th Garrison is assigned to protect and patrol the Weschali Provincial Region. At the end of 512 QR, the duty was held by Commander Evalia Wodoria.

Comstead Hall
A large banquet hall used for celebrations in Basion City, under the firm hand of Madam Comstead.

Concords of Woulofon
The Concords were supposed to be a permanent peace treaty between the Civan Empire and the Kingdom of Dawnfire. An accidental fire resulted in the death of Princess Aveve, and the riot that followed turned into the 3rd Imperium War.

Consort-Blade Leadir
Leadir is Maiden Esterveen's bodyguard, assassin, and enforcer. A talented murderer, he's not someone to willingly jump into a fight with.

Danse Festistanis
A celebration observed for "Unions of Great Importance." Typically only attended by the high and mighty of the Kingdom. Smaller dances sometimes pop up that everyone can attend.

Episturine
Minions of Istalla, they defend Her home of Tundrala at any and all cost.

Exorcist
In this world, evil things exist and the dead do not always rest. Exorcists from the Order of Love are given tasks three: To help the souls that can be salvaged find peace; To release the souls that are cursed to walk of volition not of their own; And to condemn the ones that should not have been allowed to see the light of day.

Exorcist's Field Guide
A list of instructions, Words, Wards, notes, descriptions, and other information used by Exorcists in the Order of Love

Faegoli's Bog
The Abyssian realm of the Plaguebringer, the Rotbringer, the God of Decay.

Fel'achir Forest
A huge forest that covers Kettering, the edges of Lowmarsh, Mulvette, and spreads east past the edge of the Orshia-Avagerona River, the Fel'achir serves as everything from a natural barrier to a source of fresh timber to a hunting ground and more.

(The) Fleetfinger's Guild
The Guild of Thieves in Basion City, run by a council of criminals and overseen by Liona Reanage.

Gem of Nullification
A magical gem that has the ability to absorb or neutralize the effects of magic in a localized area.

Geomancer
An elementalist that specializes in manipulating the ground, rocks, dirt, and the like.

Granalchi Annex
Granalchi Annexes are colleges where the Grand Library isn't. Study, learn, experiment, join the Granalchi or hire an Adept – at an Annex, you can do just about anything if you set your mind (and will... or coinpurse) to it.

Grand Temple of Love
Located in Mulvette Province, the Grand Temple was established in 296 QR by Mother Adrianne. In addition to serving as the home for all worship for the Order of Love, it also holds Love's Academy – a training ground for exorcists, templars, paladins, and priests of all stripe in the Order. The Sisters of Love reside here, and Holy General Johasta Fire-Eyes has her primary office there. The 1ˢᵗ Garrison and the Office of the Army is located nearby.

Holy Brazier of Eternal Light and Purity
A giant gold and copper brazier that is ever-burning, even when smoldering, and is considered a beacon of light in the darkness no matter what.

Hunter's Guild
The premiere mercenary guild in the world, the Hunter's Guild is established in every territory you can find society – and a few places where you can't.

Isamiael, Goddess of Medicine and Health

Revered by physicians of any stripe, of any Order, of every Kingdom, the Goddess of Medicine is one of the most popular of all of the Gods. Her Order, the Order of the Hand, works in subtle ways to bring health and healing to all those who need it.

Istalla, the Queen of Ice
Goddess of Ice, and ruler of the Upper Elemental Plane of Tundrala.

Keps / Crowns / Patong / Evane / Diandra
The currency of Dawnfire. 10 Keps = 1 Crown, 10 Crowns = 1 Patong, 10 Patongs = 1 Evane, 10 Evanes = 1 Diandra.

Koik
Silver coins with a crow's feather. The currency from the Midlands.

Laws of Normality
The laws governing non-magical phenomena in the world.

Loophole
A window slit in a fortress that is just wide enough to aim a bow through.

(A) Lover
A member of the Order of Love; a priest, an exorcist, a templar, a paladin, or someone with a bare minimum of training in executing Her will.

Lowmarsh Province
Lowmarsh borders the Missian League to the north of Kettering Province, and is the official start of Dawnfire's control of the Orshia-Avagerona River. The province is overseen by Maiden Lianna DeNagen and her Betrothed, Martin Stalniker. The provincial capital can be found in Elsarch.

Lythrivol
The language of the dead and damned.

Maiden / Provincial Maiden / Maiden-Templar
A Maiden is a title granted to a select few leaders in the Kingdom. Their words are law, and are often placed in charge of the Queen's primary interests, notably her armed forces. Most armies would call them "Generals" or "Admirals," but they are both more than that and less. Military-tasked Maidens answer directly to the Holy General Johasta Fire-Eyes, while any other Maiden (few as they are) speak directly to the Queen herself. Each military Company is assigned a Maiden as a matter of course.

Maiden-Templar Catherine Prostil

An Order of Love Templar, and currently controls the Repository of Miral.

Maiden Sanlian Esterveen
Maiden of Kettering Province. Rarely interferes in civilian manners, and is only concerned with rooting out corruption wherever she can find it in the ranks of the military. That said, Kettering Province rarely has a threat in it, so most of her time is spent lounging about and complaining about her Betrothed's drinking habits.

Makaral
The God of War.

Malik Odinal, aka the Bastard of Odinal
Malik is the son of Warlord Nemok Odinal, one of the unaligned tribal leaders along the southern edges of the Midland wastes. He is destined to be a great leader of his peoples. His mother is of Civan decent, which only fosters the hatred some people in Dawnfire have for his lineage.

Man of the Red Death
Very little about him is known. He interfered in the Coldstone Incident, killing several people and maiming Mariah-Anne for no reason that has yet been discerned.

Melia, Lady of Destruction and Reformation, the Queen of Ashes
The Goddess of Destruction and Reformation. Estranged sister of Illiya, and Matron Goddess of the Kingdom of Dawnfire.

Melian Deconstructionist
An upper-level priest in the Order of Destruction and Reformation; Melian worshiper.

Merchant-Master / Overseer Notif Hannock
Notif Hannock is the Blackstone-Trading Company appointed Merchant-Master and Overseer for Basion City.

Merchant-Master Tos Eran
Tos Eran is, like Hannock, both the Merchant-Master and Overseer for Port Cableture.

Mulvette Province
The capital provincial region of Dawnfire, and the seat of power for the Queen. The Queen's Capitol, the Grand Temple of Love, the Great Dawnfire Annex of the Granalchi, the chief Guild Office for the Southern Hunter's Guild, the Master

Tower of the Blackstone Traders and more can be found here.

Nia'valth, the Dreamer, Demi-Goddess of Dreams and Nightmares, the Valth, the Nightmarion and Nia, Daysteed, the Twin of One
Much like Her mother, Lethandria, Nia'valth is one of the most powerful Gods of the Abyss who doesn't actually reside in the pit. While most realms of dual-nature exist separately in the Upper and Lower, Nia'valth is one entity that can manifest in three different forms – either as Nia, as Valth, or as Nia'valth combined. One person's dream is another person's nightmare, after all...

Nayli
A horse that Order of Love Exorcist Akaran DeHawk found and adopted in Toniki. She did not enjoy the trip by boat from Gonta to Cableture, and has spent most of her time being cared for by various stable boys at Medias Manor while he recovers.

Neph'kor, the Rotbringer, God of Decay
The God of Rot and Decay. One of the most repulsive beings in the world... in any world. He is said to have a special hatred for things that cannot rot, and often can be found in conflict with the Heavenly realms.

Niasmis, Goddess of Love
Banished from Her rightful place next to the top of the Mount of Heaven by the other Gods and Goddess for an infraction against the Goddess of Flame that She truthfully is not guilty of, the Goddess of Love is considered by nearly everyone to be the least of the Divine, and as such, holds power only in the lowest regions of the Heavens, and... well... ...She has a bit of a chip on Her shoulder because of it...

Niasmis's Three: Miral, the Guardian of Love
Miral is one of the three Archangels of Love, and is the patron saint of Her paladins, exorcists, and any that take up a sword in Her name.

Odinal Tribe, aka, the Whoretribe of the Midland
Despite what the locals to Basion are calling it, the Odinal Wartribe is one of the strongest, and most stable, of the Midland factions. Considered slightly less barbaric than some of the other clans, their sphere of influence covers the southwestern edge of the Equalin Mountains.

Offices of the Dean
The head offices of the Grand Granalchi Library, overseen by The First Orbit, the Understudies of the Arcane, and the Grand Dean-Adept.

Ogibus Bay
A chain of three islands in the Alenic Ocean, and home to a seafaring Kingdom.

Order of the Hand
Followers of the Goddess Isamiael, they practice medicine anywhere and everywhere there is need.

Order of Love (Oo-lo)
Followers of the Goddess Niasmis. They are the only Order to operate a school specifically to hunt and destroy the minions of the Abyss – instructions divinely ordained and aggressively carried out.

(The) Origin
The God of all Gods. The Faceless One, the Alpha. His realm is high above the rest of the Pantheon, and the River of All Souls flows from his feet.

Orshia-Avagerona River
The Orshia-Avagerona River is a major waterway that starts as a series of underground streams and overground tributaries in the Equalin Mountains and flows through Lowmarsh Province where it gains steam and thunders down through Dawnfire, effectively splitting the Kingdom as it flows out into the Alenic Ocean. The Orshia splits in two once it hits Basin City at the Orshia Falls, with the Orshia River flowing through the western side of the walls before pooling into the Orshia Overflow and vanishing underground. The Avagerona river follows east, then goes south into Yittl Canyon.

Orshia Overflow
A lake in the south-western portion of Basion City. The Orshia River pools here before disappearing underground.

Paladin-Commander
One of the highest ranks attainable in the military arm of the Order of Love. They answer directly to either their provincial Maiden, or to the Holy General.

Paladin-Commander Steelhom
Mentor and father figure to Exorcist Akaran DeHawk. For some unexplained reason, his notes can be found in nearly every entry chronicling the events of the Age of Misfortune, under the name Sir Steelhom, Office of Oversight, New Civa – a title he doesn't have and a place that doesn't exist in 513 QR. Chronomancy... it's a headache.

Panidillic
Capital of Imall Province, west of Lowmarsh

(The) Pantheon
The Gods of the Heavens.

Paralidrieam
A type of nightmare that involves feelings of paralysis, shrouded figures, terror, and hallucinations.

Para psiphonic
Transferring magic from one person to another.

Priestess of Stara
A speaker for the Order of Stara and frequently for the Order of Light. They answer to Lumina, the Demi-Goddess of Stars, the Lightbringer. While the Order of Light oversees and aids the worshipers of any God or Goddess of the Pantheon, the Order of Stara communes directly with Lumina herself. The Order of Light answers to them.

Princess Aveve
A princess of Civa. Her accidental death in a fire at Castle Woulofon resulted in the 3rd Imperium War.

Pristi's Gate
The entrance to the Heavenly Mount, and the realm where Pristi holds court.

Pristi, Goddess of Purity
The Gatekeeper. The Guardian of the Mount of Heavens, the Crystal Goddess has no patience for anything other than perfection, and considers those that are not as beneath Her.

Port Cableture
More of a military outpost than an actual city, Port Cableture is home to around six thousand of the Queen's citizens, and another five thousand members of the Queen's Navy. Port Cableture serves as the home for the 2nd Naval Armada.

Purgalaito
The language of the Pantheon. Most, but not all, of the Holy Orders use it in their spellworks.

Queen's Army
The Grand Army of the Dawn.

Queen's Capitol
The seat of the Queen's power in Dawnfire. Located in Mulvette, it isn't just one palace. It's a slew of them in an entire complex that is grander than one would

assume it needs to be. The people that assume such things, of course, are not as sophisticated as the Queen. They are, however, likely more humble.

Queen's Law
The Law of the Queen and the Law of the Land. All Agents of the Crown are beholden to see that it is upheld in any situation and at all times. Justiciars are responsible for passing judgment on disputes regarding the law or to punish offenders.

Queen's Royal Wavecrasher (Q. R. W.) Hullbreaker
A military transport ship carrying a shipment of sylverine destined for the capital of Dawnfire. It departed Gonta in mid-Hearthbreak, and hasn't been seen since. It is believed to be lost at sea.

Raechil Lamar
One of the aids of Medias Manor.

Reformed Order (of Love)
After the Order of Love was effectively destroyed by the Hardening, Mother Adrianne re-established the Order nine years later, and rebuilt it from the very Tenants and up. After a century, the Order lost the 'reformed' moniker, as nobody was left alive to remember what it used to be prior to her efforts.

Repository of Miral
The Repository serves as a library, a vault, and a pit of secrets for the Order of Love. Not much is known about the inner workings of the outpost, but it is just that: a military outpost. One of the most heavily guarded locations that the Order of Love directly owns, it is believed that any record of any encounter the Order has eventually winds up buried somewhere in the sprawling hallways and chambers underground.

Rise of Queen Dannivette
The story of the 1ˢᵗ Queen of Dawnfire, practiced, embellished, and gotten horribly wrong over almost five centuries. The proctors at the Grand Temple of Love think that it's a wonderful story for the children to act out, and they force all of the students in the Temple to watch them to offer their support.

Rishnobia
A vile little beast, a mote of a demon, and the 'favored acolyte' of the Man of the Red Death.

River Solindal
The River of All Souls. It flows from the feet of the Origin and through the entirety of eternity.

Rmaci
A Civan spy who worked tirelessly in Toniki to uncover the secrets of Usaic's work. A liar, a thief, an adulteress, and a murderess to boot – she came to a very bad end in Gonta. Her current plane of residence is believed to be Frosel, the Lower Elemental Plane of Ice.

Runes of Alloyance
A specialty of the Granalchi, Runes of Alloyance can modify the base properties of an object they are in direct contact with. A word could gain the ability to ignite at will, for example, or a silk gown could develop a surface strength of cold iron. They are expensive, they are difficult to manage, and they do not last forever.

(The) Sands
The World immediately beyond the Veil. The sands expand for eternity, with only the Abyss behind them and the Heavens in front of them. Known for nothing but bright blue cloudless skies and sand that is abrasive (if you are destined for damnation) or soft (if you are destined for heaven). Other than that, for all that mortal men know, the Sands are a great nothingness.

Scriptures of Geshalda
A truncated version of the Affirmations of the Covetous. Geshalda craves more of everything, and thus, required two tomes of Her words.

Seal of Order
A restriction handed down by the Order of Love preventing certain documents, information, reports, or experiences from being repeated to those that don't need to hear it.

(The) Second Queen of Dawnfire
Daniia Mulvette, who ruled from 300 to 379 QR. She is responsible for a great deal of the Kingdom's growth, defenses, and infrastructure.

Seline Valdin
A healer in Medias Manor. Though a follower of the Goddess Niasmis, she doesn't have a great understanding of the workings of the Order.

Shiverdine
The polite title for 'slaver' in Sycio. As slavery isn't strictly forbidden in Dawnfire, you can find them from time to time in larger cities and provinces, usually hunting for prisoners that the Crown would like to get rid of.

Signostica of Stara

A symbol showing rank in the Order of Stara. The Signostica is a clear vial with four materials inside, each separated by a thin layer of resin. Ash at the bottom (representing the lives of those that come before us), topped by soil (representing where life begins), topped by sand (representing the Eternal Sands), and then empty air (representing the distance a soul is from the Heavens). The vial I sealed with a tar plug (representing the way we are trapped to this world).

Sisters of Love
Seers, priestesses, soothsayers – it's hard to say exactly what the Sisters are. The only thing that's known for certain is that they hear whispers on the wind, and their words are to be followed at any cost.

Solinal, God of Peace
Solinal oversees the Ascent to the Heavens, and is tasked to help unburden souls of whatever weight that may be on their shoulders as they prepare to pass through Pristi's Gates at the top of the Heavenly Realms.

Southern Midlands
The southern side of the Midland Wastes/Equalin Mountain region. Generally hospitable, the Odinal Wartribe exerts control over most of it, much to the chagrin of a few other nomad groups.

Stilamatheric, The Stonehewn
The God of Orcs, Dwarves, Goblins, and anything that crawls underground.

Syicdac
The common language of Sycio.

Sycio
The continent across the Alenic Ocean to the southwest of Dawnfire. The north-eastern region is believed to be the only inhabitable territory... and it's a desert. The rest, or so travelers say, is impassible jungle and mountains.

Sylverine
An ore that is known to amplify magical properties.

Thesd Estate
Recently owned by Winslex Thesd, he offered the entire estate to Lady Anais Lovic a few days after her arrival in Basion City. The why is unknown, but he decided to move towards Ogibus Bay after she expressed an interest in it.

Thravstil

A very rich, flavorful, and often pungent red wine. A skilled alchemist could hide all manner of herbal concoctions in it if they tried.

Tiaxadin
A small township in Kettering Province.

Tidesinger Quinchecco
Tidesinger Quinchecco is the high priest of Aqualla for the Hall of Sea's Song in Mardux. As his Order routinely cares for the waters of the Orshia-Avagerona in and around Basion, he's frequently seen inside the city and is considered local nobility for all intents and purposes.

Toniki
A village in the far east of Dawnfire, this otherwise unremarkable frozen pile of rocks was the site of what is now being referred to as the "Coldstone Incident."

Tundrala
The upper elemental plane of ice, a plane on the Mount of Heaven. Istalla, the Queen of Ice, holds sway here.

Underwars
A series of battles between the Crystal Kingdoms and the subterranean race of the Damians.

Undlajunct
Priests in the Temple of Light/Order of Stara that are of lower rank than Ladjuncts.

(The) Union of Bankers, aka the Uob
The Uob operates in slight contention with the Blackstone Trading Company. They provide financial services to anyone and everyone willing to pay interest. They are primarily focused in Dawnfire, and primarily in the Mulvette, Imaii, and Kettering Provinces.

Usaic's Cabin
A nondescript cabin in the woods around Toniki that held the path to Usaic's Tower... and secrets that nearly ended the world.

Valina Gorosoch
Daughter of Telburn and Elsith Gorosoch, born 506 QR.

(The) Veil
The fabric of ether that separates the mortal world from the Worlds Beyond, and it prevents those worlds from crashing into each other.

Wedding of Dusk and Dawn
The talk of the town, the celebration to end all celebrations, or the worst disaster ever to strike the province. It's the wedding of Malik Odinal, from the Odinal Wartribes in the Midlands to the Golden Baronessa, Hylene Tessamirch.

Weschali Province
The easternmost provincial region of the Kingdom of Dawnfire. It holds immense strategic value to the Kingdom, as the primary passageway through the Equalin Mountains between the Kingdom of Dawnfire and the Civan Empire. Among other villages and cities, it encompasses Anthor's Pass, Triefragur, Gonta, and Toniki. It is under the direct oversight of Maiden Piata and her Consort.

Woodmason's Guild
Much like the Mason's Guild, the Woodmasons serve as carpenters, woodworkers, and artists throughout the Kingdom.

Worlds Beyond Worlds aka the Worlds of Others
The planes of existence past the mortal plane where Gods dwell.

Writs
Writs are the lifeblood of the Hunter's Guild. They are legal contracts issued by the Guild with permissions from the regional judiciary that allow a Huntsman to carry out a contract to the extent that the law allows. A Writ of Investigation is to determine who, or what, or where, or when something was done; a Writ of Naming to secure the name of a person who did it (if applicable). A Writ of Execution is a legally-authorized assassination contract.

Wveld-weed
A decorative plant with green vines and red flower buds. It only grows in the presence of ilmalcium, a toxic mineral. The weed is known to have a calming effect on damned spirits, although decades have study have never revealed why.

Yittl Canyon
A ten mile long canyon that connects Basion City to Port Cableture. The walls of the canyon scale between ten feet at the lowest mouth and around two-hundred feet where it meets the entrance to Basion City.

THE MAGE'S HANDBOOK OF SPELLS, INVOCATIONS, AND OTHER FLASHY EFFECTS

Invocations

Naffin, naffin, Almed Isamiael; vetchins takint uldas beneal
"Please, please, Goddess Isamiael; bones mend bodies heal."
- A healing spell that invokes the Goddess Isamiael to mend minor and moderate wounds. It can be invoked by most priests or healers in the Orders of Light, as Isamiael lends Her ability across the pantheon. That said, healers themselves must have appropriate training to mingle calls to the Divine that aren't their own patron/matron.

Almed Isamiael, Almed Isamiael, rodel solin rodel lumin rodel nia rodel kayba'a proppa!
"Goddess Isamiael, Goddess Isamiael, bring peace bring light bring love bring pain's anathema!"
- A healing spell that invokes the Goddess Isamiael to mend difficult, stubborn, or otherwise grievous wounds. This invocation requires both a devotion to Isamiael and an understanding of how medical-based magic works.

Eberenth, aiy covax proshadi; Eberenth, aiy covax stensavi; Eberenth aiy covax mastadi ya al zalbat.
"Eberenth, please grant sight; Eberenth, please grant understanding; Eberenth, please grant confusion to the ignorant."
- Invokes the Goddess of Knowledge. Enables translations, but does the opposite if the person reading it has no connection to Eberenth, or if the person is not a seeker of knowledge.

"Washer of Souls, may Your breath calm the turbulent, may Your touch soothe

the chaos of the Mind."
- *A spell written in Queen's Common, instead of the typical purgalaito. This invocation to Solinal is designed to inspire peaceful presence and mindfulness.*

"Trespass against the lost and Love will trespass against you."
- *An invocation that screams a warning to the damned from the Goddess of Love. It's less of a 'spell' as it is a 'blatant threat with Divine ramifications.'*

Granalchi-Taught Spells
Donola... donola... donola-CHA
- *This spell summons a bolt of lightning that is both violent (against the subject) and taxing (from the caster). This is considered an ether-kenetic spell.*

Isava, annoia, castata
- *This casts an etheric net over a subject to help either visually display the ether around them or to help contain someone or something. This is considered an ether-kenetic spell.*

Pheknit
- *A spell that causes a buildup of air-pressure around a subject. This spell is considered mattanic in nature, but is also used by elementalists.*

Edsfion
- *A spell that channels ether into another object in a stable fashion, both charging the receiving subject or draining it from the emitting subject. This is an ether-kenetic spell*

Instada
A word used to make sure a spell effect only targets the caster.

Words or Wards
Enlidoam
- *Light dome of privacy and protection. This is a Word used by Templars in the Order of Love.*

Distruvas-Instada
A disruption spell. Interferes with channeling ether. Mostly used by Order Templars, but sometimes used by other magic wielders. A similar spell is used by ether-kenetics from the Academy.

Instabilisist Spells
Manabomb
A short-lived, explosive, ball of mana that detonates either on direct contact or after a few moments of landing (depending on the type of bomb) causing

explosive-style damage.

Shadowbomb
A short-lived ball of shadows that explodes on contact with the target, but instead of causing physical maladies, it intensely disrupts the magical aura of the victim; this either drains their ability to use magic outright or inflicts lethal damage to their aura.

Magic and the Granalchi Academy
The Granalchi Academy has spent centuries developing themselves as the one and only licensed sources of practitioners of the *Grand Allegiance of Schools of Ether-kenetics*. In short, if you plan to study or use magic (let alone make a profit from it), you ally yourself with the Granalchi Academy. The rare school that appears outside of their control never lasts more than a few years before they inexplicably shut down. The only other option is to follow one of the Divine Gods and be taught through priestly studies – but divine magic and any type of ether-kenetics are two different beasts.

Magic is broken down into six schools. In order to use magic of that discipline, you first need to have an affinity for it (born into it) and then trained to master it. It's entirely possible to have an affinity for two or more types of magic; but the broader your affinity, the harder you need to work to control it.

Granalchi identify themselves by a disk that they wear on their necks with six circular paths (orbits) that have gemstones on each path depicting what school and sub-school they are a student or teacher of.

The schools and their corresponding sub-schools and identifying gemstones are as follows:

Magical Schools
1st School: *Elementalists* – Water, Fire, Land, Air (Aquamarine, Ruby, Amber, Sapphire)
2nd School: *Ambianists* – Light, Dark, Aura (Diamond, Onyx, Opaline)
3rd School: *Psyanists* – Illusion, Psychic, Dream, Emotional (Pearl, Fluorite, Zircon, Bloodstone)
4th School: *Ether-kenetics* – Etheric, astral, siphon/transfer (Moonstone, Lapis Lazuli, Pyrite)
5th School: *Mattanics* – Conjuration, Teleportation, TKE (Carnelion, Beryl, Amethyst)
6th School: *Ulta-Kenetics* – Healing, Time, Veil & Beyond (White Agate, Hematite, Uranium)

Magical Ranks of Competency
Null – No magic affinity.
Affinitist – Has affinity, but no skill.
Novice – Can use magic at a basic level.

Journeyman – Has a wide understanding of magical concepts and can use spells that are more complex than a novice.

Journeyman-Adept – Has been studying for an extended period, has learned to use more than one school of magic with a strong degree of proficiency.

Adept – Has begun to learn how to use magic without relying on inscriptions, extended invocations, or extensive preparation.

Arch-Adept – Rudimentary knowledge of extra-planar interactions and can access either the elemental planes for brief periods of time or the Veil.

Master – Can craft their own unique spells and abilities, can access the elemental planes for longer periods of time.

Obit-Adept – Responsible for overseeing the study and practice for one of the six schools across the entirety of the Academy.

Grand Dean-Adept – The Dean of the Granalchi Academy, and is responsible for the well-being and studies of the entire Academy. The first, and the final, authority on magic.

Granalchi Identification (pendants)

Every Granalchi carries a flat copper disc, with six concentric circles that designate which school an Adept follows. The center of the disk itself designates their rank.

Grand Dean-Adept: A platinum polygon
Orbit-Adept: A platinum square
Collector: The center of the disk is cut out, leaving the disk hollow
Headmaster-Adept: Inverted gold triangle
Arch-Adept: White gold triangle
Instructor-Adept: Gold triangle
Adept: Gold square
Journeyman: Silver square
Scribe/Archivist: Copper hexagon
Annealist: Iron chip

Magic Outside the Academy
Divine

The most commonly-seen magic outside of the Academy comes from members of the priestly orders (Divine or Otherwise) and follows an entirely different set of rules from the where, the how, and what limitations are established on the user. With that being said, a priest that can use flame is a mage using flame, and *some form* of pyrokenetic affinity is required. The same can be said for priests that influence auras, use light or shadows, and more.

Alchemetic

Alchemy is considered, by some, the 7th School of Magic. In 472, an internal schism resulted in the then-Orbit-Adept of Alchemy splitting away from the

Academy and forming the Fellowship of the Alchemetic in the Free Cities of Ameressa. Ever since, the Grand Dean-Adept takes a hostile stance to anyone even suggesting that herbs, minerals, or the like can be considered worthy of study (outside of using them as simple reagents for the other schools).

Necrosia

There is an additional school – Necrocrosia – that is an offshoot of the 6th School. It's illegal to practice in most of the civilized world, but it does include manipulation of death magic, blood magic, animation, and deadspeak. The vast majority of necromancers, necromongers, and other affiliates can be found in Sycio; that said, most of the Fallen Gods give their followers powers over the damned in one form or the other.

Instabilisist

A magical school *not* taught by the Granalchi, it's still typically one of the first learned. Otherwise known as destruction magic, an Instabilisist channels elemental and etheric magic into an unstable form and sends it away from their bodies at a target. Otherwise formless, the ether detonates in some fashion, destroying or damaging a subject. It's *exceptionally* popular in the Hunter's Guild and in the armies of several different nations and nation-states.

THE SAGA OF THE DEAD MEN WALKING
Available in Digital and Print!

Year 512 of the Queen's Rule
The Snowflakes Trilogy
Book I: Snowflakes in Summer
Freshly minted by the Order of Love, a young exorcist is sent to the edge of the Kingdom of Dawnfire to deal with a 'small, simple haunting.' Between a winter that won't end, a girl that doesn't belong, and people being eaten in the woods, only one thing is for sure: he's over his head, and utterly out of luck.

Book II: Dead Men in Winter
As the search for the Coldstone continues, new allies enter the fray in the mountains around Toniki, and in the streets of the City of Mud. But new blood only means new bodies, and Makolichi seeks to provide those in excess...

Book III: Favorite Things
It's time for Usaic's Tower to ascend. Truths will be revealed, blood shall be spilled, and suffering shall become legendary. But it's not just the living who should fear the Coldstone being set loose. For though the dead will rise, the damned had best be ready for Who comes next...

Year 513 of the Queen's Rule
The Auramancer's Exorcism
Book I: Insanity's Respite
Beaten, broken, and battered, Akaran is sent to the Safest City in the Kingdom to recover from his battle against Makolichi, Daringol, Rmaci, and the rest. What he expects is peace and time to heal. What he finds instead is that insanity knows no bounds and offers no respite...

Book II: Insanity's Rapture
Akaran's worst nightmare has just come true, and he's the only one that can stop her from setting the world on fire. But how can he fight a demon only he believes is real – before the city is consumed in chaos?

Book III: Insanity's Reckoning (Summer 2021)
Pity the instruments of madness, for they answer to the one that calls down Love.

Origins of the Dead Men Walking
Year 510 of the Queen's Rule
Blindshot (Release date: TBA)
A self-professed Merchant of Secrets enlists the help of the Northern Hunter's Guild to trek to the Cursed Continent of Agromah to recover a relic lost to time In this land of the dead, what chance does a blind man have against a demon

king?

Year 512 of the Queen's Rule
Slag Harbor (An Interruption in the Snowflakes Trilogy)
After battling Makolichi in Gonta – and before facing him down for the final time in Toniki – Akaran decides to leave Private Galagrin behind in the City of Mud to make sure that nothing got missed in his sweep. What he finds is more than just stray shiriak; it's an answer to an unasked question...

Year 513 of the Queen's Rule
Lady Claw I: Claw Unsheathed
Who's to blame when a young girl is accused of murder? Did she do it, or did her father? And when she's cornered and the claws come out... does it matter?

Year 516 of the Queen's Rule
Fearmonger
Years after Toniki, a grizzled Akaran serves as a peacekeeper to the Queen – and nothing wants the peace to be kept.

Year 517 of the Queen's Rule
Blindsided
Stannoth and Elrok couldn't be any more different. Trained mercenaries in the Hunter's Guild, they absolutely hate each other – but they don't have a choice but to work together.

WELCOME TO A WORLD WHERE GOOD THINGS HAPPEN TO BAD PEOPLE AND THE GOOD PEOPLE ARE QUESTIONABLE... ...AT BEST.

Good things come to those who wait, but I'm impatient as the fires in the Abyss are hot (or cold, depending on Frosel). I'm working on the next book as fast as I can (I promise!) and I've got some stuff for you.

Please be sure to follow me on social media to find out where I'm going, what I'm doing, how I'm doing it, and the occasional stupid meme just to laugh. Plus, get some random business insights on the self-published side of the coin AND see what I'm doing when I dress up for charity purposes.

There's also a newsletter you can sign up for!

You can expect free stories, character information, special promotions, extra information about the World of the Saga, and more! Be sure to visit and subscribe (it'd mean a lot to me if you did)!

Amazon.com:
https://www.amazon.com/author/sdmw

Facebook.com:
https://www.facebook.com/sagadmw

Website:
http://www.sagadmw.com

Twitter:
@Sagadmw

Instagram:
@Sagadmw

Dead Men Emailing Newsletter
http://www.sagadmw.com/email.html

AND!

Please don't forget to leave a review. Your opinion on the story (and the series!) MATTERS. Loved it or hated it, thought it was amazing or thought it was garbage, your feedback helps me be a better author and helps me provide the best experience that I can for not just you, but other readers in the future.
To leave a review, please hop to:

https://www.amazon.com/gp/product/B085B8KLQS/
ref=dbs_a_def_rwt_bibl_vppi_i0

Printed in Great Britain
by Amazon

32076653R00179